THE
MEMORY
INDEX

a novel

JULIAN R. VACA

THOMAS NELSON
Since 1798

The Memory Index

Published in Nashville, Tennessee, by Thomas Nelson. Thomas Nelson is a registered trademark of HarperCollins Christian Publishing, Inc.

Thomas Nelson titles may be purchased in bulk for educational, business, fundraising, or sales promotional use. For information, please email SpecialMarkets@ThomasNelson.com.

Publisher's Note: This novel is a work of fiction. Names, characters, places, and incidents are either products of the author's imagination or used fictitiously. All characters are fictional, and any similarity to people living or dead is purely coincidental.

Any internet addresses (websites, blogs, etc.) in this book are offered as a resource. They are not intended in any way to be or imply an endorsement by HarperCollins Christian Publishing, nor does HarperCollins Christian Publishing vouch for the content of these sites for the life of this book.

ISBN 978-0-8407-0066-7 (hardcover)
ISBN 978-0-8407-0072-8 (e-book)
ISBN 978-0-8407-0075-9 (downloadable audio)
ISBN 978-0-8407-0080-3 (trade paper)

Library of Congress Cataloging-in-Publication Data

CIP data is available upon request.

Printed in the United States of America

22 23 24 25 26   LSC   5 4 3 2 1

For our daughter Lyvia,
whose light was taken too soon,
but whose memory brightens our lives daily

Everybody needs his memories. They keep the wolf of insignificance from the door.

—SAUL BELLOW

If you only have memories of the ones you love, the only way to bring them into the now, and to ensure they are part of your future, is by talking about them.

—ZOË CLARK-COATES

PROLOGUE

November 1986

Emilia Vanguard hadn't considered that she might die until Mr. Lear said so.

"You might die," he said conversationally, as one might remark about the turning of leaves in autumn. They walked in stride toward the massive hangar. It was dawn—the kind of cloudless, purply dawn that paints skylines in swaths of shadowy light—and Emilia thought she would very much like to avoid dying, if she could help it.

"Does that frighten you." His questions always seemed like statements, especially when he talked of life and death (which was quite often, times being what they were).

"No," Emilia answered. Her tone sounded like a shrug even though she hadn't shrugged.

"Of course not." He put a steady hand on her shoulder as they marched toward the row of cars in the hangar. "How could it. You're special."

There's that confounded word again. She rolled her eyes. *Special.*

Emilia wasn't special. She was just Emilia.

And I would kindly thank you to remember that.

Now in the high-ceilinged hangar, they briskly walked toward a black '86 Audi Quattro at the center of the lineup. It was a beautiful specimen, unblemished by fingerprints or smudges of any kind; its black sheen was supremacy-like, a boastful proclamation to the rest of the sports cars that here lay—for all to behold—the Superior Vehicle.

Now that's special. Emilia clicked her tongue.

"Envelope's in the glove box," said Mr. Lear. He reached for the driver's-side door, but Emilia said thank you and opened it for herself. Once seated, she turned the key in the ignition and the vehicle growled, a great beast disturbed from hibernation and now hungry— starved, frothy at the mouth—for the road.

We'll get you there soon enough. Emilia wondered if this was how cowboys felt before mounting their stallions and riding across the desert, the sun bearing down on their leathery necks.

"You know your route, yes?"

"Yes," Emilia replied, shutting the door. She caressed the steering wheel reverently, familiarizing herself with the reins. Then she saluted Mr. Lear with two fingers, put the Quattro in Drive, and shot out of the hangar and across the abandoned airfield. She watched Mr. Lear shrink in her rearview mirror until—like an extinguished afterimage—he was gone, *poof,* out of sight.

The sun was a half thumb at the horizon. One hour from now Emilia would reach the interstate, where her path would turn precipitous as it snaked through the mountain. There, Mr. Lear's words would finally catch up with her: *You might die.*

"She's a woman of few words," said Ashley Molaison, greeting Mr. Lear as he approached. They turned and stood, practically shoulder to shoulder, on the top floor of the empty air-traffic control tower and watched as Emilia Vanguard sped off toward the horizon. As the sun continued its slow-burn ascent into the sky, Mr. Lear caught their reflection in the dusty glass.

He noted the streaks of gray in his brown hair, which had seemed to double since he last observed his reflection in a mirror. *I'm getting old.*

Ashley consulted her wristwatch. "The Transference is set to begin in ninety minutes."

"Yes." Mr. Lear sighed. When Emilia and her vehicle were completely out of sight, he turned from the view. *Godspeed, Special One.* "Everything's in motion."

"All we can do now is wait and pray." This would prove difficult, as Ashley did not possess a proclivity to waiting *or* praying.

"And drink tea." Mr. Lear flattened his tie as he walked over to the column at the center of the octagonal room. Here, beneath the hanging first-aid kit and portable defibrillator, was a small cart upon which sat an electric teakettle, two porcelain mugs, and a straight-sided glass jar containing several tea bags.

And one of those tea bags contained tiny yet effective traces of benzopint, a concoction of Mr. Lear's own making.

It's for her own protection, Mr. Lear thought in a tired, desperate attempt to convince his conscience. He asked, his back to Ashley, "Have a cup with me, won't you."

"I'm convinced you drink your weight in tea every day," she said in a good-natured tone, still gazing out the dirty, tinted windows of the control tower. She fingered her cognition wheel idly, tracing the tattoo on her right palm with her left pinky.

Mr. Lear prepped two cups. "There are only two basic tenets of Philip Lear, the first being: A day hasn't actually begun unless it's marked by a hot beverage. For some, that's coffee. For me, that's—"

"Lavender chamomile."

Mr. Lear joined Ashley at the windows and handed her one of the two mugs. The other he raised toward the cigarette smoke–yellow ceiling tiles. "To Emilia Vanguard and the Transference."

Ashley, too, raised her cup, the wispy steam dancing between them in the dawning light. "And to Joshua Cohen . . . may he receive the message and act." *Before it's too late*, she seemed to imply.

They both sipped their tea.

In minutes, Ashley Molaison would drift into a deep sleep. She would awake hours later to find herself in her apartment with no memory of the last twenty-four hours and only vague images in her mind of the previous two weeks. Depending on how much benzopint she had consumed, even those vague images would eventually be snuffed out, like a candle burned down to the base of its wick.

But, for now, the two continued sipping mutely.

What tragic irony, Mr. Lear reflected solemnly, *that in the age of Memory Killer, I still need to take matters into my own hands and delete this poor girl's memories.*

It felt plain wrong.

The memories Mr. Lear was trying to erase from Ashley's mind could possibly be recovered and then archived onto memory tapes for her to play back and remember. But it was a risk he *had* to take; paper trails, especially paper trails of the mind, had to be expunged where possible.

"What's the other basic tenet of Philip Lear?" Ashley asked, clasping the warm mug at her chest.

Mr. Lear smiled, perhaps for the first time in days, and answered—knowing full well she would not recall this conversation: "That Arnold Schwarzenegger movies are the greatest of all the movies."

She let out a soft chuckle. "I'm not familiar with his work. Where should I start?"

"He's only starred in a few," Mr. Lear replied, playing along, "but I'd start with *The Terminator*, a modern classic about a time-traveling soldier sent to the past to protect mankind's only hope for salvation."

"It sounds . . . epic. I'll have to remember to rent it," she said, hopelessly unaware she would *not* remember.

"Yes." Mr. Lear forced down the guilt that welled up in his throat and reminded himself that this was, after all, for Ashley's own protection. "You should."

❖ ❖ ❖

Emilia clicked on the radio. "Rhymin' and Stealin'" by Beastie Boys came on.

She smiled and turned up the volume so loud that the plastic speaker encasings rattled in the car doors, the rearview mirror shook, and her bones vibrated. It was like she had her own personal earthquake inside the cab of the Quattro, looping continuously. She absorbed the noise, rapt with wonder and determination.

She needed Earthquake Loop in the sort of all-consuming, life-giving way that Fish needs water.

No, Emilia thought, *like Bird needs air.*

She sped up and passed an eighteen-wheeler on the narrow highway. On the shoulder, a sign indicated that Interstate 24W was up ahead. Two miles. Almost go time.

Stay sharp. Emilia soaked up the blaring rap music. *Be sharp.*

Emilia slammed her foot on the gas and crested the uneven on-ramp. Interstate 24W reached out before her—a long, concrete frontier that narrowed to its vanishing point with innumerable skyscraping trees on each side. A few cars and SUVs rode the interstate already, morning commuters. Early birds trying to get the worms, as it were.

Emilia prayed none of them would get seriously hurt.

With flagrant disregard for blinker etiquette, she swerved in front of a shuttle van and sped across two lanes toward the passing lane, inciting a barrage of angry honks. She gripped the steering wheel, the taut leather squeaking beneath her sweaty fingers. Her eyes darted from the interstate to the rearview mirror and then back to the interstate a few times, as if trying to spy some phantom pursuer.

Seventy miles per hour.

Eighty miles per hour.

At ninety, she closed in on a white Toyota 4Runner in the passing lane. The driver remained put, annoying Emilia greatly. Yet rather than honk or flash her headlights, she checked her blind spot and then jerked out of the passing lane. She flew past the SUV just as the sun appeared over the tree line, just as the faint sound of police sirens rang out in the distance, *just* as the semitruck with the red cab came into view. On the back of the gray tractor trailer, written into the dust and grit by someone's finger, were the sloppy words, "To Forget Is to Die."

"Here we go," Emilia said, turning up the music in her cab even more.

Milo Pruitt had driven tractor-trailer trucks (without incident, he'd proudly say) his entire adult life. No parking violations. No speeding tickets. No accidents. In fact, his was a life fraught with many nos: no friends, no hobbies, a no-frills existence with no events of real importance.

That all changed that November morning.

Interstate 24W was awash in the magic, glowing light of sunrise. There wasn't a cloud in the sky; the cool, crisp air legally guaranteed a fair-weather day—the kind of wonderfully perfect day that grace-fully straddles summer and autumn.

Milo hunched over the wide steering wheel, adjusted his pos-ture, then glanced at his side mirror. In the middle lane, a black Audi Quattro approached at an alarming speed.

That was Milo's cue.

He sucked in a deep breath through his nose. He pictured the briefcase of cash that had been promised to him by the Man Who Smelled Like Lavender—the man in the paisley tie who'd approached him last week. How and why he'd selected Milo was still a mystery, though Milo was willing to leave it unsolved. The sum of money awaiting him on the other side of this was . . . well . . . it was enough to make Milo Pruitt—a man plagued by nos—say *yes*.

He exhaled.

He winked at the Dale Earnhardt bobblehead mounted to his dash.

He pulled the steering wheel hard left and slammed on the brakes.

The lumbering semi jackknifed, sliding across all three lanes while it folded in on itself.

Rubber burned against asphalt; rancid smoke filled the cab and rose in the air outside the semi in foglike plumes.

And the black sports car deftly dodged Milo Pruitt and his tractor-trailer truck a fraction of a second before chaos ensued.

Emilia quickly took to the left shoulder of the interstate in anticipation of the semitruck's maneuver. Whoever Mr. Lear had hired did their part with marvelous skill. In fact, the truck driver actually managed to steer the massive vehicle as it slid across the interstate.

Then the cab and tractor trailer toppled. Cars screeched to wild halts. Horns honked. A cacophony of metallic crashes, booming collisions, and shattering glass resounded.

In total, only six seconds had elapsed.

Emilia shouted and laughed, her heart threatening to burst like an overblown balloon. She glanced at the rearview mirror: traffic was completely stalled behind the mangled semi. Tendrils of smoke began to rise in the blue sky.

Pedal to the floor, she accelerated, passing a sign that warned of a steep grade and another that read BEWARE FALLING ROCKS.

❖ ❖ ❖

Miraculously, she encountered no other drivers. Twice she almost swerved out of control as she barreled around the sharp bends. But she managed to right the Quattro and maintain control each time, her tongue clamped between her front teeth.

Mere minutes after she left the semitruck behind, the helicopter came into view, swooping down near the craggy cliffside up ahead.

Nice of you to show up. Emilia allowed her body to go slightly lax. *And just in the nick of—*

Colorful, flashing lights caught her eye in the side mirror: a small fleet of highway patrol vehicles were closing in on her, as if they'd appeared out of thin air.

Emilia swore.

Wild-eyed, she kept her foot on the pedal and pushed the Quattro to its limits. The next bend in the interstate was a sharp one—nearly a switchback—but Emilia didn't slow down as she approached.

C'mon, c'mon . . .

She checked her side mirrors again: it was working. She was managing to open the gap between herself and the highway patrol. In truth, she was only buying herself seconds, but seconds were a precious commodity, and right now Emilia Vanguard was in the business of buying seconds.

Here came the hairpin.

Emilia eased off the gas at the last second and compensated with the brake, pulling back on the steering and gliding around the sharp turn. She only narrowly missed the railing on the left side and the nightmare-inducing drop-off and the acres of treetops beyond. As Emilia came out of the bend, she exhaled—morning sunlight coloring her in a warm-orange glow.

She merged right, sliding off the interstate and onto a slim shoulder, where she ground to an abrupt halt. She put the Quattro in Park, yanked open the glove box, and snagged the envelope. With the car still running, she leapt out the passenger door, stuffed the message into her back pocket, and began to climb the side of the cliff—hand over hand.

A sudden, loud whirring of helicopter blades tousled Emilia's deep brown hair. She was halfway up the cliff, nearly twenty feet above the interstate, and did not look down once.

The highway patrol finally arrived, encasing the Audi Quattro in a semicircle and demanding—through loudspeakers—that the driver show themselves, put their hands on their head, and all that business.

The helicopter's loud rotor blades drew their attention upward, and the officer in charge would later describe the scene thus: A midtwenties woman in a dark T-shirt and gray pants scaled the side of the cliff toward a rope ladder that hung out of the cabin of an unmarked helicopter. The woman pushed herself off the side of the cliff and leapt toward the rope ladder, only barely catching one of the rungs, and hauled herself up as the helicopter flew toward the horizon.

Highway patrol never identified the woman, and the reason for her reckless stunt confounded them. The vehicle, purchased anonymously secondhand and unregistered, was not stolen. Nor was any contraband discovered in the trunk. So why the daring, theatrical escape?

The patrolmen who filed the report had no substantial theories, and so the event remained a mystery.

1

FREYA IZQUIERDO

Before, people said their biggest fear was dying. Today, we die before we're actually dead, when all our memories are consumed by Memory Killer.

Now—in this great apocalyptic now—many say their biggest fear is either forgetting or being forgotten. *To forget is to die,* some have elegantly said. *To be forgotten is to be killed.* Or, as my dad once put it, *Olvidar es la muerte.*

Poetic, right?

And look, I get it. I *really* do. Memory Killer is an enigmatic plague that has loomed over the globe for nearly a decade, slowly and methodically collapsing economies, crippling world governments, poisoning society, confounding medical scientists, and so on and so forth.

Pretty scary stuff.

Even in the face of all this uncertainty, we still get to make some choices. And I've made mine: I'm not going to expend energy on being afraid.

I've got too much work to do.

Like breaking and entering.

❖ ❖ ❖

"It's two more streets up," I tell my foster sister from the back seat of our stolen car. "Then take a right."

I should reword that: It's not *stolen*, it's *borrowed*. We *borrowed* our foster parents' car—an acid-green clunker that no one has any business driving much less borrowing or stealing. But beggars can't be choosers, so here we are.

"This is grand theft auto," Nicole says dryly. "If we get caught, we're dead." My bespectacled foster sister is a hopeless alarmist. She also has a driver's license that *isn't* revoked, so here we are. She pushes up her square glasses and eyes me through the rearview mirror disappointedly. "Not to mention we're minors, out in the city without a handler. Do permanent records mean nothing to you, Freya?"

"I've forgotten . . . what are those again?"

Nicole blinks. "That's not funny. Memory loss is *not* funny, Freya."

I was really hoping Nicole would have gotten this out of her system at the house when I initially asked her to be my driver.

A hopelessly persistent *alarmist.* I smile to myself wryly.

"All you have to do is circle the block five times." I grab my heavy rucksack from the floor and set it on my lap. "I'll be in and out in ten minutes, tops."

"I cannot believe I agreed to this." She heaves a weighty sigh. "María"—one half of our foster parents, a high-energy middle-aged woman with a penchant for serious talks of the future, *fútbol*, and votive candles—"is gonna kill us if we're caught."

"Which is why we *won't* get caught," I say breezily. "There. Pull over by that dumpster."

After the car rolls to a stop on Fifty-Third, Nicole turns on the hazards and I clamber outside. The sun-kissed, graffitied buildings cast long shadows across the broken sidewalk. Overhead, the streetlights switch from yellow to blue, flickering two times in programmed synchronization with each other, before returning to their original warm glow.

It's the citywide curfew warning. I set an alarm on my wristwatch as Nicole rolls down the passenger window.

"Is the paint dry?" she asks, gesturing toward my right hand. I nod and flash her my palm. I have altered my cognition wheel—a tattoo that every sixteen-year-old gets after they're scanned by a MeReader (or memory reader)—from a two-quarter mark to a three-quarter mark. Clockwise, the first quarter is inked a beige-yellow, the second a beige-orange, the third a beige-red, and the fourth quarter is blank—leaving a quadrant of my skin visible. If a cop stops me on the street and asks to see my wheel, the fake ID should convince him or her that I'm a recollector—a blessed individual who can remember up to three-quarters of their memories and only has to use artificial recall once a day.

In other words, a privileged person who can be out past curfew without a handler.

The risk I face (or one of them, anyway) is that not many recollectors would be caught dead in this degen-infested part of Long Beach. Degenerates, or "degens," are those who can only recall up to half of their memories on their own and need the aid of artificial recall for the rest. They're branded with a two-quarter mark and must be accompanied by a handler (essentially hospice workers, many of whom are sixteen- and seventeen-year-old recollectors earning community service credits) on every basic errand imaginable.

It's some pretty Orwellian stuff.

"What happens if . . ." Nicole says, trailing off. "What happens if you have another spell?"

"We can't worry about what we can't control."

Nicole deadpans, "You're so wise."

"And you're holding me up!" I lightly tap the roof of the car with my fist. *"Sal de aquí!"* She shakes her head, mumbles something about needing a pocket Spanish translator, then reluctantly puts the car in Drive. As she merges back into the flow of city traffic, I fling the rucksack on my back and march forward into the crowd.

It's just around the corner. Adrenaline courses through my veins.

I only walk a few steps across the busy downtown sidewalk before pondering Nicole's words. *What happens if you have another spell?*

Here's the thing: I dream in half memories when I'm awake.

I know, I know—it sounds crazy. But these fragmentary visions from my past, these broken scenes of long-since-gone days, visit me frequently and unexpectedly. It's a nauseating experience. One second I'm walking to class or killing time in the library, minding my own business, just trying to get through another insipid day, and the next thing I know I'm blinded by some powerful headache. Then there's this flash of me on the Belmont Veterans Memorial Pier at dusk. I'm laughing hysterically, trying to stay balanced on my roller skates but having little success, awkwardly gliding through a gaggle of annoyed people and squawking seagulls. Someone—who's also laughing, their voice muffled in the throng—trails behind me in the almost-twilight, cheering on my

13

childlike efforts while "Lovely Day" by Bill Withers plays over the loudspeakers on the pier.

Before I can remember who I'm with on the pier, the half memory is gone, just a sloppy, unfinished painting in a gallery, and then my headache intensifies—flecks of splotchy light dancing around my periphery.

The school nurse is troubled by my "half-memory dreams." He once told me it sounds unnatural, that it could be a strange side effect of artificial recall.

He warned me to speak of my half-memory dreams to no one.

"In a fear-based society like ours, where your inability to remember decides your fate," he said, checking my eyes with a small flashlight, "having inexplicable flashbacks like the ones you've described could get you committed to the Fold."

Great, I remember thinking, *should've kept my big mouth shut.* The Fold are controversial "hospitals" located all over the country that are privately funded and shrouded in mystery. The kind of places one should avoid like the Bubonic Plague.

The nurse, who noticed that I started to panic, softened his face and changed the subject. "Have you found yourself misremembering things, like important dates or class assignments?"

I shook my head and told him no. Although, even if I *was* misremembering stuff, I wouldn't tell a soul. Misremembering could be an early sign that artificial recall isn't working anymore, and it would almost certainly land you in the Fold quicker than you can pluck a forget-me-not.

"I'm sure it'll sort itself out, Freya," he said, handing me two painkillers in a paper cup. "Just because I've never heard of half-memory dreams doesn't mean it's abnormal."

But I feel abnormal, especially when those half-memory dreams turn into nightmares.

I chuckle inwardly, clutching the straps of my rucksack beneath the twinkling city lights. Nightmares don't have the same sting when you're living in one.

❖ ❖ ❖

Dad once said that the nighttime attracts the crazies. As I shuffle through downtown Long Beach toward my destination, I see what he meant.

The streets are lined with aggressive vendors whose makeshift tents block boarded-up, vine-covered storefronts. Shuttered drugstores, RadioShacks, and pawnshops are nothing more than an ominous, historic backdrop of a not-too-distant past.

Simpler times, like when lawn care and trash pickup were commonplace.

So many vines! I regard the untamed web of thorns and greens. The vines swallow entire sides of nearly abandoned buildings, like spider veins spread across swatches of skin. Thick weeds sprout out of cracks in the sidewalks, where so much filth and trash is strewn about you can practically see lines of toxic fumes wafting in the air. Many people wear disposable surgical masks.

It really is *a jungle out here.*

The street vendors peddle all kinds of wares, but the most common products are homemade, "holistic" remedies that the sellers promise will fight Memory Killer in ways that artificial recall cannot. How they manage to sell these medical cocktails, these "memory enhancers," is a mystery for two reasons: (1) the contents inside the glass jars look like muddy water, urine, or muddy urine, and (2) most of the people on the sidewalk—the vendors' potential clientele, who shuffle along with their handlers in tow—have their headphones on and their eyes downcast.

Which reminds me . . .

I pull my Walkman out, press Play, and then slip my orange

headphones over my ears. "Strong Island" by JVC Force starts to play. Perfect. This is my hype song. This is going to get me where I need to go. I return my cassette player to my back pocket and pull the hood of my sweatshirt over my jet-black hair.

A few years after the almighty, invisible enemy known as Memory Killer stormed the beaches of human consciousness, a Harvard study found that playing "mood-matching" music around the house or while doing homework or other menial tasks greatly benefits the working memories of adults—both young and old. Something about the pairing of emotional cues in songs and the "affective state" of the person listening improves their ability to recall.

I just take it as an excuse to listen to my Walkman more.

Naturally, classical and ambient and atmospheric genres became the popular choices for people, but I don't need any of that.

I approach a homeless woman sitting on the curb, rocking back and forth. She fumbles with one of her memory tapes—an old videotape-looking brick with a white label and crude handwriting on it. Her Restorey (a yellow, government-issued tape player that's slightly bigger than a Walkman) is scratched and dented. I'll be shocked if the portable device even works. And yet, by the time I pass her, she has inserted her memory tape and affixed the small suction receivers to her temples just above her crow's feet. Her eyes roll back as her own memories return to her.

It's a strange feeling artificially recalling memories you didn't know you'd forgotten. At seventeen I'm still not used to the grating sensation. The jolt of energy is knifelike at first, and then it trickles into your head in a slow burn as a particular memory reenters your consciousness. It feels like . . . How do I describe this? Like getting punctured with an infernal needle and then injected with millions of microscopic spiders that pitter-patter across the surface of your skull. And then—*poof!*—the memory is back, and you exhale.

They say you never get used to artificial recall. *Qué emocionante!*

What's more? Because Memory Killer is an erratic sort of phenom-enon, a real cancer of the mind that cannot be eradicated, no one knows how long artificial recall will keep memory loss at bay and preserve one's agency. One day you're plugging into your Restorey and following your artificial recall schedule, and the next you're an aimless wanderer with no recollection of your past.

And that's being let off easy.

Sometimes, Memory Killer swallows your mind and spits out something dangerous . . . something *inhuman* . . .

I absently pat my sweatshirt pocket, where I keep my own Restorey already loaded up with the evening's memory tape. My fos-ter parents gave me the hand-me-down piece of junk when I moved in a couple of years ago. It eats up batteries like they're going out of style, but otherwise it works just fine.

I don't have to artificially recall for another two hours, long after I've grabbed what I came here to get.

The factory, or what's left of it, sits starkly against the violet sky. Even from across the street I can see its hollowed-out center . . . the caved-in ceilings . . . the blown-out windows . . . the mounds of rubble encased by graffitied walls . . . and the vines.

The deadly explosion happened over two years ago, and yet the fire-scorched site remains untouched save for the barbed-wire fence and NO TRESPASSING signs.

I waste no more time.

I pull my headphones off and hang them around my neck.

I sprint toward the fence.

I scale it quickly and hop to the other side.

I land on shaky feet and immediately pull my Sony Betamovie video camera out of my rucksack.

I cross the soot-covered ground toward the nearest busted-out window and turn on my video camera.

"Hey, Dad," I say under my breath, climbing inside the decrepit factory, precious seconds counting down on my wristwatch. "I made it."

2

FLETCHER COHEN

In the white room, the only thing more sterile than the stiff antimicrobial chair or the shiny linoleum floors was the lab technician's smile. She removed the heavy, bulky MeReader from Fletcher's head and set the helmet on its stand beside a poster of Molly Ringwald, who was exhorting folks to Never Forget: Memory Readers Save Lives!

"Anyone ever tell you that you look like Molly Ringwald?" Fletcher asked the lab tech as his chair returned to its upright sitting position. He caught his reflection in the mirror above the sink and tried to style his wavy mullet back into place with his hands.

"Molly Ringwald?" the lab tech said, plopping down on her stool and then rolling over to the sleeping machine beside the closed door. Here, she inputted a code into the keypad and the boxy computer moaned to life, immediately setting to work imprinting one of Fletcher's at-risk memories onto a memory tape. "She's pretty."

"Yeah, you are."

And then that sterile smile of hers filled with color.

The computer *blipped* and spat out Fletcher's fresh memory tape. The lab tech took it, placed it inside a plastic case, and then slipped it inside a manilla envelope along with an updated, laminated recall schedule. She handed this to Fletcher, completing his download session.

Downloading happened here once a month, at the county repository his family was zoned for. First, the high-end technology in the MeReader conducted a CT head scan. Then it drew out any memory or memories he couldn't recall that hadn't been completely swallowed up by Memory Killer. Finally, it imprinted that memory or memories onto a tape.

Voilà.

After sitting in on dozens of downloads, Fletcher was still amazed by the whole process. The MeReader navigated the neural map within his brain's temporal lobe and rescued memories that he didn't actively remember but hadn't completely forgotten. It was like using a metal detector on a shoreline, sweeping the sands of his mind in search of lost trinkets that were holed up just below the surface.

From start to finish, the download took about one hour.

"You're new here, aren't you?" Fletcher asked, swinging his feet around and standing. He grabbed his denim jacket off the coatrack and put it on, glancing at the name badge clipped to her lab coat. Andie Parker.

"I just transferred from the Riverside County repository," she said, getting up from her stool. "Been trying to get out of the desert since I graduated from college."

"Well, on behalf of the city of Los Angeles, welcome, Ms. Parker," Fletcher said, bowing. Andie rolled her eyes, but not before her pretty smile deepened. She shook her head and opened the door.

On his way out, Fletcher gave her a friendly side hug and added, "It's quite a relief knowing that my memories are in good hands!"

Her cheeks flushed and Fletcher winked, taking his leave.

Outside the repository, Fletcher jogged down the wide steps toward the street, where his parked Ducati awaited. Beside the black motorcycle, Denise Meyers—his girlfriend of eleven months—paced on the sidewalk.

"I got your page," she said, stuffing her beeper inside her pocket and then tucking a strand of yellow-blonde hair behind her ear. "What's up?"

"Hop on," he said, gesturing toward his motorcycle. "I'll show you."

They mounted the motorcycle together and Fletcher fired up the engine. Then he accelerated, weaving through the labyrinthine LA traffic. Overhead, the late afternoon sky had turned blood-orange, thanks to the dense smog that hung above the skyscrapers.

After turning up a few streets, nearly running a red light, and passing through Little Tokyo, Fletcher rolled to a stop outside the four-story office building.

"This your idea of a date?" Denise asked, getting off the seat. Fletcher pocketed his keys, grabbed Denise's hand, and led her up the steps toward the entrance.

"Something like that."

Before they could reach the doors, they had to contend with a small gathering of protesters. Effusive men and women who fancied themselves Memory Ghosts and insisted they knew the truth about Memory Killer, the unethical origins of artificial recall, and damning information about its unscrupulous architect.

"Your first memory tape," said a woman with bulging eyes. "Think about your first memory tape, son!"

"*No hablo ingles,*" Fletcher said, sidestepping past her with Denise in tow. Once inside, they approached the concierge, who was seated behind a wraparound desk and was deeply engrossed in a crossword puzzle.

"Hey, Fletcher," said the hulking man whose name Fletcher could not remember. This he did *not* chalk up to Memory Killer; the poor man had a hopelessly forgettable name. "Your dad just left."

"All good," Fletcher said, improvising. "He left his billfold in his office and sent me to pick it up for him."

The security guard's eyes fell on Denise, who blushed and looked at her bow flats. Eventually, though, he said gruffly, "Fine. Make it quick."

Fletcher led Denise down the hall, past some conference rooms, and inside an office. He flipped on the light, revealing rows of tall filing cabinets and a single computer in a corner.

"C'mon," he said, briskly walking toward the computer and turning it on.

"We're not here to grab your dad's wallet, are we?" Denise asked rhetorically, looking around the office anxiously.

A pop-up window appeared on the computer screen, prompting Fletcher to scan credentials in order to proceed. He pulled Andie Parker's name badge out of his jacket pocket, the one he secretly swiped off her lab coat earlier.

"Where did you get that?" Denise asked, coming up beside him. Fletcher ignored her, flipped the badge over, and examined the barcode. Then he slipped the badge into the square reader beside the monitor. After a moment, pixelated words flashed across the screen, confirming admittance.

Fletcher smiled.

Quickly, without even a breath to spare, he sifted through the unlabeled folders and records on the desktop.

"Fletcher?" Denise said, her voice low, intense. "That concierge is going to come looking for us—"

"Do you know what happens if Memory Killer attacks someone's mind while they're using artificial recall?" he asked, trying his best to multitask.

"Um . . ."

It was a question Fletcher had wondered since he'd had his reading at sixteen, when everyone was first scanned by a MeReader and subsequently diagnosed a degen or recollector. Lack of public information only amplified this burning question. As far as Fletcher could tell, no one was talking about this on the news; no one was actively researching this; no one seemed to care what would happen if Memory Killer intersected with artificial recall.

Why?

"One time," Fletcher said, his fingers flying across the keyboard, "I asked a technician who was servicing my Restorey. The old woman wouldn't answer me . . . She barely looked me in the eye!"

Denise glanced over her shoulder at the office door.

"Why aren't people talking about this?" Fletcher muttered. He found a folder housing public records from a recent probing into Memory Frontier, the global conglomerate behind the Restorey and artificial recall.

Bingo. His heart fluttering, Fletcher opened the folder and entered a search command for "Memory Killer" and "artificial recall."

Unexpectedly, a new pop-up window appeared, alerting him that his credentials were restricted. He wouldn't be able to access the records—

The doorknob to the office turned, and Fletcher pulled Denise into a long kiss.

"Okay, okay," the concierge said after Denise broke away. "You've had your fun. You should probably leave."

Fletcher stood awkwardly, feigning surprise—making sure to obstruct the security guard's view of the computer. "Oh, uh, Stanley . . . we . . . we were just leaving."

The concierge blinked. "It's Spencer."

Ah. There it is!

❖ ❖ ❖

"You were using me," Denise said, standing beside Fletcher's Ducati with her arms folded.

"Well, I can see why you'd say that . . ."

"And?"

"And what?"

"You trailed off," Denise said, cocking an eyebrow, "like you had more to say."

"Oh, no. That was it. I get why it seems like I was using you. I kind of was."

"*Kind* of?"

He shrugged because it was all he could do.

"You're *awful*." Her tone was now decidedly indignant. "Why do you want to know *everything*? Who cares about Memory Killer and artificial recall and all that? Don't you think the experts have that all sorted out?"

"I don't want to know everything," Fletcher clarified, trying to mollify his now ex-girlfriend. "I want to know the truth."

"Well, here's a truth," she said, whisper-yelling. "You're a real jerk, Fletcher Cohen. If I could choose which memories to lose, I'd choose every single one with you."

For a moment, those big blue eyes of hers grew distant and glassy. It was as if Denise was deep inside her head, rifling through the moments the two of them had shared over the past year. It was like she was taking inventory of the memories right then, standing on the sidewalk, *willing* herself to lose them to the great big void that resided in her consciousness, where memories took a forever sleep and had no chance of being awoken. Everyone had that ravenous void: Memory Killer, the bottomless ocean of the mind that consumed memories before they were stored onto tapes. And to lose one's memory to the void was to lose a part of one's makeup . . . a part of the fabric of their identity . . .

A part of one's soul, some said.

The moment passed, and Denise blinked.

"Enjoy spending senior year alone," she said. "I'm calling a cab." And then she stormed off. Fletcher watched her leave, and then he felt a sudden, unexpected pang of remorse. Denise was beautiful. An incredibly smart and gifted girl with all kinds of amazing things in her future. *Just not me*, Fletcher reflected. But she was popular and resilient. Fletcher wouldn't be surprised if she was seeing someone else by the time school started next week.

Yes, Denise would be fine. And, more importantly, so would Fletcher.

Fletcher pulled up to a red light and planted his boots on the pavement, attempting to sort through his overlapping thoughts. In the darkened sky, ephemeral lines of pink streaked west toward the coast.

His thwarted plans to investigate Memory Killer's potential impact on artificial recall only deepened his curiosity.

For months—almost an entire year, in fact—Fletcher had been on-again-off-again writing down questions and theories about Memory Killer, the elusive enemy of the mind that had scourged mankind since he turned seven. He couldn't put his finger on *why* all of these questions nagged at him like small rashes beneath his clothes that refused to heal and demanded to be scratched. But nag at him they did. And so Fletcher, ever the dutiful Itch Scratcher, would journal about his thoughts in his Memory Killer File; he simply couldn't chance forgetting these urgent thoughts.

That was the maddening thing about memories: a society could build a robust infrastructure to keep hyper memory loss to a minimum, and yet every so often a memory slipped through one's mental fingers like a vapor, and all that remained was the faintest memory *of* a memory—not the memory itself.

Too often, Memory Killer devoured a scene from one's past before they ever had the opportunity to archive it.

Fletcher tightened up whenever he thought about Memory Killer. His body's protective instinct kicked in like he was bracing for an impact tantamount to a car crash. So he rolled his shoulders and loosened up as if shaking off weighty, invisible ropes.

To his right, on the street corner opposite him, an elderly man with long, wispy hair stood atop a crate. The man wore a large sign around his neck that read SLAVES TO OUR PAST, and he was vociferously preaching the Gospel of Forgetting to passersby.

Fletcher had seen his kind before; theirs was a cultish movement that embraced Memory Killer. They rejected artificial recall altogether and believed forgetting the past paved the way for an enlightened present, even at the cost of losing oneself in the future.

Fletcher was sure they would also contend the earth was flat and the moon landing was staged.

He rolled his eyes and turned away. To his immediate left, he saw a dark-complected, middle-aged woman in the passenger seat of a white sedan. Her window was rolled down, and Fletcher could hear "Running Up That Hill" by Kate Bush faintly playing on the stereo. The woman leaned her head back against the headrest as she removed two suction receivers from her temples and set them in her lap, where Fletcher assumed her Restorey was. This meant she must have just completed artificial recall mere seconds ago.

Now, she stared unblinkingly at the evening sky. The red stop-light cast a delicate glow across her smooth face.

That was when Fletcher noticed her deep green eyes clouding over and turning solid gray, like smoke filling a beaker.

He knew what this meant.

Memory Killer was at work.

Right now, the woman had no idea her eyes had gone opaque. Her vision, in fact, was perfectly fine. But unbeknownst to her, she was in that exact moment actively losing some memory from her past—like the air from her lungs was subtly being siphoned off.

Fletcher knew what this meant because it happened to him too.

It happened to everyone, some far more than others.

He watched this woman and found he could not look away, even though he'd seen this very thing occur countless times . . . to friends . . . to teachers . . . to his parents. The bizarre phenomenon caused no discomfort. In fact, if it weren't for the strange symptom of eye discoloration, no one would know when Memory Killer was present and silently wreaking havoc.

The woman eventually noticed Fletcher watching her.

Her gray, lifeless eyes met his.

The edges of her mouth began to twitch, flirting with a smile. The driver (her handler) was a guy probably Fletcher's age in scrubs, whose features were hidden in the evening shadows. The handler slowly brought a lit cigarette to his pursed lips, took a long drag, and exhaled an undulating puff of white smoke. The ghostly cloud hung in the air, interplaying with the cold, red glow of the traffic light.

The woman held Fletcher's stare.

The traffic light turned green. The handler flicked his cigarette out the window and drove off. Fletcher watched the car disappear into the traffic, still mesmerized by the unsettling scene.

The SUV behind him honked. He revved his engine before accelerating and then zoomed forward, wending and weaving around crawling cars. He took side streets all the way back to his house in the heart of Manhattan Beach, and the Woman Who Lost Her Memories was all Fletcher could think about the entire drive.

Being a recollector meant that Fletcher Cohen was part of the 50 to 60 percent of the world's population who could recall up to three quarters of their memories on their own. It also meant that he only had to use artificial recall once a day (in the morning, promptly at 7:00 a.m.) to fill in the gaps.

This was a short, mostly painless process: Each day, Fletcher inserted a different memory tape into his Restorey, ensured the memory was rewound and queued up, affixed the receivers to his temples, and then pressed Play. Memories materialized in his mind's eye like scenes in a movie, only it was much more than that. Regaining a moment in time that one had lived was markedly different from watching actors on TV. But the imperfect comparison was more or less adequate.

The state of California mandated that all minors recall in the presence of their parents or legal guardians. This meant that every time Fletcher recalled, either his mother or father was there, and usually they conducted their own recall as soon as he finished his. He'd sat with them countless times over the years and not once had either of them been visited by Memory Killer *while* they were hooked up to their Restoreys.

At least . . . that he was aware of.

A person's eyes were closed during artificial recall, so he wouldn't know if their pupils or irises had turned gray.

Fletcher gripped the handlebars of his motorcycle, hoping and praying he didn't forget these thoughts before he made it home to log them in his Memory Killer File.

He turned up his street, which was flanked by lit palm trees, and then slowed down as his house came into view. It was a forest-green bungalow with a perfectly manicured lawn—the kind of annoyingly well-kept yard that landed on the cover of periodicals that no one read but stocked in waiting rooms.

Fletcher saw his father's black '87 Mercedes-Benz 420SEL in the driveway. A white SUV he didn't recognize was parked behind it, its engine running, driver at the wheel. Because Fletcher's father was a congressman, it wasn't uncommon for their house to become a meeting place of sorts. In fact, his parents often threw soirées where businessmen and socialites and changemakers from all over the state descended upon their backyard and drank too much. A variety of state and federal politicians made appearances throughout the year too; the governor had been over twice that year already.

So Fletcher cut off his engine, flicked off the headlight, and dismounted.

The front door opened.

A young woman Fletcher had never seen before, in her twenties, he guessed, stepped outside. She wore a navy business skirt and jacket, and her black hair was pulled back into a taut ponytail. His father appeared in the doorway a second later but remained in the house just beyond the threshold. He looked uncharacteristically . . . anxious.

Fletcher was suddenly very aware of his mother's absence.

Hunched over, he walked his Ducati onto the sidewalk and stopped behind the wall of shrubs that encased his neighbors' front yard. From here, Fletcher had the perfect vantage point for watching the front door, which was illuminated by a hanging lantern. He slouched and peered over the shrubs just as his father took off his wire-rim glasses and slowly leaned forward.

Fletcher lowered himself even more, feeling his heart pounding. It was too dark—and he was too far away—to tell if they'd kissed or if they were just talking in hushed voices.

Fletcher bet the latter was just wishful thinking.

The woman eventually headed toward the passenger side of the SUV. Fletcher quickly dipped his head so he was completely hidden behind the shrubs. He could hear the distinct clicking sound of the vehicle switching from Park to Reverse, and slowly the young woman's driver pulled out of the driveway.

Fletcher paused to collect himself.

Who *was* that?

And had his father arranged for them to meet in his mother's absence?

Fletcher didn't want to go too far down that rabbit trail. Not right now. He just needed to get inside and gather his thoughts. He walked his motorcycle toward their driveway . . .

. . . and found his father still standing in the doorway, shrouded in half shadows, watching him expectantly.

3

FREYA IZQUIERDO

Nothing evokes a visceral reaction like standing in my dad's tomb.

For a moment, I lose sight of my goal. I just stand in the empty, wide-open factory, tears burning at the edges of my eyes, feeling every bit as broken as the shards of glass I'm standing on. Yes . . . I lose sight of my goal, which is to say that I lose a part of myself. I am stricken with fear and grief and sadness in the belly of this beast—this beast that killed my dad, along with many others.

The beast threatens to swallow me whole too.

Even though I've been planning for months to visit the site where my dad took his last breath, what I *didn't* plan for was the overwhelming sense of enormity. I'm not talking about the factory, of course, which has been reduced to a fissured shell of its former self. (Explosions possess an uncanny ability to do this.) I'm talking about the enormous guilt that suddenly rattles me: guilt for not coming to this factory-turned-graveyard sooner; guilt for not being able to prevent him from dying; guilt for not feeling guilty all of the time.

I know the feeling's misplaced, but I allow myself to feel these things anyway.

Grief is unlike memories in that way. It's not linear. There may be a beginning to it, sure, but there's no middle or end. Grief just *is*, and I hate its inherent ubiquity.

I blink back the tears and shake out of it. I only have minutes, and I need to act.

I bring the Sony Betamovie's viewfinder up to my right eye and peer inside. The Record icon flashes red at the bottom of the grainy screen. Quickly and carefully, I walk over the grime-covered rubble and pan my video camera across the wreckage.

They said it was an accident. That some of the machinery malfunctioned. That there was no warning. The fire started and seconds—*breaths*—later the explosion came.

But I have a different theory, because this wasn't just your average factory.

This is where MeReaders first went into production.

My video camera is my third eye—it's an extension of myself, of my being. With Memory Killer ever looming, there's literally no telling what moments from my past could be unexpectedly consumed. Having a Betamovie around and burning through videotape after videotape of footage has become a sort of contingency plan. I often play back VHS tapes and watch them through the plastic viewfinder, reliving some insignificant afternoon at the beach with my foster sister just because.

Having a Betamovie also makes solving the mystery of my dad's death easier. Video evidence, as they say, is irrefutable.

I duck underneath a fallen doorframe, tilting my video camera up toward what's left of the ceilings. Moonlight falls through in columns, casting the interior in spectral light. A thickness hangs in the air, something I can both see and taste, a kind of space dust suspended in the atmosphere. My footfalls echo loudly, startling a flock of pigeons. They flap their wings angrily and exit through one of the many holes in the enormous half roof.

There have got to be some clues around here . . . anything!

I approach the charred remains of a conveyor belt. It's covered in bird droppings, grit, and moss. I zoom across the machinery slowly, my heart racing, fully expecting to discover *something* hidden in plain view.

So far, a whole lot of nothing.

My inner critic laughs. *What did you expect, Freya? Did you really think you'd just waltz into this place, turn your video camera on, and find something that the first responders missed?*

I curse at myself and lower my Betamovie. I try to guess where the offices might have once been. But hardly any of the interior walls still stand; so much of this factory has been flattened, and I assume anything remotely valuable was pillaged long ago.

Think, Freya . . .

The timer on my wristwatch goes off. I have one minute to hop the fence and jog back to where Nicole dropped me off. If I'm even a second late, she might panic and come looking for me.

"I *will* be back," I mutter, accepting defeat. For now. "I promise, Dad."

I stop recording and switch off the video camera. I stride back the way I came, climb through the window, and retrieve my rucksack.

Once I'm back on the other side of the fence, I turn around and take one last mental picture of the factory.

Yes, I will be back. And next time, I'll give myself more time.

I turn around. But before I can take one step, a police car flashes its red and blue lights, and then I'm swallowed by a blinding searchlight.

❖ ❖ ❖

The East Division Precinct is loud and bustling, a revolving door of felons and prostitutes and alcoholics.

My home away from home.

"Welp," Nicole says beside me on the stiff bench. "I just hope they spell my last name correctly in the obituaries."

I stifle a laugh.

"You think I'm joking," she snaps. "But I've lived with María longer than you. When she gets here, she'll be riding a pale horse—"

"Hi, Freya," a passing policeman says, raising his Styrofoam cup of coffee to me.

"Hey, Danny," I say, half waving. "Haircut looks good."

Officer Danny smiles, flashing his gap. "Did it myself."

"Oh, it shows," I reply without skipping a beat. He laughs a jolly laugh before turning a corner. I smile after him and then turn back to Nicole, who looks incredulous.

"You're unbelievable."

"Look," I say, lowering my voice. "Everything's gonna be fine. Just stick to the story. Next time, we'll be more care—"

"*Next time?*" Now Nicole's the one who laughs. "Oh man, you're full of jokes tonight. You're also full of—"

"Nicole Dickman?" a male voice booms.

"It's *Diekman*," Nicole corrects, sliding up her glasses and rubbing her eyes irritably. On the list of the world's all-time worst names, Nicole's is *definitely* near the top. She stands up, shoots me a peevish glare, then shuffles off toward the policeman who beckons her toward his office.

Once the door shuts behind her, I distract myself with the small television on the wall across from me. A commercial's wrapping up. A young blond guy in a colorful windbreaker is brandishing his new Restorey with glee, while a boisterous male announcer declares, ". . . because everyone knows that artificial recall is only as effective as your Restorey. With the all-new Restorey Edge from Memory

34

Frontier, don't just recall your memories, relive them! Available in stores now. Accessories sold separately. Batteries not included."

I roll my eyes.

A news story comes on next.

"Our top story this evening comes from rural Tennessee, where Memory Frontier—the Fortune 500 company responsible for the first line of Restoreys—has just announced what they're calling 'ground-breaking medical technology that will revolutionize our fight with Memory Killer.' Diana Short has more on the story."

I lean forward, intrigued.

"Thanks, Zach. I'm in Foxtail, Tennessee, standing in front of a sprawling, new boarding-school campus that's nestled deep in the woods and borders Land Between the Lakes—a beautiful national forest. In two weeks, five hundred randomly chosen students from all over the country will arrive, enroll in their classes, and settle into their state-of-the-art dorms." The news camera zooms out, revealing a serious-looking man in a suit and tie. "Right now I'm joined by Frontier spokesman Marshall Kendrick. Marshall, just what makes this boarding school so special?"

"Well, Diana, the students lucky enough to be chosen for enroll-ment will receive an all-expenses-paid tuition, and they'll be a part of our historic efforts to combat memory loss and potentially reverse it. You see, under the leadership of our cofounder and CEO, Alexander Lochamire, we've developed an all-new piece of medical technology that could very well retire the Restorey altogether and pave the way for a more effective, more streamlined way of recalling."

"Those are some pretty audacious claims," the field reporter says, chuckling.

"Well, sure, but Memory Frontier was also the first major corpo-ration audacious enough to experiment with artificial recall. And that groundbreaking experimentation led to the world's first Restorey."

"Fair enough. So how exactly will these students be involved?"

"After receiving consent from their parents or guardians, each student enrolled at Foxtail Academy will be required to wear a device for a set number of hours. We'll monitor the technology's performance and efficacy throughout the school year and publish our findings to the public in tandem with a wide release sometime next fall."

"And I don't suppose you can offer any details on what the device is?"

The spokesman smiles. "I cannot, no. But I'll say this"—he turns and looks into the camera—"students who lottery into Foxtail Academy are going to be a part of history. Diana, thank you, I gotta run."

The field reporter shrugs as the news camera centers her in the frame. "Well, there you have it." She brings the microphone closer to her mouth. "A part of history."

Officer Song calls out to me.

"You just never learn, do you, kid?" he says, folding his thick arms across his chest.

I glance up at him from the bench, forcing a smile. "What can I say? I'm forgetful."

Officer Song's office is tiny—a glorified broom closet—and it's not until I've taken my seat across from his desk that I notice someone standing in the shadows beside a metal filing cabinet. The man looks to be in his late fifties, with salt-and-pepper hair and stubble. He wears a grayish suit with dark suspenders, projecting the air of someone very important . . . or at least someone who *thinks* he's very important. He hardens his face, brooding so much that I begin to wonder if he has a medical condition that makes it impossible for him *not* to brood.

Officer Song sits down in his creaky chair and holds up a piece of paper. "Unlawful tampering with your cognition wheel. Violating curfew. Hijacking a vehicle. Visiting a metropolitan area without a handler or adult guardian. Trespassing." He sets the paper down and meets my eyes. "And that's *just* tonight."

"That sounds like a really impressive résumé, if you ask me."

"You're in serious trouble this time, Freya," Officer Song says gravely, and I believe him. The problem? I don't really care. "I've always told you that, at a certain point, I'd have to stop sticking my neck out for you. Did you think I was bluffing? And what are you doing breaking into abandoned factories anyway?"

"When will I get my video camera back?"

The man behind him shifts his weight.

"That's another thing." Officer Song picks up the paper again. "That Sony Betamovie was reported stolen four months ago. What's a kid like you need a video camera for, huh?"

I shrug. "I'm a degen lost in the foster system, and I don't have a whole lot to look forward to." I give him an apathetic look. "When I turn eighteen next February and leave my foster home, I'll be assigned to a handler, and then I'll have to find some minimum-wage job that I'm sure I'll hate. At that point it's just a coin toss to see what kills me first: my dead-end job or my deteriorating brain. So I figure a video camera isn't the worst way to pass the time."

Officer Song blinks. "That's very . . ."

"Sardonic?" I ask. "Yeah, my guidance counselor says that too. Been meaning to look that word up." I harden my tone. "Shouldn't María be here with me? I've seen enough movies to know that I don't have to talk to you without a legal guardian present."

The man behind Officer Song clears his throat.

"Look," Officer Song says, straightening up, his kindly eyes locked on me. "That was private property you trespassed on, Freya. Property owned by Memory Frontier. But they're willing to drop the charges against you if you accept . . . *this.*" He slides another piece of paper across his desktop. I give both Officer Song and the mysterious man a blank stare before picking up the sheet of paper.

It has a Memory Frontier seal at the top—a colorful *M* designed to look like an intertwining marriage of brain cells and flowering vines.

To Freya Izquierdo,

It is my pleasure to extend to you this formal invitation to enroll at Foxtail Academy. I believe we are on the cusp of something truly remarkable—something that could save countless lives. And the only way we can achieve this is with help from students like YOU.

This is going to be a school year unlike any other, marked by exciting innovation and the promise of real change for mankind.

To accept your enrollment, please have your parents or legal guardian sign the back portion of this letter and mail it *no later than August 11.* (A stamped envelope with our return address has been provided to you along with this letter.) When you opt-in for enrollment, we'll immediately mail you a welcome packet.

We hope to see you on move-in day at Foxtail Academy.

Sincerely,
Alexander Lochamire
Co-founder and CEO,
Memory Frontier

I read the letter twice and then flip to the back, where both of my foster parents have already signed on the dotted line. My thumb smudges the fresh ink, and I can practically hear my foster mother María whispering breathily to her husband as they debated this decision: "Getting her out of Long Beach could be *just* what she needs."

"Putting aside my personal feelings about all this 'trial' and 'testing new technology' stuff," Officer Song says, leaning back in his chair, "I can't deny that this would be a fresh start for you. A chance to get out of Long Beach and—"

"Please don't pretend to know what's best for me," I interrupt, tossing the paper down. "You don't. *Neither* of you do." I eye the mysterious man, who unexpectedly replaces his scowl with a restrained smile.

I want to tell them both that I reject this deal, that they can stick it you-know-where. That I'd rather take my chances in juvie than be shipped out to the middle of nowhere to become a lab rat for some billion-dollar corporation.

But then I think of Nicole, who didn't ask for any of this. Nicole, who was just being a good foster sister . . . a good friend.

I take a beat, compose myself, and say, "Nicole gets off scot-free. And I'd like my video camera back."

Officer Song snorts. "You're not really in a position to make demands." But he rubs his chin, considering me with visible amusement. "Your foster sister doesn't have any priors. I'll see to it that she gets nothing more than a slap on the wrist. As for the video camera . . . it's not yours, it's stolen. But . . . you can have the tape back."

I grind my teeth. "Fine."

Officer Song rises to his feet, and I follow suit. "C'mon, your foster parents are in the lobby." He walks around the desk and opens the door. "Dean Mendelsohn here needs to make a few phone calls."

I pause in the doorway and turn back toward the man, who procures a boxy cell phone from his pocket and pulls out the long antenna with pinched fingers. "I'll have my eye on you this year, Freya Izquierdo," the dean says contemptuously.

❖ ❖ ❖

Officer Song doesn't accompany me to the front of the precinct. I know my way around this place like the back of my tattooed hand. As I walk, my thoughts rush around in my head in a turbulent storm: Why did Memory Frontier select *me* for this trial? Why would they send the school's dean all the way to Long Beach for my little interview? I don't think for a minute it's a coincidence that Frontier "randomly" selected me the very day I trespassed on their property.

Don't they have more important things to do than enroll a seventeen-year-old delinquent degen in their stupid boarding school?

A wild shrieking interrupts my thoughts. A guy in handcuffs is flailing on the linoleum floor in the hall, kicking the air as two police officers try to restrain him. I gasp and flatten myself against the wall, unable to look away from the kid's agony.

"My window! My window!" he screams out, large veins bulging out of his forehead like fault lines. "I missed my window! Please, please!"

My mouth and throat go dry. He missed his window, as in he missed his next window for artificial recall.

I hear the distinctly haunting, three-octave wail of a MACE vehicle approaching the precinct. The US Memory and Cognition Enforcement is a federal law-enforcement agency whose aim is to "protect" citizens of this fine nation from the erratic men and women whose rapid memory loss makes them a danger to society.

This delirious kid, who doesn't appear much older than me, is likely destined for the Fold. I've heard that in the time before Memory Killer, those with dementia or Alzheimer's were cared for by family or checked into nursing homes. Theirs was a tragic fate to be sure, but did they descend into violent hysteria like many degens do today?

Like this poor soul here?

My breathing quickens. I start to hyperventilate as the scene plays out: Two MACE agents decked out in smoke-black armor race past me. Their apparel looks like riot gear, and as they thunder by, I catch my reflection in one of the agent's shiny, militaristic helmets.

I look small.

I look lost.

I look like the terrified little degen that I am.

The two MACE agents, forceful and precise, yank the hysterical guy off his back and to his feet. He jerks around, seemingly unable to control his faculties, as one of the agents violently injects him with a torpedo-looking syringe.

I can almost feel the ice-cold tip of the syringe as it punctures his twitching neck. I can feel the sedative set to work as his shrieks taper off and his body goes lax. I can feel—

"Freya." I flinch away from Officer Song, who had placed a soft hand on my trembling shoulder. He watches me with a look of deep concern. Behind him, Dean Mendelsohn stands in the doorway, his penetrating eyes also trained on me with one eyebrow cocked.

They both watch me, not the two MACE agents, who drag the unconscious guy off to who knows where.

I swallow and meet Officer Song's eyes. "When does my flight for Tennessee leave?"

4

FLETCHER COHEN

"I expected you later," Fletcher's father said evenly, hands clasped behind his back. He wore his customary black three-piece suit and tie, meticulously knotted around his clean-shaven neck—as if he *just* tied it. Fletcher pretty much only saw his father dressed like a politician, like he was forever bound by some contract to dress a certain way all of the time. Even when he was home and not in DC, he only ever wore suits, including around the house. Fletcher was not convinced he owned a T-shirt. "How was dinner?"

"Fine," he replied, avoiding his father's eyes. Easier than explaining he and Denise hadn't eaten after all. He unlatched the garage door, slid it open, and walked his motorcycle inside. He leaned his Ducati against its kickstand and turned around to find that his father had silently followed him into the garage.

"I see you forgot your helmet," he said, standing between

Fletcher and the driveway. The streetlights in the distance backlit him, creating an eerie shadow that draped across his nose and down the side of his hard jawline. The whites of his eyes cut through the darkness.

"Oh, right," Fletcher said, unsettled. He cleared his throat. "My bad."

"Your mother hates when you forget to wear your helmet."

"She *is* a stickler for rules, huh?"

Fletcher's father nodded and took a step, narrowing the gap between them. "I sent her for takeout. She should be back soon."

"You guys sure do love your pad Thai."

"But don't worry, son," he said, lowering his voice to a whisper. "When she comes home, I won't tell her you forgot to wear your helmet. It can be our secret."

His father possessed a razor-sharp enunciation, as if every sentence he spoke had been drafted on paper at a lamplit desk and then reviewed by a team of proofreaders. It was undoubtedly what made him so successful at politicking. Though Fletcher was used to him talking in such a pointed manner and with such a pointed cadence, tonight the underlying intensity in his calm and collected tone was alarming.

Fletcher swallowed. "Cool. I'm gonna crash." And without another word he brushed past his father and walked through the still-open front door, across the foyer past the credenza, and then down the hall into his bedroom. He locked the door and then leaned against it, letting out a long breath.

If it was so important for his father to meet with that woman in private, why in the world did he risk getting caught here, at home?

He shook his head and crossed the bedroom to his desk, which sat beside a pair of french doors. Past the half-drawn curtains, Fletcher could see the fading pink sky expanding over the infinity pool, across the hills, and toward the ocean like watercolors spilled across textured paper. He'd lived in this house most of his life, and that view still gave him pause.

He pulled out the desk chair and pushed aside his Walkman, a handful of cassette tapes, and some issues of *National Geographic*. With the desktop clear, he began to root inside one of the drawers for a sheet of lined paper and a pencil. Next, Fletcher played "Running Up That Hill" on his boombox to help strengthen the memory of what he'd witnessed at the traffic light nearly half an hour earlier. As he journaled, he tried to capture every single detail so it was here, on paper, should this memory ever unexpectedly fade. He quickly jotted down everything, from the woman's features, to the grayness of her eyes, to the faint smell of her handler's cigarette smoke.

And at the very bottom, he wrote down the burning, million-dollar question and underlined it several times: *Can Memory Killer strike during artificial recall?*

Fletcher heard the front door of his home open, followed by the muffled sounds of his mother's voice.

At any moment, she would inevitably come knock on his bedroom door to ask if he'd like to join them for dinner, even though she knew he'd had plans with Denise earlier. He shut off his boombox, folded the paper in half once, then a second time, then walked over to his bed. He got on both knees and retrieved the *Raiders of the Lost Ark* tin lunchbox he'd kept since middle school.

This little box had become Fletcher's go-to "safe."

He flipped back the latch with his thumb and opened the lid, revealing a soft pack of cigarettes, a worn copy of a Pacific Northwest road atlas, a faded Polaroid of him and his parents at Disneyland when he was maybe six or seven, and four other pieces of folded paper—each containing his stream-of-consciousness questions about memory loss.

Are animals afflicted by Memory Killer?

What happens when someone who already has dementia is attacked by Memory Killer?

What came first: the Fold or Memory Killer?

The scientists on the news say Memory Killer isn't a pathogen, something visible in CT scans, so what is it?

Et cetera, et cetera.

Fletcher placed the folded paper on top of the others, shut the lunchbox, and slid it back underneath his bed. He kicked off his boots, jogged back to his desk, snatched his Walkman, and jumped into bed. He slipped the headphones over his ears and pressed Play. The cassette tape rolled to life, and R.E.M.'s ethereal "Pilgrimage" flooded into his ears—picking up from the last time he listened, right smack in the middle of the second verse.

With any luck, his mother would think he'd passed out and leave him alone. So he closed his eyes and pretended to be asleep. Before he could shut off his brain, he thought back to the pretty lab tech from the repository. Molly Ringwald's double. What was her name again? Alex Something? Or was it Andrea? Fletcher strained to recall, but the detail was fading . . .

No matter. The staccato keystrokes in "Perfect Circle" lightly carried him off to dreamland.

The next morning, the obnoxious ringing of Fletcher's digital alarm clock sliced through his dreams, and he was up and at 'em after only a few seconds.

He smacked the Off button, rubbed his eyes, and tossed his headphones aside. He took off the clothes he'd slept in and threw on a

T-shirt and shorts, then practically stumbled out of his bedroom and into the hall—still yawning.

His father stood at the wide island separating the expansive living room and kitchen, fully dressed and sipping his black coffee. With one hand he clasped his bone-white mug and with the other, the day's edition of the *Times*. His glasses rested on his head, and he didn't look up as Fletcher walked past him and opened the fridge. He glanced at the headline as he passed by. HIGH-SPEED CHASE ON 405 LEAVES 3 DEAD. MALE DRIVER STILL AT LARGE.

"Morning," his father said, taking a long sip.

Fletcher said hey and poured himself a glass of orange juice. He could hear his father opening his mouth, but he was cut off by his mother's entrance.

"Morning, hon," she said delightedly, rubbing her son's back as she made for the cabinets. "Missed you last night."

"I was beat," he said, avoiding his father's eyes. "Decided to call in early."

"Beat?" she repeated, setting her glass down and touching his forehead with the back of her hand. "You're not ill, are you?"

"Mom, no, I'm not ill." He shook his head.

"He broke up with Denise," his father said coolly.

Fletcher's mother gasped. "What?"

"I . . . How did you know that?" Fletcher's ears reddened with either embarrassment or anger. Probably both.

"Well, yesterday was Friday, wasn't it?" he said, not looking up from his newspaper. "And you're usually out late with her and your friends. So either you're in a fight or you broke up."

"Are you two fighting?" his mother asked earnestly, staring at the side of his face.

Fletcher scowled at his father, annoyed beyond words that he was in his business, before finally murmuring, "No. He's right. We broke up."

"Hon, I'm *so* sorry. Can you two repair things before school starts?"

Fletcher shrugged and left the kitchen, staring his father down as he walked into the dining room. He *hated* how well his father was able to read him and that situation. If his ability to observe and perceive wasn't so sharp, Fletcher would have guessed he was spying on him.

He ground his teeth as he sat down at the dining room table, where his Restorey awaited. Beside it was a leather bag with a dozen slots, each containing a memory tape. These were the archived memories Fletcher was currently cycling through.

Every morning, he recalled a different memory according to the MeReader's regimen. For example, the memory tape he received in March had to be recalled precisely 117 times over the span of a year before it was considered a fully restored memory, at which point the memory tape could be "wiped" with a magnetic tool and discarded, then replaced by a *new* memory tape at his next monthly visit to the repository.

It was a cruel cycle that made basic things like travel or camping a real pain in the ass.

As much as Fletcher was looking forward to turning eighteen, at times he wished he was still fifteen or younger—when he didn't have to be bothered at 7:00 a.m. for artificial recall.

Fletcher reached for the laminated paper that detailed his recall sequence for the month. This morning he was to recall the memory tape from last November. To date, he'd recalled this particular memory 216 times and, per the notes, only had to artificially recall it four more times. He grabbed the memory tape labeled *11.01.86*, took it out of its case, and loaded it into his black Restorey.

His mother joined him at the table, setting a plate of buttered english muffins between them. She set to work uncoiling the wires attached to two receivers, which looked similar to electrode stickers.

Once she was done with this, she plugged them into the Restorey and carefully fastened them to Fletcher's temples.

"I really am sorry to hear about you and Denise," she said, still gently holding both receivers against his skin. Behind her, the faintest hint of morning sunlight began to creep in through the venetian blinds.

"It's fine, Mom, seriously," he said, trying to sound convincing. While that was true, there was a reason he didn't tell his parents about his dating life: to avoid conversations like these.

She frowned and dropped her hands. Then she picked up the laminated piece of paper and scanned it. "You've got the tape from November?"

"Yeah."

She flipped over the paper and read aloud. "'Have you consumed any psychoactive substances such as alcohol in the last six to eight hours?'"

"No."

"'On a scale of one to ten, how well can you recollect the memory you're about to recall without the use of the memory tape: ten being vividly, one being not at all.'"

"Seven," he replied.

"'What elements of this memory are still foggy: the setting, the people present, or'—?"

"My emotional state," he said guardedly.

His mother's eyebrows rose, as they did every time he had to give this answer. But she refrained from prodding.

"Don't worry," she said, setting the laminated paper aside. "Once you're eighteen, you'll be able to recall without this irksome checklist."

"I know." Fletcher checked to make sure the Restorey's volume was set to his liking before slouching in the high-back chair.

"Okay, hon. Let's begin."

He nodded and gave her a half smile. Then he clamped his eyes shut and braced for the recall. The last thing he heard was the soft *click!* of his mother pressing Play on the Restorey, which was swiftly followed by a hot stabbing sensation on his temples. A near-suffocating pressure briefly enveloped his head, like his skull had been wedged between the closing grip of a steel vise. After that uncomfortable moment passed, an icy feeling started behind his eyes and then trickled *upward*, behind his forehead, before cascading deep into the core of his brain.

And then there was a brilliant, blinding whiteness that washed away any lingering thoughts. Just like that—like someone had snapped their fingers—Fletcher was inside his memory.

Afterward, he heard the distant *clack!* of his memory tape finishing playback inside the black Restorey.

Fletcher blinked his eyes open and slowly removed the receivers from his temples. He set them on the dining table and noticed his parents were both seated at the table and hooked up to their Restoreys—eyes closed, heads leaned back, deep in their respective artificial recalls. A mug of coffee steamed in front of his father; a half-eaten english muffin hardened in front of his mother. The soft, almost peaceful hum of their Restoreys was the only sound in the dining room.

Fletcher stood up and steadied himself, feeling light-headed after that emotional recall. He knew he should remain seated and reflect for a moment (it was highly encouraged that one sat for a time with emotionally complex recalls), but his stomach felt like it was going to eat itself.

He made his way into the kitchen and grabbed a box of cereal. The TV in the living room played the disturbing music video for "Land of Confusion" by Genesis on the MTV channel.

He grabbed the remote off the island and clicked away.

A story was running on the morning news about some boarding school that Memory Frontier had founded so the corporation could test its new, groundbreaking medical technology on randomly selected kids.

Fletcher tossed a handful of cereal into his mouth and chewed, listening as the field reporter interviewed people on the street.

"It's outrageous."

"No parent should consent to shipping their kids off to be tested."

"Focus groups are one thing, but these kids are going to be away from their homes and their families for an entire year!"

"If you're a parent watching this and you're considering it, ask yourself: Could you sleep at night knowing your kid's a glorified lab rat?"

Fletcher chuckled. Alexander Lochamire, the cofounder of Memory Frontier, made headlines just about every month for some controversial statement, business decision, or questionable investment. His name came up a lot around the Cohen dinner table, and Fletcher's father had even played golf with the man a couple of times—for charity, of course.

Fletcher flipped off the TV and set down the remote, feeling mildly sorry for the unsuspecting kids whose parents were dumb enough to sign them up for that.

Honestly, he thought, munching on more cereal, *the worst part about that boarding school—aside from it being a boarding school—is probably that it's in some Podunk town in the South.*

He returned to his bedroom and shut the door, where he finished off his breakfast, listened to the album *The Queen Is Dead* by the Smiths, and made the difficult decision to lie in bed until around lunchtime.

❖ ❖ ❖

On Monday, Fletcher went to the movies and saw *The Lost Boys* with a couple of friends, and when he came home, he found a letter waiting for him on his desk. There was a Memory Frontier seal on the back, and his heart sank at once.

"You gotta be kidding me," he said to himself, collapsing on his bed.

His father appeared in the hallway, and he loitered by the door when he noticed his son. "You're home," he said, pushing his glasses up his nose. He gestured toward the letter in Fletcher's hands and added, "So you've been selected?"

He glowered at his father, immediately wondering if he was responsible for this. "I'm not going."

Fletcher's father smiled. He flattened his black tie and said, eyes glinting behind his glasses, "I'd pack a lot of shorts. Tennessee gets very humid in August."

5

FREYA IZQUIERDO

Right before the plane begins its descent, as I'm wrapping up my head-phones and getting ready to stuff my Walkman into my backpack, my eyesight starts to haze, then my mind is violently transported to a scene outside a baseball park. Here, in the parking lot, I squint against the setting sun, watching my silhouetted dad. He stands only a few yards off, hands at his hips, with his back to me and looking out toward the baseball park in the distance. I can hear "Eye of the Tiger" by Survivor playing scratchily over the loudspeakers. After a few moments, the great tall lights over the field flash on, mystical clocks signaling the twilight, and my dad expels a large breath. He smiles, his skin gleaming in the dusk. I sense him opening his mouth to say something, but before he can turn to face me the half memory abruptly ends and I am back on the plane. The lingering, unfinished scene presses me into abject discomfort.

A flight attendant, whose winged badge says he is Billy Watkins, pauses in the aisle to ask if I'm all right.

I nod. "First time flying," I say, blaming my nausea on motion sickness. I look up from his name badge to meet his eyes and find—with a stifled gasp—that they're solid gray orbs.

Memory Killer.

"Miss?" he says, cocking his head, his eyes a sideways hourglass of storm clouds. I want to tell him what I see, but I know that won't change a thing. In moments it'll all be over and the color will return to Billy Watkins's eyes. Whatever memory is being erased from this flight attendant's mind will be erased, and he will never know the difference.

I feel a kind of anguish for this man who, like all of us, is losing a precious picture of his past. His first kiss? That Christmas morning when he received his favorite gift? That indescribable moment when he first listened to music through headphones? Of course, he *could* be losing a traumatic memory. Perhaps something he subconsciously suppressed. I remember hearing this doctor on the TV talk about how the latest-model MeReader still has some difficulty differentiating between a *suppressed* and a *repressed* memory. He said that while they've come a long way since the MeReader was invented ten years ago, there's always room for improvement. And that—

"Would you like some water?" the flight attendant asks.

I nod, avert my eyes from his colorless ones, and tell him that would be nice.

After I shuffle off the airplane with my carry-on (still nursing a smarting headache), I follow the herd of passengers through the wide terminal halls toward baggage claim. Along the way, I pass a WEL-COME TO THE VOLUNTEER STATE! sign, as well as a series of neon-colored

PSAs that advise people to call a hotline if they're experiencing para-
lyzing headaches or recurring spells of misremembering.

When I arrive at baggage claim, it takes a while before I spot
the softside, floral-patterned suitcase my foster parent loaned me—
floating by on the conveyor belt amid a sea of other ear-tagged
suitcases. The boxy bag on wheels is ratty and faded, and contains
my every possession. Not a whole lot, which is just the way I like it.

I lug the suitcase toward the exit, and as soon as I step outside, a
humid afternoon heat such as I've never experienced rushes me. I can
feel my skin glisten with sweat. The thick and muggy air smells . . .
different. I don't really know how else to put it. It's definitely a *good*
different. It's weighty and wet, and it carries a kind of rich summer
sweetness that tingles the inside of my nose. It's like I've uncapped
some perfume and unleashed an intoxicating aroma. I smile dumbly,
savoring the fresh air, when—

Someone brushes past me, nearly knocking me off my feet. The
young, blond-headed guy wears large headphones and is completely
oblivious. "Hey!" I shout. "Watch where you're going!"

He stops and turns, pulling down his headphones and letting
them hang around his neck. "What's up?"

"Watch where you're going," I repeat, adjusting my backpack.

"Oh, right, my bad," he says, flashing a toothy smile. His long,
parted hair falls past his ears, and he runs both his hands through it,
tousling it casually. He wears a pastel-colored polo with the collar
flipped up, jeans, and expensive-looking Nike high-tops. So, in other
words, he looks like every other guy from my high school. His smile
broadens. "You're that girl from my flight."

"What do you mean 'that girl'?"

"The one who almost hurled."

"What?"

"Yeah, no, you're *definitely* her. I was in the row across from you."

"I don't know what you're talking about."

"You get used to it," he says, pocketing his hands. "The flying. I fly all the time. When I was ten, I would pretend I was the pilot to distract myself from being scared"—and then he actually protrudes his lips out and makes a noise that doesn't *remotely* sound like an airplane engine—"But mostly it would just annoy the parentals."

"'The parentals'?"

"My dad and stepmom, yeah. They're funny." He pulls a small bag out of his pocket and proffers it. "Sunflower seed?"

"I'm good."

"Nice to meet you," he replies. "I'm Chase Hall."

I blink, staring at him blankly.

"I'm kidding!" he says, scooping out some sunflower seeds and tossing them into his mouth. "I don't *actually* think your name's *good*. Unless, of course, it *is*, which would be kind of cool."

I stare at Chase, trying to decide if he's real. He must've been dropped as a kid. No one's *this* cheery. I clear my throat. "I'm Freya Izquierdo."

He nods, like he was somehow expecting me to say that. "That's a really pretty name. You're Hispanic then?"

"Mexican," I correct, wondering where this is going.

"Our pool guy's Mexican too!" And there it is, people's irresistible urge to say they know another Mexican. "I don't think I've ever known a Freya. 'Course, I could've forgotten. But not you, no. I'd never forget you."

Somehow that golden-retriever smile of his deepens, but I just continue my deadpan stare.

"Huh," he eventually says, "that usually works."

I dig into my front pocket and retrieve the folded-up pamphlet that Foxtail Academy sent me. I flip the pamphlet to the back, which details the day's itinerary. According to this, I need to wait by—

"Arrivals," Chase says. I look up to find him waving the exact same pamphlet. "C'mon, it's this way."

Chase marches off, stepping around and between throngs of people with the confidence of someone who's navigated an airport before. I grab my suitcase and drag it on its wheels, jogging to catch up.

"This is all so wild, isn't it?" he says after I'm at his side. "I mean, has it really sunk in for you? Of all the millions of kids out there, *we're* the ones chosen for this. Luck of the draw, or fate? Who's to say?"

I grunt. "I'm just glad I don't have to spend my senior year at Victory High."

"Long Beach?"

"Yeah."

"Newport Beach," he says, pointing at his chest with his thumb.

I realize he's not lugging a suitcase. "You crammed everything you'll need for a whole year in that backpack?"

"Huh? Oh, yeah, no. My stepmom had my things shipped directly to campus."

Oh, right. Pool guy. Newport Beach. Duh.

"The news is calling us a 'chosen generation,'" he continues, lost in the fog of his own little world.

I shrug. "That has a better ring to it than 'lab rats.'"

Chase and I emerge from beneath a concrete overpass, which I assume is the path taken by those headed toward departures, and the intense sun reminds me that I'm not in Southern California anymore. Chase whips out a pair of iridescent sunglasses and slides them on importantly. As he does, I catch the cognition wheel tattooed to his right hand.

It's the three-quarter mark. He's a recollector. I switch from dragging my suitcase with my right hand to my left so I can casually slide my right hand into my pocket, keeping my own cognition wheel hidden. I'm not ashamed of who I am. I don't even think this dumb tattoo defines me. But I'm exhausted from that four-hour flight and sweating from what feels like every pore in my body. I don't want to get into the recollector/degen discussion right now.

"Anyway," he says, fidgeting with his backpack straps. "I can't help but feel like this is all a big deal. They're saying that whatever we're going to be trialing will replace artificial recall. Imagine that! Ha! A world where we don't have to do recall every morning!"

"Or multiple times a day," I add under my breath. Speaking of which . . . I check my wristwatch. It reads 12:23 p.m., which means it's 2:23 here. Shoot. I've never had to recall in a different time zone. My next recall isn't until 1:00 p.m. Pacific Time, which is in half an hour, so I'll likely have to do it on the drive to campus. After I get settled into my dorm room, I'll need to find a faculty member and ask them how to reorder my recall schedule.

"Here we are," Chase says, nodding toward a long row of shuttles and taxicabs up ahead. At the very end there's a white bus, which is parked beneath a giant billboard that reads DON'T FORGET TO PULL OVER BEFORE YOU RECALL. I nearly laugh out loud.

As we approach the bus, which has the academy logo emblazoned on the side, a man in his thirties hops out to greet us. He wears khaki shorts and a tucked-in beige polo. He has an infectious smile, straight brown hair, and a well-groomed mustache.

"Whew, sun's hotter than a fire ant," he says with a slight twang in his words. He pulls out his *Top Gun* aviators and puts them on as Chase and I reach the shade of the bus. "I'm Ben Williams, your campus counselor. And you must be"—he points at Chase—"Freya. Which means you're"—he points at me—"Chase!"

On cue, Chase laughs enough for both of us.

"Nah, I'm only foolin'," Mr. Williams says as if he needs to clarify. I smile despite myself. "Listen, you two are my stragglers. Let's get y'all out of this heat and aboard the SS *Foxtail* so we can make our way to campus!"

He takes my luggage and loads it into the bottom compartment of the bus while Chase and I clamber inside. It smells about how you'd expect a hot, humid bus filled with a handful of sweaty teenagers to smell. A gaggle of white girls near the front begin to whisper among themselves when they see Chase. I sidestep past him in the narrow aisle and head for the back. The last six or seven rows are completely vacant, so I swing off my backpack and slump down into the hard-backed seat at the very end of the bus. I wipe the sweat from my face with the sleeve of my T-shirt, watching as Chase tells the girls some story while making animated hand gestures. They reward him with raucous laughter, his personal live studio audience!

I roll my eyes.

Mr. Williams appears at the front of the bus a second later and says something to the driver. Then the long vehicle rumbles to life, the doors shut with a *hiss*, and we start to roll forward. Mr. Williams scans the bus. With his aviators still on, it's pretty hard to tell where he's actually looking. But the next thing I know he's making his way down the aisle and headed straight my way. He collapses in the seat across from me and lets out a long sigh from the bottommost part of his belly. "You can live here your whole life and still never get used to these humid afternoons!"

I give him a half smile just to be polite. There's another burst of laughter from Chase's small crowd, and I find myself increasingly annoyed.

"It's crazy what a little fame will do, ain't it?"

"Huh?"

"You know, the attention it gets you," Mr. Williams says, tilting his head down and glancing over the top of his sunglasses in Chase's direction. I'm thoroughly confused at this point.

"You mean you don't recognize him?" Mr. Williams cries, baffled. "He's that kid from those Memory Frontier commercials! 'Don't just recall your memories, relive them!'"

Huh. I didn't see it at first, but now I guess Chase *does* look familiar.

"Bah, that won't matter much soon, I guess," Mr. Williams says, pushing up his sunglasses.

"What do you mean?"

"Well, that's one of the exciting things about Foxtail Academy, isn't it? We got students coming from all over the country. And, well, it doesn't matter where you been or where you come from, because everyone's starting from scratch. You know? This isn't just *your* first day . . . it's *everyone's* first day."

"Yeah, sure, I guess."

"You don't sound convinced."

"It's just, well, for me it'll *always* matter where I've come from. People will *always* see me as different." I turn in my seat to face Mr. Williams, and I can see him starting to get a little uneasy. "Plus, I've had a lot of first days, and I kinda think they're overrated."

"Oh?"

"First day on this earth and my mom died giving birth to me. Then there was the first day someone called me a beaner. Think it was in sixth grade. *No bueno, verdad?* Oh! And then there was my first day as an orphan. That pretty much sucked. Then my first day as a foster kid"—I exaggerate a gagging noise—"And who could forget (no pun intended) my first day as a degen?" I hold up my two-quarter mark for him to see.

Mr. Williams stares at my cognition wheel and, to my surprise, his body goes visibly lax.

"So forgive me if I don't gush over first days."

After a very long pause, he says, "You know, I'm sorry. I guess I don't think on any of that very often. Well, at all, if I'm being honest."

I start to say more, but my wristwatch beeps, reminding me that I have fifteen minutes until my artificial recall.

Mr. Williams gives me a knowing look. "I may not understand

what it's like to be . . . to be *Mexican*," he whispers as if it's a curse word. I let it slide. "But I do know the sting of being called a degen." He shows me his cognition wheel: a two-quarter mark identical to mine.

Now *I'm* the one who goes lax, releasing tension in my shoulders that I didn't realize was there.

"*You?*"

He nods.

"Where's your handler?"

"Every state's different, Freya," he explains, sounding grateful. "In Tennessee, I can work my job and perform my duties so long as at least *one* recollector is present." He makes a gun with his hand and points at the bus driver. "My next recall is in a couple of hours, so I'll have to do that first thing in my office when we get to campus. And, speaking of recalls, I should probably leave you to it."

He slaps his knees before rising to his feet, but before he leaves he says, "You should know something that I think's pretty darn cool: I pored over the student registry with our teachers and staff all week long. We've got freshmen, sophomores, juniors, and seniors with all different kinds of backgrounds enrolled at Foxtail Academy. And every one of 'em is a recollector. Every single one, Freya, except for you."

I raise an eyebrow skeptically. "That supposed to make me feel good?"

"I dunno," he admits, wiping his mustache with his bottom lip. "But I know it makes me feel kinda proud. It's like, however random they say this whole selection process was, I get the sense they saw something special in you. Some kind of promise in you. I'm pretty excited to see what that is."

I know Mr. Williams means well, but I feel he's putting a kind of implied expectation on me, an expectation I want no part of. I'm not here to prove that degens can roll with recollectors. I'm here because I have to be. And since I have to be, I might as well (1) see why I was selected to trial this mysterious technology, and (2) try to track down someone who has answers about my half-memory dreams.

Mr. Williams chuckles. "I'm getting ahead of myself. You just focus on having a fun senior year. And, with the help of this tech, you might get to make some lasting memories—you know, like a normal kid."

"Speaking of tech . . ." I tilt my head.

Mr. Williams shrugs. "Memory Frontier's been keeping it under lock and key. Even the faculty don't know what to expect. But I'm told a Frontier spokesman is gonna unveil it at our first assembly today."

It's hard to tell if he's actually in the dark or just saying that because he's not supposed to divulge anything to students.

He smiles and starts to leave, but first I ask, "Wait. I need an adult to go over my checklist before I—"

"You'll be eighteen in a year, right?" He laughs and pushes up his sunglasses. "Those checklists are pointless anyway, if you ask me. Oh, and don't worry about this bunch." He gestures toward Chase and the other passengers. "You recall in peace. I'll make sure no one bothers you."

Before I can ask him what that means, he's walking down the aisle, awkwardly balancing himself on the backs of the bus seats. "All right, gang!" he proclaims in a singsongy voice. "Who knows every word to 'Take on Me'?"

I fight it for a second, then give up and smile. Nearly every time I have to artificially recall, I'm beset by these sharp pricks: reminders that I'll never measure up in society. Recollectors will never understand the burden of relying on a Restorey so much. It's a societal disconnect that might never be repaired. All this to say: when I get the chance to recall by myself without someone watching me like I'm a fading patient on a ventilator, I'm beyond thankful.

Mr. Williams is all right, I conclude, watching as he conducts with his hands—leading Chase and the other students through that catchy A-ha song.

I seize my moment alone and pull out my Restorey, attach the receivers to my temples, and then cue up the right memory tape. After getting settled and triple-checking my recall schedule printout, I lean my head back. Before I press Play, a thought occurs to me. In many ways, heading to Foxtail Academy positions me to continue investigating Dad's death. Memory Frontier employed my dad, and now I'm trialing Memory Frontier's precious new invention. The company will likely have a base of operations on campus, fully staffed. If I keep a low enough profile, I just might be able to do some digging . . .

Heading to Tennessee isn't a setback, I realize, my forefinger hovering over the Play button. It's potentially my inflection point.

6

FLETCHER COHEN

The taxicab rolled to a stop on the gravel road canopied by huge trees. In fact, Fletcher saw nothing *but* trees. Green behemoths that touched the sky. Everywhere. As far as the eye could see.

That and a small crowd of reporters and rabid protesters.

The cameramen, field reporters, and vocal objectors came alive in front of the iron gate when they saw Fletcher's taxicab turning up the road. The protesters waved painted signs that read, STUDENTS TAKE TESTS, THEY'RE *NOT* TEST SUBJECTS, and KIDS AREN'T LAB RATS.

That's the best they could come up with?

A security guard appeared. She did her best to fan the protesters and reporters aside while the motorized gate creaked open. The driver rolled through slowly, taking care not to hit anyone. The men and women descended on the passenger windows and shouted things like, "You don't have to do this, kid!" and "Don't let your parents force you to do something you're not comfortable with!" Some even pounded on the glass with their fists. Fletcher recognized one reporter, a young man in a tan suit, from the nightly news. The man shouted a question through the window, but of course his voice was lost in the shouting.

The gate began to close behind them, shutting out the impassioned dissenters and field reporters. Fletcher turned his head and watched as they banged against the gate, thrusting their signs into the air with even more fervor.

"I *love* getting to meet my fans," he joked to the driver, who didn't so much as glance back at him through the rearview mirror.

Tough crowd.

Fletcher looked out his window, gaping at the wooded expanse. *We're really off the grid now*, he realized. The sunlight fell through leaves and branches, spotlighting the tall grass, moss-covered roots, and clusters of dense thickets. Birds swooped down every so often, perching on large rocks or fallen trees, and the occasional acorn fell and thudded lightly against the cab.

After a brief, silent drive, Fletcher spotted the carcass of a small animal lying in a patch of weeds. As the cab rolled by, he saw the distinct features of a fox: its auburn fur, too-big ears, and coal-black paws. And under its head and across the neck, its fur was hardened with dry blood, where swarms of flies feasted and lay eggs.

Fletcher swallowed. Even in the hot cab, he got the shivers.

Fletcher didn't have to dwell on the dead animal too long, because the driver was slowing to a stop at the edge of an immense clearing.

The Foxtail Academy campus was a sprawling collection of squat, single-story buildings with dark green siding, wide porches, and timber columns. The largest of these buildings stood equidistant from the others and had a wraparound porch and a massive, pointed roof.

This must be the auditorium, Fletcher guessed. Beside the big structure was a patch of hackberry trees, and in the shade students milled about laughing. Some threw a Frisbee. Members of the faculty shook hands with parents. Groundskeepers watered the pristine landscaping.

If he didn't know any better, Fletcher would have said this whole thing was staged to look as appealing as possible.

Reluctantly, he flung open the cab door and got out. The unbearable humidity washed over him, assuring Fletcher that it wouldn't be long before his T-shirt and jeans stuck to his skin with sweat. He grabbed his duffel, slung it over his shoulder, and shut the door. He slid on his round-framed sunglasses and scanned his surroundings while the driver unloaded his two suitcases. Fletcher thanked him and handed him his fare, wondering if he could pay the man to take him somewhere else—anywhere but here.

Yet before Fletcher could form an escape plan, the cabdriver was back in his car, making a U-turn, and disappearing down the road back to civilization.

"Sweet," Fletcher said under his breath, grabbing his suitcases and dragging them toward campus. He followed a newly paved sidewalk toward the admissions office, a small building with a prairie barn roof. The wooden directory planted in the grass showed him the dorm rooms and library to the east, the dining hall and lake to the north, and the auditorium, classrooms, and faculty housing to the west.

He approached a folding table outside the admissions office, which had a bold WELCOME, CLASS OF '88! banner hanging from the porch columns. A bespectacled woman in a beige polo and shorts waved him over.

"Well hey there," she said in a Southern accent, looking about as friendly as a job-fair volunteer. "Name?"

"Fletcher Cohen," he replied, standing across the table from her. She picked up a clipboard and scanned the list, mumbling to herself, before spotting his name and thumping it excitedly.

"Here we are!" She made a note with a blue pen, then instructed him to set his suitcases in a pile of other suitcases beside her. "We'll be taking y'all's stuff to the dorms during the assembly that's about to start. And speaking of dorms, you're in room 25W, and your dormmate is"—she consulted her clipboard again—"a Mr. Chase Hall!"

"About that." Fletcher raised his sunglasses and rested them on his head. "I'd like to respectfully ask for a room by myself. See, the thing is . . ." He searched for a lie she just might buy. "I sleep with this really loud humidifier. Thing's a real pain in the you-know-what. Anyway, I'd *hate* to subject . . . Chase, was it? Yeah, I'd hate to subject Chase to that. Really."

The young woman stared at him for a second, then laughed through her nose. "They got a different brand of humor out in California!" She slapped a name badge sticker on his chest with a little more force than necessary. Next, she slid Fletcher's class schedule and a travel-size bottle of mosquito repellent across the table.

He sighed, then took both things and stuffed them into his front pocket.

"Why don't you go ahead and make your way to the auditorium?" She beamed. "Assembly's fixin' to start."

Defeated, he nodded, adjusted the duffel slung over his shoulder, and left the table. As he approached the large structure at the center of campus, he heard "Everybody Wants to Rule the World" by Tears for Fears playing inside the auditorium. The remaining students outside began to file in eagerly, and Fletcher jogged toward them—bringing up the rear.

The air-conditioning offered a wonderful respite from the grueling humidity.

Fletcher took a brief pause to enjoy the coolness before deciding where to sit. The auditorium had amphitheater seating and looked to be at capacity. Indeed, the excited chatter was reaching fever pitch and nearly overpowering the loud music on the PA system. Fletcher glanced up, noticing the exposed ceiling trusses and mounted speakers. The recessed lighting began to dim.

He scrambled down the nearest aisle and spotted an empty seat about six chairs in. He pulled his duffel off and sidestepped toward the seat. He plopped into the chair right as the light on the stage brightened and the music faded. This was met with hearty applause.

"Made it in the nick of time!" the kid beside him said, flashing his braces in a wide, goofy grin. He pushed up his black-rimmed glasses before leaning in uncomfortably close. "I'm gonna call you Nick."

"Please don't do that."

"Nah, I'm not gonna call you Nick." The kid laughed, and before Fletcher could fully appreciate the weirdness of the interaction, a young guy appeared onstage with a microphone in hand. Behind him was a wide row of seated faculty members whose faces were mostly silhouetted.

"Hey, everyone! Let me be the first to welcome y'all to Foxtail Academy's inaugural school year!" The students cheered, whistling and clapping. "I'm Mr. Ben Williams, the senior counselor here at Foxtail. I'll be Dean Mendelsohn's boots on the ground, working with your teachers to ensure that both you *and* they have everything y'all need on a daily basis. Look, obviously this school year is gonna be very different, and in a second, I'm gonna bring Memory Frontier spokesman Marshall Kendrick to the stage to explain just *how* different. But first, I wanna underscore something.

"I know the buzz out there in the world is all about this mysterious memory-technology stuff. I mean, how could it not be? But, at the risk of minimizing y'all's important role in this trial, I also want to invite you to have a little fun."

Mr. Williams paused, squinting in the light and gazing out at the students. He slowly paced the length of the stage and continued: "Out there, we confront the harsh realities of memory loss every single day of our lives. It's a kind of silent warfare that we're all engaged in. And some of us bear the brunt of the battle more than others.

"Yeah, it's a wildebeest of a problem that none of us asked for. But within the walls of Foxtail Academy . . . on these sunny grounds, in the shade of our trees . . . on the Juniper Lake pier, in the frothy water . . . in the noisy dining hall, and yes, even in the stuffy classrooms . . . try to enjoy yourselves, won't you? You are just kids, after all, and shouldn't be bothered by all that." Mr. Williams flipped his free hand as if warding off a swarm of bees.

"Our theme this year is simple: Don't forget to have fun. Say it with me now!" He cupped his ear. *"Don't forget to have fun!"* Everyone around Fletcher chanted in unison. To his surprise, he found himself muttering those words too.

Don't forget to have fun!

Mr. Williams laughed. "All right then, let's give a warm Foxtail welcome to Memory Frontier's Marshall Kendrick!" He handed off the microphone to a clean-shaven, middle-aged man in a blazer.

"I, uh, wow. That's gonna be tough to follow, Mr. Williams," he said sheepishly, forcing a chuckle. He cleared his throat and composed himself. "Well, on behalf of Alexander Lochamire and the entire Memory Frontier board, I want to extend a grateful thank-you to every student here. Your decision to accept enrollment and help us cross the finish line with our new tech is nothing short of brave, admirable, and inspiring. And, speaking of tech, shall we get to it?"

An overhead projector clicked on.

A gigantic image of a sleek black device that reminded Fletcher of his father's pager materialized across the stage backdrop. The advertisement looked like it belonged inside a magazine or on a billboard. The device had only one button and a small display. Beside the device, the pink cursive copy read, "Introducing the Reflector from Memory Frontier."

And below this, in a smaller font: "Remember what it's like to remember."

The whispers began subtly at first, but in no time they rippled throughout the entire auditorium until everyone was having to talk at full volume to be heard. Fletcher watched Marshall, wondering when the spokesman would rein everyone back into his presentation. But he took his sweet time, clearly pleased with the response.

Finally, "This, as you can see, is the Reflector. It's a state-of-the-art, pocket-sized device worn a minimum of eight hours every evening while you sleep, effectively rendering your Restoreys obsolete." After another audible *click*, the image flashed to the next slide. This picture showed a pretty woman lying under the covers and smiling in her sleep. The Reflector sat on her nightstand beside a glass of water and an alarm clock. The two suction discs securely fixed to her temples were noticeably smaller than the ones Fletcher used with his Restorey.

"Gone are the days of fumbling with memory tapes, adhering to strict recall schedules, and having your lives and routines dictated by a MeReader's diagnosis. And, speaking of memory readers . . ." A new slide. This image framed a park, where a bunch of smiling teenagers huddled together held out their right hands. Their cognition wheels included three-quarter marks, two-quarter marks, and even a few one-quarter marks. These were unfortunate individuals who suffered from accelerated loss of short-term memories. Usually these people were shipped off to the Fold, where doctors and hospital staff monitored them intensely. Rumor had it that *those* degens had to artificially recall every hour . . .

The whispers returned, but the Memory Frontier spokesman cut in quicker this time. "That's right. It doesn't matter what your cognition wheel says. It doesn't matter what results you received at your reading. Each Reflector is calibrated uniquely to the wearer and works specifically with that individual's special needs, intricately collaborating with your own cell bodies to *regenerate* the gray matter in your brain. In short, the Reflector is effectively retraining your brain to remember, and shielding your memories like a garrison. Early testing has been very positive, with every single person exhibiting *at least* 70 percent retention in short-term memory, long-term memory, sensory memory, and working memory—month over month. You could say that, as a species, we've reached a cognitive zenith."

Another *click*. Another slide.

Here, the Reflector sat atop a pile of old, broken Restoreys like some mythological warrior posing majestically atop the bodies of felled enemies. There was even purple lightning and plumes of storm clouds. The bold copy read, "Coming Soon: The Reflector," and underneath this in italics, *"Because the only thing worth forgetting is your Restorey."*

Marshall Kendrick stretched out his arms, his eyes sparkling in the spotlight. "It's time we reclaim our right to remember."

The cacophonous applause was deafening.

The students around Fletcher rose to their feet, hollering. Fletcher *felt* like he should be joining in, but something held him back. Something he just couldn't put his finger on.

Sure, this revolutionary technology changed everything. If it worked like Memory Frontier said it did, it would have positive, sweeping effects in the world. People less fortunate than recollectors would experience a level of normality they hadn't tasted in a long, long time.

Fletcher sighed. *I mean, what's not to be excited about?*

But a few persistent questions just wouldn't leave him alone. What were the implications of Memory Killer striking during artificial recall? Or, now: What were the implications of Memory Killer striking while hooked up to these Reflectors?

Fletcher scratched his chin, watching as Mr. Williams shook hands with Marshall Kendrick. They exchanged a few words while the house lights brightened, then the spokesman disappeared off-stage. Once the cheering died down, scattered pockets of conversations erupted around the auditorium.

Mr. Williams spoke into the microphone. "All right, y'all. Pretty exciting stuff! Why doesn't everyone head to their dorms now to get acquainted with your roommates, and then y'all take the rest of the day to get familiar with the campus grounds. Campus staffers will stop by your rooms with your personal Reflectors before our kickoff barbecue and bonfire, which is at 7:00 p.m. sharp!"

Fletcher opened the door to his dorm room to find his roommate lying on the bottom bunk, making out with a freckled girl in a pink tank top and cutoff shorts. Fletcher sighed, tossed his duffel on the floor, and slammed the door.

The young girl rolled off the bed and stood, looking positively mortified.

"Hi," Fletcher said, stuffing his hands into his pockets.

"Yeah, um, hi, I mean, bye," she said, adjusting her ponytail and then practically flying out of the room.

"So I guess that means you've claimed bottom bunk." Fletcher turned in a circle and took in the room. It was modest-sized, with one full bathroom, a single closet, a couch, and a brand-new TV that sat atop an oak dresser. The windows on either side of the bunk bed let in a *ton* of natural light. As far as dorm rooms go, this one was quite spacious.

It was a pity Fletcher wouldn't be staying the night.

"Wow, yeah, sorry about that." His roommate got to his feet. He grinned and held out his hand. "I'm Chase!"

"Fletcher." They shook hands. He spotted his suitcases on the floor next to the dresser, so Fletcher crossed the room, set the suitcases upright, then rolled them toward the door and parked them against the wall.

"Honestly, it's impressive that you guys made it back that quick." Fletcher turned and faced Chase. "I left right after the assembly and came straight here."

"Yeah, ha-ha, that assembly was wild," Chase said, unzipping his own suitcases. He started absently tossing his boxers into one of the dresser drawers. When he finished, he unfurled a Cindy Crawford poster and set to work taping it to the wall above the couch. "Really . . . wild."

Fletcher folded his arms. "You dipped out early, didn't you?"

"It's *very* possible that we did, yeah." Fletcher could actually *hear* him smiling. "It's my curse, man. I'm a sucker for girls named Alicia."

"Her name badge said Maddie." Fletcher raised his eyebrows.

Chase turned slowly, his nose crinkled in embarrassment. "'What's in a name? That which we call a rose by any other name would smell as sweet.'" He winked.

Fletcher shook his head and suppressed some laughter.

"Aren't you gonna unpack?" Chase asked, nodding toward Fletcher's suitcases.

"I would, yeah, only I'm not staying."

"You're not staying?"

"I am *not* staying." Fletcher ripped off his name badge, crumpled it into a small ball, and tossed it overhand toward Chase, who didn't bother attempting to catch it.

"So, what, you're gonna stroll off campus, hop the fence, and—"

"And hitchhike to literally anywhere but here? Yup. That's the plan." Fletcher scooped up his duffel. "I made up my mind on the walk from the auditorium. This trial thing . . . it's not for me"—plus, Fletcher felt he'd been summoned to Foxtail just as he was making incremental progress with his Memory Killer File—"So it is with deep sadness that I bid you adieu."

Before Chase could reply, there was a firm rap on their door. They exchanged a glance.

"Did Maddie forget her Chapstick?" Fletcher asked, reaching for the doorknob. His roommate snort-laughed as Fletcher swung open the door, revealing a nervous-looking kid who wore a backwards baseball cap and a large Darth Vader T-shirt.

"Hello." The guy waved awkwardly.

"Hi."

"I'm Adam McCauley, one of the school prefects." He pointed at the Foxtail Academy pin above his name badge.

Fletcher sniffed. "Okay."

"Yeah. Anyway. Dean Mendelsohn wants to see Fletcher Cohen in his office."

7

FREYA IZQUIERDO

I'm one of the last ones to leave the auditorium after the assembly. My head's spinning, my heart's fluttering in my chest, and there's an impossibly big grin plastered on my face.

No more artificial recall!

It sounds too good to be true. If there's one thing I've learned in life, it's to never let your guard down. The second you do that, the *split second* you get comfortable or excited, the rug gets pulled out from under you, and you're somehow worse off than before.

And yet . . .

And yet I can't help but get swept along in the buzz of this life-changing news! My backpack bounces as I quickly descend the auditorium steps. The sun doesn't feel that hot anymore. The humidity's not as oppressive—it's bearable even. The hundreds of students who fan out toward the dorms chatter and laugh. Some even smile and wave at me. Everyone appears to have a pep in their step, myself included. There's definitely a magic in the air, dispelling the doubt about this place that formed when my bus rolled in. I clasp my backpack straps and head off to find my dorm room, wondering when I'll be awoken from this incredible dream.

That's when I hear Dad's words in my head, clear as the day he uttered them some five years ago: *In a world where memories are like currency, dreams can be a complicated business.*

He was always skeptical of the MeReader's ability to discern the difference between memories, dreams of memories, and just regular old dreams. According to the spokesperson for Memory Frontier, this Reflector is going to operate while I sleep, which begs the question: Will this new technology also increase my ability to recall dreams? I remember my dad talking about how our dreams are stored in short-term memory. He said the MeReader's main goal was to pinpoint meaningful, "at risk of deteriorating" memories—both short- and long-term. This all begs yet another question: Will the Reflector make it difficult for me to know the difference between a memory and a dream? Surely not . . . Dreams certainly *feel* different than memories. In fact, in a lot of dreams that I can recall, many details and elements are off, like the arrangement of my bedroom or the layout of a familiar place.

But then, some of my dreams are vivid, blurring the lines of reality until I wake up and have to tell myself I was dreaming.

I pause in the shade of a tree, maybe fifty yards from the girls' dormitories, and attempt to corral my questions. If this Reflector works, if it's actually successful at fighting the rapid memory loss that has plagued our world for nearly a decade, will it also eliminate the half memories that I've been dreaming when I'm awake? Those flashes that strike me like lightning, leaving me with searing headaches and random snippets from my past?

I really wish I could call you, Dad. I wonder what he would make of all this if he were alive today. Would he be as skeptical about the Reflector as he was about the Restorey? And what would he say about my half-memory dreams, which didn't start until I began artificial recall?

So many questions. I lean against the tree and watch my elated peers flock toward their dorms. *Do any of them have questions like mine? Am I the only soul on campus with a complicated past and an even more complicated present?*

I scold myself. I can't get down on myself. Just because I harbor all these questions doesn't mean I can't let myself enjoy the moment.

I exhale, then march off with a renewed focus to find my room. *Take it one day at a time.* That's all I can do.

After I organize my clothes, I take inventory of my most prized possessions, inspecting them closely to ensure nothing was damaged during the flight.

First, there's my VHS copy of *Bruce Lee, the Legend*. Not only was this one of Dad's all-time favorite documentaries, but Bruce Lee was a hero to him. He would go on and on about Lee's "freakish athleticism," and I would tease him about this. "You sure you don't have a crush on the man?" I pull the tape out of the sleeve and turn it over carefully. Convinced it's damage-free, I put it back in its case and display it on top of the TV.

There's also the VHS tape that Officer Song returned to me, the one containing the footage of the abandoned factory. I almost left this in my shared bedroom at my foster home, but at the last second, I decided to bring it to campus. After working so hard to get that footage, I didn't want to chance one of my foster siblings messing with it.

Next, there's my Fernando Valenzuela bobblehead. When I think about my dad's passion for Fernando, the words *childlike reverence*

76

come to mind. I mean, I could see ballpark fireworks in his eyes whenever he'd tell me how Fernando had won the Cy Young Award, Rookie of the Year, *and* the Silver Slugger. "And he's from Navojoa, *mija*," he'd say, swooning. "Navojoa!" And God forbid I should ever try to talk to my dad when the Dodgers were on TV. I roll my eyes with affection, then flick the enlarged brown head and watch it wobble, feeling satisfied. I set the bobblehead beside *Bruce Lee, the Legend*.

Then there's my leatherbound photo album with the frayed spine. I heft the heavy book out of my suitcase and set it in my lap, running my hand across the cracked surface. I briefly contemplate flipping through but ultimately decide I don't need myself getting all teary-eyed on the floor and giving the worst first impression in the history of first impressions to my roommate (who still hasn't shown). Instead, I walk my photo album to the bottom bunk and slide it underneath the gray pillow until it's completely concealed.

I return to my suitcase, bend down, and grab the last thing in there: a baseball wrapped in construction paper. I trash the paper and clutch the ball in my right hand, bobbing it up and down as if I'm learning its weight for the first time. In high school, my dad struck a home run with this very baseball on the day he was first scouted by Major League Baseball teams. I close my eyes and try to imagine what that must have felt like for him: cracking the ball out of the stadium in front of friends and teammates . . . hearing the spectators roar . . . confidently jogging across those hard plastic, sun-warmed bases . . . all while knowing professional baseball scouts had eyes trained on him the whole time.

When your bat hits the ball outta the park, Dad would say, oohing like he'd just tasted something delicious, *there's a feeling like no other feeling on this planet that courses through your veins.*

I smile and open my eyes to find my roommate, I presume, standing across the room staring and grinning. She wears hot-pink spandex and an oversized Adidas T-shirt. A bright yellow scrunchie holds her highlighted hair in a ponytail.

"Heeey," she says, biting down and showing her white teeth. "You need a minute?"

"I—"

"Looked like you were praying or something. Definitely don't want to interrupt you if you're praying or something."

"I . . . I wasn't." I hold the baseball behind my back.

"Oh, good!" she declares. "I'm Hoa Trang, but you can just call me Ollie." She points to her name badge with both index fingers and cocks her hip to the side.

"I'm Freya, Freya Izquierdo."

"Freya, I *love* your outfit, so fashion forward!" she says. I glance down. I'm wearing my dad's oversized Dodgers T-shirt with the sleeves cuffed, and a pair of thrift-store jeans and sneakers.

I can't tell if Ollie's being sarcastic or sincere.

She walks to the window, unlocks it, and slides it open. Then she retrieves a soft pack of cigarettes from her purse, which sits atop her mound of suitcases next to the bunk bed.

"I have *so* much to tell you, roomie," she says, steadying a cigarette between her lips and lighting it.

"Oh?" With her back momentarily to me, I take the opportunity to hide my dad's baseball in my underwear drawer. I join Ollie by the window, folding my arms across my chest and leaning against the wall.

"I just spent the last half hour meeting some other kids and scoping out the grounds." She pockets her lighter and offers me a drag of her cigarette. I politely decline, and then she continues with theatrical exasperation: "Everyone is just so fascinating in their chronic pursuit of fitting in. We've been here, what, an hour? And they're *already* gravitating toward like-minded individuals and forming cliques. It's *fascinating.*"

"Cliques? Already?" Great. I guess you can't escape inevitabilities.

Ollie takes another puff of her cigarette. As she does this, I see the three-quarter mark neatly inked onto her palm. "Cheerleader types. Jocks. Musicians. Computer nerds. Band geeks." She chuckles to herself. "I wouldn't be surprised if this whole trial isn't part anthropologic study. Just *so* fascinating. Oh! Love that T-shirt. You're from California?"

Her pivot catches me off guard. "Hmm? Oh, yeah. Long Beach."

"Irvine!" she says, hand to chest. "Wow, okay. So if there's five hundred students here, I guess that breaks down to exactly ten from each state. That's so . . ."

"Fascinating?"

"Mhmm." Ollie gazes out the window.

I watch her watching some small cardinals flit around in figure eights beneath the trees. I'm really taken by her contagious, high-energy personality. "So, what, you like to people watch?"

"Definitely," she says. "My grandparents are restaurateurs, and they raised me, so I basically grew up popping from steakhouse to steakhouse. Now *that's* an interesting crowd, steakhouse frequenters! Anyway, whether we mean to or not, we all live our lives making microassumptions about people we know and don't"—she half shrugs—"So I guess I just kind of lean into that."

"Microassumptions?"

"Mhmm. For example . . ." She leans her head back so she can size me up and down. She squints, takes a drag, and exhales out the side of her mouth. "You don't care what anyone thinks. You're pretty independent. And, well, *pretty*. Oh"—she glances past me at the TV—"and you're super into sports. Although that's kinda obvious."

I smile. "Three out of four. Not too bad."

She faux gasps. "You don't consider yourself pretty? Have some self-respect . . . You're beautiful."

I roll my eyes, but I can't keep myself from laughing. Ollie joins in and lightly touches my arm, like she's supporting herself so she doesn't topple. Wow, even her laughter is infectious.

"So," she says, once our laughter tapers off. "What'd I get wrong?"

"Sports," I answer. "I'm not really into them. My dad is. The Angels drafted him in high school, but he never played professionally."

Ollie forms a knowing look. "Ah. That explains the baseball."

My eyes widen.

"Oh, come on," she says, looking affronted. "You think someone with *my* acute observation skills wouldn't have noticed you clutching that ball like a holy relic?"

For the second time in the short span of a minute, I roll my eyes. Ollie winks at me.

"I wanna show you something," she says, pinching the cigarette between her lips. With her hands now free she pops the screen out of our window. It lands on the grass and pine needles with a soft *thud*. Ollie pulls herself up, swings one leg outside, and straddles the sill. "Watch your head," she mumbles.

"Um . . ." I glance at our door, then back at Ollie just as she hops down. "Pretty sure our door's still in working condition. You *did* just use it."

"Leave through the front and risk a teacher catching me smoking?!" she yells, incredulous.

"Well, if they don't *smell* it, they *heard* you."

"You coming or not?"

I shake my head but awkwardly clamber out of the window all the same.

Once I'm outside, I close the window and leave it partially cracked, just in case we decide to come back in the way we left and need help remembering which room's ours. The back of the girls' dormitories borders an expansive wall of trees. With the sun on my neck and shoulders, I follow Ollie down the narrow sliver of grass between the dorms and forest, occasionally having to sidestep past the noisy air-conditioning boxes.

"You're gonna love this," Ollie calls back to me, small clouds of smoke trailing behind her. Several girls, who happen to be beside their windows as we pass by, watch us curiously. Ollie casually waves to them. One girl bumps her face into the window trying to get a good look at where we're headed.

Before we emerge from behind the dorms, Ollie grinds the butt of her cigarette against the wall and buries it under a patch of gravel. Without checking to see if I'm still behind her, she continues along the tree line, keeping to the shade.

The Foxtail Academy campus spreads out before us under a cloudless sky, green and majestic. The sun brightens the lawn; the tin-roofed buildings cast shadowy shelters from the heat; kids congregate and laugh and exchange magazines; a tall flagpole looms, the American flag drooping in the breezeless air. Honestly, the grounds are strikingly similar to some of the golf courses I'd seen on TV with my dad: the blades of grass are finely combed, as if done so with a hair pick, and the surrounding landscape is tidy and well watered with not so much as a clod of mulch out of place.

A wide sidewalk snakes across the grounds, linking the buildings and stand-alone classrooms. To my left I see the back of the tall auditorium, and up ahead—past Ollie and a collection of picnic benches, at the edge of Juniper Lake—the school dining hall. "The Foxhole" is painted in vibrant orange cursive over the entrance.

Just when I start to think that Ollie is leading me toward the dining hall, she veers right, heading in the opposite direction toward a thick stand of trees.

"Those are hackberry," she tells me conversationally, pointing at them. "I heard Mr. Williams telling some sophomores that after the assembly. And those are juniper bushes. Apparently, there's *tons* of them all around the lake. Isn't he hot?"

"Huh? Mr. Williams?"

"Yeah, he's got a Tom Selleck thing going on."

"Got a thing for mustaches?" I ask, finally joining her side.

She shrugs. "I got a thing for hot guys."

I gently shove her. "Please refrain from telling me which teachers you think are hot."

She smiles sweetly. When we reach the thicket, Ollie stops and looks behind us, as if checking that we're not being followed. Convinced no one's paying attention, she ducks under the low-hanging branches of a vine-smothered tree and disappears.

"You're not taking me in there to kill me, are you?" I call. Ollie's head reappears through the leaves, looking like it's perched on a leafy branch.

"No one *would* be able to hear you scream."

"Ha-*ha*."

"Come on." She disappears again, then adds (her voice now muffled), "We're almost there."

I sigh, wondering what the heck I've gotten myself into, then forge ahead. The wooded area is cool and tranquil. Just a few paces in, the sounds of commotion and laughter wane. In here, birds sing loudly and squirrels frantically scale the trees, chattering about our presence. I run to catch up with Ollie, who has made her way toward the muddy edge of the lake. Slippery pebbles crunch beneath our sneakers, and three times I slip and almost fall. I have to catch myself on Ollie's shoulders. She giggles deviously, like she took this path just to see how I'd fare.

"Here we are!" she announces at last, skipping forward and turning in a full circle. She's led me to a small clearing at the banks of Juniper Lake. She hops up onto a large, fallen tree and spreads out her arms. "Whatcha think?"

I don't reply at first. I just take it all in. From this vantage point, we have a stunning view of the still, expansive lake, which reflects the bluest, most entrancing sky I've ever seen. All along the shoreline, and as far as my eyes can see, old-growth trees encase Juniper Lake like celestial hands cupping a puddle of water. In the distance, I see a long pier and the Foxhole, radiantly lit by the late-afternoon sun.

"It's perfect," I say breathily. "It looks like a picture from a calendar."

"Right?"

"How'd you learn about this spot?"

"Now, I can't reveal *all* my secrets," she says mischievously, hands at her hips. "We did just meet after all." She sits down on the mossy bark and pats the spot beside her, inviting me to join.

I smile. As I stride toward the tree, a blinding headache rams into my forehead like an eighteen-wheeler. It *literally* takes my breath away before casting me into a half-memory dream.

It's nighttime, and I'm outside near train tracks, crouching beside someone I can't identify. I can't even tell how long ago this is supposed to be, or what I and this other person are doing hiding in the shadowy woods!

I hear panting.

I smell smoke.

I see a man whose features I can't make out, wearing a lab coat and walking fast. A small group of MACE agents appear from behind a building and he brusquely directs them. They're wheeling something toward the train tracks . . . and with a sharp gasp I realize it's a body bag on a gurney.

The man in the lab coat freezes and turns my way, clicking on a flashlight and shining it in my direction.

8

FLETCHER COHEN

The door to Dean Mendelsohn's office was half open, so Fletcher let himself in.

The room was wide and airy. Floor-to-ceiling windows and sky-lights let in generous amounts of afternoon sunlight. An enormous bookcase stretched the length of one of the four walls. Books, diplomas, and accolades on stands adorned the shelves, as well as framed pictures of a gray-haired man shaking hands with dignitaries.

Two movers in jumpsuits worked to hang a piece of artwork on the wall between two of the many windows. The man from the pictures (whom Fletcher presumed to be the dean) sat at the edge of a mahogany desk, instructing the movers to level the picture. Once he was satisfied, he clapped once and rubbed his hands together. The movers gathered the empty boxes from the floor and then showed themselves out.

The dean noticed Fletcher loitering beside the door.

"Ah, Fletcher, good to see you," he said evenly, gesturing for him to close the door. Fletcher did, then took a seat in one of the chairs that faced the desk. Dean Mendelsohn was average height and had perfect posture. He wore a pressed button-down shirt with suspenders and a checkered tie. He rolled up his sleeves, revealing wet stains under his armpits.

It was all Fletcher could do not to stare.

"Flight was okay then?" he asked Fletcher casually, uncapping a thermos and pouring some steamy coffee into an enamel mug.

That explains all the sweat. Why in the world he's drinking hot coffee when it's a hundred degrees outside is unfathomable.

Dean Mendelsohn must be clinically unbalanced or something.

"Yeah, flight was good."

"Good, that's good," the dean said, sitting down in his wide-backed chair. He shuffled some papers aside, clearing the surface of his desk. "My, it's like you've grown an entire foot since last I saw you."

Try as he might, Fletcher couldn't cover up his confused expression. The dean laughed a guttural laugh, then slowly sipped his coffee. "You don't remember me."

Fletcher shook his head.

"I don't blame you," he said. "Memory loss or not, I'm a pretty forgettable guy. Two years ago. Fundraiser in Orange, at the Marriott on North State College Boulevard. You were with your folks."

"Oh, right," Fletcher lied, drawing up the most convincing look of realization he could muster. "Sorry. I meet a ton of people through my dad's work." He mostly remembered that evening. Lots of expensive suits and dresses. A revolving door of boring speakers. But Fletcher could've sworn it was a ribbon-cutting ceremony for a new hospital wing or something—not a fundraiser.

The dean nodded as if lost in a brief moment of thought, then he set his mug on the desk and interlaced his fingers. "Do you still find the sensation of forgetting to be strange?"

"Um . . ." Dean Mendelsohn's question caught Fletcher off balance. "What do you mean?"

"Well, take us, for example," the dean explained. "You clearly don't remember meeting me at that event. So in that moment of panic when you realized I knew you but you didn't know me, did you chalk it up to memory loss? Or did you think our meeting was so fleeting, so insignificant, that the interaction never planted a lasting memory in your subconscious?"

"I . . . guess I didn't really think about it that much."

"It's funny. These are the very things that keep me up at night, Fletcher," he muttered, sighing through his nose. "You know, in those early days, when rapid memory loss first began to spread, I naively thought I'd be immune to it. I think a part of me believed my being engrossed in academia rendered my brain impervious to Memory Killer. I was so very wrong. No one could've foreseen just how plague-like this phenomenon is in its pursuit of annihilating humankind. Indeed, those early days seemed hopeless."

The dean pulled open a drawer, dug around inside for a moment, then found a yellow pencil. It was unused, unsharpened. He set it down on the desk between them and closed the drawer.

"I was shopping for a new watch the first time I felt Memory Killer's sting," the dean continued, leaning in. "And the only thing worse than experiencing that feeling was having to relive it countless times via artificial recall. Of course, I've come to sort of appreciate that memory tape, and still can't bring myself to discard it even though it's been a fully restored memory for some time. Anyway, my first encounter with Memory Killer: I'm at the mall, shopping for a new wristwatch. I *hate* shopping. And malls. But my wife insisted that I upgrade. So I'm in the store with the clerk, zeroing in on this Rolex here"—he held up a fist, flashing his gold watch—"when

suddenly"—he snapped his fingers—"I felt a gap open in my consciousness, as real as the smarting sensation after a paper cut.

"I had to leave the store, it was such a bizarre, unnatural experience. I *knew* I was forgetting something . . . something pertinent . . .
but I had no idea what or who that thing was."

His anecdote gave Fletcher pause. It reminded him what a terrifying reality that must have been for so many: losing memories
without any hope of regaining them. Before the MeReader and the
Restorey were introduced, before artificial recall was developed, the
memories one lost were lost for good. Period. Ever since his reading
at sixteen, Fletcher had been on a strict recall schedule. And if he
felt himself forgetting something, something potentially important,
he hardly ever panicked. He just had this blind faith in eventually
regaining whatever he was forgetting the next time he picked up a
memory tape.

Fletcher would have been the first to confess that he took his
situation for granted.

"That weekend," Dean Mendelsohn said, luring Fletcher back, "I
took up illustration." He opened another desk drawer and retrieved
a novelty pencil sharpener. Slowly—deliberately—the dean began
to sharpen his yellow pencil, and spiral shavings soundlessly rained
down onto his clean desk. "I realized I needed a method of preserving
precious moments from my past. Artificial recall was still months
away from trial completion, and I didn't want to risk losing another
memory before the technology was available. So I made a shortlist
of memories and began to draw them. They're crude things, with
lots of lines and disproportionate details. But it didn't matter; I found
them helpful."

He stopped sharpening his pencil and held it up, inspecting it
with one eye closed. The tip was perfectly pointy and spearlike.
Dean Mendelsohn gave a grunt of approval, then set the sharpened
writing utensil on top of the shavings. That's when Fletcher realized

that the framed picture behind the dean—the one the movers hung on the wall moments ago—was a pencil drawing of a faceless child standing at the mouth of what appeared to be a waterfall. The dean's self-assessment of his drawing abilities was spot-on. The illustration was messy and wild and raw, with continuous lines connecting the child to the untamed water.

The drawing gave Fletcher the creeps.

"I call it 'memory anchoring,'" the dean said, picking up his mug and drinking. "Some people pen their memories in a journal or a song. I find drawing them to be the most effective. Plus, my illustrations are vague enough that no one but me can interpret their meaning. Memory tapes—or, say, journal entries—could be illegally possessed by individuals with nefarious intentions."

Fletcher's eyebrows rose involuntarily. The dean's words reminded him of his *Raiders of the Lost Ark* lunchbox, where he stored his own handwritten memories along with his pressing questions about Memory Killer and its relation to artificial recall.

He adjusted his posture, suddenly feeling uncomfortable in his chair. He made a quick mental note to check his suitcases for his lunchbox as soon as he was back in his dorm room. "If your drawings are *too* vague, though, don't you risk misremembering stuff?"

Dean Mendelsohn smiled. But there was an emptiness to his smile . . . a sort of colorlessness to his expression, like he was a wax doll displayed in a museum. His dark eyes seemed to grow *darker*, as if all light and life had been drained from his irises.

Fletcher swallowed a lump and forced it down his throat.

"Misremembering one's past is a danger we all face, Fletcher Cohen," he said quietly, "even after we recall. I mean, it *is* called artificial recall, isn't it?"

"Yeah. Guess you're right."

"'Course I am," he said, relaxing a bit in his seat. Whatever harrowing tension hung in the air between them dissolved. "Now. I'm sure you're wondering why I summoned you here."

Oh. Right. "Yeah."

Dean Mendelsohn rose to his feet and crossed the room toward his bookcase, talking with his back to Fletcher, hands clasped behind his waist. "I graduated top of my class at MIT and then spent nearly a decade consulting for the Department of Defense before ultimately leading the task force responsible for MACE's inception. You could say I understand our battle with Memory Killer better than most. Unlike Alzheimer's or dementia, the phenomenon we face does not appear to abide by scientific laws, rules, or biases. I've seen Memory Killer poison even the most promising of minds seemingly at random.

"So, until we can cure whatever this is, our best hope is to contain it. Enter Memory Frontier's latest technological initiative: the Reflector."

Wow. What's a guy with a résumé like that doing in the private sector? Fletcher had eavesdropped on plenty of conversations between his father and his cohorts. He assumed a paycheck was what likely drew Dean Mendelsohn from the hallowed halls of DC to the backwoods of the South. And yet, this man had so much ambition Fletcher could practically smell it.

Either the payday's astronomical, Fletcher mused, *or something else lured him to Foxtail Academy.*

He just couldn't see a man like this content to play the role of high school dean for an entire year.

Dean Mendelsohn turned around to face Fletcher. "I was quite humbled when Alexander Lochamire enlisted my help. He and the board needed someone with a specific track record to ensure this trial goes smoothly and things remain copacetic at Foxtail."

"So you're gonna interrogate each student individually, starting with me?"

The dean laughed, running a hand through his silvery hair. "While that sounds appealing, I'd likely reach a point of diminishing returns. Five hundred students, you know? No, no. Given my relationship with your father, I made an assumption about you. And while it's often true what they say about assumptions, I'm hoping this instance is an exception to the rule."

Fletcher cleared his throat. "I'm sorry. I'm not really following."

The dean smiled crookedly. "Let's just say I've helped shepherd your father to where he is today. And believe me, it's been my pleasure. He's doing great work for the state of California. But as far as mentoring goes, you can only disciple someone insofar as they are willing to be discipled."

Fletcher tilted his head sideways, trying to infer what the dean was saying. He wished he would spare him the fluff and come out and say it.

"I need a set of eyes and ears out there," he said, finally getting down to brass tacks. "I'd be foolish to assume I can perform my job well alone. The *second* I approach a gathering of students, they'll scuttle away like roaches spooked by light."

Any doubt that Fletcher's father was responsible for his enrollment at Foxtail Academy vanished. "You want me to spy on other students and report back to you."

The dean returned to his desk, keeping his eyes trained on Fletcher. "I'd like to mentor you. And that would require us meeting frequently. Now, along the way, if you were to offer a report about the goings-on on campus, I wouldn't oppose it. At all."

Of course you wouldn't. This was almost unbelievable, but he connected the dots. His father—ever the politician—was indebted to this man. Before Fletcher could answer, the dean glanced at his Rolex.

"I need to get to a meeting, but do give it some thought, would you?"

He lied with a smile and got to his feet as Dean Mendelsohn

said, more to himself than to Fletcher, "You know, I'll always be struck by a pencil's marriage to death and creation. You chip away at a pencil, grinding it down to a nub before ultimately discarding it, all so you can breathe life onto a page." He lifted up a wastebasket and wiped the shavings off his desk.

The weird, unsettling observation was enough to get Fletcher out of the dean's office as quickly as possible. However, as he opened the door to show himself out, he thought of a question. The dean had mentioned needing to play back a memory tape of his first encounter with Memory Killer, and he said on that day in the mall he knew he was forgetting something . . . so did artificial recall repair that secondary memory too . . . the thing the dean said he'd forgotten at the watch store?

Fletcher turned to ask this, and saw the dean twist the cap off an orange pill bottle with a white prescription label. Fletcher shut the door hurriedly, wondering if it was allergy medicine or something else entirely.

9

FREYA IZQUIERDO

The strange man's flashlight beam illuminates my face, and the blinding light cuts the vicious half memory short. Dizzy, I nearly collapse on the ground beside the fallen tree. Ollie has the presence of mind to reach out and steady me. She carefully helps me sit beside her on the tree as I grind my teeth against the all-too-familiar white-hot headache that torments my skull. This unwanted visitant that I wish would leave me alone already.

"Whoa, whoa, you okay?" Ollie asks me softly, rubbing my upper back.

"Um . . . *fine*."

"That didn't look fine," she says seriously, staring at the side of my face.

That's two in one day. I think back to the half-memory dream I had on the flight. *They're getting more frequent.*

"I get these migraines." I massage my temples. Slowly, the throbbing pain begins to abate. I plant both my elbows on my legs and support my face in my hands. "I'll just snag some Tylenol from the nurse."

Ollie arcs an eyebrow, looking askance. "My grandmother gets migraines. Migraines don't knock her off her feet and she's old. *Really* old."

I chuckle. "I'm jet-lagged too. That's probably not helping. I'm fine, really."

"Mhmm," she says, side-eyeing me skeptically.

A man in a lab coat. MACE agents. A motionless body in a bag stretched across a gurney. These haunting images are cracking my head open. Even though I work to shake myself from the half memory, it burns as it lingers, like it's branding my subconscious with a cattle iron.

I look out at the lake and surrounding foliage in search of something on which to fixate my attention, at least until the headache passes. Almost immediately, I notice a tree in glowing-white blossom that stands, proudly, a short distance off in the opposite direction Ollie and I came from. The tree kind of looks self-aware, like she knows full well she's a beautiful rarity in a forest inhabited by ordinaries. About a foot above the ground, the trunk splits into four or five thinner branches, which reach toward the sky like upturned fingers, then fan out like an umbrella.

I stare at the white, regal tree for what feels like forever before telling Ollie I'm good to head back.

Ollie and I barely talk on the walk back, for which I'm grateful.

We head into our dorm through the front door. Two small, black boxes sit on the coffee table in front of our couch. The boxes each have our names on them, scrawled in blue ink on sticky notes.

"Wow, so *this* little thing here's gonna change the world, huh?" Ollie plops down on the couch, grabs her box, and pries apart the packaging.

I sit beside her and slide my box toward me, savoring the details: the glossy Memory Frontier label imprinted on all four sides, the deep purple hues and illustrated clouds, the jagged words: *The Reflector*. The bottom tip of the *t* in *Reflector* is designed to look like a bolt of lightning.

I swallow. The device inside this very package is going to remove my need for artificial recall. No recollector will be able to understand just how significant that really is. I carefully take off the sticky note and set it aside, then slide the cardboard tongue out of the top of the box and open the package. Inside, nuzzled in a fitted foam nest, is a black device encased in plastic. Slowly, *gently*—as if to avoid startling a sleeping sparrow—I pinch the Reflector with my thumb and index finger and remove the black device. Ollie has already set her Reflector on the table and is lazily leafing through the white instruction manual. I continue to take my time, breathlessly slipping the little piece of technology out of its wrapping and then palming it in both hands.

I cradle my Reflector for a few moments. It's incredibly light, almost surprisingly so, with a thin display strip on the front above a single round button. I press this a couple of times and it gives a faint, satisfying *chrick!* in response, sounding (and feeling) like the popping of bubble wrap.

"Says here we're supposed to leave it charging on its base during the day." Ollie flips a page. "And we're to affix the discs to our heads 'no later than eleven each night.'" She grunts, sounding bored, and tosses the manual onto the table. She unboxes the rest of her package, which includes a power adapter, a gray charging base, and the discs that look like electrode stickers. She collects these, along with her Reflector, and finds an outlet on the wall beside the bunk bed. After she plugs it in, three sharp notes ring out softly, confirming that the device has begun charging.

Ollie heads over to her bulging suitcases and begins to unpack. I hear her attempt to make small talk, but her voice is distant, like she's speaking through a wall. She plugs in her boombox and blasts some music—something by Prince. "Raspberry Beret," I think. But everything around me seems to get drowned out and go out of focus, except for the tiny, black Reflector in my hands. I stare at the device, a little motherboard of wires and batteries encased in smooth plastic, and it stares back.

How could something so small and so insignificant-looking hold so much incredible, restorative power?

I ruminate on this question for some time before getting to my feet and plugging my Reflector into an outlet. Ollie enlists my help to hang a few things on our walls, one of which is a wrinkled, well-worn *Teen Wolf* movie poster. "I always travel with Michael," she says, planting a kiss on the actor's cheek. "Plus: Michael J. Fox *and* Foxtail Academy? Serendipitous to the max, right?"

Before I know it, the sunlight outside our windows begins to dim. I glance at my wristwatch: it's shortly after 6:00 p.m., which means the kickoff bonfire and barbecue that Mr. Williams mentioned is fast approaching.

"We'd better change," Ollie announces, opening our shared closet and rifling through her hanging shirts.

"For the bonfire?"

Ollie doesn't answer at first. After selecting a turquoise top and a pair of high-rise jeans, she turns around and flashes a confused look. "I'm sorry, I thought that was a statement. Freya, yes, *of course* we need to change for the bonfire." She shakes her head and crosses to the bathroom, where she quickly undresses.

I fold my arms across my chest and follow her inside. "Why? Why do we *need* to change?"

"Okay, look, I get it. You don't care what others think about you. Anyone who knows you for two seconds can draw that conclusion."

"But?" I lean against the doorframe, returning her gaze through the mirror.

"But to us mere mortals, first impressions are a big deal," she says, replacing her Adidas top with the turquoise one. "Look, when I would hang out at my grandparents' restaurants, I witnessed a *bunch* of first dates. Some were even *blind* dates, Freya! And you could always tell that when she was meeting him for the first time, whatever he was wearing and how he carried himself set the tone for the entire date. We're about to meet the other seniors, people we're going to be sharing the whole year with. A year's a long time, Freya, so I wanna make a good impression. It's not unlike how we judge books by their covers."

"They say you're *not* supposed to do that."

"And yet we do it anyway, don't we?" She dumps out her toiletry bag on the sink and ferociously grabs her purple brush. Then she pulls out her scrunchie and begins to work on her hair, brushing with great, long strokes. I mean to argue, but she's actually right on that point. Nearly every time I check something out of the school library for recreational reading, I base my decision on the cover as much as the description that's on the back.

I refrain from telling Ollie she has a good point, though, and leave her in the bathroom to finish. I walk to our closet and stare at my side. I have maybe three or four tops that aren't T-shirts: pastel-color blouses that María insisted on sending with me with in case I'd need to "dress nice for a special occasion."

Whatever the heck that means.

I tap my chin, contemplating if changing into other clothes is worth anything. After a few seconds I sigh, frustrated with myself for even considering it, when Ollie appears beside me.

"Here, at least try this on." She pulls a bleached-denim jacket off its hanger and hands it to me. I take it and she heads back into the bathroom to finish getting ready.

"It's gotta still be like a hundred degrees, Ollie."

"It gets cool in the evenings."

"Where'd you hear that?"

She starts whistling.

Fine, whatever. I put on the jacket—left arm first, then right. *Just because I don't care what people think doesn't mean I can't wear something nice.*

I join Ollie at the bathroom sink and begin to comb my long black hair, which nearly reaches my lower back. It's not until I'm finished wrapping my hair in a firm high bun that I realize Ollie's watching me with an ear-to-ear grin.

"What?"

"You're gonna kill in that jacket." She winks.

I resist a smile as best I can, but one expands across my face all the same. "Thanks."

She squeezes my free arm and then exits the bathroom. "So you don't really like sports, but you're a Bruce Lee fan?"

I hear her lie down on the couch. "Oh, um, no. I just . . ." I hesitate to say more, so I settle for half an explanation: "I'm really into documentaries. A few months ago I"—I clear my throat and choose the right words—"I *bought* a Sony Betamovie. I was just getting ready to start a documentary project, actually, but my video camera was . . . stolen."

"That's cool." She sounds legitimately interested. "Sorry—that you're into documentaries, *not* that your stuff was stolen."

"Yeah. Sucks."

"I'll have to introduce you to my friend Chase. He's like an actor and does commercials and stuff."

"Chase Hall?"

"Yeah. You know him? He's hilarious. And hot. It's kind of a lethal combination."

"We met." I suppress my real feelings on the guy. "He seemed . . . neat."

Ollie laughs from the other room. "Yeah. He's great. My grandparents have a beach house next to his parents'. We used to take sailing lessons together. Anyway, he's got a video camera. Probably brought it with him too."

I almost drop my hairspray in the sink. I turn around and stand in the doorway, staring wide-eyed at Ollie. "Chase has a video camera here, on campus?"

"Um . . . probably?" She shrugs. "He self-tapes for auditions and stuff."

My heart races. I can feel butterflies in my stomach.

Ollie says, "We should catch up with him at the bonfire!"

I smile and head back into the bathroom, dumbfounded by this stretch of good luck. I even have to lean against the sink to steady my breathing. First, my need for artificial recall is eliminated; then I meet someone on campus who owns a video camera. If I can convince Chase to lend it to me, I just might be able to use it in my Memory Frontier investigation on campus.

Lo siento, María, I say inwardly, thinking back to earlier today at LAX when I promised my foster parent I'd stay out of trouble. *I gotta do what I gotta do.*

"Yes," I tell Ollie, joining her on the couch when I'm ready to go. "We *should* meet up with Chase at the bonfire."

10

FLETCHER COHEN

"Wait, so he *actually* asked you to spy on us?"

"More or less," Fletcher told Chase, walking alongside him toward the grassy expanse behind the auditorium. Strings of lights hung from tree to tree, creating a wide net of glowing bulbs that glinted against the twilit sky. Beneath the lights, long folding tables bore countless catering-sized trays of barbecue.

Students formed multiple lines and eagerly loaded their paper plates with steamy pulled pork, potato salad, and baked beans. They gathered at groupings of folding chairs and picnic blankets beyond the food tables. Fletcher saw a handful of staffers beyond the eating area working to light an impressively tall arrangement of firewood. "Don't You (Forget About Me)" by Simple Minds started to play through the loudspeakers, and this was met with scattered cheers.

"So, like, what did you tell him?" Chase asked as they migrated toward one of the food lines.

"To get lost," Fletcher said, pocketing his hands. "More or less."

"No waaay."

Fletcher shrugged. "I don't care what my father thinks he owes Dean Mendelsohn. I didn't get shipped halfway across the country to be the dean's patsy."

"That's wild," Chase said under his breath. "And you don't remember ever meeting this dude before? Like, how sure are you that he actually knows your old man?"

Chase raised a great question. However, in Fletcher's father's line of work, it made total sense that the two of them would have crossed paths. Plus, Fletcher *had* been at that event in Orange. If the dean was lying about something or only telling Fletcher half-truths, he didn't get the sense it was about knowing and working with his father.

"I'm pretty sure," he told Chase, who shook his head and clicked his tongue.

They progressed down the food line, and Fletcher contemplated telling his roommate about the off-putting moment when it felt like the dean was implying that he'd read Fletcher's journal entries.

After his meeting with the dean, Fletcher had returned to his dorm room and checked his *Raiders of the Lost Ark* lunchbox while Chase was in the shower. He found all the contents of his "safe" inside, undisturbed.

He had a real gut-check moment when he realized he was being irrational and paranoid. There was no way the dean could have rifled through his belongings; he was likely present at the assembly. And if he wasn't, he was probably seeing to other administrative things. Plus, even if he *had* read Fletcher's pages, it would've been incredibly violating and infuriating, sure, but it wasn't like he would have discovered something incriminating.

So, instead of mentioning this to Chase, Fletcher decided to share another thing Dean Mendelsohn said that piqued his interest.

He kept his voice low. "He did sort of imply that someone's memory tapes can be, like, illegally recalled by someone else."

Chase, who was standing slightly ahead, snapped his head back so quickly his blond bangs whipped his eyes. "Duuude. He *did*?"

"Um . . . yeah. You've heard of that happening?"

"Have I!" Chase caught himself, reining in his emotions. The girl in front of them turned around and, when she saw Chase, instantly flushed and faced forward. Chase continued with quiet excitement. "It's called memory knifing. How have you *not* heard of this? There's this whole black market for stolen memory tapes. People pay a high premium to try to artificially recall someone else's past."

"I thought safeguards made it impossible to do that. My dad helped pass the legislation requiring them."

"I don't know if anyone's been able to do it successfully," Chase admitted, his wide eyes unblinking. "But I know people try. I worked with a chick at a casting agency who knew someone who knew someone whose memory tapes were stolen."

Fletcher held up a finger. "Hang on . . . trying to follow that . . . okay, I think I caught up."

"It's fine, you don't have to believe me." Chase grabbed a plate and fork as they finally approached the folding table. "But don't be surprised if it comes out that Memory Frontier pivoted to Reflectors because memory knifing was running rampant."

Fletcher chuckled. "I'm just messing with you. Honestly, I'm shocked Dean Mendelsohn just casually threw that out there. You'd think if memory knifing is actually happening, a seventeen-year-old student is the last person he should tell. Right?"

Chase tapped his cheek with his fork as they inched closer to the food. "Unless . . . he told you on purpose."

"Why would he do that?"

"Quid pro quo." He shoveled a hefty portion of pulled pork onto his plate and then drizzled it with coleslaw. "Think about it: if he wants you to report back to him—to be his 'eyes and ears'—then maybe he extended you some top-secret info in good faith."

Fletcher stared at the back of Chase's head. "What?"

"He scratches your back, you scratch his."

"While I'm *really* grateful for that visual"—he picked up the serving spoon and served himself—"I just don't see a scenario where a guy like Dean Mendelsohn offers some student classified intel in exchange for gossip. Like . . . what am *I* supposed to do with anything he tells me? Nah . . . I think it was more of a threat than anything else."

"It's possible." Chase snagged a Coke from the cooler at the end of the food table. "But that's for us to figure out. It's a good thing you decided to stick around, roomie!"

"Who said I'm not still planning on sneaking out tonight?"

But Chase was already walking off. Fletcher grabbed a chilled drink and followed his roommate toward the eating area.

Nightfall had arrived, and the dark blue sky was speckled with countless stars—vivid, bright particles fixed on an infinite canvas. The incredible view reminded Fletcher of his childhood camping trips. Unlike in the city, here the stars were not only visible, they actually brightened one's surroundings, like they were boasting or showing off just how lustrous they were.

"Chase! Hey!"

Fletcher and Chase perked up as a girl jogged toward them. She had almond-shaped eyes, highlighted brown hair, and a smile so big it rivaled Chase's.

"Ollie!" he proclaimed as he hugged his friend, careful not to spill the food piled on his plate. "When I didn't see you on my flight, I figured you got cold feet or something."

"Blow off the chance to get away from my grandparents for a year?" She scoffed. "You do remember I'm Vietnamese, right?

Somehow they managed to get *more* overbearing the closer I got to senior year. Yeah, no thanks. I couldn't mail in my acceptance for this trial fast enough." She met Fletcher's green eyes and asked, "Who's this?"

"I'm Fletcher." He smiled back. "The poor soul who's forced to room with Chase."

"Ah," she said, feigning empathy. "Question: How long did it take him to sneak a girl in?"

Fletcher laughed. "I walked in on them, so I'm guessing under thirty minutes."

Ollie laughed, too, pulling her hair to one side. "Wow. It's like he's trying to break some personal record. I don't know if I should be impressed or concerned."

"*Definitely* the latter." Fletcher turned to Chase. "I like her."

Chase deadpanned. "I'm glad that was so special for you guys."

Ollie and Fletcher exchanged another laugh.

"Where you sitting?" Chase asked her. "Believe it or not, I *still* wanna hang with you, even after that display."

Ollie beamed. "C'mon, I'll introduce you to my roomie."

Fletcher and Chase tagged along after her toward a collection of picnic tables just as Billy Ocean's "Caribbean Queen" came through the PA system.

The bonfire had been successfully lit at that point, and orange-hot flames voraciously lapped up the firewood and expelled dancing embers into the summer air. As they got closer to Ollie's table, Fletcher saw a girl standing off to the side—her back to them, hands pocketed inside her bleached-denim jacket. She watched the bonfire flames roar in the distance. The flickering glow silhouetted her intensely, outlining her inklike hair and brown skin with a ruddy light. It was like she was posing, but also like she wasn't . . . She wore a cool and casual demeanor as confidently as her high-rise jeans and sneakers.

The girl turned slowly as they approached. Her face was round and beaming in the fire- and starlight, and her taut bun accentuated her curved hairline, which seemed to frame her long eyebrows like an arbor.

Fletcher felt a stupid knot forming in his throat. He swallowed it and tried his hardest to appear nonchalant.

Her radiant, knowing eyes lingered on Fletcher for only a tenth of a second before she noticed Chase. Her face lit up, a reaction just about every other girl on campus exhibited when she saw Chase.

"No way!" he said. "Freya, right?"

Of *course* they'd already met.

"Yeah, hey." They gathered at the picnic table, where Freya's and Ollie's plates and drinks were waiting. "Good memory. Bet you won't even need to use a Reflector."

Chase laughed hysterically and then cracked open his soda, which fizzed and bubbled.

"Wait, so how do you two know each other?" Fletcher asked, hoping he didn't sound like he cared that much. He took a bite of his barbecue sandwich and savored the flurry of tangy-sweet flavors.

"We were on the same flight," Freya explained, "though we didn't meet until after we landed. Chase here nearly knocked me off my feet."

"I have that effect on women." He shrugged. Freya rolled her eyes.

"He's impossible," Ollie said, scooping up some potato salad with her spoon.

"You're from California too?" Fletcher asked Freya.

She nodded. "Long Beach. You?"

"Manhattan Beach."

"You know, you look really familiar," Freya said, pointing at Fletcher with her plastic silverware.

"I get that a lot. Actually, no, I don't know why I said that. I've *never* gotten that."

Freya's smooth lips formed a smile—more of a smirk, actually—and he felt his neck getting hot.

Get it together, moron.

"Hiths dad's a congrethman," Chase said with a full mouth. He quickly swallowed and switched to a British accent for no apparent reason: "You've probably seen ol' Fletch here on the telly with his pops. Famous, in' he?"

Ollie perked up on the bench beside Fletcher. "You're Joshua Cohen's son?"

"Why does that sound like an accusation?" he joked, sipping his soda.

Ollie chuckled. "Ha, it's not. I'm really into public service actually. I was gonna apply for an internship with the mayor's office before I got my letter from Memory Frontier."

"You might've dodged a bullet," Fletcher said seriously. "I've been to city hall before with my dad . . . it's a pressure cooker."

"Well, sounds like they need more able hands," she replied, brushing off his pessimism. Fletcher smiled.

They took a few moments to chow down, Billy Ocean's lilting voice echoing across the lawn.

Freya set her fork down. "So, Chase. You're an actor?"

"Ah, so you've seen my work." He planted his elbows on the table and rested his chin on his fists. "Big fan?"

"I don't know why I tolerate you." Ollie lightly punched him in the arm. "Freya's into documentary filmmaking. Her video camera was stolen shortly after she started her project on . . . actually"—she turned to Freya—"what *is* your documentary about?"

"Oh, you know," she said, looking down at her plate. "Just this personal project I've been trying to get off the ground. I just wondered if you brought your video camera with you, Chase."

"Sure did," he said. Fletcher watched as Freya's face brightened, like someone had just told her all of her community service credits had been met. "But first you gotta tell us more about this project of yours. If you need a dashing leading man for your protagonist, I know a guy."

No one at the table replied.

"Guys," Chase said, annoyed. "I was talking about me."

"When *aren't* you?" Ollie asked. "Plus, documentaries don't have leading men since they're about real-world subject matters, numbnuts."

Fletcher was intrigued by Freya's video project. As he leaned in toward her to ask a question, a tall, pretty, vivacious-looking girl with dark, permed hair approached their table. Her luminous features were perfectly proportioned, as if she had been manufactured by the same power surge Gary and Wyatt used in *Weird Science*.

She sauntered right up to Chase and placed her hand on his upper back, not so much as glancing at anyone else at the table.

"Chase Hall, right?" she said in an impossibly sweet voice.

"Correctomundo." He looked up at her, perpetually Mr. Cool.

"A few of us are gonna ditch the bonfire and have some drinks on the pier. Wanted to see if you'd join us. I'm Ave Maria, by the way."

Ollie leaned in. "Oh! Like the song? I had to play that at one of my piano recitals in middle school."

Ave Maria stared daggers at Ollie. "Oh, so you *can* speak English. A few of us were wondering."

Instantly, Fletcher could hear his own heartbeat thrashing in his ears. But before he could so much as open his mouth, Ollie replied, a twinkle in her eye: "I'm glad I could help settle a bet. Now if you'll excuse us, we were just about to go watch some paint dry, which will be infinitely more fascinating than sitting here with you."

Fletcher's jaw dropped. Ave Maria looked like she had just been told she had one week to live. She was dumbstruck, her hand lingering on Chase's back. Eventually, though, she composed herself and walked off.

Chase waved at Ave Maria's back before raising his Coke and clanking it against Ollie's can. They both took a long drink and then smacked their sodas down on the picnic table.

"Nicely done," Freya said to Ollie.

"Yeah, well, when you deal with that kind of BS regularly, you build up an arsenal of comebacks." She returned to her food as if nothing had happened.

"Are you okay?" Fletcher whispered, turning toward her. "That was . . . I'm really sorry."

"Why?" She sounded genuinely confused. "When people level hate toward me it's only because they're compensating for their own crippling insecurities."

"Hear, hear," Chase said. "Also, she was a brunette and *so* not my type."

"You're *disgusting*." Ollie threw some food at him, which he easily dodged.

"Well." Chase cleared his throat. "Anyone look at their class schedule yet?"

Fletcher reached into his pocket and pulled out his folded schedule. Freya and Ollie did likewise. It was nothing Fletcher hadn't expected: poli-sci, AP lit, calculus, a free period afforded only to seniors. But at the bottom was a course entitled—

"Memory Theory?" Ollie groaned. "That sounds heady. Seniors don't do heady."

"Which period do you guys have it?" Freya asked the table. It was fourth for everyone. "Well, at least we'll all be stuck in there together."

The music playing through the loudspeakers abruptly paused. They all turned their heads to see Mr. Williams standing on top of a picnic table and holding a microphone. He smiled at everyone.

"Does he go everywhere with that mic?" Chase whispered, snickering.

"How good is that barbecue, friends?" Mr. Williams asked. "Shout-out to Mr. Herschel Jones, our school chef, and the entire kitchen staff!" Clapping and rowdy shouting filled the air. "Now, I wanna make you aware of two things really quickly: One, make sure y'all are back in your dorms no later than 9:00 p.m. School staffers will be accompanying Memory Frontier representatives to each room to go over protocols for using your Reflectors. And two, since tomorrow's Sunday and officially the last day of summer . . . make sure you sleep in and take it easy. Deal?"

Faint laughter. Mr. Williams thanked everyone for listening before stepping down. The music and chatter returned in a steady crescendo.

"Soooo," Chase said, dropping his voice. "I'm thinking Ave Maria might've been on to something when she mentioned drinks on the pier."

The girls exchanged a mischievous glance.

Ollie whispered, "You grab the beer"—she gestured toward Freya with her thumb—"and she and I will provide the spot."

Like a team breaking a huddle, they all got up from their spots, threw their plates away, and slinked off toward the dorms.

11

FREYA IZQUIERDO

When we reach the viny hackberry tree that marks the entrance to our hideout, Ollie flicks on a flashlight and leads the way into the darkened forest. Chase lights a cigarette, and the two begin to pass it between each other, engaging in hushed conversation while occasionally gasping or laughing, like they're exchanging news that's either too titillating or too funny to believe.

"How do I know you and Ollie aren't luring us back here to kill me?" Fletcher asks.

I almost tell him I made the same joke earlier, but instead I whisper, "You don't, Fletcher Cohen. Hope your affairs are in order."

He shakes his head. "Getting axed by a cute girl in the backwoods of Tennessee is *not* how I thought I'd go."

"You know what they say about life."

"That it could one day be cut short in a random forest at the hand of a total, albeit cute, stranger?"

"That it's full of surprises." I make sure I sound unimpressed. "Also. You said 'cute' twice. Kinda laying it on thick, aren't we?"

"Just wanted to make sure you heard me."

I catch him smiling in the starlight, coolly clutching a six-pack of beer under his arm. (How he and his roommate managed to get alcohol so quickly is kind of impressive.) While we walk, I conspicuously learn his features: Fletcher's tall, probably a little more so than me, with medium-length, curly black hair styled back in a mullet. His hard jawline connects with his round chin, which has a deep dimple in it, and—

"What, do I have barbecue on me?"

I quickly improvise. "No, just a leaf." I reach out and brush away an invisible leaf from his firm shoulder and then look straight ahead, playing it cool.

"You're not burning up in that jacket?" he asks.

"It's Ollie's, not mine. She insisted I wear it. First impressions mean a great deal to her, apparently."

"Looks good. The jacket, I mean. On you."

I tell him thanks. "So, what's it like having a congressman for a father?"

He shrugs. "I dunno. Weird, I guess. Like, he's busy *all* the time. My father's always on the job: taking phone calls, traveling, and whatever."

"Oh. I bet that's hard."

"Yeah, when I was younger it was, but now it's great. Means I get more time to myself."

He sounds like he's trying to convince himself. I attempt to change the direction of the conversation so he doesn't ask anything about my dad. "Do you get to travel a lot?"

"Yeah, actually, as much as we can." His voice brightens. "We like to visit national parks. Did you know that California has nine? It's more than any other state."

"I didn't know that."

"Yosemite Falls, Kings Canyon, the Redwoods . . ." He trails off, apparently cycling through some fond memories. "They're unreal, and you somehow feel insignificant in different ways at each park."

"What do you mean?" We amble toward the shoreline, then take the slippery path along the water's edge. I can barely hear the laughter and music from the bonfire at this point, like someone turned its volume to the lowest setting.

"Well, at Yosemite Falls, I felt a sense of . . . I dunno . . . comfort. Like the bigness of the waterfall gave me a kind of assurance that we're all in this together. We're all little hopeless specks on a map who can't really outdo one another, even if we try. At the end of the day, our shadows are all basically the same length under a mammoth, godlike waterfall. Now, conversely, the Grand Canyon kinda terrifies me. It's awe-inspiring, don't get me wrong, but in a terrifying way."

I stifle a laugh. "You sure you're not just scared of heights?"

"Ha-ha." Even in the dim moonlight I can see him blush a little.

"I've never been," I tell him.

"To the Grand Canyon?"

"To any of them."

"Well." Moist pebbles squish beneath our shoes. "I'll have to make a list for you. And I'll make sure my favorite park is at the very top."

"Which is?"

"You'll have to wait for the list."

I smile. We walk in silence for a bit. I listen as crickets sing, frogs croak, and small animals dive into the lake, making sporadic splashes. The atmospheric soundtrack is so vivid it almost sounds artificial or man-made, and I realize, a grin cracking across my face, that I am a stranger in a strange place that is altogether different from my home, and in all the best ways. There's a rhythm to this place, a kind of old-earth heartbeat that pumps life into the forest.

You ever think your girl would be hanging out in the woods, Dad? I imagine the look of pride on my dad's face, the thick delight in his voice were he to say, "Okay, okay. This city girl ain't afraid of no woods!"

But of course I'm not afraid. Why should I be when I carry my dad with me always? His spirit burrows down deep into my soul, a warm light that burns around the clock within my innermost core. And I need that warm light, the memories of my dad, to never be extinguished.

As we walk along the lapping lake water, I decide that—when it comes to the Reflector and me—the stakes are very high. Memory tapes will soon be phased out, rendering Restoreys pointless. So when that time comes, it'll be on the Reflector to ensure memories of my dad don't slip away forever.

I really need this new technology to work perfectly.

What happens if they haven't worked out all the bugs? What happens if some unexpected issue arises along the way? This is a trial after all, and it's called a "trial" for a reason. Is there any risk of me losing all my memories once I stop using artificial recall and switch to the Reflector?

I can't get worked up. A billion-dollar company like Memory Frontier has surely done its due diligence. They wouldn't risk the minds of five hundred students on a device that's not ready. I'm sure if there was any kind of risk, the board or decision-makers would have shut down this whole operation.

Right?

"You know." Fletcher stalls my thoughts. "I never thought about this until now, but in a weird way memory loss is kind of a gift."

"What do you mean?"

"Well, without Memory Killer, we'd never have artificial recall."

He sounds like he's still working through his thoughts. "Where before, memories were unreliable and only *barely* clear with a lot of fuzzy details, now we can recall with sharp specificity."

I stave off the urge to tell him how insanely privileged that sounds. A person who only has to do artificial recall once a day doesn't have the same experience as those of us who aren't beholden to unjust laws and restrictions. Plus, the less you have to artificially recall, the less likely you are to miss a window. I think back to that guy at the East Division Precinct who is just one of the many ill-fated degens to miss a window and get racked by the painful consequences.

There's also the matter of cognition wheels. Fletcher hasn't been branded a literal degenerate. Not only does being a recollector unfairly earn him elite status, but his family's probably swimming in wealth because of his father's post as congressman.

I pause. Without even trying I made a quick microassumption about Fletcher. Ollie was right.

I compose my emotions. "I disagree. But we're gonna come back to that later."

Fletcher, reading my tone loud and clear, opens his mouth. Thankfully he swallows his words, and it's just as well. We've arrived at the small clearing. At the edges, fireflies dance and dazzle, conjuring up a magical, pulsing, low-lit incandescence. Somehow, this little spot of ours is even more beautiful at nighttime. Fletcher freezes, admiring our surroundings, and I jog ahead toward the fallen tree.

"Whoa," he mutters. "Breathtaking."

"I've graduated from cute to breathtaking already? You need to work on your game."

"I wasn't . . . I meant," he stutters, and I just laugh and leave him lingering at the shoreline.

"Nice work, ladies," Chase proclaims, hopping up onto the tree and beating his chest.

"Good grief," Ollie says. "Please don't mark your territory."

I chuckle as Fletcher catches up, prying apart the beers and handing us each one. Chase gets down and sits on his haunches, and I take a spot between him and Ollie. Fletcher cracks open his drink and looks out at the glassy lake, which crisply mirrors the moon.

He eventually sits beside Chase. "Gotta admit, there are worse places to be on a Saturday night."

On either side of me, Ollie and Chase agree with soft grunts, and I, too, find myself in agreement. In less than twenty-four hours, I went from practically friendless to meeting and befriending this bunch. Maybe, just *maybe*, if I can get over my misgivings about the trial, my senior year won't be that bad.

Imagine that. I take a sip of my beer, smiling as the cold drink fizzes down my throat. *A normal year of high school.*

"Oh, guys, you *have* to hear about Chase's nickname," Ollie shouts.

"*Et tu*, Ollie?" he says, slouching. "*Et tu?*"

"Wait," Fletcher says. "Should we guess?"

"Sunflower," I blurt out, which is promptly met with laughter.

"He *does* eat an unseemly amount of sunflower seeds," Ollie admits, wiping tears from her eyes. "But sadly, no. You ready? It's *Chase*."

"What?"

"I don't get it." Fletcher looks back and forth between Chase and Ollie.

"He gave himself the nickname *Chase*. His actual name's Christopher."

"I thought someone else had to give you your nickname," Fletcher says, to which Chase closes his eyes and takes a long swig. "Isn't that the point of nicknames?"

"I'm gonna kill you, Ol," Chase mumbles, his eyes still closed.

"And," I add, suppressing more laughter, "I'm not 100 percent certain, but isn't *Chris* the shortening of Christopher? Again, just me guessing here . . . stab in the dark."

Ollie almost sprays her beer.

"I'll have you know that plenty of actors use stage names," Chase says, abandoning the embarrassment. "Marilyn Monroe's actual name was Norma Jeane. So. Yeah."

"Why *Chase* though?" I ask, genuinely curious. "And not, say, Bob."

Fletcher and Ollie snicker.

"This won't help my case," he admits. "But, well, I dunno . . . I just felt like since I'm *chasing* this Hollywood dream, Chase kind of represented that."

Silence. Fletcher and I sit with this, and I find Chase's reasoning a little sweet, albeit childlike. But Fletcher snort-laughs loudly, and Ollie joins in.

"You guys are the *worst*," Chase says, finishing off his drink. I keep waiting for him to divulge the story behind Ollie's nickname. I imagine she's told Chase why she ditched Hoa in exchange for Ollie. And yet as I watch Chase, who good-naturedly smiles at us, taking the ribbing in stride, he never once hints he's got any dirt on Ollie. Instead, he picks up another beer off the ground and offers it to each of us before snapping it open for himself.

Maybe there's more to that debonair smile of his than meets the eye.

The four of us fall into natural silence as we sit beneath the dome of bright constellations I don't recognize but that are spectacular nonetheless. Across the lake, far in the distance and beside the Foxhole, we see the shadowy, ant-sized figures of Ave Maria and her gang collecting their stuff and making their exit off the long pier, which means it's probably getting close to time for us to all head back to our rooms. I wait to see who's going to suggest this first, and when no one does, I feel a warm tingling in my chest. These three here, sitting beside me on the mossy tree, are just as content as I am to do nothing but mutely look out at the rippling lake. No one wants to disrupt this moment, and I'm okay with that.

In fact, I'm *more* than okay with that. I pray I remember this evening . . . that the insatiable Memory Killer would leave these moments untouched.

"Who needs a star on the Hollywood Walk of Fame when you have these?" Ollie cranes her head back, staring reverently at the night sky.

"I've always felt the Walk of Fame stars were more like grave-stones than monuments." Chase sounds forlorn, not contemplative. "Feels unnatural, you know? Stars were created to burn in the skies . . . not get trampled on beneath our feet."

I hear Ollie smile. "It's just a dumb tourist attraction."

"True." Chase blinks up at the stars. They twinkle back. "Plus, time doesn't care about the distinction between a gravestone and a monument. Everything we try to memorialize on Earth will eventu-ally crumble and fade over time."

Fletcher takes a swig. "Not stars, though. Guess they're both gravestones and monuments by nature of how they're formed, huh? And since the sky is constantly giving birth to new stars, starlight feels eternal."

I nod, following their train of thought, then add musingly, "Down here, we try to memorialize everything. A kind of doomed endeavor. Up there, the stars memorialize themselves. It's beautiful . . . and kind of tragic at the same time."

As we stumble through the darkened woods back to campus, giggling and talking in whispers, I'm hit with déjà vu. The knotty

116

trees—seeing them in the nighttime, their blackening shadows—possess a sense of familiarity.

Have I been here before? As in . . . before Ollie brought me here earlier today?

That's impossible, though. I've never left California before coming to Foxtail Academy.

And yet . . .

The half-memory dream I just had, the one where I was hiding in the woods and watching the man in the lab coat and—

"What do you think, Freya?" Ollie asks between laughs, scattering my thoughts like sand in the sea breeze.

I pretend to sound engaged and ask her to repeat the question, only I can't help but be distracted by the possibility that I've been in these woods before, long ago, and I just can't remember when . . . or why.

12

FLETCHER COHEN

"I just blabbered on about national parks and didn't even think to ask her one thing about herself," Fletcher confessed to Chase as they ran toward the boys' dormitories. It was already five after nine, which wasn't exactly a good look. Hopefully the curfew was a "soft" 9:00 p.m.

"She asked you though, right?"

"Yeah, I mean, she asked if I traveled, which kind of sent me on a tangent."

"Then I don't see what the problem is." Chase gasped. "Unless, of course, you like her?"

"What? Who, Freya?"

"No, Ave Maria," Chase said dryly. "Yes, Freya. You like her?"

"Dude, Chase, we *just* met—"

"Yeah, because that's stopped love before," he said, prodding

Fletcher with his elbow. The boys reached their dorm room, and Chase quickly opened the door.

A school staffer and Memory Frontier representative were waiting inside. They were seated on the couch, legs crossed, each wearing a look of annoyance. They rose at the boys' arrival.

The Foxtail staffer, a midforties woman with curly brown hair, a tucked-in beige polo, and pressed khaki shorts, mumbled something as she made a note on a clipboard. The representative was a broad-shouldered man in a suit with greasy black hair matted to his forehead.

Apparently he didn't get the memo about Tennessee humidity, Fletcher thought, sizing up his expensive-looking suit.

The staffer handed the representative the clipboard, which he took without breaking their gaze. "Fletcher Cohen and Chase Hall, I presume."

"The presuming is most accurate, good sir," Chase said jovially.

"Sorry we're late," Fletcher added.

"So am I," the man said, remaining stalwart, his tone unapologetically deep. "Have a seat."

Fletcher and Chase exchanged a glance before walking to the couch and slumping down. The staffer, whose name badge read Tama Rose, stood beside the boys' bunk beds, channeling a disappointed-parent look.

Fletcher swallowed. *This feels more like a disciplinary meeting than an introduction to our Reflectors.*

"I'm Oswald James." The representative tucked the clipboard under his arm and clasped his hands in front of him. "Memory Frontier has appointed me cognicologist—"

"Not to be confused with a gynecologist, right?" Chase interrupted, chuckling at his own stupid joke. Fletcher shook his head, leaning away from his roommate and creating as much distance between them as he could.

Tama narrowed her eyebrows into a deep scowl, really giving Mr. Strickland from *Back to the Future* a run for his money.

The representative cleared his throat. "There are twenty cognicologists who've each been assigned twenty-five students. You two are in my jurisdiction. I'll be checking in with you quarterly to get readings and to map your progress in confidential reports, which will be privately shared with you and your legal guardians and no one else. It's our solemn duty at Memory Frontier to uphold the integrity of the study and your confidentiality throughout the entirety of this trial. Are there any questions so far?"

Fletcher saw Chase start to raise his hand. But he shot his roommate an exaggerated glare and Chase slowly dropped his hand back into his lap.

"Good." Oswald emphasized the word like a staccato note. "Now. On to the Reflectors."

Fletcher was so embarrassed by their tardiness that he hadn't even noticed the two black boxes on the coffee table until now. Yellow sticky notes with their names were stuck to the boxes. Fletcher and Chase leaned forward and set to work unpackaging the devices.

"Included you'll find your personal Reflector, a pair of receivers, and a charging station," Oswald explained. Fletcher pulled each item out of the small box almost in perfect sync with Oswald's words. "Listen carefully: Memory Frontier has leveraged data points and memory insights from your personal records and carefully calibrated your Reflector to your cognitive needs. This required a joint effort with your respective repositories to ensure optimal recall. And before you ask"—he arched an eyebrow at Chase—"if you wear each other's Reflectors, absolutely nothing will happen. As I've said before, the devices have each been programmed to address your brain's specific memory deficits. I will also add that you should experience no side effects whatsoever after each use. None of the dizziness or light-headedness that you might've experienced after artificial recall. Nothing. On the off chance that you *do* feel something unfamiliar, report it immediately. Just alert one of the school staffers, who will put you in touch with me."

Fletcher picked up his Reflector and examined it. It was no bigger than his father's pager and had one lone button and a thin display, which was currently blank.

"Don't just give that owner's manual a cursory glance," Oswald said, nodding toward the thin booklets inside the boxes. "Read it thoroughly. But for this evening, I'll give you the basic rundown: Plug your charging stations in, dock your Reflectors, and firmly place the receivers onto your temples just like you would with your Restoreys. After the display turns on and greets you, press the button once. The Reflector will set to work immediately."

"What if I don't fall asleep right at eleven?" Fletcher inquired, checking the clock on the wall. It was a little after nine thirty.

"The Reflector is operational for eight straight hours, even in the liminal space between consciousness and dream state."

"Good, because I'm an insomniac," Chase said, chuckling. His inability to read the room was *painful.*

Just how many beers did he have?

"Insomnia is no laughing matter," Oswald said solemnly. He pulled out the clipboard and thumbed through a couple of pages. "A few of your peers suffer from it. One student has sleep apnea and will require a very . . . er . . . *specific* trial. We take sleep disorders very seriously, Chase Hall."

Tama made a *hmph!* noise like she was adding an exclamation point.

"For sure, for sure," Chase whispered, a whipped puppy relegated to a cage.

"Now, if there are no further questions," Oswald said, a sense of finality in his voice, "I encourage you both to have a wind-down period around ten each evening, starting tonight. While it's not required, we find that some subjects have off-the-charts results with their Reflectors when they spend about sixty minutes clearing their heads before retiring. Of course, for those who don't have a lot to clear"—he eyed Chase—"sixty minutes may be overkill."

Oswald James glanced back at his stoic enforcer, and the two silently took their leave.

"Welp," Chase said, jumping to his feet, seemingly unaware of Oswald's harsh jab, "hopefully video games count as a wind-down activity, because I'm *not* about to meditate or something." He pulled out a SEGA Master System from one of his many suitcases and then started to hook up the console to the television.

Fletcher took his Reflector and plugged the charging base into the wall, then set everything on his pillow on the top bunk for later that evening.

"You get a weird vibe from that Memory Frontier rep?" Chase asked, flicking on the TV. White snow filled the screen.

"Weird?" Fletcher asked. "Or annoyed?"

Chase grinned. "C'mon, man. You gotta keep these suit types on their toes."

"What?"

Chase unzipped a small vinyl bag and emptied a collection of video game cartridges onto the coffee table, lazily sorting through them in search of a specific game.

"Give me more cred than that, Fletcher," he said, sounding truly offended. "You think I'm that crazy or oblivious? Okay, look, don't answer that."

"You were *trying* to annoy him?"

Chase stopped what he was doing and looked up at Fletcher, paling slightly. He wordlessly grabbed his portable boombox off the carpet and set it atop the TV. He pressed Play, and "Silent Running" by Mike and the Mechanics filled the dorm room, midchorus. Chase grabbed him by the wrist and sat him down on the couch.

"I wasn't trying to *annoy* him," he said underneath the music. "I was trying to *stump* him. Catch him off guard. Throw him off. Pull the rug out from—"

"Okay, I get it." Fletcher furrowed his brow. "But *why?*"

"Fletcher, dude. These guys aren't telling us everything—about the trial *or* the Reflectors."

"I mean, sure, I have my doubts, too, but—"

"At first I was stoked," Chase continued, wide-eyed. "I mean, the news is calling us the 'chosen generation.' Hard not to be excited when you're called *that*. Hard not to get swept up in all the buzz. But between Memory Frontier's presentation at the assembly, and then Dean Mendelsohn propositioning you, it just seems like maybe Foxtail Academy isn't all it claims to be."

"Hmm . . ."

Fletcher thought back to that afternoon when the cab dropped him off. Everything on the grounds was neat and tidy and orderly. Happy Place, USA, home to the nation's cheeriest teenagers and teachers this side of heaven. In this brief moment of reflection, Fletcher finally realized what was bothering him about Marshall Kendrick—the Memory Frontier spokesman—and the talk he gave at the school assembly. In fact, there was one pretty big thing that both Marshall Kendrick and Oswald James had failed to explain about Reflectors.

Fletcher linked his thoughts as he spoke. "When the MeReader scans us once a month, the at-risk memories it locates are imprinted onto physical tapes and then given to us, along with our updated recall schedule."

"Uh-huh." Chase's eyes darted around in their sockets. "Reading you loud and clear, Captain Obvious."

"And as far as we know, that's the *only* copy of that particular memory in existence," Fletcher continued. Chase nodded. "The MeReader does not duplicate or archive our memory tapes. To do so would be a massive privacy violation that would result in an even *more* massive malpractice lawsuit. Not to mention, duplicating memory tapes is illegal."

"For sure, yeah." Chase leaned in, now clinging to his roommate's every word.

"So." Fletcher lowered his voice, buying into Chase's paranoia. "When Memory Frontier prepped our Reflectors in anticipation of this trial, who gave them—a billion-dollar corporation—access to our individual memory insights, or whatever Oswald called it?"

"Our parentals, probably."

"Did any of your memory tapes go missing in the last month . . . or year . . . or ever?"

Amazingly, Chase managed to widen his eyes even more. "Nooo. And, like you *just* said, memory-tape duplicates are illegal."

"Bingo. So just what are these mystery memory insights that Memory Frontier has supposedly calibrated our Reflectors with?"

"You don't think they've been"—Chase couldn't bring himself to say it out loud, so he mouthed the rest—"memory indexing?"

"I don't know what I think," Fletcher confessed. Memory indexing was a very serious accusation, one that seemed to fill Fletcher's mouth with a hot, bitter taste.

It is a possibility though. His heart somersaulted. *If Memory Frontier doesn't have people's memories indexed on secret, expansive digital archives, how else are they managing to pair us with these Reflectors?*

Chase leaned back into the couch, breathing, "Whoa!" and really drawing out the word.

"I can't believe I'm saying this," Fletcher admitted, "but your instinct to stump that Memory Frontier representative was spot-on, even if it was a little . . . messy."

"Yeah?" Chase blinked.

"Think about it, man," Fletcher said, turning on the couch to face his roommate better. "This is one of the biggest companies in the world. They *for sure* have dotted their i's and crossed their t's.

They've looked at this from every angle, and their legal team has likely spent countless hours working to ensure this trial is bulletproof, at least from a legal standpoint."

"Yeah . . . ," Chase said a third time, tapping his knees anxiously.

"We're not going to find out their secrets by reading the fine print or listening to canned explanations." Fletcher's heart continued to race. "We're going to find out by catching one of these suits in a lie."

Chase laughed through his nose. "I need another drink." He shook his head. The cassette in his boombox softly scratched to the next song. Hearing the music playing from the tape gave Fletcher an idea.

"Did you bring your Restorey?"

Chase gave him a grave look, like he knew where this was going. "Yeah. My stepmom packed it, along with all my memory tapes. You?"

"Yup. Have mine."

Fletcher's tiny, black Reflector sat in the soft imprint of his gray pillow. He stared at the device, his head spinning with so many thoughts he was starting to feel woozy.

"What if we *skipped* the trial?" Fletcher whispered. "At least for a couple of weeks, or until we can see if we're able to track down any info on how Memory Frontier is actually calibrating these Reflectors."

Chase leapt to his feet, as if the couch cushions were suddenly hot to the touch, and started pacing in front of the TV.

"Skip the trial," he said, so quietly that Fletcher had to read his lips. "Dude, that's insane. *Insane.* They'll find out and kick us out!"

"Oswald said he's checking in with us quarterly. That's in like two months. So we take a couple of weeks to do some digging, see if we're on to something here, and keep using artificial recall in the meantime."

"I dunno . . ." Chase ran his hands through his blond hair. He walked over to his backpack, pulled out a bag of sunflower seeds, and munched on a handful. "I was just hoping to catch Oswald off his game . . . get him to slip up or something . . . But skip the trial?"

"You said it yourself, Chase: maybe Foxtail Academy isn't all it claims to be. What's the worst thing that could happen? We get kicked out for not participating and sent back home?" Fletcher smiled wryly, picturing the look on his father's face as he stood on their doorstep, suitcases in hand—thwarting his father's plan to get Fletcher out of the house for nine months.

Chase didn't reply for a while. Eventually, he returned to his spot on the couch beside Fletcher and said defeatedly, "Should've kept my trap shut. I could be schooling you on my SEGA right now."

Fletcher laughed inwardly, realizing just how quickly their roles had reversed. Chase's hesitancy to skip the trial did make Fletcher question himself, though.

Are we . . . am I . . . making a big deal out of nothing?

Tomorrow, after breakfast, if the two of them were to track down a Memory Frontier representative and ask them to explain the technology a little better, would they get a satisfying answer?

Am I looking for a bombshell secret that doesn't exist?

In other words . . . was Fletcher's skepticism really about this trial, or was it rooted in his desire to get back at his father?

"Fine. Let's do it." Chase leaned his head back. "But only for one week."

"Deal. And . . . I think we should keep this between us, man. Not tell Freya or Ollie."

"You sure?" Chase asked. "Ollie's sharp as a tack. And Freya seems—"

"No," Fletcher said firmly. "The fewer people who know, the better. Plus, if we get in trouble, I wouldn't want them guilty by association." Fletcher didn't care how controlling he sounded; keeping the girls out of this seemed absolutely necessary.

Chase nodded.

As the two sat there, Fletcher realized what *else* had to be done if they were to have any shot at learning what was going on behind the scenes.

"I have to take up Dean Mendelsohn on his offer." Fletcher tasted bile on the back of his tongue. "I need to ingratiate myself with the dean. There's no telling what kind of info it could afford us if I'm meeting with him regularly."

Chase gave him a look of pity before declaring they were *both* going to need another drink now. He returned to his suitcases and opened the smallest one. After briefly digging around in his belongings, Chase produced a six-pack.

"It's most *definitely* warm," he warned, setting the beer on the coffee table and separating two cans. Fletcher and Chase cracked them open simultaneously, and the drinks erupted with mini, frothy explosions.

"No no no!" Chase said, exasperated, leaning forward and slurping the foamy drink. Fletcher laughed at his roommate, wiping away suds from his forehead and cheeks, then raising the can like a toastmaster would.

"Here's to uncovering Memory Frontier's secrets!" They clanked cans.

"And to warm, flat beverages," Chase declared.

Their laughter doubled, and for a fleeting second Fletcher didn't think about anything else—not the trial, Dean Mendelsohn, or his father's secrets. He just tried to keep his laughter at a reasonable volume so a prefect didn't file a noise complaint against them.

13

FREYA IZQUIERDO

I wake to a thin piece of morning sunlight draped across my cheek. That was easily the best night's sleep I ever had. Outside the window birds chirp noisily, and above me Ollie softly snores. On the wall, the clock reads 7:19 a.m. I pick up my Reflector, which didn't move from its spot beside my pillow, and check the display. The word *Complete* flashes in pixel letters.

I sit up, stretch, then carefully remove the suction receivers from my temples and roll out of bed.

I brush my teeth, then take a hot shower. As I stand in the steamy water beneath the showerhead, I hold up my right hand and watch droplets of water bubble down my fingers and over my cognition wheel. For the better part of a year and a half, I have *loathed* this mark and prayed that one day, miraculously, I'd wake up to find it gone.

In a lot of ways, that prayer has been answered.

But cruelly, *painfully*, as if some scales in the universe needed to be balanced, this answered prayer has come with a price. Had the Reflectors come out two years ago, expunging the need for artificial recall when my dad was still alive, things would have been different. His recall schedule wouldn't have dictated our weekends. He wouldn't have needed a handler. This freedom would have enabled me and my dad to go anywhere and do anything. I'm sure we would have traveled, like Fletcher and his family. Sure, we were so poor that some nights Dad didn't eat dinner so I could, but you don't need a lot of money to go on road trips.

With access to Reflectors, there's no telling what my dad and I would have done.

The hot water runs down my back and I start to tremble. My breathing quickens and my chest violently contracts. And then the tears flow.

This is my harmonious grief dance. When I'm happy, when a small moment of joy reaches out and lightly kisses me on the lips, guilt hollows me out and empties me. And when I grieve, when I'm alone in the shower or my bedroom or at the beach—when even my thoughts abandon me coldly—guilt condemns me for not being more grateful, because many people out there have it *far* worse than me, after all.

And so the dance goes, tugging me this way and that, at once rehearsed and improvised—a synchronicity of light and shadow.

I compose myself, then flip off the shower and get dressed.

I blow-dry my hair and tie it back in a ponytail in anticipation of the ruthless humidity. This morning routine of mine is magnificently elevated by the fact that I don't have to use my Restorey today—or ever again, for that matter.

Today is the beginning of the new normal. I smile at my reflection.

I leave the bathroom and wake up a groggy Ollie, who uses colorful language to tell me how much that annoys her. Her grumpy face doesn't begin to melt away until we leave our dorm room, enter the loud, vaulted-ceiling dining hall, and grab our trays of pancakes.

"I forgive you for waking me up." She douses her breakfast in maple syrup.

I smile at my roommate, watching her devour her fluffy pancakes, and an unfamiliar wave of gratefulness and contentment washes over me.

Thanks to Memory Frontier and the Reflectors, I have a whole new future I didn't think was possible. I don't care why Memory Frontier dropped the charges against me so I could attend Foxtail Academy. In fact, I don't even care about the cursed half-memory dreams.

I don't care because I'm just thankful to be in this massive dining hall, on a morning free of artificial recall, eating pancakes with students from all over the country, wondering how I ever got this lucky.

On my way to drop off my empty food tray, a conversation between two girls catches my attention.

"Did she leave a note?"

"No, nothing."

"That's weird."

"*So* weird, right? And after only one night on campus!"

"Maybe she got super homesick?"

"You think?"

"Well, sure, I mean . . . why *else* would your roommate vanish in the middle of the night with all her things?"

They sound young, probably freshmen or sophomores. Melodramatic. It's not like her roommate was abducted.

Yeah. She was probably homesick.

14

FLETCHER COHEN

Fletcher's alarm clock shrieked at 6:45 a.m.

It took him a long, dazed minute to remember he was in a dorm room on the Foxtail Academy campus, thousands of miles from home. He smacked off the alarm on his wristwatch, emerged from the covers, and found Chase seated on the couch. His Restorey and bag of memory tapes rested on the coffee table.

"Hey," Chase said, yawning, his hair disheveled and his left cheek covered in liny pillow imprints.

"Hey." Fletcher hopped down from the top bunk, rubbed the sleep from his eyes, and staggered toward the closet, where he'd put his Restorey and memory tapes yesterday. After grabbing his things, he joined Chase, who was scanning his laminated schedule.

"Should we, like, stagger this?" Chase asked, locating the day's memory tape.

"I'm fine going at the same time if you are." Fletcher quickly pinpointed the day's date on his recall schedule. He was due to play the same memory tape he'd viewed on the day he received the Foxtail Academy invitation letter.

Fletcher snagged the memory tape from his bag, loaded it into his black Restorey, and made certain it was rewound.

"Okay, well," Chase said, sticking the suction receivers to his temples and leaning back. "See you on the other side, then." He pressed Play and his eyes slowly rolled back in his head.

Fletcher sighed, glancing at his Reflector and its charging base— completely unused, the receivers and wires still spooled together like they hadn't even left the factory.

Well, no time for second thoughts now. He slid his Restorey closer and firmly pressed the receivers against his temples. He pressed Play and ground his teeth together.

◈ ◈ ◈

The sound of bacon sizzling in a skillet.

The sound of sleety rain falling sideways against a window.

The smell of that bacon, and also musk and old carpet and pine.

I hear "Fire and Rain" by James Taylor softly playing.

I observe a hallway lined with strange artwork encased in ornate frames. No, it's not artwork—it's maps. Dozens of them. (Ancillary recollection: My grandfather adored these things and, despite my grandmother's constant bemoaning, collected them at flea markets and antique shops and hung them around the house. And he didn't bother to use a level or give any thought to how best to arrange his precious framed maps. He'd just find a free space on a wall in a random room and then unholster his hammer and drive a nail into the drywall.)

I continue down the hallway and turn into the kitchen, where my mother (her back to me) stands at the stove and prepares breakfast. I observe

triptych windows above the farm sink. It's cold and wet and gloomy outside.
Swelling clouds show no sign of relenting.

(Ancillary recollection: When my mother and I would stay at my grand-
parents' home in West Linn, Oregon, she would wake up before anyone else in
the house and cook her self-proclaimed "specialty" of scrambled eggs, bacon,
english muffins, and a berry medley topped with a pinch of powdered sugar.)

My taste buds tingle.

My mother turns around. She is startled by my appearance. I see tears in
the corners of her eyes, thick masses that hang like rainclouds. She nervously
blinks them away and throws on a brave face.

You're up early, hon. *In her voice I hear a fragility that she mostly*
holds in check.

I could hear the bacon and the rain.

She smiles down at me. Ah, two of my favorite things. *She sets the*
tongs down and invites me in for a hug. I lean into her embrace, and she
has to bend over slightly. I am six or seven, perhaps younger. (Ancillary
recollection: we stopped visiting my grandparents when I was around thir-
teen, about the time my father's career began to accelerate and my mother
and grandfather grew distant. To this day they're still estranged, my mother
and grandfather, though we receive holiday cards every year, and my grand-
parents call on my birthday.)

Why were you crying?

She pulls away but remains hunched over at eye-level with me. Her
green eyes stare into mine, unblinking, and I feel her words materialize in my
subconscious before she says them aloud: Well, hon, Mommy just misses
Josephina right now.

What do you mean?

Well, you know how we told you about your baby sister growing
in Mommy's tummy?

Yeah.

My mother visibly steels herself. Well, she, um, she stopped growing
last week.

I know I should feel something. My mother never talks with such a serious and soft tone. "Stopped growing" must be very, very bad to make my mother cry.

How can you miss her if you've never met her?

A smile breaks across her weary face, and I feel a warmth from that smile that instantly gives me gooseflesh. I have met her, hon. She reaches forward and cups the side of my face in her hand. (Ancillary recollection: on that cold morning, my mother's touch warmed me all the way down to my bones.) She continues, watery-eyed: In my dreams I see her face, like I see yours now, and hers is a radiant face with radiant eyes and radiant hair that assures me it's all going to be okay, even to the end of time.

I let her words sink in—I really ponder them in the way kids analyze new words or unfamiliar turns of phrase—before I ask, Do you think I will ever meet her?

The grin on her face deepens, and I know the answer is yes without her having to say it. But a chill of sadness fills me as I realize I likely won't meet Josephina for a long, long time.

Maybe I'll dream about her too.

My mother nods. Yeah, hon, maybe you will.

The kitchen goes white, washing away the appliances, the windows, the smells, the sounds, and my mother's kind and hopeful face. The smile lines beside her green eyes are the last detail I observe before even those, too, are gone.

"Look who decided to wake up," Ollie said in a bombastic tone, her brown eyebrows raised. Beside her, Freya, whose smooth skin glowed in her loose-fitted tank top, smirked and then took a swig of orange juice.

"Ha," Chase said as he and Fletcher sat down in front of the girls at the long table, the boys' respective trays piled with eggs and pancakes. A deafening din filled the dining hall: forks and spoons clanked; laughter rang out. Fletcher grabbed the bottle of syrup beside Ollie's tray and drizzled his pancakes. His stomach grumbled impatiently.

"How'd you sleep?" Freya asked.

"Good, yeah." Fletcher cut into his pancakes with the side of his fork. "Really."

"Yeah, really good," Chase added.

Freya and Ollie exchanged a drawn-out glance.

"Um, okay." Ollie pressed the tips of her fingers together. "You two are *awful* guilty. Fess up. Did you drink more last night after lights-out?"

"You got us."

"Nailed it."

Ollie clicked her tongue with a *tsk-tsk-tsk*, but Fletcher guessed she was more disappointed that they drank without her. Thankfully, Ollie and Freya seemed to buy it because Ollie was now lowering her voice and changing the subject.

"Check out Gordon Gekko," she muttered, gesturing toward the cafeteria doors with a flick of her head. "Straight off the set of *Wall Street*." Fletcher and Chase turned, trying to spot who Ollie was talking about.

"Dean Mendelsohn," Freya said under her breath.

The dean was standing in a pool of morning sunlight, hands in his pockets, leisurely scanning the dining hall. He wore a new set of suspenders over a blue button-down shirt that had a white collar. Mr. Williams walked up beside him, wearing his customary Foxtail Academy uniform of khaki shorts and a beige polo.

The two of them created quite a contrast.

"Now there's a pair," Chase said as if reading Fletcher's thoughts.

Mr. Williams chuckled at something the dean said, then absently brushed his mustache with his finger. He gazed out at the students and, when he spotted the four watching him, waved like he was signaling for a helicopter to land.

Fletcher and Chase quickly turned away. Freya and Ollie giggled. Before either of the girls could give them grief, someone one table over loudly shouted, "Hey, Nick! Hi!"

The kid who sat beside Fletcher during the assembly rushed over, a stack of orange papers in hand.

"Nick, hey, it's me, Skipper! From the auditorium!" His black, square-rimmed glasses slid down his nose as he panted like he'd just run a marathon. He sat his stack of papers on the table beside Chase's tray, looking flat-out drained.

Chase, Ollie, and Freya slowly turned to Fletcher. He closed his eyes, annoyed, and when he didn't reply the kid continued, offering an explanation to the group: "He arrived *just* before the assembly started yesterday—right in the nick of time!"

"Ah," Chase said, nodding. "Nick. Got it."

Fletcher scowled at his roommate as Freya asked, "Your name's Skipper?"

"Matthew Skipper," he replied importantly, hands on his hips like he was about to take flight. "But Skipper sounds cooler."

"*Way* cooler," Ollie agreed. "What's with the flyers?"

"So glad you asked . . ."

"Ollie."

"Hi! So glad you asked, *Ollie*." He licked a finger and then carefully slid four pieces of paper from his pile. He proudly handed them out. Fletcher took one and scanned it. The bold, comic-book font read "MOVIES AND MEMORIES!"

And beneath this, "A weekly movie-club watch party and discussion in which we'll watch movies and discuss the intersection of movie plots and memories!"

"Really glad you clarified what the club's about," Chase quipped, setting the flyer down and returning to his pancakes. Fletcher skimmed the details of Skipper's meet-up, which included the time and location.

"We have a senior lounge?" Fletcher asked, looking up at Skipper.

"Sure do! It's in here, actually. Second floor. It's decked out with a big TV, pool tables, darts. The works. It's pretty radical, if I do say so myself. Anyways, we're going to start with Robert Zemeckis's contemporary classic, *Back to the Future!*"

Ollie's eyes widened dramatically, and Freya gave her roommate a knowing look.

"Did you know," Ollie began, her voice hushed with excitement, "Michael J. Fox was actually the *second* choice to play Marty McFly?"

"Yes!" Skipper shocked Fletcher by managing to look even more elated than before. "This will be great fodder for our first discussion next weekend!"

"I'm just impressed you started a club on the second day of school," Fletcher admitted. "I mean, we haven't even gone to our first class yet and you've already designed and printed off these flyers."

"Well, if *that* impresses you, just wait until our first Movies and Memories meet-up!"

"I'll think about it, man," Fletcher said, scratching his chin, unable to avoid sounding noncommittal.

Skipper laughed, flashing his braces. "Classic Nick. See you next Saturday evening!" He scooped up his flyers and left as quickly as he arrived, off to another unsuspecting table.

"Does he even know your real name?" Freya asked, sounding amused.

"Honestly," Fletcher said, picking up his fork, "I don't think it would matter if he did."

15

FREYA IZQUIERDO

After breakfast Ollie and I follow the boys outside, where billowy clouds undulate in the blue sky like riptides at sea, shielding us from a scorching sun that seems bent on boiling everything in her sight.

"The humidity here is *awful!*" Ollie moans, pinching at her T-shirt and fanning herself. The four of us head toward the sandy shoreline beside the pier. When we reach the "beach," not a single one of us delays in ripping off our sneakers, rolling up our pants, plopping onto the sand, and sticking our legs in the cool water. I can almost hear our skin sizzling with relief.

Mere seconds after we get comfortable, Mr. Williams's charged voice loudly echoes through the campus PA system: "Happy Sunday students of Foxtail Academy! Wanted to let you know that y'all need to stop by the library with your class schedules before dinner to collect your textbooks for the fall semester! Teachers will be present to answer questions. We'll go by grade, starting with freshmen at 3:00 p.m., sophomores at 4:00, juniors at 5:00, and seniors at 6:00 to close us out!"

"Ollie." Chase leans back on his elbows. "You're *such* a doll for offering to pick up my textbooks for me!"

"Mhmm." She kicks some water in his direction.

"Ahhhh." He throws his head back, his wavy blond hair bouncing. "That's the spot."

Ollie and Chase begin to bicker playfully.

After a while, Ollie exhales energetically. "You know the first thing I thought about yesterday in the auditorium, after they unveiled the Reflector? No more scholastic gaps!"

I nod, feeling yet *another* weight lift. Scholastic gaps are aspects of certain school subjects that become at-risk memories. They're of course identified by the MeReader and imprinted onto memory tapes, making for an incredibly boring, taxing artificial recall.

The only thing worse than learning about linear equations is having to artificially recall how and what they are over and over.

Chase and Ollie lament to one another about their dullest memory tapes. Fletcher slides on his round sunglasses, and before he and I can get a word in, a few younger students (likely freshmen or sophomores) race across the pier. They're barefoot but with their clothes still on, and they cannonball into Juniper Lake. Chase and Ollie begin to quietly criticize them like two crotchety retirees.

"At least take off your shirts, you absolute *rubes*." Chase flips his hand.

"I meant to ask," Ollie says to me, later, after we've split from the boys and are heading back to our room. "How'd you sleep? You know, with the Reflector and all."

We merge off the grass and onto the paved path toward the girls' dormitories. "Really good. Soundless and dreamless. Plus, I used to get light-headed after artificial recall, so spending the morning without having to deal with *that* has been great."

"Same." Ollie puts her hands in her back pockets. "Probably could've slept longer if not for a certain roommate of mine."

"You're welcome."

"So . . ." She clears her throat. "Have you gotten any more of those migraines?"

Ah. That's what she's really getting at. While I appreciate her caring, she doesn't need to expend an ounce worth of worrying on me. "Ha. No, actually. And don't think twice about that. I'm fine—"

"I know you say you are. But, Freya, you looked like you were about to pass out. You looked . . . like you were somewhere else. I've been thinking about it ever since it happened."

"Well, don't." I'm probably firmer than I need to be. "Look, it means a lot that you care. But you're blowing this up."

She nods and throws on a smile. I sigh inwardly. I know there's no real harm in telling Ollie about my half-memory dreams, but I'm just not comfortable divulging them to her because I don't want to burden her—or anyone else—with this problem of mine. I learned this lesson after letting Nicole in; not a day went by after I told my foster sister when she *wasn't* checking on me, asking if I'd had another spell.

It became Nicole's problem too.

I don't want that happening again, not to Ollie.

"Sorry," she says as we approach our dorm room.

"Don't be. You care, and that's never anything to apologize for. Just don't want you worrying about me."

She says okay, then opens the door. Ollie doesn't say another word as she picks out some fresh clothes from the closet and heads into the bathroom to shower. I'm worrying I might've been too hard on her when something catches my eye.

It's my leatherbound photo album. Its worn, peeling corner sticks out from beneath my pillow.

Did I flip through it this morning before waking Ollie for breakfast?

I . . . don't remember. But if I had, I *definitely* would have concealed it beneath my pillow when I finished. This personal window into my past is very intimate, something I've never shared with others, and I wouldn't chance my roommate asking about it.

Of course, I could've been careless. I could've nudged it askew when I got out of bed this morning and just forgot to cover it back up.

But. No. Not with this. It may seem insignificant to someone else, perhaps even a little obsessive, but I'm *certain* I would've covered my photo album back up.

Unless . . .

❖ ❖ ❖

It used to be that existential threats were the scariest kind of threats, Dad said once as we walked to the video rental store. *You know: inclement weather, recessions, the nuclear wars. Then Memory Killer came and changed all that. Suddenly the scariest threat came from* within *our very minds.*

He took my tiny eleven-year-old hand in his giant one. I could feel his cognition wheel against my skin, like the two-quarter mark was somehow radiating a kind of cold heat.

I hated that tattoo even before I fully understood its implications.

But I think all this memory-loss business isn't even our primary enemy. He looked down at me as we walked. *To be honest, I don't even think it's secondary or tertiary! How about that?* He lowered his voice, like someone afraid of being overheard: *I think humanity's real enemy is misremembering.*

❖ ❖ ❖

I walk to my bed. I slide my photo album underneath my mattress this time, taking extra care to ensure it's hidden, anxious I *did* thumb through it earlier and have misremembered.

16

FLETCHER COHEN

The campus library was a glass, octagon-shaped building that stood between the boys' and girls' dormitories. Countless windows refracted the late-afternoon sunlight, dazzling the long aisles of books that stretched the distance of the library's interior. Deep armchairs sat in various corners of the giant room, and a few desks held state-of-the-art Apple IIGS computers that appeared to have just been unboxed.

Fletcher, Freya, Chase, and Ollie loitered near the entrance as the last handful of juniors collected their textbooks for the semester.

Above the checkout counter, a gold plaque read: LOCHAMIRE'S INCUBATOR FOR BRAINSTORMING, RESEARCH, AND ACADEMIC READING FOR YOUTH.

"Alexander Lochamire turned *library* into an acronym about

himself," Freya said beside Fletcher, staring at the plaque. "Why does that seem like a whole new level of narcissism?"

"Because it *is*," Fletcher replied, his mouth hanging slightly open in disbelief.

"We need to come up with an acronym for our dorm room." Chase lightly elbowed Fletcher. "Like . . . how about: Dungeon of Rowdy Misfits."

"*Dungeon?*" Ollie snorted. "What are you, a Disney witch?"

"Dungeon of Rowdy Misfits it is," Chase repeated sourly.

The foursome followed a lengthy queue of their senior peers toward the checkout counter. Campus staffers busily referenced class schedules and divvied out the appropriate textbooks to students.

"You guys think Alexander Lochamire will make an appearance on campus?" Freya asked, still staring at the gaudy plaque.

Ollie sighed. "Doubt it. The only thing more enigmatic than Memory Killer is Alexander Lochamire."

Chase popped some sunflower seeds into his mouth. "Really? You don't think Willy Wonka will come visit his memory factory at least once?"

"He's a pretty strange guy," Fletcher said. Slowly, Freya and Chase and Ollie directed their eyes toward him.

"Have you *met* him?" Chase asked, raising his eyebrows.

"Well, no, *I* haven't," Fletcher clarified, feeling like he was suddenly called to the stand by a team of prosecutors. "I just . . . my father has. At charity event . . . things."

Ollie pushed Fletcher in the chest, nearly smacking him into an unsuspecting classmate. "You're holding out on us! What's he like? He looks *really* old on TV. Did you meet his daughter too? Wait, no, I think they're estranged—"

"He has a *son*," Chase said dismissively, turning to Fletcher: "I heard Alexander lives in a mansion on a remote island. And that he sleeps hooked up to this memory ventilator device that preserves all his memories. Can you imagine?"

Fletcher couldn't get a word in, and Freya grinned at this. "Well, Fletcher? *Are* you holding out on us?"

Fletcher glared at her, but before he could reply a saccharine voice said, "Back of the line, hm?"

Ave Maria appeared wearing a bright pink top and a jean skirt. She carried her textbooks as if she were modeling for *Seventeen* magazine, and she was flanked by a tall, blonde girl with fair skin and a pointy nose, and a guy with a head of hair so curly it might have been permed. He wore aviators and chewed gum with obnoxious, open-mouthed chomps.

Ave Maria added coolly, "It's almost as if you four are used to bringing up the rear."

Chase chuckled, but Fletcher and the girls deadpanned. Chase cleared his throat and straightened up.

Fletcher gestured toward Ave Maria's armful of textbooks. "I don't see your copy of *Living with Chronic Traumatic Encephalopathy*."

She narrowed her eyes.

"You know," Fletcher continued, without a modicum of insincerity in his tone, "CTE? Brain damage caused by multiple head injur—" Fletcher embellished a gasp. "Oh no. Do you not realize the extent of your head injuries?"

Ollie snickered and Freya was completely unreadable. Chase, on the other hand, frowned as if sorting through a complicated math theorem in his head.

Ave Maria's fake grin deepened. "That's clever. Anyway, we don't want to hold you up." She turned to her lackeys and, like two dogs commanded by their master, they subserviently followed her lead and exited the library.

Chase, as if suddenly emerging from underwater, said, "Wait, so Ave Maria has a concussion?"

"Laid it on kind of thick, huh?" Freya folded her arms, sounding borderline accusatory.

"Let him do his thing!" Ollie snapped as they finally reached the checkout counter and slid their schedules across the table. "Girls like her are emboldened by silence."

"It's called fighting fire with fire," Chase said, agreeing, leaning against the counter lazily. But Freya didn't appear convinced, and Fletcher's ears reddened. "You guys happen to notice Ave Maria's friend?"

"Who, Sunglasses?" Ollie snorted. "I'm sure you two could bond over hair products."

"Ha," Chase said. "No. Her lady friend. I'm feeling like there might've been some electricity between us." He bit his lip and whipped the bangs out of his eyes.

"Please, for the love, don't fraternize with the enemy." Ollie took her textbooks.

"She had one of Skipper's movie club flyers," Chase said. "Suddenly methinks we should all go check it out."

Ollie made another remark, something about being both disappointed and unsurprised, but Fletcher tuned it out.

He worried Freya was right—that he *had* come across too strong against Ave Maria. He tried to catch her eye, but Freya was too busy stacking her textbooks to notice.

Outside, Fletcher and the gang found the campus uncharacteristically quiet. Everyone who was on the grounds tilted their heads back, frozen under a powerful spell, and stared at the sky. Naturally, the foursome looked up. A triplane cut across the pink firmament with a long banner whipping at its tail.

Fletcher mumbled the words aloud. "'Memory Frontier is the arbiter of our fates.'"

Ollie sighed. "The Memory Ghosts *are* relentless . . . gotta hand 'em that."

"Relentlessly crazy." Chase laughed under his breath, though Fletcher noted a hint of unease in his roommate's tone.

No one spoke on the walk back to the dorms.

17

FREYA IZQUIERDO

At breakfast the next morning in the Foxhole, Dean Mendelsohn approaches our table with his enamel coffee mug in hand. I avoid his eyes and focus on my cereal, but it's no matter—he's not here to see me.

"I wonder if I might borrow you for a chat after final period?" he asks Fletcher, who instantly pales.

"Yeah, sure. Should I come to your office?"

"I'll find you," the dean answers ominously. Then, to the group, he adds, "Have a wonderful first day of classes."

Once he's out of earshot, Ollie whispers, "What was *that* about?"

"Nothing," he says. I'm surprised Chase doesn't prod. Ollie and I exchange a glance, but with it very clear that Fletcher doesn't want to talk about it, we resume eating.

After breakfast, we take our empty trays to the designated drop-off zone by the kitchen and walk to our first class.

The classrooms, a collection of a dozen or so stand-alone buildings with vertical siding and square windows, are on the west side of campus beyond the colossal auditorium. As we get closer, each of us consulting our class schedules while trying to balance our too-heavy textbooks, Mr. Williams rattles off the morning announcements through the loudspeakers. He ends with a boisterous, "Have fun learning, y'all!" to which Fletcher remarks that *fun* and *learning* should never, under any circumstances, be paired.

Eventually, we all figure out where we're going, and my first two classes of the day (economics and literature) are bittersweet bites of reality that remind me I'm still in high school with nine months' worth of reading, research, and testing ahead of me. As great as this past weekend has been, it's back to the semi–real world for me, which means working harder than most to maintain a 3.0 GPA.

Lunch with Fletcher, Ollie, and Chase (none of whom I shared my first two classes with) is like being handed an oxygen mask after trekking up a very high and very steep mountainside. We laugh, cut up, and each make a case for why our first two periods were more boring than anyone else's. As it turns out, the three of them are stuck in AP lit together. I force a smile at the table, trying not to feel left out as they complain about the teacher's nasally voice and excessive nose hair. Chase even turns to me at one point and says, exasperated, "Just be glad you're not in there with us, Freya. The required-reading list feels like a literal assault on our free time."

I chuckle and lie. "Good luck . . . I'd hate to be stuck in there with you guys."

Wow, I think, as we gather our things and start to head to third period, *I never thought I'd have a reason for feeling left out of an advanced placement course.*

Next up is Algebra II, a class I thankfully share with Chase.

"Math has never been my strong suit," he tells me as we claim two desks at the back of the classroom. He brushes the bangs out of his eyes and slouches in the stiff metal chair. "So thank you for your service."

"My service?"

"Letting me cheat off of you during exams." He actually rolls his eyes. "Freya. C'mon."

I blink. "I've barely known you two days and I'm already questioning why we're friends."

He smiles and shoots me his customary wink.

Algebra II proves to be a slog, a ninety minute carousel ride filled with inequalities and polynomials, and by the end I feel more nauseous than if I had *actually* been riding a carousel for an hour and a half. The teacher, a well-intentioned woman named Ms. Schneck, whose dry-erase board scribblings are only barely legible, teaches with a droning, monotonous voice that seems to send half the class to sleep.

When the bell rings, Chase and I can't leap out of our desks quick enough.

I inhale the hot air and hug my textbook as the two of us cross the grounds.

"So, um, Chase."

"So, um, *Freya.*"

"I've been wondering . . . think maybe I could borrow your video camera at some point this weekend?"

"Color me intrigued." Chase smiles as we near the Foxhole. "One, how'd you know I had a video camera, and two, what do you need it for?"

My heart sinks a little. He's completely forgotten about our talk at the bonfire on Saturday. Chase, reading my silence, shakes his head. "We already talked about this, didn't we?"

"Mhmm."

"Memory Killer's a cruel mistress." He puts on a confident face, his eyes squinting in the sun. "'Course you can borrow my camera. Bring it by your room Sunday?"

"Perfect." As Chase pulls open the door to the dining hall, I add, "I guess I'll consider letting you cheat in Algebra II."

We meet up with Fletcher and Ollie in the senior lounge, where we intend to spend our free period before closing out the day with Memory Theory.

As we gather at a table, I only barely listen to my friends' banter. I realize with a start that I haven't had a single half-memory dream since Saturday afternoon. That bizarre, unnerving memory about the train tracks at night . . . the dead body in the woods . . . the shadowy man in the lab coat . . . marked the last time I've been hit with an unfinished scene from my past. If I make it through the rest of the afternoon and into the evening, that'll be *two whole days*.

That's the longest stretch since they first started when I was sixteen.

"You good?" Fletcher asks, watching me carefully.

"Hm? Oh, yeah."

"Got kinda introspective on me." He smiles.

"I'm known for that."

His smile turns into a chuckle. "Duly noted."

I lean back in my chair, deciding it's time I take advantage of my clear head. With Chase agreeing to lend me his video camera this weekend and my half memories at bay, I need to carve out some time to secretly locate and explore Memory Frontier's base of operations.

If there are any answers here, Dad, I will find them.

The four of us mingle in the senior lounge, and the hour breezes by. The lounge is filled to about quarter capacity: a few seniors play foosball; a couple of girls order iced drinks from the coffee bar; a handful of our classmates sit around the TV, watching *MTV News*.

Before I know it, we're reluctantly gathering our books and making our way back toward the classrooms for Memory Theory.

"Let's all please settle down," a kind yet commanding voice says. "Thank you. Good. Good."

A woman in her midthirties walks down the aisle toward the front of the classroom and sets her leather briefcase on the desk. She flicks open the brass latches and opens the briefcase, then pulls a few things out, including a large stack of papers, which she places beside a collection of framed photographs. As the chatter in the classroom fades to a lull, she turns and writes her name across the large dry-erase board with wide, sweeping strokes. She wears a black skirt hemmed just above her knees, a charcoal-gray blazer over her white blouse, and shiny, reflective pumps. Her straight, blonde hair—it almost looks like gold—falls to her shoulders, where it curls in slightly at the ends.

I decide the woman belongs in high fashion, not education.

"I'm Dr. Brenda Sanders," she says, capping the marker and turning to face us. "I have worked for Memory Frontier since 1984 leading a small division that specializes in the overlap of memories and dreams. Before that, I was a cognitive psychologist who spent most of my time writing and publishing boring papers. I've always romanticized lecturing in a classroom to a group of young, budding minds, so please don't disappoint me." Dr. Sanders winks after that last part. She gracefully moves to the front of her desk, leaning against it and scanning the classroom. Now that we can see her face, I observe her dark brown eyebrows, hydrangea-blue eyes, faintly freckled skin, and upturned nose.

Not high fashion. More like the runway.

Indeed, Dr. Sanders is beautiful, and on each side of me Fletcher and Chase all but drool in their desks as our teacher continues to talk with the ease and confidence of an accomplished woman who knows where she's going and, more importantly, how to get there.

"In the mid-eighteenth century, fleets of ships would sail across stormy waters in search of the ocean's most majestic creature: the sperm whale." She rolls up the sleeves of her blazer. "These seafarers, aptly named *whalers*, would hunt these mammoth animals with harpoons, heft them onto their ships, and then take them back to land so they could be harvested. And, while there were a few uses for their bodies, can anyone tell me what these ninety-thousand-pound animals were primarily utilized for?"

The classroom is silent. Either no one knows the answer, or everyone is too enraptured with Dr. Sanders to respond.

"Lighting." Her tone is sorrowful. "The heads of sperm whales contain a rich oil that men burned for indoor lighting. Benjamin Franklin wrote that these oil lamps 'afford a clear white light; may be held in the hand, even in hot weather, without softening; that their drops do not make grease spots like those from common candles.' In short, whales were slaughtered to the point of near extinction so men and women could read by lamplight."

She lets us sit with that brief, harrowing history lesson for a few moments.

Still seated at the edge of her desk, she continues, "You think that's disturbing? How about this? It wasn't that long ago that barber shops offered a service called *bloodletting*. Patrons would pay to have their blood drawn while they were getting a haircut or having their beard trimmed. It was thought to be a cleansing." This is met with subtle gagging noises from the class. "It's true. It's why those classic barbershop poles have a red stripe."

Dr. Sanders smiles at our collective discomfort and walks back to the dry-erase board. "I share these two factoids with you to illustrate an important point. We, as a species, have made some pretty foolhardy decisions in our past. However, as our scientific discoveries and understandings continue to advance, we change course. Learn from our mistakes. Find a better way. Or that's the hope, at least, isn't it?

"That's why you all are here—because, in the case of Memory Frontier's Reflector, we *have* found a better way."

Dr. Sanders takes a red marker and begins erratically dotting the board, seemingly at random, and when she's finished half the surface is covered in small red marks.

"Who knows how much data can be stored on a memory tape?" She sets down the marker and clasps her hands behind her back.

A hand at the front of the classroom rises slowly into the air. Dr. Sanders calls on the redheaded boy with a smile. "Yes, Lucas Childs, is it?"

"Yeah," he says, shifting uncomfortably. "Um, so the average memory tape can hold up to two gigabytes of storage, which is about the same as a VHS tape."

Someone in the back coughs the word *nerd!* The classroom erupts into laughter. Lucas blushes and sinks into his chair.

"That's enough, that's enough," Dr. Sanders says firmly, her nose twitching irritably. Then to Lucas, "You're absolutely right. Let's quickly compare that to the human consciousness. Our brains possess roughly one billion neurons, and every single one of those neurons creates hundreds and *thousands* of interconnected pathways, totaling well over a trillion unique connections. And our neurons actively work together via this network to form a storage capacity of up to a million gigabytes. That's an awful lot more than a single memory tape, wouldn't you say?"

Heads nod throughout the classroom.

"When Memory Killer was first discovered, it confounded medical scientists the world over. In fact, to this day it is still somewhat of an enigma. It's not some pathogen that can be studied in a petri dish beneath a microscope. Memory Killer . . . just *is*. One day you're watering your garden or walking your dog or balancing your checkbook, and the next thing you know a cold wave visits you, like an apparition, feeding on your memories slowly . . . little by little . . . day by day . . . until you are nothing more than a passengerless vessel."

The classroom is dead silent. Dr. Sanders isn't necessarily presenting new information to the class about the phenomenon of Memory Killer, but it's *how* she's communicating it. Her voice is laced with reverence and fear, a kind of awe, like someone talking about an enemy whose power they cannot deny.

I feel my blood run cold.

Dr. Sanders returns to the dry-erase board and sets to work nimbly connecting the dots with a continuous line. "For years now, our only means of survival against Memory Killer has been to identify vulnerable memories in our minds and then imprint them onto memory tapes. This way we can *relearn* and then *restore* these precious moments to our consciousness before the memory is swallowed whole. But how can memory tapes, which can only provide two gigabytes of storage, possibly hope to contain something as profound and complex and vast as a single human memory?"

She connects the last dots on the board and steps aside. Some of my classmates let out soft gasps. Dr. Sanders has drawn an ancient ship, complete with three masts, three sails, and a bowsprit. A likeness of the type of vessel, I assume, used by whalers. We stare at the drawing, likely all wondering how the heck she managed to connect those seemingly haphazard dots into art.

"Memory tapes"—she gestures toward the board—"are much like these dots. They contain tiny yet pertinent details—memory landmarks, if you will—and when you artificially recall, your brain connects the dots to complete your memory."

Now *this* is something no one has ever explained to me, and I wonder how many in this classroom are learning about the technology behind memory tapes for the first time too. Before I can think on it too much, Dr. Sanders pulls a stack of papers out of her briefcase and hands it to one of the students on the first row, who dutifully takes one copy and hands the rest over his shoulder. This continues down the rows until finally the class syllabus makes it into my hands.

Dr. Sanders's eyes fall on each one of us. "In Memory Theory, I aim to present just how important of a throughline memories play in our history, and why the fight to preserve our ability to remember is more urgent than ever. Further, each of you will work across the span of both semesters to answer the most important question that looms over a society plagued by memory loss: Are we more than the sum of our memories?"

After class, we file outside into the late-afternoon heat, our first Memory Theory assignment dashing all hopes of an easy first week. I decide to talk to Dr. Sanders about my half-memory dreams. Maybe someone with her training will have answers. Maybe she can help me understand why I get them and—more importantly—chart a course of action for preventing them.

Now I just need to figure out how to do it without sounding crazy.

18

FLETCHER COHEN

Before dinner, Fletcher grabbed a notebook and pencil and meandered around the campus grounds between the classrooms and the faculty housing. The latter was a cluster of small, uninspiring brick buildings with chevron-patterned doors and tiny windows. It was as if the builders poured their entire budget into the rest of the campus and then realized they needed to construct housing for the teachers too.

Fletcher picked a patch of grass beside the sidewalk, plopped down, and started to list new questions for his Memory Killer File.

First, there was a question he thought of yesterday after breakfast: *Do MeReaders know the difference between suppressed and repressed memories?* Beneath this, he wrote the question that had popped into his head during Memory Theory: *Why does Memory Frontier have a monopoly on artificial recall?*

❖ ❖ ❖

Fletcher had hazy memories of sitting in the back seat of his parents' car and listening to them speculate about the pharmaceutical industry—conspiracies that took on a whole new life after Memory Killer's arrival and the subsequent need for artificial recall. The conspiracies had long claimed massive pharmaceutical companies were this insidious force that actively placed profit above public safety. Soon people were saying that a cure for Memory Killer existed but was in fact being withheld so Memory Frontier could generate revenue off the production and sale of Restoreys.

Something like that, anyway. Fletcher was only half listening at the time.

After his father was elected congressman a couple of years ago, those kinds of discussions were quelled in the Cohen household. From that point forward, Memory Frontier and artificial recall were never again called to task. In fact, Fletcher's father spoke of the corporation and its work only with a kind of reverence, and he was quick to condemn naysayers and "radical activists"— his words—who insisted Memory Frontier's policy-management team needed to be scrutinized by federal committees. Chief among these activists were the self-proclaimed Memory Ghosts, an ardent and vocal group who protested Memory Frontier, circulated petitions, and insisted the corporation was built on a shaky foundation of lies.

The Memory Ghosts had some violent, rogue actors too—men and women who supposedly set fire to Memory Frontier factories and fulfillment centers. At least, that's who the news outlets *claimed* was responsible for these random, infrequent acts of violence . . .

A long shadow draped over Fletcher's notebook, blotting out the sunlight. He looked up.

Dean Mendelsohn smiled. "I didn't peg you for the diary type."

Fletcher shut the notebook and rose to his feet. "Hi, Dean Mendelsohn."

"Walk with me." The dean rolled up his shirtsleeves as he walked away, like he was getting ready to perform manual labor. Reluctantly, Fletcher followed, pocketing his journal and pencil. "Have you given any thought to my request?"

"Er . . . yeah," Fletcher said as he matched the dean's stride, the faculty housing to their backs and the classrooms up ahead to their right.

"And?"

Fletcher sighed inwardly, making up his lie as he went: "I think a mentorship is a good idea, especially if you can find some way to make it count toward my community service credits."

The dean released a soft, manufactured chuckle. "Spoken like a politician's son."

In California, every registered high school recollector was required to obtain a minimum of five hundred community service credits before graduating. Credits could be obtained in various ways, such as by volunteering in citywide lawn-care efforts, trash pickup initiatives, or—most commonly—as handlers to degens.

In short, community service credits provided free labor to a state with a rapidly crumbling infrastructure. Even his father agreed on that.

"I'll see what I can do," said Dean Mendelsohn, surveying the campus as they ambled along the winding sidewalk. The severe humidity that Monday afternoon had forced most of the student body inside. Fletcher spotted only groundskeepers and a handful of faculty members out and about. "Take the next couple of days to familiarize yourself with your peers . . . to get into a rhythm here at Foxtail. Then we can discuss you spending one or two of your study periods in my office for your mentorship."

Fletcher could think of a hundred places he'd rather be than holed up in the dean's office twice a week. But he reminded himself this was necessary if he and Chase were to uncover any secrets that might be hidden behind the Foxtail Academy walls.

"Oh, by the way," Fletcher said, hoping he sounded conversational. "I forgot to ask Oswald the other night when he was giving us the rundown of the Reflectors: Should I be worried if Memory Killer attacks my consciousness while I'm hooked up to the Reflector at night?"

Dean Mendelsohn stopped in his tracks. Slowly, he turned to face Fletcher, sweat beading beneath his gray hairline.

Fletcher continued, "Shouldn't be a problem, right? Just like Memory Killer striking during artificial recall isn't a problem either?"

A fake grin hovered around the dean's lips. "No problem."

Fletcher opened his mouth to press further, but a soft ringing cut him off.

The dean pulled a pager out of his pocket and glanced at it. "I have to run, Fletcher." He took off at an almost-sprint, cutting across the greenway and disappearing beyond the auditorium.

Before long, Fletcher had looped the length of the sidewalk and was back by the faculty housing.

A teacher—an older man with drooping jowls and an honest-to-God protractor sticking out of his breast pocket—sat beneath the eaves with his nose in a book, half reading and half sleeping.

A thought occurred to Fletcher. *You want me to spy on my peers? Fine. Might as well spy on the faculty too.*

As surreptitiously as possible, Fletcher scoped the layout of the teachers' housing in relation to the rest of the campus. He pulled out his pencil and notebook and jotted down every possible detail, no matter how small.

Fletcher wrote down his observations: twelve single-story duplexes arranged in a staggered semicircle. Their front doors all faced southeast, toward the stand-alone classrooms and auditorium. There was a sitting area, a sort of outdoor lounge comprising wooden chairs and tables, in the shade beside the rightmost building. Behind this a postal box on a stand had twenty-four compartments. There was also a payphone.

Fully convinced he would later appreciate this reconnaissance, Fletcher turned to leave.

Something caught his eye.

A faint path just beyond the payphone disappeared into the thick woods. No stepping-stones or landscaping marked the trail, just a thin strip of grass that had the distinct look of having been trampled. Fletcher was pretty surprised he even noticed it.

Someone has definitely taken this trail multiple times, Fletcher thought, adding "walking trail" to his notebook and then glancing around. Surprisingly, there were no faculty or staffers in sight. The teacher sitting outside his door was full-on snoring at that point.

So, naturally, Fletcher tucked his notebook and pencil into his back pocket and made for the trail.

As Fletcher trekked through the forest, he became aware of how loud the twigs and dry leaves sounded crunching beneath his sneakers. The forest floor worked hard to ensure all his efforts at being stealthy were magnificently thwarted.

What's the worst that can happen? I'll get reprimanded for being curious?

Yet slowly—as he ventured deeper in, glancing over his shoulder to make sure the path was still visible so he'd have no trouble finding his way back—he realized why his footfalls were so loud.

The woods were quiet. *Eerily* quiet.

There was an unmistakable absence of chirping birds. Of wind and rustling branches. Of tiny rodents scurrying under bushes. Of any kind of activity whatsoever. It was like Fletcher had stepped through a portal and into a vacuum, a peculiar corner of the universe where the rules of nature didn't apply.

His heart started to beat heavily, rivaling the sheer loudness of his sneakers smacking against the ground. For a second, he contemplated turning and running back to campus, but he'd been walking for ten to fifteen minutes and his curiosity wouldn't be quelled.

After a few more minutes that dragged out like hours, Fletcher saw an opening in the trees ahead, where wan sunlight pooled on the ground and reflected off something. His heartbeat was so loud he could practically hear it in his throat.

He slowed and diverged from the path, hunching over and staying as close to the forest floor as possible. Once he reached the edge of the trees, he peered through the branches, trying his hardest to breathe steadily and not move a muscle.

What he saw shocked him. And it took a great deal of mental effort to eventually leave the scene and race back to campus, his body shaking with adrenaline.

In the Foxhole, Fletcher pulled Chase from the food line and told him he needed to talk—that it was a real emergency. He snaked through the dinner crowd with Chase on his heels. They walked upstairs to the senior lounge, where a handful of their classmates were eating dinner in front of *Sixteen Candles* on the big TV.

There was a row of arcade games on the wall opposite the coffee bar, so Fletcher picked *Dragon's Lair* on the far end and inserted a couple of quarters. Chase gave Fletcher a puzzled look as he began to play halfheartedly, but he wanted to ensure no one overheard them as he told Chase what he found on the secret trail.

"It dead-ended at some train tracks, and there was a parked freight train. There were MACE agents there, Chase, unloading cargo under the supervision of Dean Mendelsohn."

Chase's jaw dropped open. "Dude ... . *what?*"

"Yeah." Fletcher wiggled the joystick and smacked the buttons, trying to cover up their voices with as much noise as possible. "So much to unpack. Why is the U.S. Memory and Cognition Enforcement here? What in the world were they unloading, and why the super secrecy?"

"Did you notice anything else?"

Fletcher laughed nervously. "You mean other than the train, mysterious cargo, and a squad of federal agents?"

"Touché." Chase looked around the senior lounge, like he was making sure no one was eavesdropping. "How did Dean Mendelsohn seem? Fidgety? Nervous?"

"In total control." Fletcher lowered his voice. "He actually yelled at one of the MACE agents for nearly dropping one of the crates. For a gray-haired, suspender-wearing dude, he can sure command a room."

Chase leaned in. "Tell me about the cargo. How big we talking? Any guesses as to what was inside?"

Fletcher shrugged. "I mean, they were these long crates covered in tarps that took about four agents to carry. I'd say about four feet wide and six or seven feet long. There were about five or six crates in total, from what I could see. And I can't be sure, but I think there was a building just out of view beyond the tracks."

Chase cursed under his breath. "So you think they hauled everything off to a building in the woods?"

"Yeah."

A pair of animated tentacles burst forth from the ceiling in the video game, entangling Fletcher's knight and whisking him off to his doom.

"You know what this means, right?" Chase said.

"That I need more quarters?" Fletcher was afraid he knew what his roommate was going to suggest.

Chase waved for Fletcher to follow him back to their table in the dining hall. "This means we have to go back to the train tracks tonight and poke around."

19

FREYA IZQUIERDO

I fall onto the couch in my dorm room, feeling the weight of a long first day of classes and assignments. I set my thick stack of books and folders on the coffee table, knowing full well I should spend this study period wisely but feeling zero motivation to do anything but sit and stare at the ceiling.

Ollie cracks open the window and lights a cigarette. She leans against the sill and looks out, scanning the wall of trees, taking drag after impassioned drag. "Some memories, the good memories, are like welcome ghosts."

"Oh?"

"Yeah," she continues feebly, dreamlike. I watch her profile, curious. "Think about it. Ghosts tarry in this life long after the departure of their souls, right? Our memories are just apparitions in our minds . . . echoes from the past . . . spirits who visit us whether they're called upon or not. And what's frustrating, what's *maddening*, is that these ghosts—these memories—are just counterfeits. The real deal died long ago and left behind . . . well, left behind a ghost."

I smile. "Yeah, I guess so. But . . ."

"But?"

"But that metaphor only works if you believe in ghosts."

Ollie laughs through her nose. I fully expect a witty comeback. But it's a long time before she says, "If I hadn't lived with one, I probably wouldn't believe in them either."

I keep waiting for Ollie to giggle, to give some kind of humorous follow-up, but no such response comes.

I don't reply at first. Instead, I give Ollie some space. I sense a heaviness in her voice, something that tells me she's verbally processed like this before. A lot. I want to pry, ask her to clarify what she means by "lived with one," because she can't possibly mean a *literal* ghost.

Ollie just doesn't strike me as the superstitious type.

Now, I could be wrong. I have only known this girl for three days. But when you've lived in the foster system for two years, you've had a chance to meet a colorful cast of characters. And Ollie? She has her quirks, yeah, but she's a far cry from crazy.

These ghosts . . . are just counterfeits. The real deal died long ago . . .

After some time, I call upon all the motivation I can find within myself and channel it toward my algebra assignment. Yet before I can even pry open the textbook, there's a knock at our door.

Ollie frantically puts out her cigarette, jogs to the bathroom to flush the butt down the toilet, then sprays a generous amount of air freshener around the room. I walk through the misty cloud of lavender and cough, give the air freshener a couple of seconds to settle, then open the door.

"Hi there!" the redheaded girl says. "I'm Judy Montgomery, one of the newly appointed prefects and Foxtail Academy's events lead. I got permission from Mr. Williams to pass these out during study hall!" She hands me a pink flyer, which details the school's fall dance next month.

"Senior prom isn't enough?" I ask, lowering the flyer so I can scowl at Ms. Judy Montgomery. "We need a fall dance too?"

Judy squeals. "Isn't it great? And it's themed too: Foxy Ladies (and Gents)!"

I look back at the flyer and see a black-and-white picture of Jimi Hendrix near the bottom, sporting his frilly 1960s shirt while stroking his guitar.

"Because the song 'Foxy Lady,'" Judy says, as if it needs to be clarified.

"We got it," I tell her dryly. "Thanks."

Judy brings her shoulders up to her ears and smiles, then vanishes down the hall to the next dorm room.

"A *themed* dance?" Ollie says, running a hand through her hair.

I shut the door and join her by the bunk bed. "Lame, right—?"

"I don't have a single article of clothing that even remotely looks like it's from the sixties," she says dejectedly, flinging open the closet door. She rifles through her clothes desperately. "Quick. What's the date on the flyer?"

"Um . . ."

"The date, Freya, on the flyer!"

"Hang on, hang on." I consult the piece of paper. "September 12."

"Thank *God*," she says.

"You're acting like a crazy person, Ollie." I toss the flyer onto the coffee table and return to my homework. "It's just a stupid dance."

"We'll have to get permission to head into town at some point between now and then," she says, pacing around like an addict going through withdrawals. She bites her lip and taps her cheek, lost in thought. "Surely there's some kind of mall nearby."

I shake my head as I crack open my Algebra II tome and flip to the page with my assigned problems. The equations mock me, daring me to try to solve them, so I tear off a piece of notebook paper and set to work pretending I know what I'm doing.

❖ ❖ ❖

After study hour, we have one more hour of free time before a nine o'clock–sharp curfew.

Ollie and I spend this time outside beneath the all-seeing stars. We find a quiet spot on the sandy ground not too far from the pier. We just lie there, heads on our hands, gaping up at the blue-black expanse to the song of distant cicadas and lapping water.

So who was this ghost you lived with? I mean to ask my roommate aloud. I want to go back to that conversation from earlier, before Judy Montgomery arrived bearing troubling news about school dances. I want to go back and ask her some delicate questions. Dig a little deeper and—

Beneath the starlight, I see that Ollie's eyes have turned a deep gray.

She notices me watching her. "What's up?"

I don't know what to say, so I just start talking . . .

❖ ❖ ❖

In a world where memories are like currency, dreams can be a complicated business.

Dad was always saying this when I was a kid, especially after I'd tell him about some dream I'd had the night before.

I mean, think about it, mija! He'd push his half-eaten plate of chorizo and eggs aside and talk with his hands. He would always talk with his hands when he got excited. *The more money one's got, the more respect they got too. Just like memories. Those who got the most memories got the most respect. And power.*

He used to get riled up easily over this subject. Sometimes it was funny—endearing, even. Other times it was overwhelming.

Now, dreams can muddy those waters, can't they? This is the part where he'd tap his temple with his finger and lower his voice, like he was letting me in on some secret. *How do they know what's the difference between my dreams, memories of dreams, and just plain memories? Hmm? Are we to believe that the technology they have can sift through all that noise?*

I would shrug and go back to eating my cereal, annoyed with myself for trying to have a normal conversation about a simple, harmless dream.

He'd examine his cognition wheel, tracing the two-quarter mark with his left index finger. I can still hear Javier Solís belting *"Cuando Calienta el Sol"* through our ancient record player in the other room. Dad hummed along, and just when I thought he was going to sing too—something he would often do without warning, his face straining with passion and anguish—he continued: *It's a shame how they done all this, you know? I mean, they slap that MeReader on your head when you're sixteen, and this tech supposedly determines how many memories you got, and how many you're capable of keepin'?*

Of course, at that time I was only ten or eleven.

We're supposed to take this MeReader's diagnosis without question? he'd say, throwing his hands up wildly. *No second opinion? Hmm? What that helmet says is the gospel truth about my head?*

I mean, I guess—?

It's like I used to tell Mamá, he'd say, all but shouting now. *I'd say, "Look, when your car breaks down, you can't just take it to one mechanic! If you don't know nothing about engines, they could say you'd need this, that, and the other fixed, and you'd never know better!"* You see what I mean, Freya?

At this point I would just nod, knowing full well that the only way to get his rant over with was to silently agree.

If you don't know nothing about an engine—he'd grab his breakfast and put it back in front of him—*how do you know if the mechanic's telling you the truth? What if your car engine ain't even broke?*

He'd look at me, really look into my hazel eyes with his dark brown ones, and I could feel him searching me for something. Affirmation? Probably. But I was just a kid, just trying to get through breakfast and out the door in time to catch the school bus.

My dad was my everything. Not in the unhealthy, idealistic kind of way; I mean *literally*. He was all I had, and I was all he had. We were each other's world, and we preferred it that way.

The Angels drafted him when he was seventeen. In high school pro scouts called him the "fierce phenom" because when he hit a baseball he looked furious. It's how he focused, he would tell me seriously. He would channel some kind of menacing, otherworldly concentration and then swing his bat like his teenage life depended on it.

My mother, who fled from Mexico by herself when she was a teenager, got pregnant with me a couple weeks after the draft, right around the start of Dad's senior year. He said he was more excited to find out about me than anything else, even baseball. And I believed him. Anytime he'd tell me about holding me when I was a baby, his face would just light up—more so than when he'd describe the feeling of holding his favorite bat.

But, of course, my mother died giving birth to me, and my dad dropped everything to raise me. His own parents and extended family were still in Mexico, just like my mother's.

He never finished high school.

It was a no-brainer, love, he used to tell me, smiling that huge smile of his. *There's nothing in this world that was gonna keep me from you.*

But you loved baseball! I'd exclaim, frowning with confusion.

Sí, pero, he'd say, shushing me with a sparkle in his eyes. *What I love never stood a chance against who I love.*

I miss that the most. When he'd call me *love,* it was like he was saying he loved me so much there was no time for superfluous descriptors. I was his love, all of it. Period. It was just that simple. And it was a felt love that permeated every corner of my heart, the way dawn light permeates an open-windowed bedroom.

Once I was old enough to go to school, my dad started working the assembly line at a factory outside Los Angeles that built the first line of MeReaders. It was a hard time for him. I could intuit that even as a little kid. The work was simple enough, sure, but he said he knew literally *nothing* outside his small sliver of the line. Who was drawing up the plans for this intricate, strange technology? Who was responsible for its design? Were the MeReaders quality tested after assembly and before distribution? Just how involved was the federal government in overseeing this operation?

But you didn't ask questions in the factory. You punched in, put on your polyurethane gloves, and posted up at your designated spot on the conveyor belt. The low bell would sound, echoing throughout the high-ceilinged workspace, and the conveyor belts would groan to life. This marked the beginning of his ten-hour shift.

I just put my head down and set to work, Dad would say when I'd ask him about his day. Then he'd space out. After a while, he'd realize I was watching him, so he'd shake out of his stupor and proceed to change the subject.

It's no wonder he'd get so fired up if I started to talk about a dream. Yes, it must have been a strange thing for him, working fifty hours a week for *years* on a small piece of a massive puzzle and never once catching a glimpse of the big picture. And his employers expected him to have confidence in what it was he was building, because he and his peers were solving the great insoluble problem of our time.

Looking back, I can't blame him for having so many questions. I can't fault him for being so skeptical all the time about memory loss and the effectiveness of artificial recall. I get why he was so bothered by the secrecy. If anything, his employment sparked a tendency to question everything and fueled a borderline obsession with conspiracies.

He never told me this, but I'm 100 percent certain he'd have preferred working at a wig factory.

I asked him once why he didn't just quit and go work somewhere else.

It's too late for that, he replied, his voice quiet and his eyes far off. He didn't elaborate on what he meant by "too late" and instead squeezed my shoulder affectionately before leaving the room.

However troubled he was by his work, my dad mostly hid it from me. We'd spend nearly all of our time together on the carpeted floor of our cramped apartment, watching MLB games, highlight reels, and documentaries he'd rent from the library. He was obsessed with sports documentaries. Couldn't get enough. And it didn't matter what the sport was. Yes, most of them were docs on contemporary and legendary baseball players and dynasty clubs, but we also watched specials on golfers, tennis players, and even gymnasts.

I can still see my dad's deep grin illuminated by the oscillating blue glow of our old television set. He'd just sit there beside me, his chin resting on his fists, marveling at whichever documentary we were watching, engrossed by the fluid movements of the featured athlete or team.

Documentary filmmaking is the highest form of art, my dad would say, playfully nudging me with his elbow. *It's this wonderful snapshot of reality . . . it preserves great moments in time, like a capsule buried in a* backyard. *And the* really *good ones let you examine the human condition through a microscope. They uncover the subject's makeup, what makes them tick. Not many art forms out there that are* that intimate, verdad?

Yeah, documentaries are kind of . . . mythical.

I'd roll my eyes at him but smile nonetheless. I may not love baseball or documentaries like my dad did, but I sure love that *he* loved them.

We were supposed to watch *Tokyo Olympiad* on the day my dad died.

The library's only copy had finally come available, and he snagged the VHS on his way home from work the same evening the librarian phoned with the news. He'd been talking about this particular documentary for months. It was just so different from anything else we'd seen, he kept saying, almost ad nauseum. I was eager to see what he meant by that.

He checked out that movie on a Tuesday, and we planned to watch it Friday over pizza from Buono's—so long as I finished all my homework and required reading. (His telling me this was just a formality. Nothing would stop him from watching that documentary with me. In retrospect, it's a wonder the VHS sat in our apartment for three nights, unwatched.)

Friday morning, Dad phoned my school and pulled me out of class. I remember it being such an odd thing, his calling me, because once I kissed him goodbye every weekday morning I didn't see him again, much less hear from him, until after his shift. He might as well have been on a completely different continent those ten hours we were apart.

The front desk lady, a dour, older woman named Krista Haggerty, handed me the phone.

Hey, love, you all right?

Is everything okay?

Yeah, hey, sorry. What class am I interrupting?

Geometry.

He made a hissing sound on the other end of the line. *Really am sorry about that.*

It's fine, really. Where are you?

Payphone. Near work.

What's going on?

He sighed. Not dramatically, not even loudly. It sounded . . . burdened. I can still hear *exactly* how that sigh sounded on that Friday morning two years ago. It's so cruel what things your mind decides to remember about the ones you love, and what things it decides to let slip into the dark void of forgetting—the place memories go to die.

Forgetting is an odious affair, Memory Killer or not.

Yes, I remember the heaviness of that sigh like it was yesterday. And I remember that sudden feeling of being drawn away from my dad, as if in that precise moment he and I began to come apart the way a page with a perforated center gets carefully and pointedly torn in two.

I was on the bus, he said, sounding out of breath. *I was sitting all the way in the back, like I always do. You know how I love to sit in the back where I can people watch.*

Yeah.

Yeah. So it was just me and Michael—his handler, a senior at my high school who I'd barely ever spoken to—*and then this older man and his handler come on the bus at the stop before mine. I watched them, like I watch everyone.*

My dad paused, and I heard what sounded like him switching the receiver from one hand to the other. He cleared his throat.

Yeah, so, this older man and his handler sat near the front, facing me and Michael. I think I smiled at them, can't remember at this point. Anyway, this old man gets his Restorey out of his jacket pocket . . .

Uh-huh. I wanted to reassure him I was still there.

. . . and he gets all situated for his artificial recall, right? Meanwhile his handler, a pretty thing with a stack of textbooks, notices Michael. Guess she goes to your school too, because the next thing I know they're moving to sit close—laughing and cutting up. Guess they figured it'd be all right to leave us since we were the only four on the bus, other than the driver.

I watched that old man put in his memory tape. I watched him stick his receivers on his temples. Hands were shaking the whole time (he must've been seventy), but he got himself all set up on his own. After he pressed Play, he closed his eyes real slow, almost like he wasn't ever going to open them again. And then . . . his eyelids started fluttering, like he was half blinking, and I could see that his eyes had turned gray.

Gray?

Yeah, I'm sure of it. I even got up and moved closer to see. And sure enough his eyes were gray . . . while he was artificially recalling . . . meaning Memory Killer was striking that old man while he was hooked up to his Restorey.

Is that . . . not normal?

My dad laughed. *I don't know, love. Artificial recall, Restoreys . . . none of it's "normal." But I was just frozen there like a kid who has seen something he's not supposed to on TV.*

I . . . *I don't know what to say.* It was true. I didn't. While someone being attacked by Memory Killer during their artificial recall didn't sound like that big a deal to me, my dad's reaction troubled me. Was there something else he wasn't telling me? Or was what he witnessed so abnormal that he'd risk tardiness at work to call me?

Dad groaned. *Yeah, I dunno. It was over as quickly as it started. And the next thing I knew we'd arrived at my stop, and the old man's eyes were sealed shut peacefully. I don't even remember getting off the bus, tell you the truth. One moment, I'm watching this crazy thing happening, and the next I'm on the sidewalk . . . walking toward this payphone outside my work and calling your school.*

I opened my mouth to say something but couldn't string the right words together.

He didn't say anything for what felt like an entire minute. Then, *Yeah, no, it was probably nothing. I should get to work. Tim's gonna chew me a new one for being so late. Love you.*

I . . . love you too, I said back.

He hung up. The line clicked abruptly, then I heard the soft buzz of a dial tone. I handed the receiver back to Krista, completely unaware it'd be the last time I'd ever hear my dad's voice. Later that afternoon, a freak accident at the factory took his life, along with many others.

I've heard people say if they knew they were sharing a final moment with a loved one, there are all kinds of things they'd want to say—as if knowing it's your final minutes with someone would embolden you to say things you'd never said before and express feelings you'd never expressed.

I think that's bull.

If I had known that would be my last conversation with my dad, I'm pretty sure I would have just cried. I wouldn't have been able to formulate words. And I don't care if that sounds weak. It is what it is.

Yeah, I would've cried into that receiver. I would've cried hard and I wouldn't have let go of the phone for anything. In fact, it would've taken Krista and practically the entire faculty to pull it out of my hands.

I'm sure you've heard people say that memories grow increasingly unreliable over time. Pretty sure this was the case even before Memory Killer. Anyway, as someone who's lost their dad—my life's north star—that *terrifies* me. Makes me think that no matter how certain I feel about the memories of my dad, those memories could be half-truths or, worse, untruths, and I'd never be the wiser.

It also makes me hate childhood amnesia. You've heard of that, right? Apparently we don't remember anything before the age of four, which sucks. I only had fifteen years on this planet with my dad, and those first four years were essentially a wash, meaning I only *really* had eleven years with him. Sure, I used to try to think back and recall my time with him when I was a toddler, but that proved to be a losing game, almost like trying to remember the first four innings of a baseball game when you were only present for the last five.

These are some of the things I think about when I think about losing my dad.

I finish talking, painfully aware I've been rambling for entirely too long. I assume Ollie fell asleep on the sand beside me. Instead, I find her propped up on one elbow, watching me.

The color has returned to her eyes.

"Sorry," I say. "I don't remember the last time I just blabbered on like that, especially about my dad. And we *just* met too—"

Ollie smiles and puts a hand on my shoulder. "You're free to blabber to me about your dad anytime you want."

And I smile back, because I believe her.

20

FLETCHER COHEN

Fletcher and Chase's decision not to use their Reflectors freed them up to sneak out while everyone else was tethered to their devices.

At midnight, when they were both convinced that the campus was sound asleep, they made their escape. Fletcher opened the dorm room window and jimmied the screen free, careful to catch it before it hit the ground. He climbed out first and Chase wordlessly followed.

The grassy area behind the dormitories was only barely visible in the black of nighttime. The tall trees at the edge of the woods obscured most of the natural light. After their eyes adjusted, they slinked down the skinny path past their neighbors' windows. In passing, Fletcher saw his classmates lying motionless in their bunk beds, the Reflectors' suction receivers stamped to their temples.

It was an ominous visual, his peers motionless and bonded to the little black devices, and it gave him gooseflesh. The skeptic in him wondered if the tech was farming his classmates' dreams while they slept.

Perhaps another question to add to his growing Memory Killer File.

Fletcher and Chase eventually walked out from behind the shadows of the dormitories. The vast campus grounds stretched out before them like a still-life painting. They avoided the sidewalk and jogged across the lawn straight for the library. Beneath the blue moonlight, the glass structure dazzled like a jagged iceberg. They ducked beneath its long shadow to catch their breath and scope out their next move.

Fletcher pointed to the auditorium, and Chase nodded once.

Fletcher counted down from three in a whisper, then they jogged to their next stop. Fletcher looked in every direction as they moved, hoping they wouldn't be spotted by some teacher or staffer out for a midnight stroll. Remarkably, the campus grounds were calm and peaceful, almost as if the place was uninhabited.

If the students are trialing the Reflectors, he thought, *maybe the faculty is too?*

That theory gave him a burst of confidence. He slowed his jog to a walk as they got closer to the auditorium, pretty convinced not a single soul was awake. But this split-second lapse in caution proved costly: Fletcher completely missed the motion-sensor light mounted near the roof, which blasted on like a searchlight at sea.

Fletcher and Chase gasped and then sprinted the rest of the way, dipping behind a small shed beside the auditorium. With their backs pressed against the wall, they tried to breathe as little as possible, bracing for a campus staffer to appear at any moment. As they panted in the shadows—as Fletcher started to panic and wonder what kind of punishment they'd face—he heard a small, faint *pop!* and then the light cut off. The relief was instantaneous for Fletcher. He slowly turned to Chase, whose eyes were clamped shut.

"I think we're in the clear."

Chase nodded and opened his eyes, glancing around in the semi-darkness. "Should we give it a few more minutes?" he mouthed. "Just to be safe?"

Fletcher shrugged. They kept quiet for a moment, listening . . .

Voices, in the distance.

Fletcher and Chase straightened up even more, flattening their backs against the shed with so much force Fletcher was starting to get a headache. *Please don't let them head this way!*

The voices drew closer, until it sounded as if they were *just* around the corner, near the auditorium's entrance.

". . . I am considering increasing the dosage. It's possible that's why we're off."

Fletcher's and Chase's eyes expanded. Dean Mendelsohn.

"That could work, yes." That voice was almost as distinctive as the dean's: Dr. Sanders. She sighed, then there was a brief pause. "It appears we still have much work to do, Father." It sounded like Dr. Sanders shuffled something, though it was difficult to tell with the sounds partially muffled. Regardless, Fletcher's heart soared as he heard Dr. Sanders and the dean stride off in the opposite direction.

"*Father?*" Chase whispered when they were in the clear.

"Yeah . . . I have a lot of questions about that," Fletcher confessed, peeling himself off the wall. He peeked toward the entrance of the auditorium and saw the backs of Dean Mendelsohn and Dr. Sanders fading in the darkness as they made their way toward the admissions building where their offices were located.

"And what was that about dosage?" Chase's voice was quivering slightly.

"We'll have to unpack all of that later. C'mon." Fletcher stepped away from the shed and walked to the back of the auditorium, checking above them for other motion-sensor lights. Chase followed his roommate closely, and when they rounded the corner they faced their most difficult stretch yet: the wide-open lawn between them and the faculty housing. With the classrooms off to their left and the Foxhole to their right, there was nothing in front of them but green grass, the snaking sidewalk, picnic benches, and six duplexes.

Fletcher counted three outdoor lights that were currently on—one near the dining hall and two flanking the duplexes. And even though those lights were a good distance away, the stars were as bright as ever, which meant he and Chase would be completely exposed as they raced toward the last place any student who was sneaking out at night had any business going: where every single faculty member slept.

Chase squatted, tucking his blond hair behind his ears. "This is the part where one of us talks the other one out of doing this because it's completely and utterly crazy."

Fletcher knelt beside him. "May I remind you this was *your* idea?"

"It's possible that it was, yes." He took a deep breath, as if he was disappointed in himself.

"Okay, well, let's fast-forward to the part where someone states the obvious: the entire reason we're skipping the trial for a week is so we can try to figure out what's really going on here at Foxtail. You *just* heard the dean and Dr. Sanders. They're up to something. And our best shot at investigating the hidden building beyond the train tracks is at night."

Chase nodded.

"Sure," Fletcher continued, keeping his voice low, "we could head back to our dorm room, call it a night, and then try this again tomorrow. But we've made it this far already. Let's see this to the end."

Chase rose to his feet. "You're right. It's now or never, Maverick."

Fletcher blinked.

"Ugh, it's from *Top Gun*." Chase lightly smacked Fletcher on the face. "You're so uncultured."

"I've seen *Top*—"

Chase bolted across the lawn toward the faculty housing, leaving Fletcher momentarily stunned. He cursed, then sprinted after Chase.

After seconds that felt like hours, Chase slowed down, got to his knees, and crawled behind a picnic bench where they had a perfect view of the duplexes. Fletcher all but fell down on the grass next to him and noticed with annoyance that Chase's breathing was as steady as if he'd just taken a casual stroll.

"You're out of shape," Chase said, like he was telling Fletcher something he didn't know. He threw Chase a dirty look and then scoped out their surroundings while he caught his breath. Hordes of tiny bugs swarmed the orange porch lights.

Fletcher squinted, trying to locate the payphone that marked the entrance of the hidden trail.

But . . . it was gone.

And not placed in a different spot, but *completely* gone. Vanished. There was no payphone in sight. Even the mailboxes had been moved. Now they were on the other side of the duplexes, beside a metal trash can with a sign that read NO GLASS. Fletcher was *certain* that was new. He would've written it in his pages. Somebody had rearranged the layout.

Fletcher started to pant again.

"Dude, what's up?" Chase asked. Fletcher didn't answer. Instead, he emerged from behind the picnic bench and walked to where the payphone should have been, Chase whisper-shouting behind him. The porch lights offered just enough light for Fletcher to see: a row of stones and flower beds created a neat little border between the woods and outdoor sitting area. Where before there had been only ankle-high grass, now there was fresh landscaping.

There was absolutely no sign of a trail.

Chase came to his side. "Fletcher, dude, what gives?"

"Something's wrong." He scanned the ground beyond the flower beds, hoping to find a portion of the makeshift trail intact.

But he didn't.

"What?"

"This is all different," he told Chase. "The payphone is gone. The mailbox is moved. These flower beds are covering the trail. Someone completely rearranged this whole area to cover up the hidden—!"

One of the duplex doors clicked open.

In the dead of night, when one is up to no good, the sound of a door being opened might as well be deafening. Fletcher and Chase exchanged a frightened look, then raced off toward the Foxhole, keeping to the edge of the woods. They hid near the dumpsters for what felt like an eternity, never once seeing or hearing a teacher.

When they felt like enough time had passed, they fumbled their way through the darkness and made for their dorm room.

❖ ❖ ❖

"You're positive that it was the same spot?" Chase asked.

Fletcher paced in front of the TV in their room, his thoughts racing off in different directions. "Positive. Just like I'm positively annoyed at being asked that question a *tenth* time."

Chase turned on some music and then took a seat on the couch. "Okay, so, don't get mad, but is it possible that you're . . . *misremembering?*"

The possibility had briefly crossed his mind. Misremembering could be a scary indicator that artificial recall was starting to fail. It was often a sign that Memory Killer had begun to cut through a Restorey's defenses, like water eroding cracks in a dam. But Fletcher hadn't experienced the other symptoms that came with misremembering, like debilitating headaches.

"No way," he told Chase confidently. "Plus, I wrote down what I saw behind the faculty housing. All we have to do is reference *this*." He opened the notebook, thumbed through, and found the list he'd made earlier. "Here! Payphone . . . no garden bed *or* trash can. See?"

He handed it over to Chase, who took it and scanned the page. "Um . . . okay, fine, but here's a dumb question: Why were you scoping out the faculty duplexes in the first place?"

"I dunno." Fletcher took the notebook back. "I guess I figured if the dean wants me spying on my classmates, I'll spy on the faculty too."

"Well, kudos. Turns out your little reconnaissance proved useful." Chase rubbed his eyes. "I could really go for a drink right now."

"You see what's happening here, don't you?" Fletcher set the notebook on the coffee table.

"Yes." Chase leaned back. "Dean Mendelsohn covered his tracks. No one but him was supposed to know about that hidden trail, and now no one ever will."

"But we do, Chase. We know he's hiding something because I've taken the trail through the woods. This is just a setback. It may be trickier now to find the train tracks with the trail covered up, but we *will* find it. And overhearing that convo between him and Dr. Sanders only makes me want to find it more."

Chase nodded. He got up, stood on the couch, and—with his pinkies in the air—carefully removed his Cindy Crawford poster. He then set it facedown on the coffee table and snagged a pen off the dresser.

"Forgive me, my darling," he said, his lip trembling. Using the back of the poster as a giant canvas, he set to work writing out a few categories (which he boldly underlined) near the top of the poster:

DEAN MENDELSOHN	MEMORY FRONTIER	FOXTAIL ACADEMY

Beneath these, Chase listed everything they'd discussed—every observation made, encounter had, or burning question pondered. They worked together like two research students compiling data for a final exam. Chase would recall something and jot it down, then Fletcher would do likewise, and on and on this went for nearly half an hour.

Eventually, Fletcher filled Chase in on a few other details, like seeing Dean Mendelsohn taking his medication. When they got to a decent stopping point, the back of the poster was half full:

DEAN MENDELSOHN	MEMORY FRONTIER	FOXTAIL ACADEMY
• former gov't contractor • knows Fletcher's pops • solicited Fletcher for help • on some kind of medication • oversaw secret MACE delivery • had the hidden trail covered up • illustrates his memories; calls it "memory anchoring" • told Fletcher about memory knifing • overheard discussing increased "dosage" with Doc Sanders • also . . . apparently he's Doc Sanders's dad (didn't see that coming)	• How is a Reflector calibrated? • What are memory insights? • Who okayed releasing that info to MF? • How involved is the U.S. gov't in this trial? (MACE's secret cargo delivery) • Why hasn't Lochamire stopped by campus yet?	• employs a MF staffer: the (hot) Doc Sanders, who's also the dean's daughter (did we mention how random that is?) • What happens to the school once the trial is over? Will it continue operating like a normal boarding school? • How much do the teachers/ staffers actually know about this trial? • campus borders mysterious train tracks in the woods

Chase chewed on the end of his pen, his eyes darting across the poster.

Fletcher had one more question to add.

Can Memory Killer strike when you're hooked up to your Restorey? Or, for that matter, your Reflector?

Fletcher posed this question to his roommate, unsure if it actually mattered in the grand scheme of things. But Chase picked up his pen anyway and added a fourth column titled "Memory Loss." Beneath this he wrote, "Does Memory Killer snatch up our memories during artificial recall?"

Fletcher yawned so big his jaw practically unhinged. Exhaustion started to set in, his energy fading by the second. Chase returned the Cindy Crawford poster to its place on the wall, careful not to crease the shiny surface.

"So," Fletcher said defeatedly, "not only was tonight a total bust, but we somehow have *more* questions than before. Awesome."

Chase took off his T-shirt, balled it up, and threw it across the room. He fell face-first into his bed. "We're not exactly private investigators," he said into his pillow. "It's only been like two days . . . we'll get there."

"Should we give ourselves another week?" Fletcher asked, expecting his roommate to deliver a thesis on why that was a terrible, risky idea. But Chase remained still. Was he considering it? Fletcher felt pretty confident that in another week they could really iron out a solid game plan. If he could convince Chase that—

The soft, muted sounds of Chase's snores stopped his train of thought. Fletcher sighed and glanced at the clock. It was 2:00 a.m. They'd have to be up in a few hours to artificially recall. He set the alarm on his wristwatch and collapsed on his bed, not even bothering to turn off the light.

The next morning, after Fletcher and Chase woke up, a strange thing happened.

Fletcher was the first to wake up. He groggily slipped out of his bed, still dizzy with exhaustion, and nearly fell off the ladder coming down from the top bunk. He nudged Chase.

Together, while swapping yawns, the two found their Restoreys and went through the tired motions of setting up and queuing their memory tapes. Fletcher affixed the receivers to his temples and pressed Play.

But he wasn't transported to one of his memories.

Instead, he was cast into what he could only describe as a vortex of neon lights. He felt a terrifying kind of weightlessness as the lights, the blinding and whirring colors, pulled him toward an eternal nothing.

The nightmare lasted several seconds.

Somehow, Fletcher managed to rip off his receivers. He clenched his jaw and blinked his eyes open, bracing for the headache he was *sure* would come. Only there was no headache, but that stomach-flipping sensation of weightlessness lingered.

He turned to Chase. His roommate was panting on the couch. Almost simultaneously, the two of them clicked open their Restoreys and found they had accidentally swapped memory tapes.

21

FREYA IZQUIERDO

Tuesday crawls along at a punishing, sluggish pace.

In economics, I spot one half of Ave Maria's posse—the tall girl Chase remarked about in the library the other day. I learn her name's Allison James, and she actually looks at me without wrinkling her pointy nose in disgust, so that's something. Dr. Spears, a middle-aged man whose glasses have the thickest lenses I've ever seen, spends most of the hour trying to explain to the class why logical reasoning is the most important skill to develop in his class.

I'll take his word for it. My boredom already teeters into madness.

In lit, I manage to stay focused long enough to learn a little bit about Geoffrey Chaucer, and in Algebra II, Ms. Schneck holds my attention for most of the period—that is, until she starts talking about radical expressions. I glance at Chase, who is pretending to take notes by ranking his favorite action movies. I suppress a smile.

Free period zooms by, as does all time spent doing enjoyable things. Ollie and I whip the boys in a couple of foosball matches in the senior lounge, and before we know it, we have to head to fifth period.

"It's just as well," Fletcher says, scrambling for an excuse: "I think our side of the foosball table is jacked up or something."

"Yeah," Chase mutters. "Jacked up."

Ollie and I exchange a smile.

❖ ❖ ❖

Dr. Sanders starts her lecture the moment the last student finds her seat.

"It was once theorized that, in order to recall a memory, one had to reach across a spectrum of remembrance. This is simply not the case. Our memories don't exist on a spectrum at all, but rather in a matrix. Stay with me: there exist any number of variables that impact the memories we form every single minute of every single hour of every single day, and so on and so forth.

"For example, you're likely to forget all the insignificant moments in your life between the highs and lows. That's why it's more difficult to remember what you ate for lunch last Tuesday versus what you ate for dinner on your last birthday. One meal was just another part of your daily routine, likely filled with passive emotions, whereas the other meal was on a day of celebration—filled with excitement, cake, gifts, and in my case, lots of wine."

The class laughs.

"The way we emote—the way we feel when a significant memory is formed—deeply impacts our chances of recalling it later on. It also affects the level of detail preserved within that memory. In short, varying levels of anger, love, fear, sadness, and every other human emotion affect what we remember and how well we remember it."

She pauses so we can take notes, and I try not to paraphrase a thing even though my hand cramps so much it feels like it's going to fall off. I want all of her lecture in writing, word for word, so I can review and ponder it during study period. There is just so much here to consider, especially as it relates to my half-memory dreams.

While we jot down our notes, Dr. Sanders's tone takes a somber turn. "Of course, when Memory Killer arrived on the scene, this was all upended. In another time, those stricken with Alzheimer's or dementia were among the only ones afflicted by accelerated memory loss. But of course, this is a new world, a dark world where our memories are like fading light. And as of today, our best shot at fighting the surging shadows lies within a small, unassuming piece of technology."

She holds up her Reflector, spinning it in the air in front of her face like a jeweler might inspect a glittering diamond.

Without even realizing I'm doing it, I raise my hand.

"Yes." Dr. Sanders places the device back on her desk. "Freya Izquierdo."

"How does the Reflector . . . or the MeReader, for that matter . . . parse out the dreams from the memories?"

Dr. Sanders smiles. "The interplay of memories and dreams is a topic that's been discussed and researched ad nauseam by authorities in neurology, psychology, psychiatry, and—arguably most of all— philosophy. Here's what we can say for certain: we dream in memory *fragments.*

"Memories, for the most part, are finite and rigid, and our brains understand this. Dreams, however, can be maddeningly elusive things." She chuckles. "Some of my peers even postulate that the more intense dreams we have are actually a training ground for problem-solving in future dangerous situations."

I and a few other students write this down.

"It's a great question, though," Dr. Sanders says. "And while I could bore you with the mechanics behind the MeReader's design, I'd rather just bore you with my lesson plan. But rest assured that the world's top scientists have labored over this technology to make certain that memories are the only thing it's detecting—not dreams, and certainly not nightmares."

Unless your memories are nightmares.

I set my pencil down and turn to whisper this to Ollie, but she's staring out the window—her expression distant, her posture tense.

When the class bell rings, echoing across the Foxtail Academy campus, I shuffle outside with Ollie, Fletcher, and Chase. But Dr. Sanders calls out to me before I make it all the way down the steps.

"Would you stick around for a moment?" she asks, and my eyes widen involuntarily. "I've seen that look before! Don't worry, you're not in any sort of trouble."

I glance at my friends, then tell them I'll meet up with them later. I follow Dr. Sanders back inside. Being in a classroom with no other students—just your teacher—is among the most uncomfortable experiences I can recall. It's hard to explain. The room is designed and intended to be filled with loud and restless teenagers. Even when it's quiet it's not *really* quiet.

This feels like watching baseball on TV with no fans in the stands.

She sits behind her desk and gestures for me to take one of the seats in the front row.

"I was struck by your question, Freya, because it's one I wrestle with daily."

I lean forward in my tiny desk. "It is?"

She nods. "In fact, it's one of *many* questions. Have you ever heard of the 'overview effect'?"

I shake my head.

"It's a fairly new concept. The overview effect happens to some astronauts in spaceflight when they see our fragile planet from above for the first time. Some say that kind of perspective—observing Earth from space, this blue-green ball that's insignificant in its place among the cosmos—causes them to have a 'cognitive shift.' At once, things in their lives that were previously consequential now seem trivial. And when these astronauts return, that new perspective of our planet lingers, as does their newfound understanding of just how fragile everything is in relation to the immeasurable universe.

"To an extent, I believe that's what has happened with artificial recall. At least, for my part. You see, even before Memory Killer, no one had control over how much they remembered of their past. And while people made conscious efforts to commit certain things in their life to memory, at the end of the day, some events rooted significant memories while others just evaporated—up to 70 percent a day, in fact.

"Enter artificial recall. Now, thanks to the technology in the MeReader, which has been integrated into the Reflector, we are remembering more than we ever have before. We've reached a sort of memory ascension. Recalling our past is less like peering through a pinhole and more like seeing a giant mural all at once. The more we can remember, the more enlightened we become."

I raise my eyebrows. "I thought the tech just saved important memories from being lost. Not *all* our memories."

"Well, sure. But due to the nature of artificial recall, our reliance on Restoreys and now Reflectors, our brains have begun to evolve. It's like when movies went from black-and-white to Technicolor."

Are we really evolving if we're dependent on tech? I almost ask this aloud, but instead I decide to get her thoughts on my half-memory dreams.

I tell her about a harmless one—the one with me roller-skating on the pier in Long Beach—because I don't want her to freak out and commit me to the Fold. I also make it a point to tell her I haven't had one of these "dreams" since using the Reflector.

Dr. Sanders rubs her chin, listening without stopping me for questions. When I'm finished, she leans back. "This is *very* interesting, Freya. And you say these began once you started using your Restorey?"

"Before then," I say. "The first dream came to me when I had my initial reading on my sixteenth birthday."

"I see." She pulls a pair of glasses from her desk drawer, slides them on, and starts to write something down in a journal.

I start to regret my decision to talk about this to a total stranger. "Could you . . . um . . . maybe keep this between us? I've really only told like two people, which includes the school nurse back home, and that was mainly to get out of class."

"Of course," she says seriously. "I'm making a reminder for myself to look into this."

"I'm crazy, aren't I?"

She sets her pen down, and her blue eyes grow soft. "Far from it. We have seen any number of unique and interesting reactions to artificial recall. I'm not downplaying what you're experiencing, and I'm not even sure it's related to the MeReader, but you're likely not alone. I'm happy to dig into this with you, Freya. Thank you for sharing."

I feel my body releasing tension. I smile and nod. I gather my textbooks and rise to my feet as a campus staffer appears in the doorway.

"Dr. Sanders?" The short man crosses the classroom and hands her a folded piece of paper. "Your father sent this."

"Ah, thank you." Dr. Sanders takes it and smiles, then turns to me. "Let's resume this conversation soon, Freya, okay?"

I tell her that'd be great and take my leave.

22

FLETCHER COHEN

"You good?" Fletcher asked Freya.

"Yeah." She scrunched her eyebrows together as if just realizing she was, in fact, good. "I am."

"Good." Fletcher wanted to ask her what Dr. Sanders needed, especially in light of the conversation he and Chase had overheard between her and the dean. But it was none of his business. Plus, until he and Chase could do more investigating, he didn't want to bring up last night to the girls and spook them until they had concrete facts to work with. So he forced down his curiosity. "That's great."

She smiled her beautiful smile—the one that exposed her perfect teeth, the one that looked like she was about to laugh until the last second, when she magically managed to keep that fit of laughter at bay—then she softly blinked her brown eyes and turned away.

Stop staring, idiot. Fletcher looked down at his sneakers as the four of them headed to their secret spot on the banks of Juniper Lake. It was Ollie's idea to kill time there before dinner; she claimed to have an emergency on her hands.

"Guys. We have an emergency on our hands."

"Oh?" Fletcher watched her pace in front of the fiery-white tree that stood at the edge of the lake.

"It's not what you think," Freya whispered to him.

"I heard that," Ollie shouted. "While *you* may not think it's a big deal, I can say with complete authority that it is a big deal, thank you very much."

Chase laughed, chewing on his sunflower seeds while sliding on his sunglasses. "What's up, Ol? Did your curling iron quit working?"

"Don't talk with your mouth full," she snapped. "It's unattractive. *Anyway.* I'm being serious, guys: this fall dance just got dropped on us like a bomb, and I'm willing to bet I'm not the only one who didn't bring sixties- or seventies-era clothes to campus."

Fletcher laughed and turned to Chase, fully expecting him to take the teasing up a notch now that they knew Ollie was freaking out over some dumb dance. But he slowly lifted his sunglasses and rested them on his head, his eyes wide as plates.

"This is officially a five-alarm emergency." He swore under his breath. "Why didn't you say something sooner?"

"You both realize this dance isn't until September, right?" Freya put her hands at her hips.

"Oh sure, Freya," Chase said, throwing up his hands. "Between classes, a stupid amount of required reading, and mounting assignments, we'll have *plenty* of time to gallivant around the local malls to find suitable clothes for this dance!"

"Honestly, Freya." Ollie shook her head, aghast.

"Just so we're all clear," Fletcher said, "you guys know this isn't prom. Right?"

Chase took Ollie by the hand and led her to the fallen tree, where they both sat down. "We need to find a mall *stat* and head there this weekend."

"There's one in Clarksville, which isn't too far," she replied immediately. "Since the four of us are out-of-state boarders, we'll need to borrow a car from a classmate who lives near campus."

Chase scratched his chin, thinking.

Fletcher turned to Freya. "Well, if there was ever a question as to why they're friends . . ."

She laughed. Chase snapped his fingers and exclaimed, "I've got it. There's this chick in AP lit . . . the one who sits in front of me . . . I think her name's Samantha."

"We've only had that class *twice* and you've barely spoken to her." Fletcher sounded more impressed than he meant to. "But you already know she lives around here?"

"You see, Fletcher"—Chase sounded downright smug—"I try to make it a point to familiarize myself with my classmates."

"The ones with boobs," Freya clarified.

Chase opened his mouth to defend himself, then conceded with a shrug. "I'm nothing if not easy to read, my dear."

Freya rolled her eyes.

"Is this really that big a deal?" Fletcher asked. Between this, schoolwork, and plans to unearth Memory Frontier's secrets, it felt like they were spinning a lot of plates.

Ollie raised her eyebrows. "We're a squad now, Fletcher Cohen. What affects me affects you, plain and simple."

Fletcher chuckled, though her response had him second-guessing his decision to stay mum about the hidden trail Dean Mendelsohn had covered up. Why shouldn't he tell Freya and Ollie about—

Chase met his eyes and, as if reading his thoughts, discreetly shook his head. Freya noticed the exchange and narrowed her eyes at Fletcher.

"Then it's settled." Chase leaned back against the tree, his legs crossed. "We'll get our permission slips this week and go to the mall on Saturday."

Ollie plopped down beside him and gave him a high-five.

The Tennessee heat in August was muggy, thick, and downright malevolent, a kind of ever-present force that lived among the trees and waited for someone to step outside and be consumed. Sure, Fletcher forgot it was there sometimes, especially in the shade. But today the humidity reminded him there was no escaping its evil reach. He was wet and needed to change clothes ASAP.

It was terrible.

Fletcher's jeans stuck to his legs as they trekked through the woods toward campus.

"Fletcher, you all right?" Chase asked, laughing. "You're walkin' kinda funny."

Ollie and Freya started giggling too. *Shoot*. Fletcher did not need Chase calling attention to him. He'd apparently forgotten how to walk normally, and he was all-out waddling.

The laughter intensified as they emerged from the forest, right into the path of Dean Mendelsohn. They all froze. He stood before them, his sleeves rolled up to his forearms, the knot in his yellow tie barely coming loose beneath the gray stubble on his neck. He held a mug of coffee.

"Well, now. It was only a matter of time before students ventured into these woods to sate their promiscuous appetites."

Chase snorted, but Ollie jabbed him in the ribs. "We were just hanging out," Chase said awkwardly. "Sir."

Dean Mendelsohn took a long drink from his mug.

The four watched him.

He watched back.

The extended pause grew more agonizing by the second, until—

"Of course," he finally said. "My dear mother always preached giving others the benefit of the doubt. I try to exercise that practice as often as I can."

"That's good to know," Freya said. "Nothing's worse than getting reprimanded for something you didn't do. Nothing's worse than getting punished because someone made an assumption about you."

Fletcher had to make a concerted effort to keep his mouth from falling open. Freya's boldness toward the dean startled him. Actually, it both scared Fletcher *and* deepened his attraction to her, which—he admitted—sounded pretty absurd. Yet all he could do was admire her out of the corner of his eye and let the tingling sensation in his body run rampant as their shoulders brushed against each other.

Freya's unlike any girl I've ever known. Anyone who met her would come to the same conclusion within minutes. He was starting to let himself admit that he liked her a lot, even though they'd just met four days prior.

"Well then," the dean said, stepping aside so they could pass. "Don't let me keep you from Taco Tuesday."

Freya thanked him and then led the four toward the Foxhole. While they were still within earshot, Dean Mendelsohn called out: "And don't make a habit of wandering too far into the woods."

Freya and Ollie snickered, but Fletcher couldn't help but feel a little unsettled by the dean's words, which felt less like a threat and more like an omen.

The rest of Fletcher's first week at Foxtail Academy proved mostly uneventful.

He and Chase decided that, since Dean Mendelsohn had caught them emerging from the woods on Tuesday, it was probably best if they lay low for a couple days. They agreed to venture back into the woods behind the faculty housing on Sunday night to look for the train tracks and check the building where the mysterious cargo was being stored.

They took extra precautions when using their Restoreys before breakfast. They stored their memory tapes on opposite sides of the room, with Chase artificially recalling in the bathroom and Fletcher on his bed.

That bizarre and unnerving exchange of each other's memory tapes—the vacuum of neon lights—had left them somewhat traumatized.

They did *not* want to risk it happening a second time.

Saturday arrived with an overcast sky and a forecast of scattered showers.

After Fletcher and Chase finished artificial recall, they swung by the Foxhole to grab some coffee to go, then went to meet Samantha Ricci in the gravel parking lot at the edge of campus.

"Did you at least invite her to come with us?" Fletcher asked Chase as Samantha parked her red Ford Cortina and waved at them energetically.

"Shut up, man, no one wants a fifth wheel," he said out of the corner of his mouth, and then to Samantha: "Sam, hiiiii!"

She got out of the car, dropped her keys on the ground, stooped down to pick them up in a panic, and then giggled nervously. "Ciao!" she said in a clunky Italian accent.

Chase walked up to her with his arms outstretched, then gave her the ol' double-cheek air kiss. "I was just telling my roommate how thankful we are for the wheels!"

Samantha flipped her hand, indicating it was no big deal. "I had to come to campus this morning anyway to help Skipper prep the inaugural Movies and Memories meet-up!"

"Of *course* you did." He beamed. "I was thinking I might go tonight. Now I definitely will." He reached out to take the keys from Samantha. "I'll just take these . . ." But at the last second, she held them out of reach and giggled.

"*Cattiva!*" Chase said, clicking his tongue. Samantha blushed and eventually relinquished the car keys.

Fletcher rolled his eyes back so far they almost got stuck.

"Try to keep her under the speed limit," Samantha told Chase, sounding like a parent rattling off rules in the driveway. "Anything over eighty and she starts to rattle a little. And the tape deck gets finicky sometimes, but it works."

"You're the best, Samantha, really," Chase said, walking to the driver's side as Freya and Ollie approached. Samantha, noticing the girls, replaced her flirty expression with a hostile one. It was such a stark change Fletcher almost laughed out loud.

"Don't mention it." She arched an eyebrow, then marched away without so much as glancing at the girls again.

"Sweet girl, that Samantha," Chase exclaimed as Ollie took shotgun and Fletcher and Freya piled into the back seat.

"Hey," Fletcher said to her, pulling his seatbelt across his chest and clicking it into place.

Freya smiled. "You ready to shop for some bell-bottoms, Sonny?"

Fletcher opened his mouth to reply, but she quickly added, "And don't you dare call me Cher."

They drove down the winding country roads with all four windows down, laughing and butchering the words to Bryan Adams's "Somebody," which roared through the cheap stereo speakers. Ollie lit a cigarette, kicked off her shoes, and propped her feet on the dashboard while Freya hung her arm out the passenger window.

Fletcher smiled and watched Freya lip-syncing as she stared up at the silvery clouds, the diffused sunlight rolling off her brown skin like glitter on a dress. She closed her eyes and leaned her head to the side, and Fletcher couldn't help but wish she was leaning on him, belting this song with her cheek pressed against his shoulder. He pictured himself holding her hand, their fingers interlaced, and the feel of her cool breath on his bare arm.

Ollie jerked Fletcher from his thoughts with an impressive air-guitar solo, the cigarette jiggling so wildly between her pressed lips he was sure it was going to fall into her lap. Chase egged her on, one hand on the wheel, one hand punching the air outside his window.

Fletcher laughed, soaking it all in, fully aware that they looked utterly ridiculous to anyone who passed them on the other side of the curvy road.

On the second floor of the mall, they located a vintage thrift store called the Flower Child, which was brimming with retro apparel. Freya and Ollie managed to find a good selection of flower-patterned dresses and go-go boots, which they tried on in the dressing room and then showed off—runway style.

Fletcher and Chase cheered them on loudly, drawing annoyed stares from the store owner.

"You'd think he'd be *thrilled* to have us," Chase whispered of the old hippie, who stroked his horseshoe mustache as he glared in their direction. "We're probably his first customers in months."

For Fletcher's part, he found a used cashmere blazer and some loud, orange-striped slacks. It was a repulsive ensemble, complemented nicely by a beige turtleneck he found on the sale rack.

Chase snagged a pair of denim bell-bottoms and a white, skintight, short-sleeve button-down.

"It's going to be *so* hard waiting until the dance to wear this," Chase said, handing the cashier his cash.

With their bags in hand, the four rode the escalator down to the food court, which was located in the mall's atrium. They split a pizza and sat beside a large collection of fake banana-leaf plants. Ollie suggested they rewatch *Saturday Night Fever* at some point before the dance, and Freya cautiously confessed that she had only seen the first half.

"What is wrong with you?" Ollie said, nearly choking on her Coke, acting like Freya had admitted to some dark, unforgivable sin.

"Outside of documentaries, I don't watch a lot of movies." She picked the mushrooms off her slice of pizza and then took a bite.

"Hey, but *Saturday Night Fever* is about disco, right?" Fletcher said. "Isn't the dance, like, Woodstock themed or something?"

"I think that movie's overrated anyway." Chase slurped his drink through his straw. "Just like all of Travolta's movies. I mean . . . *Grease*? What a terrible name for a movie. Ugh. Pass."

Ollie looked as if she might combust. Chase stood up and went to get a refill, and Ollie was quick to her feet: "Oh no you don't. You don't get to throw out some awful opinion about a seminal work of art and then just leave!"

She followed him, jumping into a diatribe against Chase's "ungodly taste in movies."

"You know," Fletcher said to Freya, shaking his head, "I can't figure out if those two are some bitter elderly couple or a pair of quibbling siblings."

"I haven't figured that out either." She laughed, then slid back in her chair and looked around the food court, scanning the surrounding shops. "They don't have malls like this back in Long Beach. Honestly, I didn't even think malls were still open . . ."

"L.A. has several." He added sarcastically, "Affluent neighborhoods sure do have their priorities sorted."

Freya gave him a grave look. He cleared his throat and, thankfully, she swooped in and changed the subject. "How great has it been starting off every day without artificial recall?"

"Yeah, no, it's great." Fletcher fidgeted with his uneaten pizza crust.

"Is . . . everything okay?"

"Hm? Oh, yeah, sorry." As hard as he tried, he just couldn't avoid sounding squirrelly. "Yeah, the Reflectors are great."

"I think so," Freya said. "This tech is going to give me a life I've never known." She held up her palm and showed him her cognition wheel.

Fletcher stared at the two-quarter tattoo for a while before saying anything. "I had no idea."

"You sound like I just told you I'm terminally ill." She smirked.

"Sorry, I didn't mean . . ." He trailed off, avoiding her eyes. "Sorry."

"There's nothing to be sorry about. These Reflectors are God's gift to mankind. If everything goes smoothly, these stupid cognition wheels will be nothing more than a scar."

For a moment, Fletcher just gawked at her hand, which she now rested on the table. "Can I ask you something?"

"Shoot."

"What's the hardest part about being a degen?" Fletcher dropped his voice. "Like, is it really that bad having to artificially recall a couple more times a day than recollectors?"

"That right there." She shook her head. "The label. Degen. That plus the segregation became a new kind of epidemic born out of the first one."

"Segregation?"

"You serious?" Freya arched her eyebrows, nonplussed. "The way these lawmakers set it up in California, if you're a recollector you hold all the cards and all the chips. The rest of us aren't even seated at the same table! We're playing a totally different game with a totally different set of rules . . . and we're playing with our hands tied behind our backs."

Fletcher blinked.

"I used to watch poker on TV with my dad." Freya looked away. "The metaphor just came to me."

Fletcher took a beat before saying, his tone decidedly sensitive, "You used to watch it with him?"

She didn't answer right away, and Fletcher panicked and wondered if he'd gone too far. Thankfully, she met his eyes again. "My dad died a couple years ago, when I was fifteen. I guess I vacillate between the past and present when talking about him. Just sort of happens."

"Oh . . . wow." Fletcher turned toward her. "I'm sorry. How did he die?"

"Not sure. I mean, they said there was an accident at his work, but I'm not convinced it was an accident."

Fletcher sat with this for a long moment. "That really is awful. How's your mom handling it?"

"Died shortly after delivering me." Fletcher all but flinched. "I'm not trying to sound emotionless, but in my experience, grief unsettles people. Over the past couple of years, I've found that expressing grief is taboo, even though we all experience it to different degrees. That's just confusing and sad. If my blunt approach rattles people, well, maybe it should."

Fletcher shifted his weight in the seat, speechless.

"You don't gotta feel bad for me, promise," she said, sounding sincere. "How about you? Only child?"

"Yup," he said, but as soon as the answer left his mouth, he felt guilty.

Freya shot him a skeptical glance. "You sure? You don't seem sure."

"No, it's . . ." He laughed uncomfortably. "I mean. Well, I guess *technically* I have a sister."

Freya blinked. "Okay, I'm gonna need you to explain."

Fletcher scratched a nonexistent itch behind his ear, then sat up and leaned forward. "Well, so, I guess when my mom was pregnant she, um, lost my little sister. It's one of the memories I have to artificially recall . . . Right now I just remember that it happened without any of the details, like how far along she was. But she never had my sister, like, what I mean is, she was never *born*, so I dunno if that counts."

Fletcher felt hot after fumbling his way through that, and he was so embarrassed that he turned from Freya and pretended to be fascinated with the water fountain on the other side of the food court, where a young boy and his mother were making wishes and tossing pennies.

At first, he watched them to distract himself from that awkward explanation of his mother's miscarriage, but then Fletcher started to fall into unexpected introspection, and the scene played out in slow motion: The mother laughs, taking her child's hand and leading him across the fountain's edge, gracefully counterbalancing his shaky steps. The boy, who can't be older than two, smiles as he gazes up at the cascading water.

Here was this young family, in a mall, in the food court, doing nothing particularly remarkable except for spending time on a Saturday beneath the great glass ceilings.

But, of course, it *was* remarkable, because the child was there . . . this woman's son was alive with budding curiosity and laughter and fascination. When she got pregnant, this woman had no guarantees her child would live to full term.

Just like Fletcher's mother didn't.

He watched the mother and her child, and Fletcher realized

his own mother likely had these moments every single day. These moments of watching and wondering—wondering what her daughter might look like and sound like and smell like had she lived.

And that girl, that child whom Fletcher's mother had carried, was his sister. She was not just the baby who died inside his mother's womb.

No. Fletcher felt a measure of defiance. *She's my sister.*

Freya took his hand. Fletcher met her gaze, realizing with a start that tears had formed in the corners of his eyes. "You know, your mom's not the only one who lost someone. You don't have to take grief cues from her."

Grief cues. Huh. I never thought of it like that.

"I lost my parents," she said matter-of-factly. "You lost your sister. The impact of the grief is different, but the gravity's the same, isn't it? Loss is loss."

"Yeah." Fletcher smiled and blinked back his tears, tears he'd hidden in a box and stored in the back of some attic. Freya was right, though, and he was all at once embarrassed to have spent all these years running from it. It didn't matter that he didn't have all the details; it shouldn't matter if he never did.

Because loss is loss, as Freya had said.

"You look at something a certain way for so long," Fletcher said. "Like, I dunno, a sculpture, and you make up your mind on the meaning of it. But all it takes is for someone to come along, to take you by the hand and lead you to the side a couple of steps . . . so you can see it from a whole new angle."

Freya smiled back, a tender smile that said a lot, only she actually said a little: "Good thing I came around then, right?"

Before he could reply, a wild shriek reverberated through the mall, and the entire food court fell eerily silent.

23

FREYA IZQUIERDO

The scream is followed by an explosion of glass shards.

A person covered head to toe in shock-absorbing armor loudly barrels through the glass wall of one of the storefronts that faces the food court. They drag something toward the center of the food court just a dozen feet away from us.

Fletcher takes my hand and pulls me back as people scream and scatter—some taking shelter underneath the tables—and a distant alarm begins to buzz.

It's pandemonium.

Fletcher and I find Chase and Ollie huddled by the wall of fake mall plants at the edge of the food court. We gather closely, watching with horror as the demonstrator takes the bag they're dragging and empties the contents onto the floor.

Dozens of new, unopened boxes of Restoreys clatter out, and

they set to work stomping on them with the heel of their boot. The demonstrator has spray-painted "2 Forget Is 2 Die" across their breast-plate, as well as a sloppy white X across the front of their cracked helmet, which completely conceals their face.

Is this a rogue MACE agent?

As the thought enters my head, two actual MACE agents storm the scene, electroshock weapons at the ready. They tackle the demonstrator, who doesn't fight back. Instead, muffled shouting cuts through the semi-silence in the food court. I expect to see some resistance, but this person is submitting as the agents violently bind them and then yank them up.

One of the MACE agents unmasks the demonstrator. It's a woman in her forties with stringy hair and weary eyes, the look of a desperate individual. "They'll call me a provocateur," she yells to no one in particular. "An agitator. But I'm here to remind you that—"

The MACE agent who unmasked her strikes his electroshock baton across her neck. I flinch, feeling like my own neck has collapsed beneath this grisly impact.

The woman goes limp, then she's carried away by one of the agents. The other one, the one who wields the baton, lingers . . . looking around the mall with his chest puffed out.

"Sorry for the show, folks." He twirls his weapon and paces, broken glass crunching beneath the weight of his heavy boots. His voice is distorted; I heard on TV that their masks scramble their actual voices so they all have a uniform quality.

They say it's for their protection, to preserve anonymity.

I think it's so they can sound more intimidating.

Fletcher takes my hand again, this time my right one—the one with my cognition wheel. He holds it securely in his. To my left, Ollie's and Chase's faces are distraught. Chase side-hugs Ollie, and she leans against his shoulder and bats away some tears.

"More agents are en route to secure the mall," the agent continues. "In the meantime, I need some eyewitness accounts for our report."

The four of us all exchange a look.

"Let's get out of here," Fletcher whispers, quickly leading us away from the food court and toward the mall exit.

It's not until we're leaving the parking lot that I realize I haven't let go of Fletcher's hand. I look down, feel a stab of embarrassment, then slowly draw my hand back toward my lap.

Fletcher meets my eyes, his gaze stalwart. I try not to look at him differently; I try to explain away his caring for me as just one friend trying to comfort another friend in the midst of a scary event. That's it. What I'm feeling right now under the watch of his soft, safe gaze is just gratitude for his coming to my side—even though I didn't need him to.

So why do I feel a pull toward him? A sort of quiet want that has me gravitating to him?

I unfasten my seatbelt and slide into the middle seat. Then, wordlessly, I take his arm and wrap it around my shoulder. I feel his chest rise up and down slowly with a sigh.

For the first time today, it begins to rain.

Chase finds a radio station with the news on it.

". . . been identified as Wesley Langdon," the female newscaster says, her voice noticeably shaky. "We're learning that Ms. Langdon's dangerous stunt at Governor Court Mall this afternoon was a protest of sorts, even though it's unclear exactly what message she was trying to send. Officials have confirmed that Ms. Langdon, who's recovering from multiple injuries, confessed to association with the Memory Ghosts—allied activists who challenge the merits of artificial recall—even though the Memory Ghosts disavow copycats who carry out violent and dangerous acts like the one Ms. Langdon—"

"Can you shut that off, Chase?" Fletcher asks. Chase complies.

No one says anything else the entire ride back to campus.

※ ※ ※

"We need a good distraction right now," Ollie says in our dorm room after dinner.

"What do you have in mind?" I'm finally getting around to hanging up the dress I purchased. My foster parents sent me to campus with a small sum of cash, and I just spent most of it on lunch and this outfit for the dance. Half grinning, I'm surprised to find I don't regret the purchase at all.

"I'm thinking that around ten, we sneak out and find a new secret hang spot. Ever since the dean saw us emerging from the woods Tuesday, it's had me worried that spot is compromised."

I shut the closet door and turn around just as Ollie walks out of the bathroom with a bottle of bug spray.

"And if there's one thing I've learned about boarding school after being here for just one week, it's that we *need* a secret hang spot . . . a refuge."

"Sure. I'm all for that. But do you think it's a good idea to try to find a new spot after curfew?"

Ollie's lips form a circle. "Um, is Freya Izquierdo actually *scared* of Mr. Dean Mendelsohn?"

I give her an apathetic look.

"You *are*, aren't you?"

"I'm not dignifying this with a response."

"So then, we're in agreement?" She tosses me the bottle of bug spray. "Ten p.m.?"

I sigh. "Ten p.m. Got a particular part of campus in mind?"

"I'm thinking the *last* place the dean would ever suspect we'd go." She sounds so sure of herself. "The woods behind the faculty housing."

The dark of night is just as hot as the daytime despite the hours of sporadic rainfall, which have managed to make it *more* humid.

And speaking of rainfall, the showers have let up, but the added moisture in the air has summoned an army of mosquitoes. Even with my whole body lathered in bug spray, I can hear the loud whirring of wings as they buzz past my ears. I swat at them in the dark, feeling ridiculous.

Ollie and I race across the quiet campus, keeping to the shadows as much as possible and avoiding the lit portions of the wet lawn.

"Over there," she whispers, pointing to the blue dumpsters outside the Foxhole. We slink along the border of the woods and dart for the shadowy side of the dining hall, my heart racing over the risk of being spotted by a groundskeeper or teacher.

We peer around the dumpsters, breathing through our mouths to avoid smelling the thick filth of discarded food and waste. From here, we can spy the front of the faculty duplexes relatively well. I hear Ollie about to whisper something just as Mr. Williams appears out of nowhere, whistling cheerfully to himself. He walks to his door, but before he unlocks it and enters, he notices some trash on the ground. He shakes his head, leaves the doormat, and goes to pick it up. Then he visibly contemplates where to discard it: the waste can on the farthest end of the faculty housing . . .

. . . or the dumpsters outside the dining hall.

Ollie and I gasp as we realize he's headed straight for us. Frozen with fear, we watch as Mr. Williams walks in our direction, balancing the trash in his outstretched hand with a look of deep concentration.

At the last possible second imaginable, *just* when I think his eyes have fallen on us, a voice calls out to Mr. Williams.

One of the school groundskeepers, an elderly man with a full head of white hair, wanders over with a turtle-like cadence. He carries with him an empty trash bag and a small rake, as well as the sharp, determined look of a man on a mission.

"Now, c'mon, Mr. Williams." He talks about as slowly as he walks. "We been over this. You got no business cleaning up. You going to put me out of a job."

We hear Mr. Williams chuckle as he turns toward the old man, and we scurry away. We double back behind the Foxhole, the portion of the building that faces the pier and the lake, and hide in a tucked-away corner beside the dining-hall doors. We hold our collective breath until—at last—the distant sound of chatter is gone. To be sure, we wait another couple of minutes before creeping out.

Before I can question the soundness of this whole idea, Ollie jogs off and makes for the dumpsters again. I follow her on the balls of my feet.

"Looks like the coast is clear," Ollie says once I settle beside her. She scans the duplexes with narrowed eyes, pulling a travel-size flashlight out of her front pocket. In a breathy voice she mutters, "It's now or never," and she bolts toward the woods.

As we sprint across the slippery grass and then leap over a row of freshly planted flower beds, my adrenaline pumping, I'm smacked with the reality of just how deranged we are. Who in their right minds would run into the stark black woods behind the snoring faculty?

If we pull this off without managing to get caught, there *is* a God.

When we're a considerable distance away from the duplexes,

Ollie flicks on the flashlight. She hands it to me, pulls a squished cigarette from her pocket, and lights it.

"Do you *have* to do that right now?"

She takes the flashlight back and gestures for me to follow her farther into the silent woods.

"Just what are we looking for, exactly?" I ask as Ollie fans the forest floor like the leader of a search party.

"The perfect hang spot." The red glow of her cigarette burns in front of her mouth.

Whatever that means.

The gargantuan trees mostly blot out the moon and stars, and the effect is pretty haunting. Even with partial light bleeding through the treetops, these woods are very dark. And quiet, I realize, as the two of us traipse beneath nature's thatch toward the unknown.

The déjà vu returns. I feel I've been here before.

"Ollie!" A stinging sense of dread wells inside me. "We should turn around!"

Voices stop her from responding. Quick as lightning, Ollie shuts off her flashlight and we crouch behind a tree. She stomps out her cigarette beneath the heel of her shoe, then falls still. My heart beats against my chest like a mallet on a drum, and I'm sure I can hear Ollie's too. On the other side of the tree, which marks a crooked border of the woods beside a clearing, the voices grow louder. They're still far enough away that I feel emboldened to try to steal a peek.

I get on my hands and knees and crawl over the tree's knotty roots. I can feel Ollie behind me, stealthily taking my cue. And at the same time, we peer through the low branches.

I see a man in a lab coat, overseeing the transport of a covered, motionless body on a gurney.

A tremor overcomes me, a feeling of being zapped by static electricity. The scene plays out just like my half-memory dream. Ollie covers her mouth with a trembling hand. The MACE agents roll the body toward a parked freight train, and as the man in the lab coat steps out from the curtain of shadows, we see that it's Dean Mendelsohn. His hardened face surveys the scene.

I grab Ollie's wrist. The dean is going to shine his flashlight in our direction seconds from now. I yank my friend away from the view at the exact same moment that Dean Mendelsohn unpockets his Maglite.

We clamber to our feet and scramble away from the train like prey being pursued by a monster.

All kinds of panicked thoughts tumble around inside my head. What is happening to me?

24

FLETCHER COHEN

"Skipper just *didn't* show?" Fletcher asked Chase, who handled his video game controller with so much intensity the plastic was bound to snap in two. "That's so weird."

"Right?" Chase bit the tip of his tongue as he furiously tapped the buttons.

After their trip to the mall, Chase had announced to the group he was going to Skipper's movie club with or without them. He said he needed a distraction after that eventful afternoon in the food court. Ollie waffled on whether to join him but ultimately decided she didn't want to chance seeing Ave Maria there.

The GAME OVER screen flashed on the TV, and Chase groaned. He shut off the game.

"Anyway, it wasn't a total loss . . . Allison James was there and Chase got to do Chase's thing. Really glad my hair does me favors."

"Don't talk about yourself in third person." Fletcher turned from his roommate. He was having a hard time wrapping his head around this. Skipper, who had flyers printed hours after unpacking his suitcases, had promoted his Movies and Memories club as if campaigning for student body president. To just no-show and leave the handful of students in the senior lounge without any note or explanation was . . . kind of unbelievable.

"Maybe Skipper got stage fright." Chase shrugged, took off his jeans, and slipped on his gym shorts.

"This is the same kid who accosted us at breakfast. He doesn't strike me as the type to get embarrassed easily."

"Fair." Chase peeled off his T-shirt, crawled into his bed, and yawned. "Come to think of it, Samantha Ricci did mention not seeing Skipper since lunchtime."

"So, like, what happened?"

Chase propped himself up on his elbow. "I dunno, I mean, we all just kind of sat there . . . waiting for him to show up. It was *super* awkward. After about fifteen minutes of that, we all just got up and—"

A flurry of knocks rattled their door. Fletcher and Chase swapped confused looks; it was 10:45. Who could possibly—?

The door swung open. Freya and Ollie spilled inside, looking as though they'd been running for miles, drenched in sweat, panic-stricken.

"Good, you two are still awake," Freya said between gasps, shutting the door and dead-bolting it.

"Hey, whoa, some of us aren't decent!" Chase shouted, covering his bare chest with his blanket. Fletcher swiped their dirty clothes off the couch so the girls could sit, which they did, taking a moment to catch their breath.

"What happened?" Fletcher asked, sitting on the armrest beside Freya. He placed his hand on her back, watching as she struggled to compose herself. Chase, realizing the seriousness of the situation, threw off his covers and grabbed two water bottles for the girls. They uncapped their drinks and took a long swig, both nearly finishing the water before setting down the bottles.

"We snuck into the woods," Freya finally said, staring off. "Behind the faculty housing."

Fletcher's heart dropped. He tried to meet Chase's eyes, but his roommate avoided him.

"Wait . . . why?" Chase asked, sitting on the edge of the coffee table across from Ollie. "Did you get caught?"

"No," Ollie whimpered, her voice frail. "At least, we don't think so."

"We were just trying to find a new hang spot." Freya's voice shook. "We saw Dean Mendelsohn. He was in a lab coat . . . There were MACE agents wheeling a body away from a building . . ."

Fletcher could tell by the way she trailed off that Freya wanted to offer more. But she refrained. "A body?"

"In a bag. On a gurney," Ollie said, nodding. "And the body wasn't moving."

Chase swore under his breath. Fletcher got up from his seat and started to pace, kicking around all kinds of wild theories in his head.

"What?" Freya said, watching him from the couch.

Chase answered first: "It's just . . . well, Fletcher found this trail leading into the woods behind the faculty housing that led to some train tracks—"

"Those MACE agents were wheeling the corpse *toward* a train!" Ollie shouted unsteadily.

Fletcher could feel his throat going dry. "You're sure it was a dead body?"

Ollie's voice rose. "Why didn't you bother to mention that to us?"

"I dunno, it didn't come up!" Fletcher said earnestly, holding his hands out in front of him. "Chase and I went back that night so I could show him the trail, but someone—I'm guessing the dean—had it completely covered up. He even moved the faculty mailbox and took out the payphone."

"When did all this happen?" Freya asked.

"Monday night," Fletcher answered. "Well, technically Tuesday morning since it was after midnight—"

"You didn't think that kind of thing was worth telling us?" Freya's eyes turned glassy. "Did you think we couldn't handle it?"

Fletcher felt like he was on trial. He had only wanted to protect them. Their protection was paramount. Now he was just dying to tell them everything, if only to prove it.

Plus, Fletcher couldn't stand the thought of Freya thinking he didn't trust her.

Chase jumped back in: "Sorry. We shoulda told you guys about that trail that Fletcher found. We were going to eventually. We just wanted to poke around the train tracks and—"

"Why are those out?" Freya pointed at the coffee table. Fletcher followed her eyes to his Restorey, which sat beside tomorrow's memory tape and Fletcher's recall schedule. Fletcher watched as Chase flushed, knowing full well he looked exactly the same.

"I . . ." Fletcher couldn't move. Couldn't speak. In most cases, he could act quickly on his feet and spin up a good excuse or halfway believable lie.

But not now.

He really didn't want to lie to Freya, but before he had the chance she was rising to her feet and looking around their dorm room intensely. Eventually she spotted their Reflectors, which Fletcher and Chase had put back in their boxes and stored in the corner beside the window days ago.

Freya met Fletcher's eyes. "Are you guys *skipping* the trial?" Her tone was heavy with betrayal and disappointment.

"No," he said quickly, his stomach lurching at the deceit. "I mean, yes, but only for a week. Not the *whole* trial. And only because—"

"Save it," Freya said, her eyes clouding with tears. "I get it. I do."

Chase got up from the coffee table. "Freya, just give us like two seconds to explain."

"Don't bother." Her words cut like a blade. She ground her teeth together and added, "I should've known . . . Fletcher was acting so weird when I brought up the trial today at lunch. You guys *hate* these Reflectors, don't you? You're about to lose some of that status of yours now that *this* doesn't matter." She held up her right hand, flashing her cognition wheel. "No more Reflectors, no more degens, no more privilege."

"Freya." Fletcher reached for her, but she jerked her hand back with revulsion. "That's insane."

"Which is what your people have always thought about mine," she said, tears now streaming down her cheeks. "Insane. Unfit. *Degenerates.* God forbid this technology level the playing field."

And with that, Freya Izquierdo left.

25

FREYA IZQUIERDO

Sunday is a long day, one fraught with loneliness.

I listen to my Walkman. I procrastinate doing homework. I eat all three meals in my dorm room, barely talking to anyone—even Ollie. When she tries to make small talk, I just flash her a listless smile and go back to my inactivity.

After dinner, I leave my dorm room by myself and head outside, walking to wherever my feet will carry me. I have so much pent-up anger inside me that I'm hoping I'll sweat it out as I wander around the campus beneath the setting sun.

Here's what I can't seem to process: not only did Fletcher and Chase prove to be just like every spoiled and privileged recollector I've ever encountered, but they somehow managed to take the stereotype to new, despicable heights. Skipping the trial? Sticking with artificial recall? Are they *that* resistant to change? Are they *that* threatened by the Reflector and how its arrival will bring down societal barriers?

Whatever their excuse for secretly skipping the trial for an entire week, whatever harebrained schemed they've hatched, it can't possibly be good.

But what burns the hottest is that I had just begun to open myself up to Fletcher. I won't soon forgive myself for that careless choice. And to think: if Ollie and I hadn't gone to their dorm room and seen their Restoreys out, I'd still be ignorant about the kind of person Fletcher really is behind closed doors. I'd probably be hanging out with him right now, foolishly letting my feelings for him grow . . .

Shame on me. *This is why you keep people at arm's length*, I scold myself, ambling toward the Juniper Lake shoreline, which is sparsely occupied. Some of my classmates splash in the water; others paddle in canoes in the distance. I find myself resenting them all for having such a normal Sunday. I pad, barefoot, down the empty pier and plop down on my haunches at the very end.

There's also the troubling matter of my half-memory dream, or whatever the hell it was. The hairs on my arms rise as I think back to that scene . . . the corpse in the bag . . . Dean Mendelsohn's chilling indifference . . . the way everything transpired *exactly* as I dreamed it days before it happened. How could I have a memory about something that hadn't happened yet? Until now, every unexpected flashback from my past has left me with a punishing headache. But that's it. The pain eventually fades, and I go on with my life.

This is the first time something has played out *after* my dream, like a prophecy or premonition coming to fruition.

Tomorrow after class, I must track down Dr. Sanders and—

My thoughts slam to a halt.

Stars in my vision.

Then white.

Then more pain.

220

Then: *nothing.* Just darkness . . . a nearly whole darkness whose edges dance with a kaleidoscope of neon lights. And then a loud, rushing, whirring sound . . . like helicopter blades. The lights swell until they become a suffocating flash, and all is still and colorful. Then the lights begin to dance in and out of focus, varying in brightness, before—with a sharp gasp—I awaken.

Back on the pier, I catch myself on the post beside me to avoid falling into the lake. With steady breaths, I tell myself that I'm okay, that the episode is over, that I'm back to reality. I repeat these truths over and over until at last I feel stable enough to walk back to my dorm room.

As I stumble off the pier and onto the sand, praying I don't draw anyone's attention, I ask myself again: *What's wrong with me?*

I've never wished my dad were still alive more than I do right now.

When I get back to my dorm, Ollie's not there, and I get pretty worked up over this. I slam the door behind me, figuring she's out with Chase and Fletcher. In fact, my annoyance boils into indignation as I realize that neither of the boys has tried to seek me out all day. The rational part of me figures they're just giving me space to cool off, but forget that.

Right now, I'm going to be irrational.

I take a cold shower to clear my head. If that strange episode on the pier was a half-memory dream, it's the most confounding one I've ever had. But what if it was a vision, like the one I had of the dean in the woods?

Why do things have to be so difficult! Why can't I just be normal? . . . Why couldn't all this have stopped once I started trialing the Reflector?

I'm only one week into my senior year at Foxtail Academy, and

I have more questions festering in my broken head than before the semester started.

And more enemies. I think of Fletcher and Chase bitterly.

Avoiding people is easy. I've spent years mastering it. Like a golfer swinging her driver after a weeklong sabbatical, I pick up right where I left off before enrolling at Foxtail.

Monday morning, I take off my Reflector receivers, put the device on its charging base, brush my teeth, and leave the dorm room—all before Ollie wakes up. I get my breakfast burrito to go, find an empty bench outside one of the classrooms, and eat in silence. Since I don't share my first or second periods with Fletcher, Ollie, and Chase, I'm able to spend the entire morning by myself. I fight off the temptation to wonder how they're doing . . . to wonder if they miss me as much as I'm pretending not to miss them.

This part proves to be the most difficult.

At lunch, I see Fletcher for the first time since Saturday evening. He's across the dining hall, his back to me, getting ready to walk into the food line. My stomach flips like I've been suspended upside down.

I decide to skip lunch. As I cross the lawn toward the library, figuring I can kill some time there under the guise of reading or studying, a friendly voice calls out to me.

"There's a strange sight!"

I turn to see Mr. Williams, waving as he walks over, clutching a brown sack of lunch with his other hand.

"Strange sight?" I pause so he can catch up. We walk in unison toward the library, which has a stand-alone swinging bench in the shade. It's usually occupied by bookworms; right now the bench is vacant.

We sit down, and he elaborates: "Can't say I've seen you without

Ms. Trang, Mr. Hall, or Mr. Cohen at your side since we arrived! You four were inseparable all last week. Where are they?"

"Is calling students by their last names, like, a high school counselor thing?" I ask, watching as he carefully and deliberately pulls out the contents of his lunch: a Saran-wrapped sandwich, an apple, a bag of corn chips. He admires his food as if it's a three-course meal.

"There is definitely an unwritten handbook for high school counselors." He unwraps his sandwich. "In fact, there's an entire chapter dedicated to prying. So humor me as I pry: Where are your friends?"

"I dunno." I shrug. "Probably in the Foxhole. Probably eating."

"I see. Allow me to pry further, then. Why aren't y'all eating together?"

I really don't want to be doing this right now, especially since I'm storing up all of my social energy for after Memory Theory. I want to talk to Dr. Sanders about the latest development with my half-memory dreams.

While I'm thinking of a proper way to dance around his question, he chuckles.

"When I was a kid, lot younger than you are now"—he wipes the crumbs from his mustache—"people in my hometown used to call my mom a man-of-war. Do you know what a man-of-war is?"

I shake my head.

"Some people have called it the floating terror," he explains between bites. "You should look up pictures in the library sometime. It's a translucent sea creature with tentacles that stabs its prey with venom. The kind of science-fiction thing you only see in movies. Anyway, my mama was a principal at my school with a penchant for making an example out of me. For some reason, a reason I don't get to this day, she made it her life's mission to rule with an iron fist—both the school *and* her family.

"One day—this would have been in fifth grade—when I was carrying my science project down the hallway, my diorama slipped out of my hands and shattered into hundreds of pieces at my feet. I was devastated! I had stayed up all night with my pops building this elaborate thing, and then in an instant it was ruined.

"My mama, who happened to be walking by in the opposite direction, didn't bother to stop to help me clean up the mess. Instead, as my classmates pointed and laughed, she took the opportunity to remind me—in front of everyone!—why I was such a disappointment. Can you believe that? My own mama. It was awful!

"Well, after that day, I decided I wasn't going to let her treat me like that anymore. I was going to stand up for myself. And I did. Sure, it was scary at first, but it got easier over time . . . After college, my mama and I began to repair our relationship, and now we talk on the phone about once a week."

I blink softly, hoping I don't look as annoyed as I feel. While it's great to hear he reconciled with his mother, I know Mr. Williams is trying to slip in some kind of life lesson.

Guidance counselors and their sage wisdom.

"Over that time, as I started to make the conscious effort not to get pushed around, I discovered something about courage," Mr. Williams continues. *There it is.* "Courageous people aren't any less afraid than those who lack courage."

I nod, then lean back against the bench. "My dad used to say something similar: 'Courage doesn't mean you're *not* afraid. Courage means you take the stand or have the talk *in spite* of being afraid.'"

"That's right!" Mr. Williams says, looking overly satisfied with my engagement. "Being courageous means doing the thing even *though* you're scared . . . even *though* it's risky and you don't know the outcome."

Yeah, yeah. You've made your point. I sigh. Embarrassingly, my stomach roars. Mr. Williams laughs and then tosses me his apple.

❖ ❖ ❖

Once Algebra II is finished, I swallow my pride, throw on a courageous face, and walk straight up to Chase. He's unable to mask his surprise.

"You guys hurt me." I don't mince words. "I wish you would have trusted me and Ollie with what you'd found in the woods, and I wish you hadn't skipped the trial."

His face softens. "I know, I know. I'm *so* sorry. We feel awful. Fletcher's all torn up."

We walk away from the classroom and cross the lawn, navigating the post-class rush. "Look"—Chase consults his wristwatch—"please just hear us out. Can you meet us at our spot in five minutes, during free period?"

I nod.

"Awesome." He hugs me. I lean in and don't push him away. "I'll see you there."

❖ ❖ ❖

I take the path along the water's edge, careful not to trip on the polished pebbles, and emerge into our secret clearing to find only Fletcher sitting on the fallen tree. When he sees me, he leaps down eagerly and all but sprints in my direction.

"I thought you might not show," he says cautiously.

"Where's everybody else?"

He doesn't reply. I understand.

"Freya, can we sit?"

"I'd rather stand."

He nods. "When Chase and I decided to keep you and Ollie in the dark on some things, we thought we were protecting you. I know that's not what you think or want to hear, but it's the honest truth."

"I don't need protection."

"I know that," he says softly. "I realize now we should face all these uncertain things *together*. I should have trusted you. And instead, the worst possible thing happened. I lost your trust."

I take a beat and let his words sink in. I walk past him and sit on the tree.

He joins me. "Before I found out about Foxtail, my girlfriend broke up with me."

I give him a look.

"Follow me for a sec." He puts his hand on my leg. "I was pretty self-absorbed and, honestly, had it coming. But I just looked at it as a gift from the universe, because I wanted my senior year to be this very specific thing: a boring transition into the rest of my life. Just a footnote. Something insignificant. And to make it happen, I was willing to hurt someone who cared about me. *That's* how badly I wanted to control my life. I deeply regret how I handled that, and I've been thinking a lot these past twenty-four hours about how I need to handle *this* . . . us."

He clears his throat and straightens up. "I'm done trying to control everything. And when it comes to you, I don't want to feel an ounce of regret. Because you've been anything *but* insignificant. I know we've only known each other a week—I know we still have so much to learn about each other—but I want to earn that right back.

"I want to earn back the opportunity to get to know you better. And that starts with me being honest about everything."

I listen to Fletcher's heartfelt tone, his words practically dripping with sorrow, and I feel the protective armor around my heart start to crack.

No guy has ever attempted to get this real with me.

Ever.

I try to remain composed, forcing down the big lump in my throat. "Go on."

He nods and starts to speak.

26

FLETCHER COHEN

Fletcher told Freya everything.

He began with the night he and Denise broke up. The mysterious woman who met with his father in secret. He told Freya how he suspected his father was responsible for his lottery selection at Foxtail Academy. He recounted his conversation with Dean Mendelsohn, how he propositioned him to spy on his classmates. He told her about his big questions surrounding the trial, Memory Frontier, and the Reflector. He posed to her the same question he and Chase had posed to one another: Just how did this corporation acquire the necessary "memory insights" needed to make a device like the Reflector technologically possible? This dovetailed into his telling her about his Memory Killer File, where he kept a running list of nagging questions, such as, What would happen if Memory Killer struck during artificial recall? He also filled her in on that night he and Chase had overheard Dr. Sanders and the dean, when the latter had said something about "increasing the dosage."

And now, with their classmate Matthew Skipper missing since Saturday, on the *very* day Freya and Ollie witnessed a body bag being rolled toward a train in the dead of night, the urgency to find answers felt greater than ever.

Fletcher finished, half expecting Freya to burst into laughter and then storm off without ever saying another word to him. Instead, she zeroed in on one thing.

"Who else have you told this to? This . . . this question about Memory Killer striking during artificial recall?"

"Umm . . ." Fletcher thought. "Just you and Chase. Why?"

"My dad witnessed this very thing happening on the day he died." She looked off into the distance. "He was riding the bus to work and described seeing an elderly man's eyes fluttering open . . . seeing them turn gray . . . while he was hooked up to his Restorey. He was so bothered by it he actually called me from a payphone while I was in class."

"I . . . wow."

"Yeah. He died in a freak work 'accident' later that day."

"Do you think his death was, like, a result of what he saw?"

"I've always wondered. He worked in a factory that built MeReaders. During his time there, he was always wrestling with something . . . So, like, I've never bought that his death was an accident. But then again, he told me about what he saw and *I'm* still alive. Unless, of course"—she got to her feet and started to walk up and down the length of the tree—"unless he told someone else at work, and it got back to the wrong person . . . Knowing my dad, he wouldn't have told a soul that he'd spoken to me that morning."

Fletcher swore, his heart pumping violently in his chest.

So there is *a chance he was killed for what he saw,* he thought darkly.

Freya's eyes widened.

"What?"

"Allison James. Ave Maria's friend. She wasn't in class this morning."

Chase and Ollie appeared, walking up from the banks of the lake.

Ollie walked straight up to Freya and threw her arms around her neck in a tight embrace.

"You good?" Fletcher heard her whisper.

Freya nodded after they broke away, then Chase pulled her into a hug too.

"I'm sorry, guys," she said, confessing, "I was wrong not to give you the benefit of the doubt. I should've heard you out. It won't happen again."

"You're good, Freya. Promise. Now did I hear you say Allison missed class?" Chase asked. Freya nodded. "I don't think she was in AP lit, either. Saturday, we talked it up at Skipper's movie club and agreed to partner up today, which is why I was on the lookout for her."

"Because I was pouting all morning, it didn't occur to me until just now how unnerving it is that two of our classmates have gone missing in a span of forty-eight hours." Freya sucked in a breath through her nose. "Come to think of it, I remember overhearing two girls on our first morning here . . . One was talking about how her roommate disappeared in the night with all her belongings."

The four of them exchanged a heavy look. Freya asked, "Just how long have our classmates been vanishing?"

"I'm really hoping the body bag we saw didn't have one of our classmates in it," Ollie said, hugging herself. Fletcher saw goose bumps all over her arms.

The group fell silent. With students vanishing in the night all week long, who was next?

"What's the word on the street regarding Skipper and Allison?" Fletcher asked Ollie.

"Well, I heard Skipper had a bad case of food poisoning." She shook her head. "They're saying he was sent home sometime Saturday after lunch. Since Allison's only just gone missing today, there's not a lot of chatter. Yet."

"Maybe Allison just played hooky," Chase offered, but Fletcher could tell he didn't really believe that. Skipping class might be an everyday occurrence at any other school, but at a boarding school, that's asking to get kicked out.

Fletcher ran a hand through his hair. "Well, whatever's going on, it's far bigger than any of us. It's far bigger than we could have imagined."

Freya broke away, heading off toward Juniper Lake. She stood with her back to them, ankle-high in the water, looking out at nothing in particular.

"Freya?" Fletcher swapped concerned looks with Ollie and Chase.

Eventually, she turned around. "It's time I told you guys about my half-memory dreams."

❖ ❖ ❖

Fletcher held Freya's hand as they left their spot and headed to Memory Theory, their final period of the day. And as Freya's soft, light hand rested in his, Fletcher felt the strength of a brave, beautiful girl who had carried a great burden she never asked for.

Fletcher told her he didn't think she should talk to Dr. Sanders again (or any of the faculty) about her half-memory dreams—at least until they could figure things out.

She told him she agreed.

❖ ❖ ❖

After dinner and their mandatory study period, Ollie booked one of the study rooms in the library. To keep up appearances, the four lugged their textbooks to the small room, which was windowless save for the thin strip of glass on the door. Chase rolled the dry-erase board in front of this to obstruct the view of anyone outside the room.

"We've got some work to do," he said as if preparing troops for battle. He pulled his folded-up Cindy Crawford poster out of his backpack and laid it on the table. They huddled around it, inspecting it like a map.

"I think we should start with a timeline," Freya said, walking over to the board. She took one of the blue markers and drew a straight, horizontal line across the glossy surface. With flicks of her wrist, she evenly spaced tiny marks across the line.

"I was born on April 27, 1970," Chase said seriously.

Freya gave him a dry look.

"Right, yeah, no," he said. "Too far back."

They decided that the beginning of their timeline should start a couple years ago, in 1984, on March 4—the day Freya's father died. From there, they moved to last year. February 8, 1986. On this day, not only did Freya turn sixteen and have her first MeReader scan, it was also the day she had her first half-memory dream.

With these two dates on their timeline, they felt like they had a good starting point, so they began to chart out every significant event or observation that had led them to that exact moment. They used the notes Fletcher and Chase had already compiled on the back of his poster as a reference, but Freya and Ollie helped to fill in the gaps.

Freya rounded out their discussion by recounting the weird, troubling vision she had yesterday on the pier.

Fletcher spotted the similarity at once. He immediately told the girls about the morning he and Chase accidentally swapped memory tapes, and how the traumatic "trip" sounded similar to what Freya had just described.

Chase snapped his fingers. "I can't believe I didn't think of this at first, but that also reminds me of a rather . . . psychedelic experience I once had."

Ollie scolded him, accusing him of being insensitive.

"No, hear me out. Look, I'm not proud of this, but I might have participated in a few memory kaleidoscopes before."

"How am I just now hearing this?" Ollie said, apparently less concerned with the fact that Chase partook in illegal activity (mixing alcohol or drugs with artificial recall), and more offended that he never told her.

Fletcher leaned back in his wooden chair, thinking back to the time *he* was crazy enough to engage in a memory kaleidoscope. He was at a beach party at night, junior year. The kid who was throwing the party on his parents' property told everyone to bring their memory tapes and Restoreys. After they had consumed too much alcohol, they simultaneously queued up their memory tapes and pressed Play.

Artificial recall was a weird and unnatural experience on its own merits. Adding alcohol—or worse, hallucinogens—was especially . . . well . . . weird and unnatural.

Fletcher didn't remember much of his experience with memory kaleidoscoping, except there was a reason he'd only done it once: the memory he was artificially recalling started to vacillate in and out of focus, and images and voices bled into reality. Fletcher started slipping in and out of consciousness, watching a dog (or maybe it was a cat?) from his memory running around on the beach beside the bonfire.

He threw up twice afterward.

Anyway, the "trip" Freya described didn't sound anything like his experience with a memory kaleidoscope.

"LSD may or may not have been involved," Chase said of his experience. *Ah. There it is.* "I was at a wrap party for an indie feature that had just completed principal photography. I had just turned seventeen, but of course I wasn't telling my fellow actors that. Yeah. So. Anyway, *hallucination* doesn't even begin to describe what I felt, and until Freya described her latest vision, *plus* what Fletcher and I experienced when we mixed up our memory tapes . . . Well, the similarities are uncanny, guys."

Ollie raised a skeptical eyebrow at Freya. "You ever partake in a memory kaleidoscope or accidentally play back someone else's memory tape?"

Freya said no, she hadn't—on both counts.

Ollie continued, "Which means you're going to do one of those things in the future?"

"Um . . ."

"Can you tell the difference between your memories and your premonitions?" Fletcher asked her before she could answer Ollie. Freya closed her eyes and shook her head, appearing overwhelmed.

"I don't . . . I can't . . . I don't know, guys. They just pop into my head at random. From what I can tell, there's no rhyme or reason to them—"

"Except that there is!" Chase said, leaning across the square table. "You had a vision of you and Ollie in the woods, spying on Dean Mendelsohn and those MACE agents. And in your vision . . . or premonition . . . or whatever, the dean shone his flashlight on you. But you were able to avoid getting caught in real life!"

Freya opened her eyes, processing Chase's words. "Didn't Dr. Sanders mention something about that in class last week?" She pulled a notebook out from underneath her stack of textbooks and flipped through her notes. "Here! 'Some have postulated that the intense dreams we have are a training ground meant to prepare us for problem-solving in future dangerous situations.'"

Ollie swore loudly. "So, like, your visions are a defense mechanism?"

Slowly, Freya nodded. "Maybe."

Fletcher had another question. "Since these half-memory dreams started, how many of them have been premonitions, and how many of those have come to pass already?"

Freya looked down at her hands in her lap. "You know," she said, glancing up at him, "come to think of it, I'm pretty sure the vision of me and Ollie near the train tracks is the only . . . um . . . premonition I've ever had. Everything else has been a half memory."

"The jury's still out on the trippy one you had yesterday, though," Chase said. Freya nodded again.

Fletcher stood up and walked to the dry-erase board, reviewing the timeline with his hands in his pockets. He stared at the scribbles for a whole minute, not even sure what he was looking for until something clicked. It was so obvious that he was surprised no one had said it out loud yet: Freya hadn't had a premonition until arriving at Foxtail Academy. *Maybe* something here, on campus, triggered this "ability" in her.

Fletcher picked up the dry-erase marker and circled the Saturday everyone arrived and Freya had her first premonition.

Behind him, Ollie gasped, putting two and two together.

"Freya's first premonition happened after she arrived at Foxtail Academy," Fletcher said, drawing an arrow from that day to the day he'd found the train tracks in the woods behind the faculty housing. "And it was about a specific location on campus."

Chase whistled.

Fletcher capped the marker and turned around to face his friends. "That means everything seems to point back to the secret building beside the tracks."

One by one, Freya, Ollie, and then Chase gave Fletcher the same grim-faced expression. They all realized what Fletcher had realized— what *had* to be done in order to find answers.

Fletcher took his seat. "If we want to find out what Dean Mendelsohn's hiding . . . if we want to find out what happened to our missing classmates . . . if we want to find out what's *really* going on here with this trial and, maybe, how it's connected to Freya's half-memory dreams . . . then we have to break into that building in the woods."

❖ ❖ ❖

234

And thus began their elaborate, intricate plan.

Their first step was easy enough: determining what actually happened to Matthew Skipper and Allison James. Tuesday during lunch, they split into twos and tracked down the roommates, who both said Skipper's and Allison's belongings disappeared when they did, sometime in the night.

"It was definitely weird," Adam McCauley, one of the school prefects, told Fletcher and Chase by the vending machines in the Foxhole. "I went to bed Saturday night with a roommate, and woke up Sunday morning without one. When I asked Mr. Williams what happened, I fully expected him to give me the skinny. You know, prefect privilege and whatnot."

Chase made a gagging noise. Fletcher asked, "And what did Mr. Williams tell you?"

"Something about not being at liberty to disclose the details." Adam shrugged. "Be honest with you guys, I kinda think he's in the dark too."

This discovery proved to be very troubling.

"How'd Skipper seem the last time you saw him?" Chase asked, feeding a dollar bill into the soda machine and selecting a Mountain Dew.

"Super giddy," Adam said. "We ate breakfast together Saturday morning. He was planning on spending the whole day prepping the senior lounge for his first Movies and Memories meet-up. That dude gets more excited about movies than I do about *Dungeons and Drag—*"

"And that'll be all, nerd," Chase said, ushering Adam away. Reluctantly, he left and made his way back to his table in the dining hall. "'Prefect privilege.' Vomit."

"So the school just had Skipper's things cleared out while Adam was sleeping?" Fletcher leaned against the vending machine. "Why? Didn't they realize that would draw *so* much more attention to his absence?"

Chase loudly cracked open his Mountain Dew and took an obnoxious slurp. "Yeah. So much more attention."

The boys got a similar story from Freya and Ollie as they all headed toward the classrooms for third period.

"I was able to track down their home phone numbers," Ollie whispered. She and Freya had gone to the payphone behind the admissions office to try to contact the Skipper and James families.

"We got nothing but busy signals," Ollie told them. "And we called *multiple* times."

"Maybe Skipper and Allison were on the phone with each other?" Chase offered, chuckling nervously. "Sharing war stories about their food poisoning?"

Fletcher and Freya gave him a dark look.

"Yeah, no, you're right." He dropped his head. "That's not a good sign."

Freya suggested talking to Mr. Williams and just asking him point-blank if he knew what happened to their classmates. The rest of the group convinced her that was probably not a good idea; it could start getting around the faculty that they were asking questions. They couldn't have Dean Mendelsohn suspecting they were on to him. He had to keep believing they were oblivious teenagers who only wanted to make out in the woods.

And speaking of the dean . . .

❖ ❖ ❖

"The homework, the reading . . . it's a lot," Fletcher told Dean Mendelsohn in the hall outside his office. "I think maybe a mentorship is too much for my plate right now."

Fletcher had decided that his missing classmates changed everything. Where before, he believed getting close to the dean could offer intel and a possible glimpse behind the curtain, *now* he wanted to keep as much distance between himself and Dean Mendelsohn as possible.

Fletcher just couldn't erase the image in his mind of the dean overseeing the transfer of a body bag in the dead of night . . . a body bag that might've contained Skipper or Allison.

"I'm very disappointed to hear that," Dean Mendelsohn said simply.

And that was that.

Next, Fletcher and the group met at their Juniper Lake spot and set to work detailing their clandestine operation. If all four of them were going to sneak past the faculty housing at night without being seen, they had to choose the perfect window.

"The night of the Foxy Ladies dance," Ollie said. She hopped up from her seat on the fallen tree and joined Chase on the ground. He sat with his back to the lake, taking notes like a focused stenographer.

"That's actually perfect," Freya said, turning to Fletcher. They sat side by side on the fallen tree, talking in low voices even though they were far from campus and well outside of anyone's earshot.

It was Wednesday of their second week at school, after dinner and nearing dusk. Fireflies hung in the air around them, and ducks lazily paddled across the lake. Since Monday, the only thing the four had been doing during meals and between classes was brainstorming. "Judy Montgomery's flyer says the dance will be held in the Foxhole."

Chase stopped writing. "If there was some kind of diversion, the four of us could slip out through the kitchen. There's an exit that leads to the dumpsters."

"And from there it's a straight shot to the faculty housing," Fletcher said excitedly.

It was actually kind of perfect, only Ollie suddenly frowned.

"What is it?" Fletcher asked.

"The dance is in September." She absently scraped the ground with the heels of her shoes. "That's nearly four weeks away, and plenty of time for the dean to snatch up more of our classmates . . . or worse, one of us."

A long silence passed between them. She was right, of course. That *was* a very long time, and Fletcher wasn't sure they could afford to wait. Lives were potentially on the line.

"Did you try phoning Skipper's or Allison's families again?" Fletcher asked Ollie.

She sighed. Yes, she had, after breakfast, but, "The lines were still busy."

Fletcher swore loudly.

"Look." Freya released a weighty sigh. "Waiting that long is not ideal. But what other choice do we have? Sneaking out during the dance is our best shot at getting to that building without being caught."

Ollie looked away, unconvinced. Chase put his arm around her.

"This may sound a little cruel," Fletcher said, hoping to console Ollie, "but we have something neither Allison nor Skipper had. Each other. We stay close between now and then, don't let each other out of our sights, and pray for the best."

Eventually, Ollie summoned a small half smile.

Chase wrote down a few more things in his journal, then rose to his feet.

"Well, we should head back to the dorms so I can give Freya a crash course on my video camera in the common room."

Freya perked up. "Huh? Why?"

"Someone's going to need to videotape what we find in the dean's secret building. And I think that should be you."

27

FREYA IZQUIERDO

In high school, nothing spreads quicker than a rumor—not even mono. It's a universal truth about all high schools, boarding school or otherwise. And right now, the rumors about the disappearances of Matthew Skipper and Allison James are spreading faster than any contagion.

Which is exactly why Fletcher, Chase, Ollie, and I started them.

Here's what we figure: if the faculty catches wind of the kind of gossip surrounding our missing classmates, those responsible for their removal (namely the dean) will assume no one is really *that* bothered by our classmates' strange and inexplicable disappearance—or that anyone's close to figuring out the truth.

The rumors are tame at first, of course. Ollie starts one that suggests Allison's parents are getting a divorce, and they need her at home with her younger siblings while they sort out custody. ("Isn't that kind of harsh?" I ask her in the girls' bathroom, and she promptly says our ends justify the means. I see her point, kind of.) Regarding Skipper, the first story goes that he had a major allergic reaction to his lunch Saturday, so we add that he needed to be hospitalized for a couple of nights before eventually returning home.

Two somewhat believable stories, sure, except no one saw them leave campus. Add to this the fact that no one saw Skipper fall ill, or spoke to Allison before she vanished, and you have the perfect recipe for hearsay.

The rumors practically write themselves.

As I walk to class, I overhear an exchange between my classmates and smile:

"I heard Allison got caught smoking pot in the girls' bathroom and was *immediately* expelled."

"No way."

"Yup. And Ave Maria's the one who ratted her out. Apparently, Allison made out with Ave Maria's boyfriend, and that *really* pissed her off."

"Well, I heard that Skipper cussed out a teacher. Apparently he was trying to smuggle alcohol into the senior lounge for his little movie club thing."

"Skipper? *No!* He seemed like a nice kid."

"Right?"

Of course, we have our own theories about their disappearance and how it's connected to the Reflector trial.

Fletcher sets a hand-drawn map on the table in our stuffy library study room. "What if something went wrong with their Reflectors? Like, I dunno, a major malfunction that could've caused Memory Frontier some really bad press." He points to the part of his map that indicates where the secret building is. "So the dean had them taken here, where he could run a bunch of tests on them. Hence his mention of 'increasing the dosage.'"

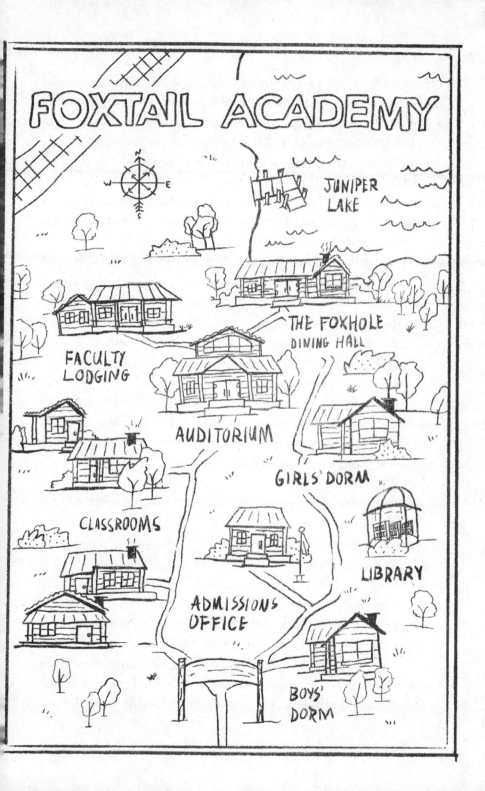

I shiver. "That's really disturbing."

"You saying you think they're *still* holed up there?" Chase asks, folding his arms across his chest.

"I dunno, maybe." Fletcher keeps his eyes on the map.

I ask the hard question: "So what about the dead body Ollie and I saw?"

Fletcher scratches his cheek. "You're right. I think until we find evidence that suggests otherwise, we may have to assume the dead body belongs to one of our classmates."

Ollie pulls a stick of gum out of her pocket and anxiously stuffs it into her mouth. We all watch her.

"What?" She balls up the wrapper and tosses it onto the table. "I'm trying to quit smoking."

"Proud of you, Ol. Now can I get a hit off your gum?"

"Why are you *so* gross?"

I pick up Fletcher's map, admiring the details. "You drew this?"

"Oh, yeah," he says coyly, blushing. "My grandfather's super into old maps. He has them framed and hung all over his house. Anyway, I just tried to make our Foxtail map like one of his."

"It's really good, Fletcher," I say.

"Thanks."

"We might just be dealing with an Occam's razor scenario," Ollie says, chewing her gum idly. "You know, the simplest explanation is the best one?"

"Which is?" Fletcher asks as I set his map down in the center of the table.

"Something along the lines of your theory. Allison and Skipper were taken to the building"—she taps the map with her index finger—"against their will so the dean could do who knows what to them."

"Okay, what about this." Chase rubs his hands together. "What if Memory Killer was actually cured years ago and somehow Skipper and Allison discovered this? Naturally, Dean Mendelsohn and

Memory Frontier can't have people knowing the truth, so he had them . . . taken care of."

Ollie blows a bubble with her gum, and after it pops she says, "Maybe . . . but what about the sophomore who went missing on day one? The one Freya heard about in the dining hall? Or, for that matter, disappearances we don't know about? They *all* learned this 'truth'?"

Chase leans his head to the side, visibly processing.

"Hold up," I say. "Don't the Memory Ghosts peddle conspiracies like that?"

Fletcher nods. "Conspirators picket outside Los Angeles City Hall almost weekly. My dad used to complain about them at the dinner table."

Ollie turns to me. "Pretty sure they also fervently believe Restoreys are a form of government overreach and control . . . a way to catalog and monitor people's secrets—"

"Those kinds of conspiracies are easily debunked." I think back to the guy at the police station who missed his artificial recall window and violently thrashed about. "If people just stopped artificial recall, eventually they'd forget everything and go crazy."

Fletcher looks a bit uncertain.

"Now that Fletcher and I are using our Reflectors at night," Chase says, collecting his thoughts as he goes, "I can say the whole process feels very . . . invasive. It makes me feel vulnerable."

That's difficult to hear. While the Reflector has been a gift to me, removing my need for artificial recall and granting me freedom, I can see Chase's point.

"Is there a better way to plumb the depths of people's minds?" Chase collapses into his chair, visibly overtaken with his theory. "Require every soul in America to hook up to this little device while we sleep . . . tell us we have to for our own good."

The study room falls silent.

Chase is right about one thing: we are at our most vulnerable when we sleep . . . when we dream.

In a world where memories are like currency, dreams can be a complicated business.

My dad's words have echoed in my head for years, following me wherever I go, reminding me to question everything I've been told about memory loss. Now I believe it was his warning to me, and I need to take it more seriously. Chase has me questioning why Memory Frontier might have been deliberate about synthesizing their technology with sleep.

If our memories can be mined while we sleep, it stands to reason that false ones could be planted too . . .

"No," I finally say, trying to be the voice of reason—trying to convince myself as much as them. But my voice quivers. "That kind of cover-up would involve hundreds, maybe *thousands* of people. Someone would definitely leak the secret. Everybody talks eventually."

No one says anything for whole minutes, until finally Fletcher says, his voice incredibly distant-sounding, "Unless those willing to speak up are . . . silenced."

I immediately infer his meaning: my dad and the question mark surrounding his death. I stare at one of the electrical outlets on the wall, just to look away from the table.

Ollie says, "In other news, I wasn't able to find out anything about the train tracks."

"What do you mean?" Fletcher asks, sitting up in his seat.

"Well, so, I looked up the Federal Railroad Administration phone number in the Yellow Pages and called their offices. When I finally got through to someone and provided the location of campus, they said there weren't any routes within *thirty* miles of here."

Chase snorts. "That's impossible. Three out of the four of us have seen the train tracks."

"Something about federal laws preventing construction of railroad tracks this close to Land Between the Lakes." Ollie shrugs.

Fletcher, Chase, and I exchange worried glances.

"What?" Ollie says, one eyebrow cocked. "The dean obviously had the route scrubbed from public record."

"Which means," Chase says, pale as a ghost, "whatever Memory Frontier has Dean Mendelsohn doing, they've also paid the federal government to look the other way."

Until now, we had just sort of assumed the MACE agents who delivered that mysterious cargo were doing some kind of "off the books" favor. Dean Mendelsohn did help found MACE after all, according to Fletcher.

Hearing that the Federal Railroad Administration is lying about the train tracks is a whole new level of disturbing.

I spend the next few free periods with Chase in the common room between the boys' and girls' dormitories, learning everything I possibly can about his Sylvania VHS camera. Handling the camera feels immediately empowering, and it helps me compartmentalize the nightmare-inducing conspiracies we discussed the other day.

For now, at least.

When Chase first brought out his black case, he set it on the end table between our chairs and opened it slowly. This big reveal might as well have been accompanied by a burst of yellow light and a chorus of singing angels.

Hello, old friend, I thought with a trembling smile.

I cannot overstate just how good it felt to have a video camera on my shoulder again, pressed up against the side of my face. My inner eye, which had been shut for weeks, now—blessedly—reopened.

"You've got a good eye for composition!" Chase plays back the footage I captured of him unloading the contents of his backpack onto the carpeted floor. "Or maybe it's just the subject you filmed . . . Man, that is definitely my good side."

I take his video camera back and tell him I want to practice the zooming toggle.

He smiles. "You're pretty passionate about this."

I remount the camera on my shoulder. "Yeah, I guess I am, huh?"

Before any of us realizes it, September is upon us, and with it comes the reddening and yellowing of the leaves. All at once the mornings are marked by wet grass, crisp air, and the swaying of colorful tree branches. It's a beautiful sight, breathtaking, even, except that it's overshadowed by the disappearance of two more classmates.

"No one's seen her in two days," Chase says of Samantha Ricci over breakfast in the dining hall one morning, keeping his voice just barely above a whisper. The other student who went missing was a sophomore named Philip Bancroft. Both had last been seen on Thursday at dinner. Friday, no one spotted them in their classes or anywhere else all day. Mr. Williams even got on the intercom before dinner to offer some BS story about how they'd gotten really bad exposure to poison ivy and needed immediate medical care, then he warned students against straying too far into the woods.

With this many students now missing—five that we knew of—I guess the faculty figured they needed to get in front of the narrative.

On the first Saturday in September we camp out in the senior lounge on the couches beside the TV. With the Foxy Ladies dance now just one week away, things are starting to get real. Thankfully, I haven't had another half-memory dream (or premonition?) since the weird, abstract vision I had on the pier. This has given me a clear head and a sharp eye; I've mostly been on top of my assignments and reading, producing a respectable 3.1 GPA. With classes under control, I've been able to focus on our objective too.

"We knew this might happen," Fletcher says of the latest disappearances. "We knew the risk when we decided to wait until the dance."

"Yeah," Ollie says, propping her feet up on the coffee table. "It just . . . sucks."

We all nod. Anyone looking in our direction right now might peg us as a sad, depressed bunch.

"Hey, so I've been thinking," Chase says, slapping his knees and then standing up. He walks in front of the TV, which is playing *The Goonies* on mute, and faces us. "We need a code name for our group. Something badass with, like, an espionage twist."

"Oh!" Ollie says. "The Fantastic Four!"

Chase points at her. "Love where your head's at, Ol, but that's already a comic. Anyone else?"

"Fearless Four," Fletcher offers. I kind of like it, but Chase screws up his face like he's just swallowed something sour.

"If we have to say we're fearless, then maybe we're not," he says. Fletcher rolls his eyes. "What else?"

We all glance up at the ceiling, quietly trying to brainstorm a suitable name. After only a few minutes, my lightbulb turns on.

"I've got it," I say casually. "We're the Forgotten Four."

Chase smiles darkly. "*Now* you're talking."

"Retrieval failure," Dr. Sanders says to the class, writing these two words on the dry-erase board and then scoring the surface with a long, thick underline. "This occurs when certain information contained in your long-term memory bank cannot be accessed even though it still exists. This happens due to an absence of retrieval cues, which are simple things like a location, smells, your mood, and so on."

On the Friday before the dance, Dr. Sanders's lecture proves to be both heady and intriguing. As always, my pencil flies across my college-ruled paper as I transcribe this new data as fast as my wrist can go. Before long, my thumb and index finger start to tingle.

"Here's an example of a retrieval failure," Dr. Sanders says, flipping the marker in her hand before setting it down. "You walk to your locker to get a piece of paper and then suddenly forget what you were going to your locker for. We've all been there, right? It's annoying and, in most cases, nothing more than a setback. Here's what's interesting, though: when you go back to the classroom and sit down at your desk, your surroundings act as that retrieval cue, and the assignment written on the board reminds you *why* you left in the first place—to get that piece of paper.

"Now, here's where we distinguish the difference between retrieval failure and the invisible enemy we all face: Memory Killer." I sit up in my chair and lean in. "Memories ravaged by Memory Killer are gone forever, even if you have all the retrieval cues in the world. But"—she points to a poster on her wall, which has a diagram of the latest-model MeReader—"the technology in the memory reader was constructed to enhance lingering retrieval cues in our subconscious *before* Memory Killer has its way with them. This makes it possible to pinpoint vulnerable memories and then imprint them onto tapes."

I write all this down, word for word. Now that Reflectors are here, this information may seem moot. Restoreys will be antiques before long. But Dr. Sanders is a wealth of knowledge when it comes to Memory Frontier, and I'm hoping something she discusses in her class proves helpful to the Forgotten Four.

She writes some page numbers on the board. "Now, how's this for a retrieval cue? This weekend's required reading is pages 77 through 151 in *The Art of Memory*."

Groans fill the classroom.

After class, Dr. Sanders stops me before I can sneak away. "I keep meaning to check on you." She sounds concerned. "But you've truly mastered your disappearing act."

"Sorry, yeah, classes have been a lot." It isn't completely untrue.

"I see." We stand in the doorway of her classroom, and I can clearly see Fletcher, Ollie, and Chase in my peripheral vision. They walk away at a snail's pace, no doubt trying to catch some of my conversation with Dr. Sanders.

She closes the door to her classroom and locks it. "I wonder if you might accompany me on the walk to my office?"

"Oh, um . . ." I scramble for an excuse.

She takes off her heels, carries them in one hand, and sets off across the grass barefoot. I sigh, then follow.

"I'll never understand why teachers need both a classroom *and* an office," she says once I stride up beside her. "I could just as easily grade papers and review my lectures in the classroom! Anyway, I've decided to view my office as something of a getaway. A place where I can read and write and think without a bunch of empty desks staring at me."

"Makes sense."

"I thought so too." I hear her smile. "So, Freya, I have a theory about the genesis of your half-memory dreams."

"Oh. You do?" My intrigue betrays me; I agreed not to talk to Dr. Sanders about this anymore, especially considering she's the only teacher at Foxtail Academy employed by Memory Frontier before the trial began. Whatever's going on behind the scenes with the Reflectors, I know Dr. Sanders is at least tangentially involved. And is she *really* the dean's daughter? Fletcher and Chase are convinced they heard her refer to him as such the night they snuck out.

But talking with a cognitive psychologist about what's happening to me is just too alluring to pass up.

We merge off the grass and onto the sidewalk, the admissions building coming into view. "With your permission I'd like to have you tested for eidetic memory."

"Er . . . like *photographic* memory?"

"Well, sort of."

I'm still confused. "When I had my first MeReader scan, I was diagnosed with hyper-degenerate memory loss." I show her my two-quarter mark. "See? Sorry, but how can degens have photographic memory?"

Dr. Sanders chuckles. "A valid point. However, I should explain something. While the terms *eidetic memory* and *photographic memory* are often used interchangeably, the former is actually something much different than being able to recall a certain image in awesome detail. Eidetic memory is a sort of strange and beautiful phenomenon where someone recalls an image or sound with such . . . with such *fervor* . . . that it actually appears as if that image or sound is being actively perceived. Does that make sense?"

My head spins a bit. "So . . . that person remembers a thing so vividly their brain thinks it's happening in real time?"

She nods. "They describe seeing an afterimage right before their eyes. Now, it's anomalous, to be sure, but I've actually studied eide-tikers, as they're called."

"Yeah, okay, but what does that have to do with my"—I lower my voice and look around—"with my half-memory dreams?"

We arrive outside the admissions building and the faculty offices. "Well, I'm still developing my theory. Suffice to say, getting you tested would either rule this out or potentially get us closer to answering *why* this has been happening to you."

28

FLETCHER COHEN

Freya caught up as the others walked through the woods to their secret spot. Red, orange, and yellow leaves rained down around them in the soft rush of a cool autumn breeze.

"What did she want?"

"She drilled me about my half-memory dreams." Freya sounded nervous. "I just kind of downplayed it as much as I could."

"Good," Ollie said before Fletcher could pry, coming up beside them and locking arms with Freya. "Dr. Sanders might be well intentioned, but let's not forget she reports to Memory Frontier."

Fletcher nodded, watching Freya's profile. She grunted, her version of a yes, and didn't say anything further as they navigated the lake's slippery edge like four tightrope performers.

JULIAN R. VACA

"Itineraries," Chase said, handing each one of them a sheet of paper with a handwritten order of events for tomorrow night's dance. Fletcher, Freya, and Ollie sat on the fallen tree while Chase paced, proudly holding his own copy.

"So we arrive at the Foxhole around seven thirty," Chase said, going down the list. "Fashionably late, of course."

"Naturally," Ollie said.

"Judy Montgomery tells me our beloved teachers and dean will be acting as chaperones," Chase continued. "And they'll likely be positioned at three of the Foxhole's four major exits. The fourth, of course, is our means of escape—through the kitchen and out the back.

"At precisely 8:15, Fletcher will set off the first phase of our diversion."

Fletcher cleared his throat. "Right. I'll spike the punch bowls."

"Now, be generous with the liquor, young Fletcher," Chase said, playing up the condescension. "Ask yourself: Am I making a drink that I could handle, or one that Chase Hall could handle?"

Fletcher rolled his eyes.

"Don't let him fool you," Ollie said apathetically. "I've seen this guy puke after one wine cooler."

"Moving on!" Chase declared. "Once the punch bowls have been spiked with a considerable amount of vodka, Freya and Ollie will slip DJ and emcee Adam McCauley a very specific song request."

"'Gimme Shelter' by the Rolling Stones," Freya said, nodding.

"An excellent choice, Freya," Chase said.

"Chase, *you* picked—"

"Moving on! This song will serve as our countdown. With the drinks spiked and our countdown underway, I will begin a dance-off, challenging our peers with awe-inspiring dance moves that will cement my legacy at Foxtail Academy. It'll be the kind of dance they write about in songs and poems . . . a sort of grand, mythos-building

252

display that will have every girl pining for my attention. Even Dr. Sanders will—"

Ollie snorted. "You? Dance? You're not *that* good of an actor."

"And finally!" Chase shouted, lowering his itinerary. "As the dancing catches on and the place goes rowdy, Fletcher will shout from within the crowd . . ."

". . . 'Hey, someone spiked the punch.'"

"With more bravado, please. Whatever. We'll work on that later. Anyway, once that happens, chaos will ensue. The teachers will frantically work to sort everything out."

"And we sneak out through the kitchen." Freya grinned. "Completely unnoticed."

"Bingo." Chase winked. "In Fletcher's duffel, which we'll hide beneath the dumpsters ahead of time, we'll have our change of clothes, my camera, some flashlights, and the bolt cutters I swiped from the groundskeepers. If everything goes according to plan, we'll be in the woods and headed toward the building no later than nine."

Fletcher reviewed Chase's itinerary a couple more times. *Wow. In just over twelve hours, we'll finally be able to get to the bottom of what's really going on.*

"Now, there is one more matter to discuss." Chase folded his itinerary and pocketed it. "Who we're going to take with us to the dance."

"We're going as a group, numbskull," Ollie said distractedly, hopping off the fallen tree.

"Sure, we could do that," Chase agreed. "But if we want to draw the least amount of attention to ourselves, I think we should pair up, like the rest of the school."

"That's actually not a bad idea," Freya said.

Fletcher panicked. *She really thinks so? Does that mean I should formally ask her to the dance?* He felt himself getting hot despite the brisk fall air.

"Good, I'm glad you agree," Chase told her. "Because I think you and I should go together."

Freya tilted her chin down and arched her eyebrows. Fletcher laughed, then abruptly caught himself.

"Sure," Chase said, shrugging. "Why not? I crashed Ollie's junior prom last spring. She can tell you firsthand I'm an unforgettable date."

"You pronounced *forgettable* wrong," Ollie muttered.

"Unless, of course"—Chase looked at Fletcher—"*you* were going to ask Freya."

Fletcher swallowed. He could feel Freya's soft eyes falling on him expectantly. So, fittingly, he panicked some more. He probably froze for only a few seconds, but it was more than enough time to miscommunicate disinterest to Freya.

"I'd *love* to go with you, Chase," she said.

"Perfect!"

Fletcher swallowed a couple more times to get rid of the dryness in his mouth. "So, um, Ollie. We can go? Like, together?"

She sighed. "You sure know how to sweep a girl off her feet, Fletcher."

Saturday evening brought an especially cloudy and gray sky, one that threatened to crack open and release a vicious torrent at any moment.

Fletcher couldn't help but worry it was a harbinger.

He and Chase walked into the Foxhole together at exactly half past seven, dressed to the nines in their thrift store finds.

"These pants are riding up," Chase said, trying to discreetly adjust himself. "Are your pants riding up?"

But Fletcher only barely listened to him as he scanned the mess-hall-turned-music-venue for Freya. He admired the Foxhole's impressive transformation. All of the tables had been collapsed and pushed to the walls, opening up a makeshift dance floor in the center of the dining hall. Judy Montgomery, the self-appointed events lead, had constructed mural set pieces and lined the walls with them. The murals included paintings of Santana, Janice Joplin, Johnny Winter, and so many more. Flower strands hung from the high ceiling with large painted signs that read PEACE AND LOVE and MAKE LOVE NOT WAR. Currently, none of their peers were dancing, and instead mingled and drank on the outskirts of the dance floor.

Adam McCauley stood on a small stage erected where the food lines usually were, manning the music controls beside a stack of loudspeakers. Creedence Clearwater Revival's "Up Around the Bend" currently played.

Judy left a group of shy-looking freshmen and approached Fletcher and Chase. "Think I did okay?" she said over the music. She had straightened her hair and wore a loose blouse, leather vest, and beaded necklace—looking every bit the part of a Woodstock concertgoer.

"Judy, this is . . . this is wow," Chase replied, soaking it in.

"I'm good with wow." She giggled. "Back home, I planned just about every major school function since I was a sophomore."

"I can see why," Fletcher said, turning in a circle. "This is incredible."

"C'mon, I'll get you a drink." She took Chase's hand and then whisked him away. As she did, the lighting dimmed, and Adam faded out the song and seamlessly brought up "California Dreamin'" by the Mamas and the Papas.

Fletcher finally spotted Freya.

She emerged from the girls' bathroom with Ollie in tow, and Fletcher felt his breathing stutter. She wore a slight amount of makeup—dark eyeliner, minimal blush—and feather earrings that drew his eyes toward her long, curvy neck. Her hair, which Fletcher was used to seeing in a high bun, flowed down past her round shoulders like a train on a dress. And speaking of dress, Freya wore the floral one and white go-go boots she had bought at the mall.

She and Ollie noticed him. As they approached, the blue and red lights flickered across Freya's face, and Fletcher continued to admire her dreamily.

Chase returned, drink in hand. "Man," he whispered of Freya. He downed his punch in one gulp and then handed Fletcher his empty cup. "Take notes." Chase walked off and met them halfway, performed a dumb curtsy, then led Freya onto the dance floor. With the ice now broken, a handful of other couples made for the dance floor, too, and then even more slowly followed suit.

"You could've asked her, you know," Ollie said, chuckling.

"Hmm?" He faced Ollie, who was dolled up beautifully in her dress and boots. Her voluminous hair was strikingly similar to how Elizabeth Taylor might have styled it back in her heyday.

Ollie gave Fletcher quite the annoyed look. She grabbed his hand and dragged him onto the dance floor, where they picked a spot and started moving their hips and shoulders to the music. They'd only been dancing for a few seconds, though, when Ollie's expression softened.

"What?" Fletcher felt around his cheeks. "Do I have shaving cream on my face?"

Ollie continued to stare at him wordlessly.

And then it clicked: his eyes were gray.

Fletcher sighed. "It'll pass, Ollie. C'mon—I've found that changing the subject helps it pass quicker."

Ollie nodded and resumed dancing. "Okay, so, how come you didn't just ask her?"

Fletcher smirked. "Is this a date or an interview?"

"It's definitely not a date." She shoved his chest playfully. "So. You going to tell me or not?"

"I . . . I don't know what to tell you. I froze."

Ollie smiled. "Well, Mr. Freeze, you could be dancing with her instead of pity dancing with me."

"Okay, first of all, this isn't pity. If you hadn't agreed to come with me as my date, you could have fallen back on any of the guys who've been courting you since last month. I count myself lucky you agreed."

"You're sweet. Adam McCauley *was* getting pretty insistent this week." They both glanced over at the stage, where Adam—who was staring in their direction—flinched and then pretended to leaf through his records.

Ollie flushed.

"And second of all"—Fletcher turned back to her—"*Mr. Freeze? Fantastic Four?* Are you secretly a comic-book geek?"

Ollie's face hardened. "Speak of this to anyone and I will end you."

"Your secret's safe with me," he replied, and then they both laughed. "Okay, so, now it's my turn to ask—"

Adam cut through the loudspeakers, doing his best radio DJ voice: "All right, Foxtail, now we're rewinding the tape to 1961 with an all-time perennial classic."

After a record-scratching noise, Ben E. King's "Stand by Me" started to play. Everyone assumed the slow-dance position, including Fletcher and Ollie.

"That was smooth," he said. "Picking a slow song to give the illusion that he doesn't care who you dance with. Give Adam major points there."

Ollie blushed again. "You think? Huh. Well, anyway, what was your question?"

"You and Chase. What's going on there?"

"Ah." She smiled innocently before leaning her head against his shoulder. "Chase doesn't see me that way. It's just as well. We've been best friends since, like, seventh grade."

"Okay, but do *you* see him that way?"

"Hmm. You know, maybe. I dunno. Chase is very attractive, funny, confident, and sweeter than he lets on."

"Great, so Freya's falling in love with him right about . . . *now*."

Ollie smiled against his arm. "Maybe at one point I had the hots for him, sure, but Chase and I will always be friends. That's it. I think I remind him too much of his cousin."

"Huh?"

"His cousin. Lyvia. The one who died when he was twelve. Didn't he tell you about her?"

Fletcher racked his brain for memories of any mention of Chase's cousin. Just as he began to wonder if he'd lost something to Memory Killer, something that maybe slipped past the Reflector, the alarm on his watch started to beep.

"Go-time," Ollie whispered.

29

FREYA IZQUIERDO

Chase and I slow dance, his hands on my hips.

"There he goes," I say when Fletcher breaks away from Ollie. As he walks toward the punch bowls, he waves nonchalantly to Mr. Williams, who sports a fake hippie wig and baggy clothes. Then, as Fletcher moves closer to the tables, doing his best to remain calm, cool, and collected, he discreetly pulls a silver flask from his pocket.

"I lent him that, you know. The flask."

"I have no doubt that you did." I grin. "But is one flask of liquor enough for all that punch?"

"Wait for it . . . ," he mutters, squinting at Fletcher. After emptying the flask into the bowl, Fletcher pulls out a *second* flask. "Lent him that one too."

That definitely looks like it'll do the trick. I laugh inwardly.

Chase gestures for Ollie to come over. "It sounds like this song is winding down. Plus, I can't have you trying to kiss me. It would crush Fletcher."

I roll my eyes as Ollie approaches. "You ready?"

"Yeah," I say, breaking away from Chase. "Let's go."

Together, she and I walk across the dance floor, and Adam McCauley visibly lights up as he sees Ollie moving toward him. "You'd better do the talking," I say in her ear, to which she shrugs, pretending that'd be no big deal.

Before we reach the stage, Ave Maria slides in front of us—halting us in our tracks. She wears a giraffe-print jacket over her lacy black dress, doing her best Mrs. Robinson impression. I gotta hand it to her: she looks pretty stunning in her Hollywood hairdo and makeup.

"What do *you* want?" Ollie says.

Ave Maria replaces her haughty face with an uncharacteristically soft one. "I . . . I want to say sorry."

I give her an expressionless look. "Sure you do."

"No, I'm serious. Look, ever since Allison disappeared, I've been looking over my shoulder everywhere I go. I know what I said at the kickoff bonfire was cruel—"

"It was racist . . . *very* racist," Ollie says, almost shouting.

"And I feel awful." At least she's earnest. "Honestly. I just wanted to clear the air in case, well, in case I never get the chance to."

Ollie and I exchange a skeptical glance.

"Thank you for your time," Ollie says, taking my hand and leading me past Ave Maria.

"I've seen you guys in your secret planning committees in the library," she says to our backs. Slowly, we turn back around. "It's pretty obvious you're doing more than studying. If you've got something in the works, I want to help. For Allison's sake."

I open my mouth to say something, but Ave Maria quickly adds, "You don't have to give me an answer right now. I get it if you'll always hate me. I just thought I'd offer. Sorry, guys." She crosses the dance floor toward the drink tables.

"How's that for a plot twist," Ollie says as we watch Ave Maria go.

"Do we trust her?" I ask. "She actually sounded pretty sincere."

"I don't want to," Ollie confesses. "Which probably means we should at least consider it."

Up to this point, I haven't had a lot of nerves surrounding our big night. Never mind that we've been planning this for weeks; there have just been so many things vying for my attention. Between classes, a mountain of required reading, tossing around theories about why our classmates are vanishing, *and* getting everything in order for tonight, it's a wonder I've had time to breathe, much less stress.

And yet, as the electric guitar in "Gimme Shelter" starts to reverberate in the Foxhole, my anxiety stirs as if awoken from a deep sleep.

"Look alive," I say as our classmates begin to shout Chase's name. He has made his way to the center of the dance floor, where he's currently revving up his audience with a scrappy attempt at a moonwalk. We form a large, crowded circle around him, clapping and laughing as he sways his hips, shakes his shoulders, and belts the lyrics along with Mick Jagger. Chase's improvised dance isn't half bad, I decide. Lucas Childs—one of our classmates from Memory Theory—slips into the circle.

He looks around shyly before facing Chase, who playfully taunts him with a wave of his fingers. Lucas nods once, then stuns us all by dropping to the floor and break-dancing. He handles himself with poise and control—spinning on his back, flipping to his feet, and slicing his arms through the air. The dance may not match the Rolling Stones' song at all, but it's still an utter joy to behold.

Fletcher appears at my side. "Holy smokes. Is that . . . is that *Lucas?*"

I laugh, nodding. Chase, not to be upstaged, immediately twirls on his heel and pulls out all the stops: he starts with the "Y.M.C.A." dance and then moves in and out of other iconic moves—threading them together seamlessly before capping it off with a near-perfect visual recital of "Stayin' Alive." It's like Chase and Lucas are both auditioning for the *Breakin'* sequel and, before long, the entire building is chanting their names—all while they both do their best to sing along with Mick Jagger.

It's altogether weird and entertaining.

"You'd better hurry," I tell Fletcher, finding myself out of breath from just watching the back-and-forth dancing. "I'm not sure how many more moves Chase has up his sleeves!"

Fletcher laughs, squeezes my arm, and then fades into the crowd. A few seconds later, once he's completely out of sight, I hear him scream, "Someone spiked the punch!" and then madness follows.

Every single student darts toward the drink tables like a mob storming a fortress. The teachers, led by the dean and Mr. Williams, hold out their hands and try to contain the situation, but their attempts are futile. The music's too loud. Our peers are too riled up.

It's pure anarchy as everyone messily serves themselves heaping portions of punch and gulps it down. One of the tables gets toppled over, knocking an ornate bowl onto the floor and shattering it. Amid the frenzy, I manage to spot Judy Montgomery, who looks like she's about to cry—an artist watching her art being crushed beneath a stampede.

"C'mon!" Fletcher shouts, taking my hand. I giggle stupidly as he tears me away from the scene. We run through the swinging kitchen doors on Chase's and Ollie's heels; behind us, it sounds like our classmates are all-out rioting in the dining hall.

Chase bumps into the industrial oven and almost trips over his feet. He and Ollie burst into laughter as she braces him clumsily.

"Hey," I say once we catch up. "I thought Travolta was overrated?"

Chase unlocks the kitchen door and flings it open. The breezy night air instantly greets us. "I said his *movies* were overrated." We spill outside. "But John? John's a national treasure."

❖ ❖ ❖

I tie my sneakers with a double knot, something I've done for as long as I can remember, then Fletcher shouts from the other side of the dumpsters, "You ladies good?"

Ollie and I tell the boys we are, and they appear a second later.

"Here," Chase says, handing me his video camera. "It's got a blank VHS tape ready to go. Might be good to start taping when we're in the woods, just in case we see something."

I nod and mount the camera on my shoulder, feeling taller with the recording equipment at my fingertips.

Finally. We're finally *going to blow the lid off whatever Dean Mendelsohn is hiding.*

Ollie stuffs our dresses and boots into Fletcher's duffel and hands it to him. He adds his and Chase's clothes, zips it shut, then slides it underneath one of the dumpsters for us to retrieve in the morning. Fletcher now wears a pair of black jeans and a black sweatshirt. I catch myself staring at him as he hands Chase the bolt cutters and Ollie a Maglite.

"Everything okay?" he whispers, meeting my eyes.

"Just trying to figure out why you didn't ask me to dance," I say, winking at him in the dark.

"Guys, this is *hardly* the time for a lovers' quarrel," Chase moans. "You ready or what?"

We all nod and put our hands in the middle, stacking them on top of one another. Fletcher and I steal a quick glance.

"Forgotten Four," Ollie says, blowing a bubble with her gum and then flashing a massive grin. "We're forgotten . . . not forgetful."

We raise our hands toward the cloudy sky and dart off in the dark toward the faculty housing.

Knowing that just about every soul on campus is still in the Foxhole—leaving us totally and completely alone in the blackening forest—is at once liberating and terrifying. Terrifying, because I feel completely lost as we cut through the woods, unsure how we're supposed to find the train tracks without directions or milestones to guide us. It's unsettling at best and disorienting at worst.

But Fletcher seems confident.

"This way," he whispers over his shoulder. "We're getting close. I can feel it."

Ollie, who shines her bright flashlight at our feet, wears a look of apprehension. And she actually jumps when an owl hoots overhead. Chase clutches the bolt cutters, holding them out slightly in front of him like he's wielding a weapon.

No matter how profoundly intimidating these dark, shadowy woods are, no matter how lost we may feel in a maze of naked trees, we're on a mission, and there's no turning back now.

At the half hour mark, things start to feel bleak. We've stopped jogging twice now so Fletcher (the only one among us to have seen the train tracks during daylight) can scan our surroundings and try to get his bearings straight.

If he has no idea where he's leading us, he doesn't say this aloud.

"C'mon," he announces both times, waving us along. "It's just up this way."

We forge ahead in the nighttime with no actual sense of direction. In fact, my heart skips a beat when I realize we could be going in circles.

The trees all look so similar in the evening, especially when they've shed nearly half their leaves, and I can't help but notice imprints in the darkness—what look like faces *in* the trees, open-mouthed expressions of frozen despair—as we stumble across the dry, crunchy leaves toward a destination just out of reach.

We're almost there. I pray to God it's true. *We're almost—*

"There!" Chase points with his bolt cutters. We all perk up and see, with giant relief, the border to the clearing. And beyond the twisty trees—beyond the roots that jut out of the ground like bent fingers—lie the thick steel train tracks.

Ollie and I sigh, almost in unison.

I click on Chase's camera, press Record, and peer through the viewfinder, keeping both eyes open. No stars shine, no moon. It's so dark that Ollie's flashlight beam seems as bright as a penetrating ray of sunlight.

We leap over the roots one at a time—Fletcher at the head, Chase at the rear—and once I'm in the clearing I zoom in on the train tracks. Slowly, I pan the camera left to right, the darkness so dense my footage is nothing but digital noise.

"Here, shine your light over here," I tell Ollie. She does, and I follow her beam across the expansive tracks.

"This isn't an official stop," Chase notes, looking around. "See? There's no flags or lights or anything."

We all nod.

"Guys, look," Fletcher says. I whip my camera in the direction he's pointing. It's the side of the white cinderblock building. It's windowless. Two stories. And most of it is tucked back into the trees, where one side of the small clearing ends. Even in the dark of night, we can tell the building is relatively new, yet the way it's positioned in the forest—like some ancient ruins partially concealed underneath old-growth trees—gives it the illusion of having been here for centuries.

"You're getting this, right?" Chase says. I flinch as I realize I lowered his camera to marvel at the building. Quickly, I remount the camera and double-check that it's still rolling. I lightly toggle the zoom button forward, tilting up from the ground and to the flat roof.

"It looks like a small hangar," Ollie whispers. "But where are the doors?"

"Guess we'd better find out," Fletcher says. He leaves the gravel mound beside the train tracks and makes off toward the building, walking with his shoulders hunched, like someone trying to avoid cobwebs in a basement.

Ollie trails after him, shining her light in a sweeping motion in front of them. I follow, doing my best to follow the beam with my camera, while Chase keeps to the back of the line.

"This place could *not* be creepier if it tried," he says. I hear genuine fear in his trembling voice, which consoles me.

I'm not the only one who's scared.

Ever so quietly and carefully, we reenter the woods and begin to circle the cinderblock building. But leaves and dry twigs snap beneath our shoes like bombs detonating in a minefield. If anyone's inside, they definitely hear us approaching. Yet not a single external light flicks on, nor do we hear any other sounds. Finally, we come to the other side of the rectangular structure, where an enormous sliding door is padlocked shut.

I pan the camera across this side of the building. It's covered in vines and, much like the side that faces the train tracks, doesn't have a single window.

"You're up, Chase," Fletcher says, signaling toward the hefty padlock. Chase nods. He joins Fletcher at the sliding door, lines up the beak-shaped blades of the bolt cutters around the lock, then squeezes the long handles together with a grunt. There's a soft *clink!* and then Fletcher catches the padlock before it hits the ground. Chase steps back as Ollie shines her flashlight on the sliding-door handle, which Fletcher grabs with both hands. I take a step back and zoom the camera out, getting as wide a shot as possible. My heart thrums in my chest like it's trying to break out, and it takes a lot of concentration to hold the camera steady.

Fletcher sucks in a deep breath, plants his feet firmly on the ground, then starts to drag the heavy door open. I'm focusing the viewfinder on the sliver of the darkened interior when a voice behind us says, "Well, now, isn't this curious?"

30

FLETCHER COHEN

Fletcher let go of the handle and raised his hands as if staring down the barrel of a police officer's gun. Ollie spun, and her flashlight beam fell on Dean Mendelsohn—who clutched a lantern in the air—and Ave Maria.

Fletcher ground his teeth. To have made it this far only to get caught outside the building was demoralizing, but to see that Ave Maria had ratted on them was infuriating. Fletcher saw her deep-red lips twist into a smile, partial lantern light spilling across her porcelain-smooth face. Fletcher lowered his hands, clenching them into tight fists at his sides.

"When Ms. Sinclair informed me you four had snuck away from the dance," the dean said, gesturing to Ave Maria, "I can't say I was surprised. But to see you've found your way to my facility is quite impressive."

Fletcher walked to Freya's side and, to her credit, she kept the camera rolling. Chase and Ollie joined Fletcher, and they formed a line, not unlike soldiers falling into rank on a battlefield. Fletcher hardened his face, bracing for punishment as the dean and his snitch stared back.

This standoff drew out for an uncomfortably long minute, Dean Mendelsohn's eyes shifting toward each one of them. Ave Maria folded her arms across her chest, smug as ever.

"Well, we might as well head inside," the dean said, walking right past the four with his lantern aloft. Ave Maria, who was left in the shadows, gasped.

Fletcher and the group watched as the dean grabbed the sliding-door handle with his free hand and walked it open. He entered the dark void of the building, his bubble of flickering light illuminating nothing except the cement floor.

Cautiously, Fletcher, Freya, Chase, and Ollie approached the threshold, and as soon as they did, Dean Mendelsohn flipped the light switch on. Long, cylindrical work lights buzzed overhead, casting the inside of the massive facility in a green, flickering glow.

"What in the world?" Ollie muttered, covering her mouth with her free hand.

At the middle of the facility was an open reel-to-reel tape machine. The black and gray device was easily seven feet tall, with sound meters, faders, knobs, lights, and four pairs of white reels. Behind the tape machine were multiple wide tables bearing boxy computers and keyboards. It reminded Fletcher of pictures he'd seen of the NASA control center, a place where scientists observed high-stakes missions. To their left Fletcher counted four doors. A bulkhead light, the kind of nautical-looking fixture he'd seen on boats, hung above each.

But the strangest thing about this place wasn't the giant reel-to-reel tape machine, the rows of computers and monitors, or the unmarked doors. It was the two reclined chairs on either side of the tape machine. Both of the sterile seats had a headrest and an extended footrest, looking very similar to the chairs Fletcher stretched out in when wearing a MeReader.

"What is this place?" Freya said, still filming. Fletcher sensed Ave Maria walk up beside him, her jaw hanging open as far as it would go. Chase was the first one to step into the building, and Ollie instinctively reached for his hand. She missed him by an inch.

"Chase!" she whisper-screamed. But he kept moving toward the device that towered over everything else in the facility. One by one, the group followed Chase inside to get a better look.

"You're a clever bunch," the dean said, appearing from behind the open reel-to-reel tape machine. He extinguished his lantern and set it on the table nearest him. "And, while it isn't your turn for the audition, I think we ought to bump you to next in line."

"What are you talking about?" Fletcher asked, his shaky voice betraying him. "What kind of sick tests are you running on our classmates? Did you *kill* them?"

Unexpectedly, Dean Mendelsohn's stern face dissolved into a soft one. "What? Here, let me explain—"

"Yeah," Freya yelled. "Explain away. Tell the world what you and Memory Frontier are *actually* doing on campus."

Dean Mendelsohn sighed. He took a step forward. They all took a collective step back. So much palpable intensity filled the air. It felt like at any moment the dean might turn militaristic and leap toward one of them, take a hostage, and subdue them.

Instead, he slid his hairy hands into his pockets and talked.

"Your classmates are safe, and in a moment, I can provide proof. But first: an explanation."

He moved closer to one of the chairs, looking at it while he continued, his firm voice resounding through the facility: "What you see here is the culmination of a years-long defense initiative designed, in concert, by the Federal Bureau of Investigation and Memory Frontier in an effort to prevent domestic terrorism and civil war. Recently, the FBI apprehended a man with ties to a terrorist organization that's plotting to attack every major MACE outpost in the country. We have intel that leads us to believe these extremists are planning their first bombing on October 31—we just don't know where, exactly. These radicals self-identify as Memory Ghosts and, as of yesterday, have mailed their manifesto to every notable news outlet in America. It's mostly hyperbole and wild claims, but in short, they believe world governments are using artificial recall as a means to spy on and, ultimately, control the people. Theirs is a misguided belief that, if gone unchecked, will lead to the slaughter of countless innocent lives.

"Our best shot at preventing the attack on Halloween is to scrub the memories of the radical whom we have in custody."

"Now *there's* some twisted irony," Fletcher spat. "You're trying to scrub the minds of the very people who claim Memory Frontier is spying."

Dean Mendelsohn blinked. He offered no rebuttal.

Fletcher's head swam. *Terrorists? This doesn't add up. It completely contradicts the image Memory Ghosts paint of themselves as protesters and truth seekers.* He thought back to the triplane that flew over campus his first week at Foxtail.

Not exactly the stuff of crazed madmen with misbegotten convictions.

Freya lowered her camera but didn't stop recording. "What . . . what does any of this have to do with us . . . or the Reflectors?"

Dean Mendelsohn dropped his hands. "Ah, yes, Foxtail Academy. After years of trial and error, we have discovered that individuals whose brains have not yet fully developed are the only candidates for successful knifing."

"*Knifing,*" Chase blurted out, laughing. "As in artificially recalling someone else's memories?"

"Precisely," the dean said conversationally. "We have been auditioning pairs of your peers to see if they can complete the first test—a simple pass/fail test that determines if they're capable of knifing."

Fletcher's face flushed. "These are students, *not* soldiers. We're . . . we're just teenagers."

"Quite right." Dean Mendelsohn gave him a grave look. "A similar argument made by those who opposed our last military draft. And yet . . . desperate times."

"This is unbelievable," Ollie said. Her hands trembled so much her Maglite slipped out of her grip and crashed against the pavement. "This *cannot* be legal."

It isn't, Fletcher realized. "Why do you think they're being so secretive?"

"What about the Reflectors?" Freya said, handing the camera to Chase, who was so caught off guard he almost dropped it. "Is this entire trial a hoax? A front? A lie? Did we lose some memories when we abandoned our Restoreys?"

For the first time that evening, Dean Mendelsohn was the one who looked intimidated. "No, the technology in the Reflectors is sound. But yes, the trial itself is a front. When Alexander Lochamire told us about his groundbreaking discovery earlier this year, we strategically coordinated Memory Frontier's trial to begin in conjunction with our counterterrorism mission."

"You told the world we're here to trial technology that will save lives. Instead"—Freya's voice broke—"Instead, you're . . . you're forcing our peers to artificially recall the memories of terrorists."

"No, not *instead*." The dean took another step forward. This time everyone held their ground. "When the school year is over, Freya, the Reflectors will be released into the world, marking a significant victory in our battle against Memory Killer. And if we can complete our mission inside these walls, we'll have prevented a terrorist attack too."

Fletcher's thoughts drifted toward his father, a politicking man deeply entrenched in his work and wholly committed to his office's cause. "Did my father volunteer me for this?"

Dean Mendelsohn shook his head. "No. In fact, he doesn't know about our mission. Few do."

"So then why spill this to us?" Ollie asked, all but shrieking. "When you've finished your little spiel, we're just going to walk out that door and tell everyone what you're doing!"

The dean remained calm. "I'm telling you five, because I believe if you know the truth about the threat we face, you'll be compelled to help."

"Then why not just tell the whole school right now, huh?" Ollie said. "Why not just give your call-to-arms speech over the loudspeakers and line up every student, one by one?"

"You may resent our secrecy, but it's essential. If word got out about our mission, it would upend everything. Working in the shadows under the guise of Memory Frontier's Reflector trial is the only option.

"There's risk in telling you everything, sure, but there's also potential reward."

A chill crept over Fletcher's mind. *Reward . . . in the form of us agreeing to memory knife for you.*

Fletcher looked at his friends one at a time. All the color was gone from Chase's face. Ollie was hyperventilating and might faint at any moment. Freya's brown eyes darted around as she visibly processed all the information the dean just dumped on them. And Ave Maria, whose recent snitching stunt still rankled Fletcher, hugged herself and breathed in soft gasps.

"It may seem random, your being here," Dean Mendelsohn said after a silence pregnant with tension. "I assure you it is anything but.

Using data points from the MeReader at your last three downloads, we were able to narrow down our pool of candidates to the five hundred students who 'lotteried' into Foxtail Academy. We are certain at least one of you is up to the task . . . that one of you can perform a successful memory knifing."

Chase laughed. "So, never mind the fact that you *just* admitted to monitoring our downloads, a highly illegal practice. How can you be so sure that one of the students at Foxtail can actually do this? Huh?"

Dean Mendelsohn swallowed, taking his time. Fletcher realized the dean was stalling for the first time. His heart throbbed. *He doesn't have a scripted answer for Chase because—*

"He doesn't know," Fletcher hazarded out loud, making his way toward the dean and standing about a foot from his nose. "You actually have no idea if memory knifing is even possible. Do you?"

The dean set his jaw and looked away.

Ollie gasped. *"What the hell.* You're putting all these kids through your . . . your *test* . . . and you don't even know if it can be done?"

"It *can* be done," the dean said, locking eyes with Fletcher again, his black and gray eyebrows forming a deep scowl.

"This is a full-blown disaster," Chase said, pacing around. "I can't believe tax dollars are funding these kinds of harebrained—"

"It can be done!" Dean Mendelsohn shouted, red-faced, silencing the entire facility in a fraction of a second. He composed himself. "It can be done because . . . you just have to trust me. It *can* be done." He walked away from Fletcher, leaning against the open reel-to-reel tape machine and keeping his back to the group.

After a quiet moment passed, Freya said, "We need to leave, guys. This place . . . these lies . . . must be exposed. They cannot get away with this."

They all nodded, including Ave Maria, and turned to leave—confused, burdened, and tired.

"If you take the test, I will give you the answers you seek."

They all stopped and turned around slowly to find Dean Mendelsohn looking squarely at Freya.

"Take my test. If you pass, then help us stop the attack. If you fail, then you can go your way and show your video footage to the highest bidder. But either way, I'll give you the answers you seek about your father."

No. He's bluffing.

And yet . . . Dean Mendelsohn was employed by Memory Frontier, and Freya's father *had* died while working at a Memory Frontier factory. But even if he did know the truth about her father's death, was he going to divulge this information to Freya?

No.

He was just trying to manipulate her emotions.

"I've seen your photo album," Dean Mendelsohn intoned. "The fragments of your past that you keep close . . . a fragmented past rife with question marks."

Freya bristled. "You . . . you went through my things?" Her voice quivered, and Fletcher felt a powerful rage manifest within.

"I came to Foxtail to complete an urgent mission," the dean said with no trace of remorse in his voice. "That required learning everything I possibly could about my recruits, and by any means necessary."

Fletcher was about to boil over; the dean's use of "recruits," his nonchalance, enraged Fletcher to the point of—

"All I have to do is take your test?" Freya said, leaving Fletcher's side and walking toward Dean Mendelsohn. "And you'll tell me what happened to my dad?"

"Like I said"—the dean placed a hand over his heart—"if you pass, you agree to help us try to thwart this terrorist attack. You fail the test, you walk away. In both instances, when it's all over, I get you the answers you seek."

"Freya, no, he's lying," Fletcher said, running up to her. "We can't trust him! This whole operation of his is built on nothing but lies! And he just admitted to violating your privacy!"

Freya looked him in the eye, her beautiful irises blurring behind quickly forming tears.

No, Freya. We cannot help him. Do not buy his lie!

She turned toward the dean and said, her voice even and resolved, "What do I need to do?"

31

FREYA IZQUIERDO

Silently, as if I'm alone, I get undressed—my hands jittering and my throat dry. I slide off my long-sleeve T-shirt and pants and drop them onto the cold pavement at my bare feet. I take the black, gray, and red jumpsuit off the metal hanger and put it on. Behind me, near the opposite wall, I hear Ollie and Ave Maria zipping up their jumpsuits, too, and when we're all finished, we turn around and face each other in the small room.

The three of us look like imprisoned astronauts; either we're going off to stamp license plates on an assembly line, or we're about to slip into heavy space gear.

Of course, we're not doing either of those things.

No.

Once we walk through that door and back into the main room, Dean Mendelsohn's going to brief us on his test. Then I imagine we'll get hooked up to the strange tape-playing machine and see if any of us manages to pass—whatever that means.

I stare at the white door, my left eyelid twitching. I hope I fail. That way, I get it over with and straight to the part where Dean Mendelsohn tells me what he knows about Dad and how he was killed.

I sense Ollie and Ave Maria watching me from the backless bench, and when I glance their way, I see they're staring at my hands. I am making such tight fists that my arms are shaking. When I stop and release my fingers, I see white fingernail imprints in my skin.

"That's a two-quarter mark," Ave Maria says softly, as if I don't realize I've been carrying around this brand since I was sixteen.

"That's some world-class investigating there, Magnum." Ollie gets up from the bench and walks over to me. "Hey. You all right?"

"You didn't have to volunteer," I tell her as she takes my hands into hers. After I agreed to take the dean's test, Fletcher, Ollie, and Chase almost immediately told him they would take it too. Ave Maria wasn't given much of a choice; she'd seen too much.

"Look." Ollie leans her forehead against mine. "We were *not* about to leave you here to do this on your own. If there's a chance the dean has some info on your father, you'd be crazy not to try to get it. We understand, and that's why we're here."

I nod, then she breaks away.

I wonder how Fletcher's doing in the room beside ours—how he and Chase are managing their nerves. I picture him sitting on the bench, controlling his breathing, while Chase walks circles around the tiny room, complaining about the temperature or lack of a bathroom.

I didn't expect them to stay and complete the test alongside me, but I sure am glad they're here.

Ave Maria pulls her knees up to her chest and hugs her legs. "You guys got lucky. I wish some of *my* friends from back home had been selected to come to Foxtail."

"Freya and I met on move-in day, ignoramus." Ollie drops my hands and marches over to her. "You know, you might have more friends than your two lackeys if you didn't suck so much."

Ave Maria looks up at Ollie, exposing the whites under her eyes, then turns away.

"It's funny how suddenly you don't have a lot to say." Ollie plants her hands on her hips. "You had *plenty* to say to Dean Mendelsohn when you ratted us out. Oh, and if you hadn't done that, by the way, we'd be racing to the nearest town right now with our video footage—evidence that would shut this whole operation down and ruin Alexander Lochamire!"

"Ollie, that's enough." I gently take my friend's elbow and lead her away from the bench. Ollie pulls her hair back into a ponytail absently, but she doesn't have a band, so she just holds her hair behind her head.

"Sorry," she eventually says, dropping her hand, her long hair bouncing down past her shoulders. There's a soft buzz on the other side of our door, and a second later it unlocks. The door swings open, revealing Dr. Sanders, who wears a white lab coat and an anxious expression.

"Hey, Doc," Ollie says.

"Hello, Ms. Trang, Ms. Izquierdo, Ms. Sinclair. Shall we?"

The facility is bustling.

Men and women—scientists, I assume—type speedily on their computers, shouting information at each other. It's chaotic, noisy, the kind of hustle and bustle you see on Wall Street on the evening news.

Dean Mendelsohn instructs a group of men, who add three

chairs to the two beside the reel-to-reel machine. The staff guide my friends to lie down in them as Dr. Sanders escorts me.

"It must suck to have your fun spoiled like this," I say bitterly. "Hopefully this doesn't throw a wrench into your precious—"

"Freya, stop it."

"No. I trusted you with my secret. And this whole time you were just counting down the days until you could drag me here against my will and subject me to the dean's test."

Dr. Sanders purses her lips.

"You probably told him about my half-memory dreams, didn't you?"

She stops me with a touch to my shoulder and lowers her voice. "Of course not. In fact, I was working to delay your turn, hoping that Dean Mendelsohn would find his candidate before giving you the test. I was trying to protect you."

"Why?"

"Well, given your condition"—she drops her voice even lower—"I have concerns about how it may impact your—"

"It's time," the dean says, waving me to the last empty seat.

Dr. Sanders rubs my arm and puts on a happy face. "I'll keep a close eye on you, don't worry, Freya."

A fresh influx of anxiety stirs in the pit of my stomach. *Great. Dr. Sanders has concerns about me participating in this test because of my half-memory dreams.*

I should probably speak up. But if I back out, I won't be keeping my end of the bargain, and Dean Mendelsohn won't have a reason to keep his.

I keep my mouth shut.

A female nurse in scrubs wheels an IV drip bag on a stand to Fletcher's chair. Fletcher glances up at the bag hanging over his head, then at me. He sits forward and calls Dean Mendelsohn over in a panic as the nurse positions IV drips beside each of us.

"You know, Chase and I already flunked this test." Fletcher's breathing accelerates. He looks dizzy, out of sorts. "We accidentally played back each other's memory tapes."

"That sounds most unpleasant," the dean says. "But one cannot perform a successful memory knifing without this key component"—he flicks the IV bag nearest him—"A sedative . . . a harmless yet effective medical cocktail that will help you all achieve a shared state of recollection."

I let Dr. Sanders help me into the cold chair beside Fletcher. "'Shared state'?"

"Yes." The dean hands a tray of five syringes to the nurse. "That's the goal, anyway."

"Shouldn't we, like, sign some kind of waiver?" Ollie jokes, chuckling nervously. But she immediately shifts her tone: "Wait. Could this kill us?"

Her question sets off a domino effect.

"You still haven't told us who was in that body bag," Chase exclaims, sitting up and glaring at the dean.

"There was a body bag?" Ave Maria shoots up in her chair too. "Who saw a body bag? No one said there was a body bag . . ."

"Please, now settle down," Dean Mendelsohn says, walking to the reel-to-reel tape machine and turning to face us all. "Mr. Hall is referring to having seen our suspect, a man who is currently in forced stasis at the Fold and being watched around the clock. He was brought here so we could download some of his memories." He taps the tall tape machine with his knuckles.

"He's not dead?" I say, surprised at how relieved I am.

"No," the dean replies. "Frankly, he'd be no good to us if he was." A man with square glasses and shaggy brown hair shuffles over to Dean Mendelsohn, and the two of them consult a clipboard.

"Lean your head back," Dr. Sanders instructs me, holding my

hand as I lie down. "The nurse is going to insert your IV lines momentarily. Have you ever received medication intravenously?"

I shake my head.

Dr. Sanders gives me a warm, comforting smile. "The worst part is the pinch of the IV line being inserted into your vein."

"Really?" Fletcher says beside me, his tone hot as fire. "I kinda thought the worst part was being lied to by the government and one of the world's largest corporations. Or maybe it was the part where the dean manipulated Freya and us into—"

"Fletcher," I say softly, reaching out and holding his hand. "Thank you."

He almost chokes on his words, looking perplexed. "I . . . For what?"

"For not letting me do this on my own."

Once all five of us are hooked up to our IV bags, the nurse and Dr. Sanders move among us and apply multiple electrode stickers to various parts of our bodies: one on each temple, one over our hearts, one on the center of our foreheads, and one on the nape of our necks.

They run tiny red wires from the stickers on our temples and plug these into the enormous tape machine at the center of the facility. When they've completed this, they run blue wires from the other electrode stickers and connect these into a square monitor on wheels, where I assume they're monitoring all kinds of readings and vital signs.

Dean Mendelsohn walks between our chairs, a surgeon checking his patients before surgery. "Once you're sedated and we turn on the Restorey, either you'll artificially recall what's on the memory tape, or you won't. That's it. That's the test." He rolls a wide dry-erase board into view. Two squiggly lines break up the shiny surface into three sections. From left to right there's a rushed drawing of a deer head with antlers, a pair of glasses, and what looks like an empty fishbowl.

"We're all set," Dr. Sanders tells the dean, leaving her monitor and joining the other scientists behind their rows of computers.

Fletcher squeezes my hand, his skin clammy with perspiration. "So, what, you're just going to throw us in the deep end and see if we can swim?" he asks Dean Mendelsohn. "See if we can artificially recall the memory of a terrorist?"

"Of course not, no." With sure and steady hands, he sets to work threading tape into the Restorey's white, open reels like a projectionist loading film into a projector. "You will be attempting to recall one of *my* memory tapes."

The facility is quieter than a library, the only noise coming from the buzz of lights and the sputtering of air vents. If I couldn't see the rows of scientists behind Dean Mendelsohn and Dr. Sanders, I'd have thought everyone had cleared the room.

But no, everyone's still here, watching us over the tops of their computers like gunmen peering out of foxholes.

The nurse takes the syringes and visits Ave Maria's chair, applying the sedative to the IV drip bag. She does this with quiet concentration, one eye squinted, and when she's finished, she moves on to Chase.

When the nurse finishes with Chase and gets to Ollie, who's on the other side of Fletcher, Fletcher turns to me and whispers, a grin spread across his tired face, "You're welcome, by the way."

I stifle a laugh and hold his eyes with mine. The nurse walks over to his chair and steadily inserts the tip of the syringe into his IV line, depressing the plunger until the barrel is completely empty. Fletcher's grin deepens, then he closes his eyes.

Finally, the nurse moves to my chair, holding the last of the five syringes. I look up at the tube lights as she dispenses my sedative.

"Let us begin," the dean says, and just like that, things are under way.

I clamp my eyes shut.

I focus on breathing.

I try not to tremble.

I brace for . . .

. . . for the unknown.

There's a *click!* and then I hear the reel-to-reel tape machine moan to life. Yet, unlike when I used to press the Play button on my personal Restorey, nothing happens right away. I only feel myself growing woozy. Nauseous, in fact, but a sensation of floating, of falling up toward the ceiling, overtakes me. The feeling is so real that my body jerks, like I'm bracing myself before violently slamming into the ceiling.

And then at once, like waves crashing into rock formations, I hurtle forward into a

spectrum of

neon

colors

and

ascend

through

an

undulating

tunnel

32

FLETCHER COHEN

The neon colors were blinding. They weren't just bright; they were *whole* and absolute, and they wrapped around Fletcher with glowing tendrils that carried him as though he were weightless. Consciously, Fletcher decided to scream, to shout with fear as his stomach fluttered and his dinner threatened to resurface.

But he couldn't move.

He was paralyzed as he fell *up* through the same light that carried him.

Unlike when he'd accidentally played back Chase's memory tape, the nightmare didn't end after a few seconds.

It raged.

It raged on with a sonorous *boom*.

Until the nightmare ended in a burst of white, like the huge flash-bulb on one of those old-timey cameras.

Fletcher squinted in pain, and then the neon colors dissolved like dust swirling in sunlight, and his vision returned.

He looked around, panting.

He was standing on a thin platform with nothing but blurry, misty, dreamlike imagery spinning around him. It was as if he had become nearsighted, and the only things in focus were his hands, which he brought up to his face to examine. They were his hands all right, only they felt detached from his body, similar to the numbing sensation he got after sleeping on top of his limbs.

Freya, Ollie, and Chase appeared on the platform, though they didn't *really* appear, because with a flinch he realized they were already there. It was so hard to explain; it was as if his brain was delayed, too slow to compute the reality of his friends' presence.

Ave Maria was nowhere in sight.

Their faces! Fletcher inhaled sharply. His friends' faces were blank canvases of skin pulled tightly over their heads. But in an instant their features dissolved into place: their eyes, mouths, noses formed as clay shaped into a sculpture. All three of his friends sucked air into their lungs as if they'd almost drowned—appearing as terrified as Fletcher felt, still wearing the jumpsuits they were issued back in the facility.

That's when the objects came flying toward them.

33

FREYA IZQUIERDO

Bus seats fly at us from every direction.

We huddle together, shielding one another from the impending impact, but the seats stop a foot or two away. All at once, the passengers, roof, and sides of the bus slide into place to form a reasonable picture. We're standing in the aisle. I think we've been in the aisle of the bus the whole time, but the formation of details is remarkably delayed.

Now I see the bus is driving through a busy street. It's twilight. It's raining. A very young Dean Mendelsohn is seated on the bench beside me. He looks out the window with a newspaper rolled up under his arm. He's clean-shaven, and his hair is jet black without a trace of gray.

He sighs.

Can you hear me? Fletcher asks at my side. I nod. But I don't *hear* his voice so much as I *feel* it materialize in my head a second after his lips move.

I can, I reply. Similarly, my voice isn't audible but rather perceived in my mind.

The bus stops and Chase points toward the front. The doors slide open and an elderly woman, her clothes soaked in rainwater, climbs on. She pays her fare and then walks down the aisle toward us.

She carries an empty fishbowl in her wrinkly hands and takes the seat across the aisle from the dean.

34

FLETCHER COHEN

The dean glanced at the elderly woman, who smiled a kindly smile.

"In the market for a goldfish?" He nodded toward her empty fishbowl.

"Oh, sadly, no." Her voice was soft as cotton. "Magnolia passed away this morning. I've just been to the river to release her small body back to the earth."

"I'm sorry to hear that. Magnolia's a pretty name for a fish."

The elderly woman beamed. "I thought so as well."

And then, like a television set unplugged in the middle of a show, everything in the bus—the passengers, the seats, the driver, the elderly woman, the dean—collapsed in on itself with a low, vibrating hum.

The neon colors rushed back, tousling Fletcher's hair every which way, and then he was back in the facility. He sat up in his chair and vomited in his lap, coughing and retching until it felt like he'd puked up everything in his system.

Then he passed out.

❖ ❖ ❖

Fletcher came to under a thin blanket on a stiff cot.

His head was pounding. Instinctively, he glanced down at his wrist to check the time, then remembered he'd taken off his watch when he changed into his jumpsuit. Speaking of which . . . It appeared someone had changed him into a clean one after he threw up on himself.

Great. It doesn't get much more humiliating than that.

A small bandage covered his forearm where the intravenous catheter had been. Two Reflector suction receivers were affixed to his temples. The tiny device was on the floor beside his shoes and folded-up clothes.

Fletcher still felt a little drowsy, but he figured that whatever that strange, hypnotic sedative was, it had to be flushed out of his system by now.

He sat up on the cot and looked around. He was in the facility still, tucked away in one of the corners beside Freya, Ollie, and Chase, who were all sound asleep on cots of their own.

The dean walked toward him with two steamy cups of coffee in hand. "You're up."

Fletcher swung his feet around and sat on the edge of his cot. "What time is it?"

The dean handed him one of the cups. "Eleven in the morning. Working inside a windowless structure can be disorienting, can't it?"

"Yeah." Fletcher took a sip of the hot drink, then glanced down at his Reflector, which flashed *Complete* across the tiny screen. He removed the receivers from his head and dropped them onto the pavement. "What happened after I . . . after I blacked out?"

The dean grabbed a metal folding chair and dragged it over, sitting across from Fletcher. He crossed his legs and drank from his mug. "Well. You passed the test. Four of you did, anyway." Dean Mendelsohn sounded as happy as a Boy Scout. Fletcher saw the dry-erase board behind him, on the other side of the facility. There was a large circle around the empty fishbowl.

"And Ave Maria?" Fletcher asked. "What happened to her?"

"Well, I suspect she had the deepest sleep of her life," he said. "She's perfectly fine, of course. When my memory tape stopped playing, she didn't wake up, just like her peers before her. Meaning, she didn't artificially recall, and instead was dreaming peacefully."

"*Dreaming*," Fletcher said flatly.

"That's correct." The dean took another drink. "Ms. Sinclair, along with the rest of your classmates who failed the test, has been transferred to another site, where we transition students out of the Reflector trial and return them to their families."

Fletcher shook his head. "So, what? You're telling them and their parents they had adverse reactions to the Reflector? That . . . that everything they saw here was just some kind of nightmare?"

"More or less."

"With as much as you guys lie, do you ever forget the actual truth?"

"We do what must be done. Lives hang in the balance."

Fletcher looked away. In the three cots on either side of him, Freya, Ollie, and Chase hadn't so much as stirred. Ollie, who lay on her side, had begun to snore softly, her right side rising and falling.

"And why can't you just do the dirty work yourself?" Fletcher asked irritably.

"That would certainly make things easier, wouldn't it?" He released a long sigh through his nose. "As I said, neuroplasticity is a key component to knifing. We need minds that have not yet fully developed and formed, brains that are malleable—"

"But *why?*" Fletcher leaned forward on his cot. "And tell me the truth, hard as that might be for you."

Dean Mendelsohn flattened his tie with his free hand. After a lengthy pause, he said, "Because of the memory particles."

Fletcher blinked. "The . . . what?"

"Fletcher, to enter one's memory is to enter their very mind," he explained. "Adults with fully developed brains who artificially recall someone else's past will wake up after knifing and find their consciousness tearing. They cannot separate their memories from the ones they've knifed. Lingering aspects of the foreign memory— memory particles, as it were—bleed into their subconscious, creating the illusion of *two* pasts. It drives them mad."

"That doesn't make any sense," Fletcher argued. "I remember what I artificially recalled from your memory tape . . . the bus and the woman and the fishbowl . . . but I know it's not *my* memory."

"And this phenomenon occurs because you're only seventeen, Fletcher. Now, if you had a mature frontal cortex, you'd be having a completely different experience . . . a rather unpleasant one. In fact, the vasospasms would have kicked in by now."

"*Vasospasms?*"

"Brain spasms." Dean Mendelsohn pulled a tiny pill bottle out of his pocket . . . the very bottle Fletcher had seen the dean grab after their first meeting. With one hand, Dean Mendelsohn opened the top, tilted the bottle into his mouth until two white pills fell onto his tongue, then washed them down with coffee.

"So, no." He rose to his feet. "Adults who can perform a memory knifing should not, under any circumstance, do so."

Fletcher swallowed. "All right, so what makes us so special? How come the four of us were able to knife when Ave Maria and our other classmates weren't?"

Freya began to roll over on her cot.

"That, I'm unsure of. But Dr. Sanders is working on discovering the common denominator among you four."

Fletcher nodded, then took another sip of the coffee.

"Wake your friends," Dean Mendelsohn said. "I've got lunch on the stove. And then we begin your training."

In the lone bathroom, Fletcher splashed water on his face and let the faucet run. The steam fogged the mirror, obscuring his reflection, and as he fumbled to open a disposable toothbrush over the sink, he found himself suddenly short of breath. He leaned against the wall and shut off the faucet, attempting to stabilize his breathing.

A knock thumped against the door.

"Yo, Fletcher, quit hogging the can," Chase said.

Fletcher let him in.

"You good, man?" Chase ruffled his own hair as if trying to get sand out.

"Yeah. Still wrapping my head around everything."

Chase crossed the bathroom slowly, muttering, "This is . . . this is *insane*, man. I gotta be honest, I'm thinking we should just bolt tonight."

"What?"

"Yeah." He joined Fletcher at the sink and grabbed an unopened toothbrush. "I mean, dude, we've spent *weeks* planning this break-in with the intent of blowing the lid off Memory Frontier's secrets. We got what we came here for, so I say we—"

"Plans change."

"Dude, Fletcher, I get why you're doing this. I do." He turned the faucet on and ran his toothbrush under the water. "But we're sheep. We're the dean's *sheep*, man. That doesn't sit well with me."

Fletcher turned off the faucet. "I can't let Freya do this on her own—*that* wouldn't sit well with *me*. So if you need to bail, bail. No one will hold that against you. But I'm seeing this through . . . for Freya."

Chase sighed. He reached out and wiped the fog off the mirror, then watched Fletcher through the reflection. After a long minute he eventually said, "Fine. Yeah. For Freya."

Fletcher, Freya, Chase, and Ollie sat around a small table in a small kitchen located through one of the four doors beside the bathroom and dressing rooms. Lunch was cold eggs, cold toast, and warm orange juice.

"Eat up," Dean Mendelsohn said, standing beside the counter and munching on his toast. "We have a lot of work to do today, and time is of the essence."

"You couldn't, you know, have food from the Foxhole sent over?" Chase asked, moving the scrambled eggs around on his plate with his fork.

"They're spoiling students in that cafeteria," the dean grumped.

"How is warm food spoiling us?" Ollie demanded, chasing a bite of her food with some juice. "That's just courteous."

Dean Mendelsohn opened his mouth, but Freya was quicker: "If you're putting us through all this, the least you could do is feed us halfway decent food." Fletcher smiled at her as he buttered his toast.

The dean composed himself, then muttered, "I'll see what I can do."

"What's going to happen with our classes while we're here?" Chase asked between bites. "*Please* tell me we're getting A's across the board for doing this."

"I'm handling that," the dean said as he abruptly exited.

"So, um, how you feelin' after last night, buddy?" Ollie asked Fletcher from across the table, snickering. He felt himself flush.

"Go easy on him," Freya said, nudging Ollie with her elbow. "We don't want to upset his tummy again."

Ollie and Chase nearly sprayed their food.

"Ha." Fletcher deadpanned, feeling redder by the second. "I officially hate every single one of you."

I'm sorry, Freya mouthed, rubbing his shin under the table with her foot. And just like that, Fletcher was over it.

"Well, I guess we now know what Freya's last premonition was about," Ollie said after their laughter faded. "If memory kaleidoscoping is similar to that, I never want to do it. Ever."

"Speaking of which"—Fletcher leaned toward Freya—"I overheard you and Dr. Sanders. She said she had concerns about you doing the test because of your half-memory dreams. Did . . . did anything happen while we were memory knifing?"

"Nothing, no," she said. The table fell quiet. "But I'm not worried about it. Since we all passed his little test, we just need to finish helping the dean so he can keep his end of the bargain. I'm not going to worry about what I can't control."

Ollie set her fork down. "Do you guys think it's a little strange that Ave Maria and our other classmates *all* supposedly failed, but the dean got lucky with us and we all passed?"

Everyone nodded.

"I asked him about that," Fletcher told the table. "He said Dr. Sanders is looking into why all four of us were able to perform a memory knifing." Everyone looked at their plates of food, clearly speculating.

After a moment of silence, Chase raised his glass of orange juice. "Well, here's to the Forgotten Four. We set out to learn the dean's secrets—mission accomplished."

"Yeah, only now it's biting us in the ass," Ollie said, and it was

Fletcher's turn to laugh. They all joined in, then they raised their cups and clanked them together.

"Forgotten," Freya said. "But not forgetful."

"The easy part is over," Dean Mendelsohn told the group, erasing his whiteboard with a rag. Fletcher, Freya, Chase, and Ollie sat in metal chairs in a semicircle, facing the dean. "Now it's time for the training wheels to come off."

Fletcher raised his hand. "I'm sorry, but what about last night was *easy?*"

The dean grabbed a black marker. "For starters, that memory of mine that you artificially recalled was stationary. Meaning, it took place in a single location—on a bus with ample space for you to comfortably tag along for the ride."

"*Comfortable* might be a stretch," Chase said under his breath.

"However"—Dean Mendelsohn pulled the cap off his marker—"had I been running in that particular memory, or driving a car, it would have been necessary for you to follow me—to not *once* lose sight of me within my memory. When you are memory knifing, if you lose sight of the host for longer than sixty seconds, you're ejected from the memory."

Freya cleared her throat. "*Ejected?*"

The dean drew a line across the board, then wrote *start* on one end and *finish* on the other.

"Every memory tape has a start and end point, like a song." He drew a thick dot over *start*, then dragged a long line over the first line, as if to indicate the dot's path, and he stopped over *finish*. "When we artificially recall a memory tape, the scene from our past unfolds around us in real time. But when someone *else* enters that memory"—he drew a second dot over the first one using a red marker

296

this time—"they're of course witnessing another person's past, not their own. There's no sense of familiarity with the scene whatsoever, which explains the jarring delay you likely experienced as the memory's framework was constructed around you. Like watching a movie with a delayed audio track."

"Something like that," Fletcher said, though he didn't feel that comparison did it justice.

"In truth, you're not artificially recalling someone else's memory at all," the dean said. "It's impossible to remember something that didn't happen to you. Which is why you must stay close to the memory host throughout the entire 'recall.'" To underscore his point, he took his rag and erased half of the second line. Then he erased the first dot and redrew it over the halfway point. Now the red dot was alone over *start* with a chasmic gap between it and the first dot. The dean gave them a minute to observe his drawing before forcefully erasing the red dot.

He turned to face them. "There's something else you should know." He put the marker and rag down, then clasped his hands behind his back. "You only get one shot at memory knifing per memory tape. So once you're ejected, that's it. You'll never be able to reenter that memory tape again."

"Why?" Fletcher asked.

"Your brain will reject it. After the first knifing, your consciousness learns that the memory tape is foreign—*unnatural*—and, like white blood cells preventing the spread of an infection, it will put up a protective barrier against the alien memory."

Ollie laughed. "So you're saying our margin for error is slim, huh?"

"No." He turned to her with a no-nonsense expression. "I'm saying there is no margin at all."

297

35

FREYA IZQUIERDO

"Let's try another," Dean Mendelsohn says, dragging the dry-erase board away. As if on cue, the sliding door to the facility cracks open, and sunlight spills in with such ferocity that we have to shield our eyes. Led by Dr. Sanders, the scientists from last night file inside and head to their stations.

"You sleep okay?" Dr. Sanders asks me as she passes by.

I nod. I still haven't made up my mind about her. While I do get the sense that she genuinely wants to help me—that she's really committed to pinpointing the cause of my half-memory dreams—I can't shake the fact that she and the dean are part of a giant web of lies. Sure, they say it's to stop a terrorist attack, but the facts remain: they have deceived the world and are secretly using teenagers as experimental spies.

The dean threads a new memory tape into the reels as Fletcher, Ollie, Chase, and I lie out on our chairs. Once he's finished, he faces us again and rolls up his sleeves.

"Since you know what to expect this time, the transition into my memory should go a lot smoother. At least . . . it *should*."

❖ ❖ ❖

"Smoother" might be a stretch. The whirlwind of neon colors yanks my consciousness forward and hurtles me through a dizzying vortex. I'm spinning out of control as I tumble upward in a sort of reverse treefall.

But hey, at least I knew it was coming, right?

I land on a patch of dirt, breathing with such intensity it feels like my lungs have forgotten how to work.

One by one, Fletcher, Ollie, and Chase appear around me, each one of them almost losing their footing. The patch of dirt expands into a wide field of fallow ground, dry and sun beaten.

Everyone okay? I ask, and they all mouth yes.

A thirteen-year-old boy races between us, chased by an angry man whose shirt is covered in manure.

Uh-oh. I realize immediately the young boy is Dean Mendelsohn. Without warning the others, I chase the teenage dean. Pursuing him may sound simple enough, sure, but the broken-up ground is so incredibly uneven that I'm forced to hop as I run.

I hear my friends struggling behind me, and since I'm keeping good pace with Dean Mendelsohn and the adult pursuing him, I steal a glance over my shoulder.

This quick risk is costly, as I trip on a mound of dirt and fall face-first onto the ground. My nose feels like it's been jammed into the back of my head, then my vision goes dark. I scream out in pain, tasting the copper of blood on my tongue, and then open my eyes.

Tears sail down my cheeks. The stars in my vision dissolve, and I sit up carefully. Dr. Sanders walks over with a blanket, which she wraps around my shivering body. I glance at the others; they're still lying in their chairs, unmoving and tranquil, wires running from their heads to the tall Restorey.

"Wh-what happened?" I ask the dean. My teeth chatter. I'm shaking so much I'm sure the IV catheter is going to pop out of my arm.

"You were ejected." He shrugs. One of the scientists calls the dean to her computer, pointing at the monitor and saying something I can't hear.

I cautiously bring my hand up to my nose, touching it gently. It feels . . . fine. Normal. I was *sure* it broke when I crashed into the ground. And yet it's not even sore.

"Did you hurt yourself?" Dr. Sanders removes the electrode stickers from my head. "In the dean's memory?"

"Yeah, I . . ." I prod my cheekbones. "I fell flat on my face. Felt like I shattered part of my skull."

Dean Mendelsohn returns, both hands in his pockets. "That doesn't sound pleasant," he says. "Because pain is processed in our nervous system, any kind of physical injury you sustain while memory knifing will feel *very* real. Did I not mention that?"

I glare at him. "I don't feel pain like that when I'm dreaming," I say.

"In REM sleep?" He laughs, almost condescendingly. "You're unconscious when you sleep, Freya, but you're *semi*conscious when you knife."

My glare deepens.

"Don't worry." He flips his hand as if to wave off my experience. "You'll catch on."

❖ ❖ ❖

When Fletcher, Ollie, and Chase emerge from Dean Mendelsohn's childhood memory, they look groggy and, frankly, a little drunk. Chase and Ollie make eye contact with one another and start snickering. The sedative they're giving us is very potent; I've only had two doses of it so far, but both times I've felt a sort of crippling exhaustion after waking up from the dean's memories, like I just spent the last three nights not sleeping a wink.

I've never wanted coffee as badly as I do now.

Fletcher blinks awake. "Th-that was quite the tumble you took."

"Yeah." I bring my blanket up to my shoulders. "What happened after I was ejected?"

"The dean's uncle eventually caught him." Fletcher touches his chin to his neck so Dr. Sanders can more easily remove his electrode stickers. "He tried hopping a fence but he slipped. And then his uncle grabbed his ankle and dragged him to the ground. Then he beat him."

"Um . . ."

"Yeah. Chase, Ollie, and I just sort of stood around. Thankfully, the memory didn't last much longer after that."

"How did you know that was the dean's uncle?"

Fletcher furrows his brow. "I . . . You know? I don't know how I know, actually."

"The memory informed you," Dr. Sanders says, removing his IV line and capping the catheter. "When you knife, not only are you perceiving the memory's setting and how the scene unfolds, but you're also perceiving the host's relation to the other people within the memory. Details and context materialize in your subconscious as if you've known them all along."

Fletcher rubs his temples. "You just made my head hurt even more."

I turn from Fletcher and watch Dean Mendelsohn, who is currently talking into a telephone at one of the computers.

"Why would he make us knife *that* memory?" I ask Fletcher, keeping my eyes on the dean, who rubs his forehead. The white glow from the computer screen bounces off his pasty face.

"Who knows." From the corner of my eye I see Fletcher shrug. "Maybe he just doesn't have a lot of memory tapes of him running?"

"Yeah," I say, not so sure. "Maybe."

The dean points to a black-and-white mugshot that's pinned to a corkboard on an easel.

"Our suspect is a man by the name of Malcolm Heckman," the dean tells us, his voice sharp with urgency. The entire surface of the corkboard is *covered* in pictures and red-yarn spiderwebs from one mugshot to another, likely indicating the Memory Ghosts' network of important players. Near the top of the corkboard, I see a zoomed-in photograph of a late-sixties, heavyset man wearing a paisley tie and fedora. In the picture he crosses a busy street, a look of determination in his eyes, and the name Philip Lear is written on a thin strip of paper and taped above his head.

"Malcolm was arrested in August after the FBI had been surveilling him for nearly a month," the dean continues, and I return my eyes to Malcolm's mugshot. He's young, probably only in his thirties, with buzzed hair, bushy eyebrows, and tiny dots for eyes. He has a thin bandage across the bridge of his nose.

Dr. Sanders brings us each a glass of cold water while the dean briefs us. Fletcher, Ollie, Chase, and I are seated in the chairs we use when memory knifing, only now they're in the upright position.

"After his apartment in Santa Ana was raided, the FBI seized and cataloged all of Malcom's belongings."

"Santa Ana?" Chase blurts, looking at us. "That's, like, our backyard."

The dean nods once. "Malcolm is from Chicago but moved to Southern California in the summer of '86. We believe last year is when the Memory Ghosts began to actively recruit radicals to their cause. Anyway, it was shortly after Malcolm was incarcerated that we discovered he was a runner."

"What's a runner?" I ask.

"A messenger. An in-between for the terrorist organization. Coincidentally, a couple of weeks before Malcolm was arrested, he was involved in a high-speed chase on the freeway. He was driving a vehicle with stolen plates and refused to pull over for the police. And while he did manage to lose the officers in a narrow escape, several pedestrians died."

I shiver, then take a drink of my water, as if that'll help ease my nerves.

The dean pushes a TV stand into a position where we can all see it. "At the time, local authorities assumed it was another routine case of grand theft auto—just some criminal idiot and a petty crime." Dean Mendelsohn picks up the remote, turns on the TV, then loads a VHS tape into the player. After he presses Play, we see aerial footage of the chase. A white sedan recklessly speeds down the freeway, occasionally scraping against the shoulder and weaving between other cars. The news footage zooms out, showing police cars a considerable distance behind Malcolm. "However, after poring over Malcom's journals and cross-referencing them with his artificial recall schedule, we discovered that on this very day—after this very chase—Malcolm delivered an important message to someone in his network. We have reason to believe this message contains information about the location of their planned Halloween attack."

The dean pauses the VHS tape, and the image of Malcolm's sedan freezes in place just as it's about to disappear beneath an overpass. The white, scratchy dropout lines at the bottom of the screen flicker over the paused footage, and it unsettles me greatly.

"Utilizing the MeReader, we've managed to capture this particular memory," Dean Mendelsohn says, putting the remote on top of the TV, "and we've imprinted it onto a memory tape. You four will be trailing Malcom to his secret destination and learning the contents of his message."

The facility falls so quiet that all I can hear is our breathing.

Fletcher shakes his head. "I'm sorry . . . you *utilized* the MeReader to *capture* this memory? I thought memory readers only obtained memories that are at risk."

The dean and Dr. Sanders swap a quick, not-so-conspicuous look of unease.

"Yes, well," Dr. Sanders says, chuckling nervously. "Certain capabilities of Memory Frontier's technology can be . . . *accessed* for times such as these . . . fringe features, if you will, that are still in R&D."

"Well, *that's* comforting," Ollie says sarcastically. "Why do I get the idea Memory Frontier's board doesn't know about these 'fringe features'?"

Dr. Sanders looks away, suddenly *very* fascinated with her shoes. I realize "fringe features" is just a roundabout way of admitting not only that memory indexing is possible, but that it's happening. It's *actually* happening, even though Memory Frontier has long sworn it isn't. How else did they locate a specific memory from Malcolm Heckman's consciousness?

If the public knew memory indexing was very much in use, there would be riots in the streets.

It's one of the biggest violations of one's privacy imaginable, and yet Dr. Sanders is standing here downplaying it—claiming the only reason this unethical practice is occurring is so they can help the FBI catch a bad guy.

I'm not so sure.

Fletcher offers another question: "Okay, so, why didn't you just find the exact moment that Malcom delivers the message? Seems like that would save us a helluva lot of trouble."

The dean says, "Unfortunately, that's impossible. Tracking down a precise moment within someone's memory is like trying to snatch a single fish in a school of fish, and with your bare hands. The MeReader works like a wide net. Once we've caught the whole school and brought them to land, it's much easier to sort through them and find the fish we're looking for."

"Okay," Chase says, setting down his glass of water, "so we have to pursue this Malcom guy. Fine. But how exactly are you expecting us to do that? Listen, I'm a fast runner, but in case you were wondering, I'm not as fast as a speeding car."

The dean smiles. "That's where manifesting comes in."

❖ ❖ ❖

Manifesting, it turns out, is the ability to bring an object or objects from your own memory into someone else's memory.

"The concept is simple enough," Dean Mendelsohn says as our chairs begin to recline. Dr. Sanders and the nurse in medical scrubs begin to prep us for another knifing. "If you are in a memory and the host is driving, you manifest a vehicle in order to follow them. But you must draw from an actual memory of yours—you can't manifest a Pontiac Fiero if you've never driven one."

"Well, *that's* a shame," Chase says. "But wait. When we enter Malcolm's memory, won't we just, like, materialize in the car with him?"

"Remember." Dean Mendelsohn holds up his index finger, like he's about to cite a rule. "This isn't *your* memory that you're artificially recalling. If it were, you'd be remembering everything from that scene as it plays out in your mind. Since this is *Malcom Heckman's* memory, you'll simply appear somewhere near the beginning and hope to catch up to him before he's out of sight."

Dr. Sanders points to the TV, which still has the paused news footage. "The good news is that we have video of Malcolm evading police. You'll be able to study this closely and learn his route, at least up until the moment he escapes. Authorities lost him when he inexplicably vanished into thin air beneath that freeway overpass."

The dean nods. "We'll prepare you for this chase as much as we possibly can, which is considerably better than not preparing you at all."

Ollie raises an eyebrow. "So when we show up in the memory, we just, like, close our eyes and tap our heels together like Dorothy, and then—poof—we're in a car?"

"Not exactly." The dean walks over to the reel-to-reel tape machine with a fresh memory tape. "Think about your memories, generally speaking. You can't control the outcome in those moments because they've already played out in your past. But you can draw things from those memories right now and imagine yourself interacting with them in new ways.

"In someone else's memory, this is only possible insofar as you are willing to relinquish control and let the desired object or objects manifest before you. Make sense?"

"Great." Fletcher covers his eyes with the backs of his hands. "So we have to get to a place of zen before we can make things appear."

I close my eyes and picture myself holding my dad's baseball in my dorm room on the day Ollie and I met. However, instead of just standing there, I imagine myself taking the baseball and bouncing it off the wall over and over again—tossing, catching, tossing, catching.

The dean chuckles, and when I open my eyes, I find him watching me with a smile. "You see?"

"Can we manifest people?" Fletcher asks as the nurse begins

applying the electrode stickers to his head. "Could one of us will *you* into Malcolm's memory with us?"

"You can only manifest inanimate objects. No people, no animals, nothing sentient. Got it?"

Everyone says yes, we got it.

"One more question." Ollie sounds scared. "What if we're struck *by* a car while we're inside the memory?"

"Moving objects that are a part of the original memory, such as people, animals, or cars, are projected 'set pieces' of the memory. You *will* be able to brush up against these things in your semiconscious state. But a word of warning. If you *are* struck by one of these memory set pieces, like a moving car, it will . . . how do I put this? It will *force* you off of it. It's like two magnets repelling one another."

"Weeeird," Chase says. He whistles.

"Now," Dean Mendelsohn says, tugging at his suspenders. "If there are no further questions, we have work to do."

36

FLETCHER COHEN

The four set to work and practiced how to manifest.

In the new memory, Dean Mendelsohn looked to be about college-aged, and he stood at a carnival ring-toss game, a beautiful, young girl at his side cheering him on with flirtatious enthusiasm. The dean wore a cardigan with varsity sleeves, and his hair was greased back with pomade. The young girl was his girlfriend, the memory informed Fletcher, a vivacious blonde with curly locks. This was their first date together: a cool fall evening in 1960 in the dean's hometown at the annual fair. Both looked like they'd stepped off the *Leave It to Beaver* set.

Dean Mendelsohn had selected a memory that was stationary, a scene where he remained fixed in a single location. This way, Fletcher and the group could step aside and spend their time working on manifesting.

The dean said we should start small, Freya said after they moved to a patch of empty grass beside a cotton-candy machine—the young dean still within eyesight. *So here goes . . .*

She held out her hand, palm up, then closed her eyes. Fletcher, Chase, and Ollie watched her expectantly. After an uncomfortably long moment during which nothing happened, she opened her eyes.

Okay, well, anyone else wanna try? As she dropped her arm, a weathered baseball materialized between her fingers. It was so unexpected that she let it slip from her hand. It hit the ground with a soft, pitiful *thud*, then rolled across the grass and stopped between Fletcher's shoes. He bent down and picked it up. It felt just as he expected it to: lightweight, worn surface, bumpy threads.

Wow. Fletcher tossed the ball underhand to Ollie. She caught it, examined it closely, then tossed it to Chase.

This is amazing, Freya, Chase said, throwing it up with his right hand and then catching it with his left. *But you couldn't have manifested some beer instead?*

Freya walked to him and took back her baseball. They all watched her study the white ball, her eyes and mouth round with fascination.

How'd you do it? Fletcher asked.

I dunno. She fingered the threads on the ball. *I just kind of . . . let go. I told myself not to try, to just let it happen, and then it appeared.*

Ollie broke from their circle and gave herself space. *Well, something tells me a bicycle isn't gonna be that easy, but here goes nothing.*

But Ollie manifested her bike almost immediately. When the bicycle appeared, resting on its kickstand, Fletcher, Freya, and Chase applauded and laughed.

I took this thing everywhere before I got my car, she told them, mounting the seat and riding in a circle.

Dean Mendelsohn's memory lasted only another ten minutes. Fletcher batted his eyes open and looked around the facility, refamiliarizing himself with their location while the girls gave a report to Dean Mendelsohn.

"Very impressive. You have officially crossed the Rubicon." He turned to the guys. "And how about you two?"

Fletcher and Chase exchanged a glance. "The memory ended before we could try," Chase said. This was partly true. After Ollie manifested her bicycle, Chase told the group to stand back so he could manifest his '87 Ford Mustang GT 5.0, what he called "the slickest sports car on the road today." Instead Chase stood before them, hands outstretched—red-faced and with a bulging vein on his forehead.

The car never made an appearance, and the dean's memory ended shortly after this.

"There's always tomorrow," Freya said beside Fletcher, winking at Chase.

The dean tapped his chin with this thumb. "Mr. Hall, might I ask? Do you own the vehicle you were trying to manifest?"

Chase blushed before pretending to cough. He grabbed the water beside his chair and took a sip.

"I see," the dean said.

"Look, I test-drove it, okay?" Chase said defensively. "I don't own it, no, but I've driven it. I have the memory of having driven it. Okay?"

"Therein lies your problem," Dean Mendelsohn said, walking over to Chase. "If you're to have any hope of manifesting a vehicle, it needs to be one from your past that you've driven multiple times. It needs to be a car that spans many memories, one you are *very* familiar with. A fancy car to impress Ms. Trang and Ms. Izquierdo that you've merely *test-driven* simply won't do—"

"You've made your point," Chase said, apple-cheeked. "Also: you could've told us that before we tried manifesting."

"Ah, but where's the fun in that?" Dean Mendelsohn laughed, and Fletcher realized it marked the very first time they'd heard him do so.

By the time evening rolled in, Fletcher and the group were so spent they didn't have it in them to talk about the day's events. Instead, when it was barely nine thirty, Freya, Ollie, and Chase hooked themselves up to their respective Reflectors and crawled onto their cots. All three of them were snoring within minutes.

Yet by ten thirty, Fletcher still had not fallen asleep.

He slid out of the cot and made for the kitchen to grab a snack. Since he was already wearing the Reflector receivers on his temples, he pocketed the small device and took it with him.

When he opened the kitchen door, he found Dean Mendelsohn sitting by himself at the table, holding one of his drawings. He hurriedly stuffed it into a folder. Before it was completely concealed, however, Fletcher saw that the hand-drawn picture was of a faceless boy holding what appeared to be a paper airplane.

The dean sniffed. "You should be sleeping, Mr. Cohen." Since the dean's back was turned, Fletcher couldn't be completely sure, but he surmised the dean had been crying.

"Um, sorry." Fletcher froze awkwardly in the doorframe.

Dean Mendelsohn composed himself and turned around. "Why are you out of bed? We have a long day ahead of us tomorrow."

"I can't sleep." Fletcher shut the door and walked to the fridge. Only a few things were inside. He pulled a banana from the bowl of fruit on the middle shelf and then closed the fridge door.

"Well, I can't say that I blame you." The dean gestured to the table. Fletcher sat. "The events of the past twenty-four hours are *plenty* to keep the brain active."

"Yeah." Fletcher idly peeled the banana, glancing at the dean's folder on the tabletop. "That, um, that drawing of yours. That's the same boy from the picture hanging in your office."

"It is. Yes."

Fletcher took a bite, chewed, then swallowed. "Was he your son?"

Dean Mendelsohn cracked a smile. "He *is* my son, yes."

Fletcher nodded, glancing back at the folder. "May I ask where he is?"

The dean broke eye contact, staring off into the distance and looking pensive. As Fletcher started to wonder if he'd crossed a line, the dean said, "He's at the Fold, stuck in a memory loop."

Fletcher swallowed, even though he didn't have any banana in his mouth. "What's a memory loop?"

"When Daniel was just barely sixteen, he was in a head-on collision. His friend, who was driving, died instantly. But my son, who was in the back seat, was miraculously spared. He was, however, in the midst of artificial recall when the van struck their car."

Fletcher's mouth fell open involuntarily.

"Now Daniel's in a coma, although it's much worse than a typical coma." The dean's voice was heavy like lead. "After multiple CT scans of his brain, and with generous assistance from Alexander Lochamire and his team of scientists, it was determined that Daniel is *stuck* in the memory he was artificially recalling at the time of the crash. Whatever scene Daniel was reliving, he is reliving it on repeat."

Fletcher was dumbfounded. He just couldn't find the right thing to say. It sounded like . . . like *hell*.

"Is there . . . is there any chance of him waking up?"

Dean Mendelsohn met his eyes again. "I have hope that there is. And as long as I have hope with me, I can face tomorrow."

Fletcher nodded. He set down his half-eaten banana, his nighttime appetite now feeling wholly inconsequential.

"I'm sure all this work keeps you pretty busy," Fletcher said quietly. "Are you able to visit your son much?"

"I fly out to see him weekly." The dean rubbed the stubble on his cheeks absently. "I bring him flowers and news from my work."

"Oh yeah?" Fletcher smiled. "What do you tell them about us? About Foxtail Academy, I mean."

"That you're all a spoiled bunch with nothing but sex and cigarettes on the mind."

They stared at each other for a long while before Fletcher was unable to contain himself anymore. He snort-laughed and, to his surprise, Dean Mendelsohn began to laugh too.

When things settled, Fletcher picked up his evening snack. "Does your daughter . . . er, Dr. Sanders . . . go with you?"

The dean's bushy eyebrows dipped into a scowl. "Dr. Sanders? My *daughter*?"

"Yeah, to visit Daniel."

Dean Mendelsohn sounded like he might laugh again.

"Oh, um . . ." Fletcher was confused. He'd heard his teacher refer to the dean as "father" the night he and Chase snuck out. But what was he supposed to say? That he and his roomie eavesdropped on them when they violated curfew?

This seemed like such a strange thing to keep hidden from Fletcher and his friends, especially with all the secrets that had come to light in the past couple of days.

Dean Mendelsohn gathered his things and made for the door. "Get some rest. You're starting to sound delirious."

37

FREYA IZQUIERDO

I'm genuinely shocked to find a stack of pancakes, a tray of bacon and sausage, and a warm jug of maple syrup waiting for us in the kitchen the next morning.

"You came through, Dean M," Chase says, licking his lips and serving himself before the rest of us even sit down.

The dean looks rather proud of himself. "Yes, well. Ms. Izquierdo was right. The task set before you all is an important one. You've a better shot at completing the mission if you're replete. So eat away."

"Aye, aye," Ollie says, saluting and then skewering a sausage link with her fork. "You don't gotta tell me twice."

"You sleep okay?" I ask Fletcher, who takes his place at the table across from me. He smiles, then glances the dean's way. Dean Mendelsohn is pouring four glasses of water, his back to us.

"Slept great," Fletcher replies. "You?"

"Yeah, great," I answer honestly.

"That's good to hear," the dean says, bringing our drinks over to us. "Because with Halloween roughly six weeks away, it's time we took your training up a notch."

The next two weeks elapse faster than any other two weeks in my life. At least, that's what it feels like. Each day, we memory knife twice—once after breakfast and once after lunch. The dean explains that one should never knife more than this, for safety reasons, and we don't question him on that.

After waking up from the dean's memories, we debrief him, Dr. Sanders, and their small army of scientists. After nearly two weeks of this, Fletcher still has not managed to manifest.

"I'm doing everything you're telling me to," he says to the dean, sitting up in his chair and ripping off his electrode stickers. "I'm . . . I'm letting go and just believing my motorcycle into existence."

"We'll try again tomorrow," Dean Mendelsohn reassures him.

"And what happens when I run out of tomorrows?" he asks. The nurse removes his IV line, and once she's capped the catheter, he gets to his feet. "What happens if we go into Malcolm Heckman's memory and I'm just left stranded on the 405, waiting to be ejected? What a waste!"

He storms off to the bathroom and locks the door.

I sigh inwardly. We have just completed another memory knifing, and the scene from the dean's past took place in a vacant parking lot. Here, Dean Mendelsohn was sixteen years old and learning how to drive his father's vintage car. Chase manifested a used gray sedan—the car his stepmom insists that he drive until he saves up enough acting money to buy something nicer. Immediately after the car appeared, he and Ollie climbed in excitedly. I stood back as they peeled off and waited for Fletcher to manifest his ride.

It was a pitiful sight. Fletcher closed his eyes and bit his tongue, looking like he was in physical pain. After he stood there for nearly two whole minutes, trembling, we were both promptly ejected.

Now only Chase and Ollie are still in there, their closed eyelids fluttering as they lie in their chairs.

"He'll get there." Dr. Sanders smiles at me. "It'll click for him soon enough."

Two days ago, it was suggested that Chase and Ollie manifest their cars, and that I ride with Ollie (since I don't own a vehicle) and Fletcher ride with Chase (since he hasn't been able to manifest successfully yet). This suggestion did not go over well with Fletcher. He doubled down and insisted he just needed a few more tries. He felt he was getting close.

"Yeah," I tell Dr. Sanders. "It'll click."

In truth, I'm not sure it will.

❖ ❖ ❖

After dinner, I find Fletcher outside.

He wears a thick jacket that's uniform with the jumpsuits we've worn every morning since arriving at the facility. He walks on the train tracks, balancing on the steel lip.

"Hey," I say, walking to him. It's barely 5:00 p.m. and the September sun is already set; the moon is a bright blue half circle that hangs in the sky at our backs.

"Hey."

"Getting some fresh air?"

"Something like that." He hops down from the tracks, sits on the gravel, and pats the ground to his left. "How you doing?"

"Good." I sit beside him. "*Really* good, actually. I haven't had a half-memory dream . . . or premonition . . . since that last one in August."

"Oh, wow, that's awesome." He puts his arm around me and squeezes gently. "Do you think it has anything to do with memory knifing? Like, is that somehow . . . I dunno . . . throttling your visions?"

"Maybe." I shrug. "I've been meaning to pull Dr. Sanders aside, but I'm waiting for the right moment. I don't want to draw a lot of attention and get the dean suspicious, you know?"

Fletcher nods. "You're worried that if he thinks you're at risk, he won't let you on the mission."

"Right. And if I don't enter Malcolm Heckman's memory and hold up my end of the deal, neither will Dean Mendelsohn."

"Well, that's not going to happen." His hand rubs my shoulder, setting free all kinds of butterflies in my chest. "Even if we're ejected from the memory and we fail the mission, we still tried, so the dean has to fulfill his promise. He *has* to."

When your life is a crooked path marred by tragedy, it's easy to default to pessimism. But I can't worry about what-ifs; with the finish line almost in sight, I just need to focus on the task at hand.

We sit in silence for a while, listening to the rhythm of each other breathing under infinite stars, whose glinting light washes the tracks in pale hues.

"I'm almost there," he says after a while. "With manifesting. I can feel it."

"You remember what you told me in the woods by the lake, when it was just the two of us?" I quote him: "'I'm done trying to control everything.'"

He draws a long breath through his nose and then exhales slowly, like someone getting their lungs checked with a stethoscope.

"Are you *really* done trying to control everything?" I inquire rhetorically.

I can tell he's processing my question. After a minute or two, though, he says, "Can I ask you something?"

"Of course."

"What's the deal with your interest in using a video camera and that special project you mentioned at the kickoff bonfire?"

"Oh, that." I grimace. "I had this plan to investigate the factory where my dad used to work. See if I could find any clues surrounding his death and then catalog my findings on videotape. It's stupid and risky, I know, but—"

"It's neither of those things." His challenge is delicate. "I think that's really smart. Whenever we get out of this place, I'm gonna help you however I can."

I thank him.

"Oh, hey, I owe you something." He pulls his arm back and then fishes inside his front pocket. He pulls out a crumpled sheet of paper and unfolds it. At the top, it reads in cursive, "Fletcher Cohen's Definitive List of National Parks."

I gasp theatrically, then fold up the paper before I can see the list.

He laughs. "What are you doing? Don't you want to—?"

"I don't want to see your list of favorite parks on a page." I hold the paper over my heart. "I want you to show them to me in person."

Fletcher laughs some more. I curve my lips into a smile, then rest my head in the crook of his neck.

"You ever stop to think about how memory loss has made us desperate for our past?" He breathes in slowly. "We're so fixed on reclaiming our memories, it's like we're living for the past, not for today. It's like we've forgotten how to be in the moment."

"Oh yeah? And how does one 'be in the moment'?"

"Like this." He tilts my head up by my chin. His piercing green eyes begin to dart between mine. Slowly, his gaze falls toward my lips, and gravity pulls our faces together. He closes his eyes, and I feel

318

his warm, nervous breathing fall across my quivering mouth. I grab his neck and pull him toward me, when—

"Well, well, well!"

Fletcher and I leap apart like middle schoolers busted on a school bus.

"What the hell, Chase," Fletcher says as he and Ollie march over, giggling. I'm so embarrassed that I can't help but laugh too.

"We just ruined a moment, didn't we?" Ollie says, plopping down next to me.

"Why yes, Ms. Trang." Chase sits on the other side of Fletcher. "I believe we did!" And then, for some inexplicable reason, he howls at the moon.

This does Fletcher in—now we're *all* laughing in the moonlight.

October arrives on a cold and rainy Thursday, and the new month brings troubling news from the outside world.

"Eyewitnesses say the armored vehicle was set ablaze by several unidentified individuals wearing stolen MACE helmets." The field reporter stands at the corner of a busy street, where a scorched MACE vehicle is wrapped around a telephone pole. Yellow caution tape has secured a perimeter around the smoldering vehicle, and several agents with white gloves move about the scene, sorting through rubble and taking photographs. "The attackers lobbed Molotov cocktails at the federal transport vehicle while it was on a routine patrol. Both MACE agents inside the armored car sustained major injuries and are currently being treated at Northwestern Memorial. The attackers fled down a side alley and are still at large. Authorities are asking that anyone with knowledge of the event please contact—"

Dean Mendelsohn turns off the TV and wheels it away, cursing under his breath. Dr. Sanders is quiet, as is the team of scientists who sit, unmoving, at their computer stations. Fletcher, Ollie, Chase, and I sit on the edge of our chairs, wearing disturbed looks.

When the dean is out of view, tucked behind the large Restorey, we hear him slam the remote control onto the ground. The plastic device shatters, and everyone—even Dr. Sanders—flinches.

"Two weeks," Dean Mendelsohn says, emerging from behind the Restorey, his voice uneven. "Two weeks from today, you four will be knifing Malcolm Heckman's memory. Between now and then, we continue to refine your manifesting abilities, and we study the aerial footage of the high-speed chase. We study around the clock if we have to. Understood?"

We all nod in unison.

"Good." He looks about the facility as if he has misplaced something important. "Then let's get back to work."

38

FLETCHER COHEN

Two days before their mission—four weeks since they'd entered the facility, learned about memory knifing, and accepted Dean Mendelsohn's offer to help him in exchange for information on Freya's father—Fletcher drew a line in the sand.

I'm giving myself one more shot.

With Freya, Ollie, and Chase all manifesting multiple times now across different memory knifings, Fletcher had to confront the strong possibility that, for whatever cruel reason, he just couldn't do it. Deep down he knew he could, but maybe he couldn't bring himself to—like a skydiver who gets cold feet seconds before leaping out of a plane.

"If I can't manifest my motorcycle this morning," he told the dean as he climbed into his chair, "then I'll ride along with Ollie in her car."

Dean Mendelsohn said that was a good idea, then left to retrieve one of his memory tapes.

For two weeks, Fletcher and the group scaled back on memory knifing from two sessions a day to one so they could study the footage of Malcom Heckman's police chase. Fletcher hoped the minor sabbatical would give him a clear head. Instead, he was distracted. As they sat around the TV, memorizing Malcom's route down to every erratic swerve, Fletcher found himself itching to memory knife. It was something he never in a million years thought he would crave.

On top of this, he developed a bizarre, recurring dream—out-of-body events where he felt like his consciousness was dividing into halves. When he'd wake up in the mornings, the memory of the jolting experience drifted from his mind quickly, and by lunch every day he'd forgotten all about it until he stopped remembering them altogether . . .

"You got this," Freya said from her reclined chair once the nurse finished applying her electrode stickers.

Fletcher thanked her, praying she was right, then took a deep breath. Dean Mendelsohn returned with his selected memory tape. As he threaded it into the reels, Fletcher glanced at Chase and Ollie. They both had their eyes closed already, having just received the sedative, and Dr. Sanders flicked the tip of the third syringe before sticking the needle into Freya's catheter.

"See you on the other side," Freya rasped before her eyes rolled back into her head. Fletcher watched as her body went lax and her breathing steadied.

322

As Dr. Sanders moved toward him with his sedative dose in hand, Fletcher noticed Dean Mendelsohn dragging a fifth chair over and parking it on the other side of Chase. The dean began to roll up his sleeves as the nurse prepped a set of electrode stickers.

Before he could ask Dr. Sanders if the dean would be artificially recalling his memory with them, Fletcher felt the powerful sedative take over. The last thing he heard was someone pressing Play on the giant Restorey before his vision faded.

Then Fletcher was cast like a doll through the neon color-rush, where he plummeted *up* toward the great nothing before eventually landing shakily on both feet.

❖ ❖ ❖

Fletcher found himself at the end of a driveway in a suburban neighborhood, standing beneath the pinkest evening sky he'd ever seen. It was so pink, so vibrant in its pinkness, that he questioned if it was real.

Of course it's not real. It's someone else's memory of the sky, not the actual sky.

At the edges of the memory's scene, a few houses away, was a great blurry curtain of distortion. Contained within this visual parameter, this dome, were the pertinent details and settings of the dean's memory. Everything outside the dome was hazy, ghostly, and mirage-like.

Fletcher noted a car in the driveway. The engine was running. Behind him, Fletcher could feel Freya, Chase, and Ollie as they appeared.

He took a deep breath, ready to attempt manifesting one last time, when Dean Mendelsohn walked out of the house. He looked to be around the same age in this memory as he was in the present, give or take a year or two. His expression was unreadable as he rolled a suitcase to the back of the small car, popped the trunk, then loaded it in. He walked to the passenger door. Before he got into the car, something caught his eye.

Is . . . is he looking at us? Chase asked. For a split second, it appeared as though the dean *was* staring straight at them. But then they realized he was looking over their heads at the brilliant twilit sky, staring at a murmuration.

Look, Freya said, pointing at the starlings. The birds twisted and bent in the sky in perfect concert, dipping and diving in slow motion. They all gaped at the beautiful display until a car door closed, snapping the four back into the moment.

Time to move, Ollie said, then they all stepped aside as the dean's transport reversed out of the driveway.

Without wasting a second, Chase manifested his gray car on the curb beside the mailbox. The vehicle's doors, wheels, and roof slid into place from nowhere, assembling on their own and then perfectly forming Chase's car.

Fletcher swallowed.

It was his turn.

His last shot at manifesting before calling it quits.

I'm done controlling, he thought. *It's time to let go and—*

Unexpectedly, as Chase was reaching for the driver's side door of his car, Freya turned Fletcher's head toward hers. Their eyes locked. She opened her mouth as if she was going to speak, only no words came. Instead she was pulling him toward her lips and into a long, passionate, heart-stopping kiss.

It was a moment he'd dreamed of for a long, long time. Yet nothing could have prepared him for how amazing—how tingly and warm—Freya's lips would feel locked against his. Because they were in the midst of memory knifing, the delayed sensation trickled down from his mouth and coursed through his entire body, like he was being filled with air all the way into his bones.

It was the best kiss of Fletcher's life even though it was happening in someone else's memory.

When Freya eventually pulled back, his black Ducati motorcycle was parked behind her.

Well done, Ollie said, laughing.

'Bout time, Chase added, rolling his eyes. It was unclear if he was referring to the kiss or Fletcher's first successful manifestation.

Ollie and Chase climbed into his car.

Fletcher turned back to Freya. *Um . . .*

She covered his mouth with her hand. *C'mon, we don't want to lose the dean.* Fletcher quickly mounted his Ducati, and Freya slid in behind him on the pillion seat. She wrapped her long arms around his waist and whispered, *You can thank me later.*

They followed Chase's car (which tailed Dean Mendelsohn's ride) at a moderate speed. Overhead, the skies were drained of wan sunset light and replaced with the icy black-blue of evening. They took a twisty road under stars and through a forest of pine trees, passing very few vehicles going the opposite way. All in all, it was one of the most peaceful rides Fletcher had ever taken—save for the eerie, frightening view of the memory scene's edges disintegrating in the rearview mirror.

It was one of the more peculiar side effects of memory knifing: the scenes in Dean Mendelsohn's memories appeared to be limited to a giant dome of details, a gargantuan bubble wherein lay only necessary set pieces. When the dean was on the move—whether by walking or driving—the "memory dome" would follow him, and everything outside this dome would be discarded with the avalanche of set pieces that violently tumbled out of existence beyond the hazy, warbling curtain—and that very much included knifers.

Hence, the sixty-second window.

It can't hurt you, Freya said in Fletcher's ear when she'd noticed him staring at his side mirror. *This isn't real. Remember? If we ever lose sight of the dean for more than a minute, we'll just be ejected from his memory. That's all.*

Fletcher smiled, trying desperately to reassure himself. *That's all . . .*

Freya leaned the side of her face against Fletcher's back, and he felt a sudden desire to show off. He accelerated, slipping into the median and passing Chase and Ollie. It was too dark to see their reaction, but he pictured Chase scowling his way and Ollie laughing. Freya tightened her grip around him, but not in a tense way. He could tell she felt secure.

I do too, Fletcher decided. *I guess my delay in being able to manifest was well worth the wait.*

With Freya at his side, he was ready to face anything.

They drove for another fifteen minutes before the back road merged onto a long main road. The twinkle of city lights materialized on the horizon, bright but distorted against the stark night sky. Before much longer, green signs announced an airport up ahead on the right, and at once the dean's memory informed Fletcher of what this evening was.

These are the last moments Dean Mendelsohn spent with his son before the accident. He turned his Ducati up the exit and followed the airport signs toward departures.

Sure enough, as the dean's ride pulled over and parked beneath the American Airlines signage, Fletcher saw a tall woman in a white blouse exit the driver's side. Fletcher rolled his motorcycle to a stop and walked it up onto the sidewalk so Chase could park beside him.

It was hard to make out the woman's features, but Fletcher perceived Dean Mendelsohn loved her deeply. After he got out of the car and retrieved his suitcase, they pulled one another into a firm embrace.

"I'll call after I land," the dean said once they let go of each other. She stroked his face and then kissed him. When she did this, Fletcher saw her cognition wheel: the two-quarter tattoo. "Tell Daniel I love him."

"Of course," she said. "And don't worry about him, hon. He's sixteen. He's *supposed* to be mad at you."

They shared a brief laugh, then Dean Mendelsohn checked his wristwatch.

"The watch looks good on you, by the way," she remarked. "Whoever insisted you upgrade to a Rolex has terrific taste."

"Indeed." They kissed again. "I should go." They broke away, and he rolled his suitcase toward the sliding glass doors. When he was halfway there, the back door of the car swung open.

"Dad, wait!"

The four watched as the dean's son, a freckled teenager with auburn hair, raced across the pavement. Dean Mendelsohn turned around and caught his son in a bear hug, practically lifting him off his feet. In this moment, this moment of father and son embracing, Fletcher and the group perceived a fierce kind of love for Daniel—an unconditional love known only by a parent, and it left them wordless, breathless.

"I love you, kiddo."

"I love you too, Dad."

The memory ended, catapulting them through waves of colors and back into the quiet present.

Fletcher blinked his eyes open, feeling the warm, biting tingle of tears. He wiped these away and glanced past Chase at Dean Mendelsohn, who was coming out of artificial recall and removing the two receivers from his temples.

The dean said nothing.

His face was completely drained of color.

He swung his feet around and stood, glancing around the factory until his eyes locked with Fletcher's.

A cold chill ran down Fletcher's spine as he exchanged this stare with the dean. In that moment, as the memory Fletcher had just knifed lingered in his mind, he perceived one last, intensely disturbing detail.

In the car on the ride to the airport, Dean Mendelsohn had been contemplating whether to use his son as a candidate for memory-knife testing.

A tight knot formed in Fletcher's throat as the dean hardened his face. The expression reminded Fletcher of the look the dean had given him in his office on the day they met. The lifeless, colorless gaze of a man stricken with pulsating shame, *not* grief.

Just what had happened to Daniel Mendelsohn? Had he been a test subject for memory knifing? Had something gone wrong? One thing was clear: the dean had lied to Fletcher about the cause of his son's comatose state.

But why?

Dean Mendelsohn silently collected his memory tape before exiting the facility.

It was the last anyone saw of him all day.

39

FREYA IZQUIERDO

On the eve of the big day, I brush my teeth after breakfast and then hold my reflection in the mirror. On the other side of the curtain, Ollie turns off the showerhead, reaches for her towel, and then dries herself off.

"You okay?" she asks, emerging from the shower, her torso wrapped in the towel.

"Just been thinking about this mission." I wipe my mouth with a hand towel. "Like, a lot."

"What about it?"

"You remember that day in the mall?" I turn and lean against the sink. "When those MACE agents arrested that protester?"

"Do I *remember* that?" she wheezes, sitting on the stool beside the toilet. "That scene plagues my nightmares."

"Yeah." I shake my head. "I've always questioned the need for

MACE . . . the need for a military-like agency like that. I mean, was that kind of brutal force necessary?"

"Of course not." Ollie pulls her wet hair to one side. "There are stories all over the news about how MACE agents often act outside the law, using questionable tactics on people. It's horrible."

"Yeah." I fold my arms across my chest. "Horrible."

A look of realization begins to wash over Ollie. She leans forward. "Are you . . . are you second-guessing if we should help the dean prevent this terrorist attack?"

I am by no means sympathizing with the Memory Ghosts. Detonating a bomb in a public place, likely around civilians, is abhorrent and evil. However, I'm afflicted by guilt and warring emotions. All our efforts this past month have been in the service of protecting heartless men and women—federal agents who hunt down artificial recall protesters, as well as those whose only crime is that Memory Killer oppresses them more than others.

What am I supposed to do with this kind of predicament?

"You are, aren't you?" Ollie whispers.

"No." I take off my shirt and start the shower. And it's not until the bathroom is filled with steam again that I turn around and add, "I may hate MACE with a kind of hate that burns my insides. But I'm no judge or executioner. They'll pay for their sins, Ollie. I just won't be complicit in that happening."

I pull the shower curtain closed and stand under the hot water. After some time, I hear Ollie walk to the sink. She clears her throat and says, "I hate MACE too, but . . . well, didn't your father die in a suspicious explosion at a Memory Frontier factory?"

I remain quiet. I know what she's implying because the thought has loomed in the back of my mind since we first learned the truth about memory knifing.

Did the Memory Ghosts bomb Dad's factory?

I think I've been terrified of exploring that as a real possibility because it would motivate me to lean into my role as the dean's foot soldier—a revenge-bent agent on assignment, here to help protect the wonderful agency known as the Memory and Cognition Enforcement!

Ay, Dios mío.

I am no one's soldier. I am here to learn the truth about Dad. That's it.

I shuffle these thoughts offstage and focus the spotlight elsewhere: the task at hand.

Just get through today and tomorrow, Freya. I'm so close.

Before dinner, I step outside for a quick walk. The dean keeps us on a tight leash, but he's pretty insistent we break up our days with time outside to clear our heads, so long as we don't wander off.

I see the backs of Fletcher and Chase as they head south, so I round the corner of the facility and veer north. I haven't walked one minute before I see Ollie up ahead, sitting at the base of a naked tree.

I sit down across from her, crisscross, and she keeps her eyes fixed upward.

After a while, she says, "My childhood was anything but idyllic. My father and mother met in Hội An and got married when they were both eighteen. She was a schoolteacher. He did manual labor at the shipyards. The way my grandmother tells it, she and my grandfather never really approved of him, my father, but my mother loved him. And he was a hard worker. Shortly after they were wed, my mother got pregnant with me, and my father left her to fight in the Vietnam War.

"I was five when the war finally ended and my father came home. He was very different, I'm told, but I don't remember him before. All I know is that I was a kid happy to see my daddy, happy to put the balls of my feet on his shoes while he danced around the kitchen. Even today, when I strain to remember, that's about all I can recall about that first year after his return.

"When I was ten or eleven, I began to notice his cold emptiness. Do you know what I mean by that, Freya? Cold emptiness? It's like seeing an empty vase on a table: you know it's supposed to have flowers in it, you know it's supposed to showcase a beautiful bouquet, and yet the flowers have long since wilted and died. Now it's just this vacant vase, like a cold house with no one living in it.

"Anyway, a lot of movies depict men who've returned from war as these raging alcoholics who lay waste to everyone and everything in their paths. I'm certain that's true of a lot of men and women, but that's not what happened to my father. No, his was a quiet and menacing kind of change . . . like he was always on the cusp of snapping . . . always on edge, a gathering storm that seems like it's approaching yet remains fixed in its place above the horizon, and all you can do is wonder when the wind and rain and lightning and thunder will come.

"Until, of course, one day they do."

Ollie's voice cracks, but she manages to hold back tears. I think to reach out and put my hand on her arm, but she's not finished.

"I was twelve the first time my father hurt me," she says, her voice small. "I don't remember anything beyond the fact that it happened when I was at home, and I told my mother the next morning after he'd left for work. I think she was in denial in the beginning, because it wasn't until it happened again that she believed me. She arranged to have my grandparents bring me to America the very next month so we could get as far away from my father as possible. I was thirteen."

"Ollie . . ."

She shifts her weight. "You want to know what's really awful? After I turned sixteen, had my reading, and started artificial recall, the MeReader kept retrieving those nightmarish memories even though my brain had worked very hard to repress them. I would pop in a memory tape and press Play, then relive those torturous moments from my past. And believe me . . . it was torture."

I don't know what to say to this. I literally can't bring myself to imagine what that must've been like for Ollie. What she's describing sounds like a deep suffering that no sixteen-year-old—or anyone, for that matter—should have to endure.

My heart aches.

"I had to spend an entire summer in the Fold." Ollie sighs. "They had to run a bunch of tests on me in the hospital to figure out how to sort those traumatic memories so the MeReader would stop locating them and then imprinting them onto tapes."

Now I place my hand on her shoulder. "I'm really sorry, Ollie."

She swallows. "Everyone's clawing for their memories. But I think some memories should remain buried."

❖ ❖ ❖

I give Ollie a side hug as we head back to the facility, and I loosely keep my arm around her as we walk.

"I've thought a lot about forgiveness over the years," she whispers. "My therapist said it would be healthy to forgive my father and let go. But I just don't agree with that."

"The forgiving or the letting go?"

"Forgiving. I used to buy the lie that you can forgive someone even if they never come to you to ask for forgiveness. That's just not how it works. Forgiveness is both relational and transactional, Freya. The person who's wronged you has to initiate reconciliation . . . they must be remorseful. Otherwise you're not forgiving them, you're just getting to a place where you *could* forgive them. There's a difference. A big one.

"If I ever meet my father again in this life and he recognizes the reprehensible pain he's caused me—the suffering he's inflicted—and then he's remorseful, maybe I'll consider forgiving him. But forgiveness can't work until he's ready to do his part."

I want to tell Ollie that's the bravest thing I've heard in a long time. That I'm moved by her resolve and resilience. That, in a way, she's just as much grieving the loss of her father as I am, and that's a bond that forever tethers us.

But I don't want to make this about me. I don't want to hear the sound of my voice. I don't want my hollow words to follow her raw, vulnerable story.

So, instead, I let the sound of our breathing fill the silence as we make our way back.

That night, after Ollie and I slip on our Reflectors and climb onto our cots, I reach out and grab her dangling hand. I squeeze it and she squeezes back, and after the boys fall asleep we softly cry ourselves to sleep.

The morning of the mission, I sit up in my cot and take off my Reflector receivers, wondering if I slept at all. Beside me, Fletcher stares up at the ceiling, blinking slowly.

"You sleep much?" I ask.

He shakes his head.

"Everything okay?"

Fletcher rolls over to face me. "Two days ago, when we knifed that memory of the dean riding to the airport, his memory informed me of something . . . troubling."

"What?"

"In the car, Dean Mendelsohn was contemplating whether to use his son as a test subject for memory knifing."

"Yeah, I perceived that too," I say, lowering my voice to a whisper. "But, and not to sound harsh, does it surprise you the dean would consider doing something like that?"

"Well, here's the thing." Fletcher leans forward, his shadowed eyes deeply concerned. "I walked in on the dean in the kitchen one night, looking over sketches of his son . . . clearly having a moment. He told me his son was in a coma, which I fully believe, but said it was because of a bad car accident. He claims his son was in the back seat, hooked up to his Restorey, when the car was struck—and that threw him into what the dean called a never-ending memory loop."

"That's . . . awful."

"It is." Fletcher blinks. "I just don't believe a car accident is what *actually* trapped his son in that memory loop."

"Okay, so what's your theory?"

"Don't have one yet." Fletcher rolls onto his back again. "But my fear is that whatever happened to the dean's son happened to him while he was memory knifing. I think the dean lied to me to avoid scaring me. And I don't think he's telling us the truth about the risk or risks involved in knifing . . ."

I sit with this for a moment, trying to digest the information slowly. "Do you want to back out?"

"I dunno," he says softly. "I just want us . . . want *you* to be safe."

"I'm sure you're right about the dean not presenting us with all the risks. But I'm doing this regardless. Because for me, the reward justifies the risk."

Fletcher nods. "I know. And we've come so far."

"We have," I agree.

"There's something else. That night in the kitchen, Dean

Mendelsohn acted like I was a crazy person when I asked about Dr. Sanders."

"What do you mean?"

"You know, how she's his daughter?" Fletcher shrugged. "The conversation Chase and I overheard between them? I don't understand why it's such a big deal that no one find out they're father and daughter."

I want to agree, only I find I don't care that much. I have plenty to preoccupy myself with, and covered-up nepotism isn't on my list.

He's silent for a while. When it seems he might say something again, Ollie and Chase begin to stir. Before long, we're all rising to our feet and marching off to breakfast.

In the kitchen, we find a serving plate of french toast, eggs, and garlic potatoes on the table. As we take our seats, Dean Mendelsohn fills our mugs to the brim with coffee.

"I figured you might need a little energy boost," he says, topping off his own mug.

I thank him before taking a sip.

"Why does this feel like the last supper?" Chase jokes restlessly.

"Yes, well, there's no denying this is a big day," the dean says, which doesn't relieve my anxiety. "But you four have impressed me greatly. Whatever the outcome of today's memory knifing, I have complete assurance that you are our best shot at obtaining the information we need."

I try to meet Fletcher's eyes, but he serves himself a portion of breakfast with his eyes downcast.

"What happens if we fail?" Chase asks. Ollie gives him a serious look.

Dean Mendelsohn clears his watery throat. "I suppose if you are unable to acquire the information from Malcolm Heckman, I will have to try."

Fletcher perks up. *"You?"* He sets his mug down. "What about all that business about your consciousness tearing apart?"

The dean smiles—not at all the response any of us expected. "If it comes to that, it comes to that. But I won't rest my head tonight until I know I've exhausted every option."

I want to argue with Dean Mendelsohn, demand why the lives of MACE agents matter so much to him. Is he really willing to risk losing his mind on behalf of total strangers, even when there's no guarantee he'll be able to get the information he needs to stop the Halloween attack from happening?

I study him. *Did you risk your son's mind too?* Maybe Fletcher's theory holds water.

But I keep this to myself and force down worries of unforeseen risks. Today's mission is about preventing an attack, yes, but it's also about learning what really happened to my dad.

Whatever information the dean has, I'm *this close* to learning it.

❖ ❖ ❖

Just like that, it's time.

Fletcher, Ollie, Chase, and I stand in a huddle beside the large Restorey in the middle of the facility. We lean our heads up against each other's, still for the longest time. Then we go around the circle, starting with Fletcher and ending with me:

"Forgotten."

"But."

"Not."

"Forgetful."

❖ ❖ ❖

Dr. Sanders connects the IV line to my catheter, which the nurse ended up leaving in my arm after about the third or fourth memory knifing.

Dr. Sanders and I haven't spoken much over the past few weeks. That's not entirely by design. Between studying the footage of the high-speed chase and all the memory knifing, we've had no opportunity to discuss my half-memory dreams. But because this has been the single longest stretch I've gone without having one since they first started, I wonder if they're gone for good.

"How did you sleep, Freya?" she asks me as she does every morning. It's become her subtle way of checking in on me—checking to see if I've had a half-memory dream since seeing her last.

"Great," I whisper. "It was a peaceful, dreamless sleep." This has become my way of telling her without telling her that I haven't had one.

"Good." She begins to attach the electrode stickers to me. Behind her, I observe Dean Mendelsohn unpacking a memory tape from a gray, hard-plastic case. He wears white gloves while he threads the tape into the reel-to-reel machine.

I shiver. That's Malcolm Heckman's memory. The memory of a terrorist.

Fletcher reaches out and holds my hand.

"We're not doing this alone," he says. "We've got each other's backs."

I nod. "Yeah," I eventually say aloud, "we do."

"I suspect you four will appear on the shoulder of the freeway," Dean Mendelsohn says once every single one of us is hooked up to the Restorey. "Do not forget: you will have seconds to manifest your vehicles and tail Malcolm's car. Once he's out of sight and the memory scene begins to collapse, you'll have less than one minute before you're ejected. So breathe. Focus.

"You know the route leading up to the overpass. Keep your eyes fixed on his vehicle and nothing else. And once you're beneath the overpass, trust your instincts and *believe* you won't lose him. There's a reason you four are tasked with this mission, and I believe it's because you are capable of completing it successfully."

When the dean finishes his speech, Dr. Sanders and the nurse grab two syringes apiece and begin to administer our sedatives. As soon as they're done, a soft buzzing rings out, and I see Dr. Sanders answer a large cell phone. "Yes, Father," she whispers into the receiver. "We're almost underway." And then she disappears behind the rows of computers.

I release a long breath. I close my eyes. Not long after that, a sluggish sensation overcomes me. The drug is in my system. In a few seconds, I will leave this facility and travel through a kaleidoscope of neon colors to the past—a past that's not my own.

Any second now . . .

40

FLETCHER COHEN

One second, Fletcher was in the facility.

The next, he was tumbling through whirling neon colors.

Then, at last, he fell up into Malcolm Heckman's memory.

Interstate 405 was an earsplitting explosion of smog and honking and sirens and sweltering afternoon heat.

As predicted, the four stumbled into the memory on the side of the freeway, their hair tossed by oncoming traffic. They barely had a moment to catch their breath before Fletcher perceived the panicked urgency of Malcolm Heckman's memory. The man's anxiety rippled across the scene like a sonic boom that gave the group a physical shove. They almost lost their footing, but the cement barrier braced them.

Here he comes, Chase shouted, pointing toward the farthest lane.

Sure enough, the white sedan they'd been studying for weeks barreled down the freeway in their direction at an alarming speed. Here at eye level with the car, they could see just how fast Malcom was driving.

Fletcher set his jaw, clenched his fists, then ran down the side of the shoulder.

As he sprinted, he exhaled through his mouth and then expertly manifested his black Ducati. The motorcycle appeared—wheels first, then body and handlebars—and as it rolled away from him he leapt into the air and mounted it. To give Freya a moment to catch up, he gently squeezed the brake lever.

When he glanced over his shoulder, Fletcher saw that Chase and Ollie hadn't wasted any time. They quickly clambered into his car, then Chase stomped the accelerator.

Freya hopped onto the motorcycle. *Go!*

Fletcher revved his Ducati and then accelerated, his tires spitting white clouds into the air. As they left the shoulder, Fletcher chanced another look back and saw the edges of the memory scene closing in like a ground-to-sky dust cloud seeking cities to devour. It sucked vehicles off the freeway, disassembled them in midair, then propelled them beyond the distorted wall.

The faster the memory host goes, the faster the edges of the memory scene collapse . . .

Fletcher weaved behind an eighteen-wheeler and merged into the center lane of the freeway, spying Malcolm Heckman's car nearly fifty yards ahead.

"Pull over immediately," a stern, booming voice commanded.

Fletcher glanced to his left and saw the fleet of police cars pursuing Malcolm, their sirens wailing. Overhead, Fletcher heard the loud whir of helicopter blades.

Over there, Freya yelled, pointing. Chase and Ollie had entered the lane beside the carpool lane, and their path was devoid of any other vehicles, who had obediently merged onto the shoulder to get out of the way.

Fletcher pulled back on the accelerator and zipped in front of one of the police cars. It was a risky move, especially at breakneck speed, but right now he didn't have time to calculate risks. He was just *doing*—acting without thinking.

Fletcher cut across one more lane before catching up to Chase and Ollie. He leaned his body to the right as they leveled out, using his weight as a counterbalance.

See if you can catch up! Ollie shouted out the window over the rushing wind, gesturing toward Malcolm's car. *Pull up beside him and see if you can look inside his cab!*

It was a great idea. Freya flashed a thumbs-up. Once more, Fletcher twisted his wrist back and sped up, passing Chase and Ollie effortlessly and closing in on Malcolm Heckman's car.

"Pull over immediately!" the police officer repeated, his garbled voice almost completely lost in the wind. Malcolm crested a small hill on the freeway, zigzagging with reckless abandon, and the dreaded overpass came into view in the far distance.

Somehow, Malcolm managed to evade authorities beneath that cement structure. How? What was his secret?

They were about to find out.

Fletcher leaned his body down and zipped forward; Freya squeezed him so tightly she constricted his breathing. Within a few seconds, Fletcher pulled up in Malcolm's left blind spot. And because he'd spent countless hours studying the aerial footage, Fletcher anticipated his quick jerk to the right. He deftly mimicked this motion and pulled up right beside Malcolm's left rear window.

Fletcher glanced through the window at the exact moment a person on the floor snuck a peek from under a blanket.

Freya, are you seeing this? Fletcher shouted, and he felt her nodding into his back.

Fletcher's heart raced. *That's how he gets away.* Malcolm's memory started to inform Fletcher of this person's identity and their role in—

A deafening crash rang out.

No! Freya screamed, and Fletcher glanced in his left mirror.

Chase's car had flipped and was rolling, top over bottom, in a brutal display of twisting metal and shattering glass.

Within moments the vehicle was consumed by the edges of the memory scene. Ollie, Chase, and his sedan vanished into the dust cloud.

Freya's breathing quickened.

They're okay. They're waking up in the facility right now, and they're okay.

Again, she nodded into his back.

We're almost there, Fletcher shouted back to her, signaling toward the approaching overpass. In the corner of his eye Fletcher caught Malcolm Heckman gripping the steering wheel, looking like he was about to do something daring.

C'mon! Fletcher's arms shook with adrenaline.

As they passed under the wide, four-lane overpass, Fletcher saw a collection of parked construction trucks on the right shoulder, as well as a row of hard-plastic barrier drums. There was a monstrous yellow paver parked beyond the trucks too.

Fletcher barely had a breath to study these details before Malcolm pulled his car hard right and crashed through the drums. He slammed on the brakes and, before the vehicle made a complete stop, the person in the back seat darted out of the car. This man had a build similar to Malcolm's and was dressed *exactly* the same—blue jeans, gray T-shirt—the perfect decoy. He rushed across all six lanes on foot and hopped the center barrier. Now on the other side of the interstate and still beneath the overpass, the man sprinted in front of the oncoming cars, only narrowly avoiding getting hit. Drivers honked and swerved, and somehow the man made it across all six lanes unscathed.

Meanwhile, the *real* Malcolm Heckman was fleeing in the oppo-site direction.

Fletcher slid his Ducati to a bumpy stop beside the abandoned car just as the squad of police cars slowed to a halt beside the center barrier. Some officers even rushed out of their vehicles and drew their guns, pointing in the direction of Malcolm's decoy. But the man was long gone.

We have to hurry, Freya said, dismounting the motorcycle first. Once they were both on foot they ran past the construction trucks and around the paver. Malcolm was still within view, but he was cov-ering ground much more quickly. He took a path around the cement columns that supported the overpass, occasionally looking over his shoulder.

If Fletcher didn't know any better, he'd think the Memory Ghost was trying to outrun *them*, not the police.

Fletcher and Freya rounded the columns, and the gravel-covered ground descended at a slippery slant toward a barbed-wire fence. Malcolm, as if he'd practiced this move a hundred times, dropped onto his side and slid down the treacherous descent with aplomb. Fletcher and Freya copied him, and the white gravel rocks scraped and stabbed at their arms. The dust they kicked up clouded their faces, and even though it didn't actually enter their lungs, they coughed.

After a few moments of this, when it felt like the skin on Fletcher's left arm had been shaved to the bone with a cheese grater, they crashed into the fence. Malcolm was already on his feet again, scaling the fence with freakish speed.

Fletcher and Freya leapt to their feet, then awkwardly climbed in pursuit of their target. The openings in the chain links were smaller than the toes of their shoes, which put most of the burden on their hands. Malcolm didn't seem to be having any trouble though, and before long he was at the top and swinging his leg over the coil of barbed wire.

We're almost there! Freya said, reaching the top a second later and mimicking Malcom's motion. She and Malcolm were on the other side, sliding down toward solid ground as Fletcher finally made it to the top. But when he stretched his leg over the barbed wire, his sweaty hands slipped.

That was all it took.

The barbed wire caught the skin above his ribs, tearing a sliver of his chest open as he fell seven or eight feet and crashed onto the ground. He landed on his side, which immediately popped his shoulder out of place. Fletcher writhed on the weeds and rocks, feeling blood pool near his stomach.

Fletcher! Freya screamed, spinning on her heel and rushing back.

Go! he yelled. Past her ankles, he could see Malcolm running toward a street. *This is as far as I go. But you can't lose him, Freya!*

Oh no . . . Freya held Fletcher's face in her trembling hands, overcome with suffocating dread.

He knew what she was looking at without having to ask her.

He'd been looked at like that before. Plenty of times.

Because his eyes had grayed over.

Memory Killer was attacking Fletcher's mind while he was inside Malcolm Heckman's memory.

And all around him, in a mad rush of overlapping visuals, Fletcher's surroundings began to pull themselves backward . . . and he felt himself leaving the ground where Freya held his face . . . felt himself fading back to the start of Malcolm's memory, on the side of Interstate 405 . . .

. . . where he feared it would begin its continuous, unending loop.

41

FREYA IZQUIERDO

Time stands still. And in this frozen moment, as I watch Fletcher fade away in my hands, his discolored eyes searching mine hopelessly, I scramble for a way to anchor him here—beside me—before I lose him.

The countdown begins.

Fifty seconds until I'm ejected.

I don't know what will happen to Fletcher now. Memory Killer is attacking his mind during a memory knife, and I know it can't be good. The way he's fading, deteriorating, tells me he's not headed back to the facility . . .

Forty seconds until I'm ejected.

I need to abandon the mission! I need to hold him tight and find a way for us *both* to be ejected and returned safely to the facility, where the dean and Dr. Sanders—

Thirty seconds until I'm ejected.

Dr. Sanders. Yes. Her lectures, her words, flood my brain, and I recall her explanation of Restoreys and memory tapes, which contain—as she put it—memory landmarks.

Twenty seconds until I'm ejected.

I speak calmly. *Fletcher, in the woods, beside our secret hang spot on campus, there's a white tree. Do you remember this luminous tree? The one with fiery-white blossoms and multiple trunks?*

Ten seconds until I'm ejected.

Fletcher, whose body has gone completely transparent now, gives me a knowing look.

Yes, he does remember. Together, simultaneously, we recall this tree in the woods. We recall the numerous times we've sat beside it, laughing and talking and—

Five seconds.

The color returns to Fletcher's eyes.

The edges of the memory scene close in like a tidal wave.

I kiss Fletcher on the lips, his body now returned to its normal state, and then I run.

42

FLETCHER COHEN

Fletcher gasped when he came to, fully expecting his broken bones to still be throbbing—fully expecting to find blood spilling out of him.

But he was back in the facility with the others, completely safe and unharmed. He jerked up into a sitting position and yanked off the electrode stickers.

"Fletcher, slow down," Dr. Sanders said, coming to his side. The second she finished removing his IV line and capping the catheter, Fletcher got to his feet and stormed toward Dean Mendelsohn.

"You knew about the risk the whole time!" he shouted at the dean, and several men leapt from their computers to restrain Fletcher. "You knew that if Memory Killer struck one of us while we were under . . . while we were knifing . . . it could trap us in . . . in a memory loop. You knew that and you didn't tell us!"

Dean Mendelsohn held up his hands. "I . . . Did this happen to you? How did you manage to get out?"

"You don't even care!" Fletcher started crying. Uncontrollably. The tears just spilled out of him messily, streaking down his face. "This mission is so important to you that you're willing to risk our minds over it . . . You were willing to risk your son's mind too, weren't you? Weren't you!"

The dean's breathing quickened. "Fletcher, please, tell me: If Memory Killer attacked you while you were inside Malcolm's memory, how did you . . . fight it? How were you able to get out?"

Fletcher pushed the men off of him and turned back to Freya. Chase and Ollie stood on either side of her motionless body. Her eyelids fluttered. The muscles around her mouth twitched.

Fletcher grabbed her hand and clasped it gently. "You got this, Freya," he whispered, wiping the tears with the back of his hand, praying that Memory Killer didn't descend upon her mind too.

Freya was alone in there. She'd somehow managed to pull Fletcher out of Memory Killer's clutches and ground him beside her before he faded away.

And now, no one was in Malcolm Heckman's memory to return the favor if something were to happen to her.

43

FREYA IZQUIERDO

I feel the edges of the memory scene collapsing at my heels, so I run faster than I've ever run before.

I am alone now.

Painfully, terrifyingly, suffocatingly alone.

If Memory Killer comes for me in here, how will I get out on my own . . . ?

I catch sight of Malcolm Heckman as he skids around a parked excavator and onto an empty street. I glance around, trying to determine where Malcolm's headed, and that's when his memory informs me that this is an abandoned construction zone.

Please let Fletcher be okay. I pray he made it out in one piece. The color *did* return to his eyes, and that unnerving occurrence of his body fading *was* reversed—all before the edges of Malcolm Heckman's memory closed in—so surely he's okay.

And how? How was I able to pull him out like that and save him from fading away?

I have no idea why a shared memory of a single tree in the middle of the woods brought Fletcher back. It was just a random, frantic attempt activated by adrenaline more than anything else.

Without slowing down, Malcolm Heckman makes his way toward an unmarked utility van that's parked beneath a palm tree. As I close in on the vehicle, the two back doors swing open. A gruff-looking man with a sleeve tattoo moves aside so Malcolm can leap into the back of the van. I follow, slipping in a second before the tattooed man shuts the doors firmly.

Instantly, the car lurches forward and begins to drive.

I lean against the wall that separates the driver from the back, sucking in air with such force that my shoulders rise and fall, rise and fall.

Malcolm, who has taken a seat across from the tattooed man and a young woman I hadn't noticed until now, is barely sweating, much less panting for air.

"Do you have it?" the woman asks, crossing her legs. She is young, probably only five or six years older than me, and wears a business skirt and jacket.

Malcolm nods. He reaches into his front pocket and procures a folded piece of paper.

This is it. I move closer so I can glance at the contents of the document. Because the van is speeding, I have to balance myself on the ceiling of the vehicle with my hands. As I stand over Malcolm and the young woman, he carefully unfolds the sheet of paper and then hands it off. When it passes between them, my heart pulsing with such fervor that I feel my chest convulsing, I see a long list of names.

I quickly scan the document and spot, with a sudden thrill of accomplishment, a single address at the bottom of the page.

There it is! I think, losing my breath all over again. I repeat the address in my mind over and over as the young woman studies the paper. Beside her, the tattooed man pulls a manila envelope out from under his seat. He opens it so the young woman can slide the paper inside.

I've done it! My head is spinning out of control, and I realize I've been doubting whether I could actually see this mission through. It's not until this very moment, as Malcolm's memory comes to a close, that I *actually* feel the prickle of warm confidence spreading through my body.

I smile to myself, letting out a hefty sigh, and wait for the memory to end so I can wake up and share the address with Dean Mendelsohn. I picture his face—I picture all of their faces—as I come to and deliver the good news. Then I imagine the dean pulling me aside after our celebratory moment and fulfilling his end of the bargain. He'll tell me what I've longed to know since I was fifteen . . . since my dad was—

A scalding-hot stab rends my thoughts into pieces. I cry out in pain.

No . . . not now . . .

My vision blackens as a half-memory dream whisks me from the van.

❖ ❖ ❖

I am seated in the driver's seat of an SUV. It's dark. I'm parked in someone's driveway.

This isn't my memory. This isn't a memory at all . . .

I glance at the rearview mirror and realize with a start that I'm not in my body . . .

I'm in Malcolm Heckman's.

Everything becomes clear in an instant: because I was memory knifing when this vision took hold of me, the vision itself is related to the memory's host—Malcolm.

This is a premonition, I realize inside Malcolm's head. I glance around the SUV's interior. *Have they . . . have they always been premonitions?*

I see the young woman—who stands on the doorstep of a bungalow—hand over the manila envelope to a bespectacled man.

It's Joshua Cohen. Fletcher's father.

No . . . I realize it's the same day after the chase on the 405, and this right here is Malcolm completing the last stop of his delivery.

The young woman leaves the congressman at the door. She climbs into the passenger seat of the SUV.

"Everything's in order," she says, fastening her seatbelt. It's at that moment I perceive her name is Alana Khan.

"Good," I hear Malcolm say, feeling his lips move as he talks. It's so disorienting being inside another person's body. His lungs pump air through his chest where *my* lungs should be; his ears rather than mine take in all the sounds in the cab of the SUV. The chipped leather steering wheel pricks his hands, not mine. And yet . . . I feel and hear what Malcolm feels and hears . . . I even perceive the cheap and musty smell of a gas-station air freshener.

Malcolm puts the vehicle in Reverse and backs out of the driveway.

"Looks like we've got ourselves a little eavesdropper," Alana says once we're in the street. She gestures toward Fletcher, who sits on his Ducati in the shadow of the neighbor's yard.

"Will that be a problem?" Malcolm asks, putting the SUV in Drive.

"No." Alana rests her hands in her lap. "I'll phone Joshua and make sure he deals with it. It's just his son, after all."

The premonition ends with a burst of grinding and piercing sounds.

I blink. I'm in the back of the van again.

Alana tells Malcolm he's done a good job, and that tonight they'll deliver this document to Joshua Cohen in person.

The memory knifing ends.

The neon colors envelop me and propel me out of Malcolm Heckman's memory.

When I come to, my back arches and I exhale loudly.

Before even a moment passes, before I can settle back down into the chair and reorient myself, I scream out the address from Malcolm Heckman's document. The facility falls momentarily quiet. I scrape my teeth together and slowly straighten myself out on the uncomfortable chair.

Everything plays out as I pictured it. There's cheering. There's crying. The celebration explodes throughout the facility and extends to the scientists stationed at their computers. They punch the air and pat one another on the back like they've just witnessed the moon landing. Dr. Sanders beams as she removes my electrode stickers, and Fletcher wastes no time pulling me into a hug. Even Dean Mendelsohn claps. He jots down the address on a scrap of paper, pulls out his cell phone, and rushes out the door.

"You did it, Freya," Fletcher whispers, holding my face. "It's over."

And you're safe. My lips quiver into a smile. *Thank God you're safe . . .*

Seeing him like this is so disorienting! The last time I held him he was bleeding out . . . so much blood . . . and his body was disintegrating before my eyes.

Ollie and Chase are with him, and the three of them form a

loose huddle around me, quietly chanting my name and laughing. I deepen my smile. Or at least I *try* to. Yes, we've managed to pull the address from Malcolm's memory. And in addition to learning the Memory Ghosts' target, I'll be able to describe Malcolm's accomplices to authorities, including this mysterious Alana Khan.

But now I have to reckon with two upsetting things. My half-memory dreams were never a mixture of premonitions and scenes from my past. They've *always* been visions of the future. The delineation between visions and memories is similar to the one between *dreams* and memories. I can sense that now as if I've known all along but was afraid to accept the truth.

So . . . *why* am I having these prophetic visions? And how? There's no telling. I have to set to work with Dr. Sanders to sort out what this means for me.

Perhaps most disturbing of all, I have learned that Fletcher's father is mixed up with the Memory Ghosts' dark efforts to attack MACE.

"You saved me," Fletcher says beneath the raucous cheering. "I . . . was slipping away. And you reminded me about the white tree. I could feel us remembering together, at the same time, and then I was okay."

I nod, wishing I could savor this moment, but knowing that—eventually—I'll have to tell Fletcher the truth about his father. The irony stings like alcohol on a cut. I'm about to learn the secrets of my dad's death at the cost of sending Fletcher's father to prison.

I can hardly bear it.

So I cry.

And I let Fletcher, Ollie, and Chase think they're tears of relief.

44

FLETCHER COHEN

The day after Fletcher and the group completed the mission marked the beginning of fall break.

Dr. Sanders escorted the four of them back to their dorm rooms, and they found the Foxtail Academy grounds completely deserted. Their peers had already left for home, leaving the campus a ghost town—a collection of buildings devoid of laughter and music and life.

"A couple of years ago," Dr. Sanders said as they walked, "one of my contemporaries—a social psychologist by the name of Daniel Wegner—submitted a hypothesis called 'transactive memory.' A transactive memory system is a means through which a *collective group* stores and recalls certain information. This mechanism . . . this shared memory ecosystem, if you will . . . makes retaining information or knowledge that much more effective. Or so the hypothesis goes."

"Transactive memory," Freya repeated. She rubbed her arms and fought off the autumn chill. "So . . . because Fletcher and I were recalling something from our memories *together*, that white tree in the woods, we were able to stave off Memory Killer?"

"Possibly." Dr. Sanders sounded unsure of herself. "Memory Killer's advantage over our minds is that it attacks us in isolation. It randomly descends upon our consciousness *individually*. Now, say, if we *weren't* in isolation . . . if we *were* able to tap into a shared memory system . . . perhaps it could bolster our defenses . . ."

She trailed off, and Chase blurted, "Sounds a lot like some science-fiction hive-mind stuff." Fletcher and Ollie chuckled, not because Chase's remark was funny, but because they'd been thinking the same thing.

"It's a crape myrtle, by the way," Dr. Sanders said to the group.

"Huh?" Freya tilted her head.

"The white tree off the banks of Juniper Lake," Dr. Sanders explained. "I explored the woods on my first day here at Foxtail. The tree is called a crape myrtle, and Tennessee's full of them."

❖ ❖ ❖

After everyone packed their things, they piled into Dr. Sanders's rental and she drove them to the airport.

On the way, Dr. Sanders shut off the car stereo. "You know, I've been thinking a lot about you four and what makes you capable of memory knifing. I think I have a promising theory. I've seen your permanent records. I've read about your losses. You have all experienced trauma to varying degrees, tragic events that have shaped your lives in unique ways. And this deep hurt and grief has fortified you—namely your mental faculties."

Chase rubbed the bridge of his nose. "I'm sorry . . . our mental *what*?"

"Faculties." Dr. Sanders smiled at him through the rearview mirror. "Your ability to imagine, intuit, choose, perceive, reason, and, of course, remember."

"What are you saying?" Fletcher asked, still confused. "That . . . that our grief made it possible for us to knife?"

Chase grabbed the handle over the passenger window and peered out, suddenly withdrawn. Ollie, too, was now reserved and quiet.

"Perhaps." Dr. Sanders parked the car in front of the departure gates. "A good deal of research shows that those with post-traumatic stress disorder exhibit increased cortisol and norepinephrine levels, and both of these naturally occurring chemicals could very well be essential for successful knifing."

"Are you trying to melt our brains, Doc?" Ollie sounded exasperated.

Dr. Sanders smiled. "Yes, well, these are just theories after all. I suspect I'll spend my break reading mounds of books and journaling."

"I'm green with envy," Chase remarked flatly.

Dr. Sanders shook her head. "Enjoy your break," she ordered them, unlocking the car. "You've truly earned it."

Fletcher, Chase, and Ollie retrieved their suitcases from the trunk and headed toward the entrance. When they noticed that Freya had lagged behind to exchange some quick words with Dr. Sanders, they waited for her.

"What's up?" Ollie asked when Freya rejoined them, dragging her suitcase.

"Hmm? Oh. Nothing. Just wanted to make sure the dean keeps his word. Dr. Sanders said he'll be in touch in a couple of days. She also said that if I don't hear from him by Tuesday, we could leak our video footage to the press."

"Wow," Chase said, munching on some sunflower seeds. "That's some serious collateral."

Freya shrugged. "Yeah. I suppose so."

"That all she said?" Fletcher asked Freya, who seemed rather guarded.

"Yeah. That's it."

❖ ❖ ❖

The day after he returned to his home, Fletcher didn't see his father or mother anywhere. He assumed his father was away for work, and a note on the fridge informed him his mother was spending the afternoon with his aunt in Laguna Beach. She'd planned for her and Fletcher to have brunch tomorrow so she could hear all about his first few months at Foxtail Academy.

This meant Fletcher had the whole day to himself.

Perfect, he thought, heading into the garage and firing up his Ducati.

❖ ❖ ❖

Fletcher pulled up in front of Freya's home later that afternoon. Her foster sister, whose name he later learned was Nicole, was reading a book in a lawn chair on the porch.

"Freya!" she shouted without even standing or lowering her book. "Your boyfriend's here!"

Fletcher laughed, and Freya appeared in the doorway a few moments later.

"What a surprise." She walked over to him with a sideways smile.

"Should I have waited another day before coming to see you?"

Freya giggled and climbed onto the pillion seat behind him. "No, I mean that I have a boyfriend. It's news to me since, you know, I'm not really seeing anyone."

"Well, that's a shame." Fletcher revved the engine.

"Tell Joaquín and María I'll be back after dinner," she shouted over to her foster sister. *"Gracias por todo."*

Nicole made a peace sign, still not bothering to glance up from her book. "Don't do anything I wouldn't do."

Fletcher took Freya up the Pacific Coast Highway, the salt-laden air whipping across their faces. To their right, the glistening ocean rolled out toward the horizon and greeted the pastel orange sky in a sort of magical handshake. The view was nothing short of a gold-framed oil painting.

With no destination in mind, Fletcher eventually insisted that Freya show him her favorite spots around Long Beach.

"Pull into that parking lot over there," she said, pointing.

Fletcher eased his Ducati to a stop and walked it into the first vacant parking spot he found. Freya took him by the hand and led him across the sand toward a pier. Fletcher suggested renting a pair of roller skates from a vendor. Freya loved the idea, and before long they were both fumbling their way up the pier, two people who had *no* business chasing each other with wheels strapped under their feet.

Freya laughed her infectious laugh, and seeing her so careless in her excitement—her mood so noticeably different than before, when they were getting ready to board their flight yesterday—filled Fletcher's heart to the brim.

She rolled to a stop at the railing, looking out across the ocean and clouds with a look of understanding.

"What is it?" Fletcher asked, sliding up beside her.

She smiled. "This moment. I . . . This was one of my premonitions."

Fletcher smiled too. "You know, when you kissed me in that memory, the one outside Dean Mendelsohn's house, that didn't really count as a kiss since it only happened in our heads."

"I see," Freya said, biting her lip. "So, like, what are you gonna do about—"

Fletcher pulled her toward him and kissed her beneath the late afternoon sky. Beneath them, the waters crashed into the pier's columns. Around them, the seagulls squawked and glided toward land. Between them, Freya raised her hands and gently held Fletcher's chest.

He savored the touch of Freya's lips against his, the sweet smell of her scent, and he made sure to note every detail. He would ingrain this moment in his memory forever. Hell, not even Memory Killer could take it from him.

Fletcher and Freya met up with Chase and Ollie at a Denny's off the boardwalk.

When they greeted each other, it felt like an entire year had passed, not a day. After they snagged a booth in the corner, "Panic" by the Smiths serenaded them through the restaurant's overhead speakers.

"How'd everyone sleep last night?" Ollie asked, taking the gum out of her mouth and sticking it to the side of her plate. She drowned her pancakes in syrup and cut into the fluffy goodness with her fork.

"Like a baby," Chase exclaimed, waving the waitress over with his empty glass of orange juice. "Like a bald, fair-skinned, button-nosed baby."

"That's not an expression," Fletcher told him, laughing.

"It is now!" he said, thumping the table.

"So, um, Chase." Freya cleared her throat, getting serious. "You gonna tell us what happened in Malcolm Heckman's memory?"

Chase's face dropped. "I do not know what you are referring to, Freya Izquierdo."

"When you flipped the car," Ollie said with her mouth full, pancakes practically spilling out. Fletcher and Freya laughed through the sides of their mouths.

Chase glared at Ollie. "It's my car. It handles poorly—"

"He was trying to get fancy," Ollie blurted as if trying to be heard over loud music at a concert. "He pulled too hard to the right, and the police car behind us smacked *right* into the underside of my door. *Bang!* After that, we rolled like dice."

Chase blinked. "Thank you so very much for the play-by-play, Ol."

"Welcome."

Fletcher dug into his eggs and sausage, and the simple meal tasted *wonderful*, like a gourmet feast fit for royalty. He couldn't have been more content if he tried.

"You guys tell anyone yet?" Chase asked the table, once they'd all had their fill and their coffee was topped off.

"No one," Freya said, taking Fletcher's arm and hanging it around her neck. "You?"

Chase shook his head. Fletcher and Ollie both said no, not a soul.

"It's gonna be weird going back." Ollie leaned back into the booth. "Just, like, pretending the only reason we're at Foxtail is to trial Memory Frontier's tech."

"Yeah," Fletcher said. "But neither Dean Mendelsohn nor Dr. Sanders explicitly said *not* to say anything."

"Maybe they think it's, I dunno, an unspoken understanding," Chase offered, shrugging.

Freya sighed. "I'm worried that when we get back to campus, the dean's gonna recruit us for more knifing. I mean, just because we stopped the Halloween attack doesn't mean the Memory Ghosts are gonna throw in the towel."

The table fell silent. Fletcher hadn't considered that.

"Well, and Halloween isn't for another two weeks," Ollie said, looking pale. "What happens if they *still* manage to pull off the"—she lowered her voice considerably—"the *bombing?*"

"We can't think like that," Fletcher said. "We did our part. Now it's up to the authorities to handle the rest. Plus, now that we know the risk . . . the risk of being attacked by Memory Killer while we're knifing . . . none of us ever has to step foot in that facility again."

Everyone nodded.

Freya slid her plate forward absently, then said, "I've been thinking. There's one thing I still don't quite understand about that day on the 405, when Malcolm Heckman was driving with stolen plates. Why was that van waiting for him off the freeway? Why did Malcolm have that decoy in the back seat? It's like he knew he was going to be pursued by police that exact day and would need this elaborate getaway strategy. If Malcolm was a carrier—a runner, as the dean put it—wouldn't he have taken more care than that? *Especially* with sensitive information on his person?"

Freya was spot-on. It didn't make any sense. What's more, Fletcher definitely had the impression that Malcolm knew he was being tailed when he and Freya pursued him on foot. But that was impossible. That was a memory . . . There was just no way Malcolm could have known someone in the future would be chasing him in that exact moment—

"Oh my gosh," Ollie said, sitting up. "Of course."

Everyone at the table turned to her.

Chase scrunched his eyebrows together. "Of course *what?*"

"The Memory Ghosts did that on purpose!" Eyes wide, she took a quick sip of her coffee. "Think about it: In a world where it's possible to access someone's memories, wouldn't people try to create, like, *safeguards?* Take the Memory Ghosts, for example. They must know that memory tapes are vulnerable and susceptible to knifing! So if they want to pass sensitive information to one another, how could they do that while making it nearly impossible for someone to knife their memory tape? By passing that sensitive information along *during* a highly dangerous and reckless stunt . . ."

The table fell silent.

"That's . . . insane," Chase said. "Which probably means it's true."

Before anyone realized it, dusk had turned to evening and the four were ordering *another* round of coffee. Their conversation turned lighter, and they eventually laughed some more. Their poor waitress grew increasingly impatient with them and their ruckus.

Finally past the point of having worn out their welcome, they paid their tab and made for the parking lot together. After they bid good night to Chase and Ollie, Freya grabbed Fletcher's hand as they walked under the streetlights toward his motorcycle.

"Dean Mendelsohn's son," she said, leaning against Fletcher's arm. "He was attacked by Memory Killer while he was knifing, wasn't he?"

"I think so, yeah."

Freya sighed heavily. "Makes me wonder about what my dad saw . . . the old man on the bus who was attacked by Memory Killer while he was hooked up to his Restorey."

Fletcher agreed. He told her about his Memory Killer File, how he'd been cataloging questions related to memory loss and artificial recall for months. "I can show you the other questions I've written down. Maybe it'll spark something. Maybe it'll provide another layer for your documentary project."

"Tomorrow," she said, pecking him on the cheek, and he felt like the rest of the street was paved with clouds as they approached his Ducati underneath the strawberry moon.

45

FREYA IZQUIERDO

I sit down at my cramped desk in my shared bedroom. The smell of garlic and onions and refried beans crawls underneath my closed door and tickles my nose. My foster parents talk loudly in the kitchen—either arguing or joking, it's always hard to tell.

I set a blank sheet of paper on the desk, grab a dull pencil from the drawer, and write out Dr. Sanders's essay question:

Are we more than the sum of our memories?

Without having to think on it too long, I let the words flow out of me through the No. 2 pencil and onto the page:

I am more than the sum of my memories, because I am not defined by moments I cannot recall.

In my life; in this crazy and tragic and scary life of mine, I have laughed. I have cried. I have grieved. I have been scared. I have made lifelong friends. And I'm starting to have these electric feelings for an inimitable someone...

All of these beautiful puzzle pieces exist and, when snapped together, make a whole—even if I can't recall each and every individual piece.

If I die tomorrow...if Memory Killer consumes every last one of my memories and drives me to madness, I won't be remembered as the Girl Who Forgot Everything.

That will not have defined me.

I should hope that I will be remembered as the Girl Who Laughed, Cried, Grieved, Was Scared, and Who Loved.

Yes...I am more than the sum of my memories.

After dinner, when I take out the trash, a beige car that I don't recognize idles outside Joaquín and María's house.

Dean Mendelsohn steps out of the driver's side looking like a new man. He's clean shaven, alert, and he's had a haircut. He sits on the hood of his car, folds his arms, and watches as I deposit the bag of trash into the waste can.

"Good evening, Ms. Izquierdo," he says as I approach him. He reaches into his pocket and produces a small piece of blue paper. "This is for you."

I take the paper and scan it quickly. It's a voucher for an updated cognition wheel, signed by the governor herself.

"Memory Frontier is still months, perhaps an entire calendar year away from releasing the Reflector to the public," the dean explains. "Since you're already using the new tech, your cognition wheel—along with your Restorey—is effectively pointless. But until the rest of the nation catches up and wheels are phased out, it wouldn't hurt to have recollector status, would it?"

"I . . . don't know what to say," I confess, looking up from the voucher and meeting his eyes.

He smiles. "You know, when we first began narrowing our pool of candidates for the knifing mission, I was *very* surprised to find that a degen had been selected. As you know, 99.9 percent of the chosen students were recollectors. And then . . . there was you. Naturally, I was confused and intrigued at once. Yet after meeting you and watching you adapt so effortlessly to knifing, it's evident why you were selected."

"And why's that?"

He blinks softly. "It has nothing to do with class. This was never about recollectors, degens, or memory loss. The common denominator among those selected to Foxtail Academy was cognitive empathy. I see that now. And while there's certainly a spectrum of empaths, your levels are . . . are *very* high, Freya. The MeReader picked up on that, even though we didn't intend it to."

I fold my voucher and stick it in my back pocket, not really sure what to say.

"You know"—Dean Mendelsohn's tone turns melancholic—"it's been said that those who empathize the most are the ones who have suffered the deepest loss."

I clear my throat. "I'm still waiting for answers about my dad."

The dean nods. "I have two last questions, though. In Malcolm Heckman's memory, how did you know a shared memory would pull Fletcher out of Memory Killer's snare? And how exactly did you two recall something in concert?"

In other words, can I walk him through each step so he can try to save his son?

I put my hands on my hips, my patience waning. I don't want to withhold this information if it'll somehow free Daniel from the terrifying "memory loop" he's trapped in. But I'm also fed up with waiting.

Dean Mendelsohn promised answers. It's time he delivered.

"Okay, well, perhaps another time." The dean opens the passenger door of his car and gestures for me to get in. "Let's go see about your father."

I take a step forward just as a throbbing headache returns with a vengeance, sending me stumbling into another premonition.

There's snow. *Lots* of snow—in the air, on the ground. I see a mansion on a hill . . . the lights are on. Smoke rises from the chimney.

It's dusk.

I glance down. Fletcher's in my arms. He wears the jumpsuit from Dean Mendelsohn's facility. His left eye is swollen and bruised. His lips are chapped.

And he's not breathing.

The vision ends. Dean Mendelsohn catches me from falling. "Freya . . . are you—?"

"I'm fine," I say. But it's a lie.

I am not fine. As long as these haunting, unwieldy visions throttle me, how can I be?

EPILOGUE

OCTOBER 22, 1987

Mr. Lear pulled the door to the phone booth shut, feeling trapped inside the metal sarcophagus, and dialed Alexander Lochamire's landline.

"This is Alex," the cold, hoarse voice said on the other end.

"It's Philip. How are you? You sound terrible."

A long beat. Outside the phone booth, it began to rain.

Dark laughter made the hairs on Mr. Lear's neck stand up. Only, it wasn't Alexander's laughter. Mr. Lear heard this other person in the background take the receiver once her laughter subsided. She ordered her father back in bed before speaking into the phone. "Well, this is a pleasant surprise."

"Brenda Lochamire." Mr. Lear grew uneasy. "Hello, dear."

"It's Sanders now," she said, almost playfully. "Missed you at the wedding."

Mr. Lear flattened his tie absently.

Dr. Sanders shuffled what sounded like papers. "That's very clever, your little method of communication . . . having your runners pass intel along while driving recklessly. *Very* clever, Mr. Lear."

"I call it Transference."

"Yes, well, our team intercepted one of your messages during a successful memory knifing." There was no more levity in Dr. Sanders's tone. "This little game you and your disciples are playing will soon be over."

Mr. Lear hardened his voice. "I wonder what game you and your father are playing at, Brenda. Feeding the media lies about the Memory Ghosts and our true mission . . . our mission to expose your dark secrets. Tell me, do you bankroll *all* the violent actors who set fire to MACE vehicles, put civilians in harm's way, and then claim to be Memory Ghosts?"

Dr. Sanders breathed into the receiver. "That's very rich, coming from you. How many innocent people died on the 405? Was it two, or three? My memory's not what it used to be."

Mr. Lear took a beat, silently conceding.

Oh, that civilian casualties in war could be avoided!

"Why did you tell your team they were knifing Malcolm Heckman's memory tape?" Mr. Lear continued. "So they could prevent an assassination?"

"A bombing," Dr. Sanders said smugly. "And look . . . it worked. We have the address we need."

Mr. Lear gripped the phone receiver. He'd have to warn the others. He could tell Alexander's daughter wasn't bluffing, which meant the Memory Ghosts would need a new safe house.

"This isn't over."

"It ended when you stormed out of that boardroom all those years ago!" Dr. Sanders thundered, panting wildly. "It ended when you stepped away from everything you and my father built, then threatened him! *No one* threatens my family, Mr. Lear . . . no one."

"The world must know the truth about indexing," Mr. Lear said simply, his voice measured and confident. "Those of us who know Memory Frontier's secrets bear the burden of exposing your empire."

"And who helped Father build this empire, Mr. Lear?"

Mr. Lear swallowed.

"Has dementia seized your mind? Or are you using selective memory?" Dr. Sanders gritted her teeth. "Your fingerprints are all over the company that *you* cofounded."

"My mission is my penance," Mr. Lear replied. "And don't think I've forgotten about the corners your father cut . . . the sacrifices that have been made to accelerate Memory Frontier's exponential growth. I will *never* forget, Brenda. To forget is to die."

Mr. Lear hung up the payphone, stepped out of the booth, and hailed a cab.

Yes, this is far from over, Mr. Lear thought, fastening his seatbelt and then regarding his cognition wheel. The four-quarter mark gleamed dully beneath the streetlights. *It's just the beginning.*

STREAM THE AUTHOR'S PLAYLIST

Every song referenced in *The Memory Index* has been compiled by the author in this exclusive playlist to enhance your experience with the book. Novels are wonderfully immersive, and the author hopes that your immersion is amplified by the book's playlist.

"Remember Me" —Jessie Villa (feat. Stephen Keech)
"Rhymin' and Stealin'"—Beastie Boys
"Lovely Day"—Bill Withers
"Strong Island"—JVC Force
"Running Up That Hill (A Deal with God)"—Kate Bush
"Land of Confusion"—Genesis
"Pilgrimage"—R.E.M.
"Everybody Wants to Rule the World"—Tears for Fears
"Take on Me"—A-ha
"Raspberry Beret"—Prince and the Revolution
"Don't You (Forget About Me)"—Simple Minds
"Caribbean Queen (No More Love on the Run)"—Billy Ocean
"*Cuando Calienta el Sol*"—Javier Solis

AUTHOR'S PLAYLIST

"Silent Running"—Mike and the Mechanics
"Somebody"—Bryan Adams
"Up Around the Bend"—Creedence Clearwater Revival
"California Dreamin'"—The Mamas & the Papas
"Stand by Me"—Ben E. King
"Gimme Shelter—The Rolling Stones
"Panic"—The Smiths

ACKNOWLEDGMENTS

Sitting down to list out every person with whom I am indebted is a hopelessly impossible task. But boy is it a huge honor to be at this point. So, here goes nothing.

I'd like to first thank Lauren Langston Stewart, my longtime friend, for believing in my writing and sticking her neck out for me. I would not be published if it wasn't for her. To Jocelyn Bailey, for taking a chance on this story and acquiring it based on some crude work-in-progress sample chapters. You helped make my dreams come true.

To HarperCollins, namely Becky Monds, Amanda Bostic, Caitlin Halstead, and my insanely talented editor Laura Wheeler. Laura challenged me (and this story) in many ways, and the book you're holding wouldn't be *half* the story it is today without her tireless laboring. I'm forever grateful. Many thanks to the brilliant Erin Healy, a line editor whose skill is unmatched. Specials thanks to Matthew Covington for the incredible map illustration and to Halie Cotton for my heart-stopping cover. I have to acknowledge the insightful work of one Linda Washington . . . her perspective was pivotal. And to my army of beta readers, who took my ugly first draft and helped elevate it in countless ways: Hai Anh Dinh, Megan Haggerty, Hannah Liberty Hatchett, Khalela Hatchett, Ali Hudson, Jenni Ivers, Will Mitchell, Josh Stewart, and Sonja Settle. Sonja, in particular, is a wonderful librarian whose suggestions and feedback were ingenious. To my life-long brothers, Rusty Shipp and Jeremy Grondahl, who celebrated this story in its infancy, and to Chris Gouker, one of the sharpest writers, collaborators, and critique partners a friend could ask for. I must also thank my tía Theresa M. Gallardo, an amazing proofreader and an even *more* amazing aunt. *¡Gracias por todo!*

Grateful to the SCBWI for welcoming me with open arms, as well as fellow writers Andrew Maraniss, Elizabeth Foscue, Jeff Zentner, and Jonathan Evison. And to David Arnold, for becoming my mentor and providing necessary insight into the crazy world of book publishing. You da best.

To my earliest supporters: Saralee and Larry Woods, the undis-puted bookman and bookwoman of Nashville; Rae Ann Parker and everyone at Parnassus, a true gem of a bookstore; to Pam Sherborne and Sue Gazell, close friends and wise book buyers; to my boy Kyle Martindale for booking my first speaking engagement when I was self-published. A massive thank-you to my dear friend Tama Powers McCoy and her infectious enthusiasm and kind heart. You're one of the good ones. To Joseph Williams for poring over my book contract and being the coolest attorney ever. (No, seriously, like *ever*.) And to my friend Kelli Wisthoff for being AMAZING, but specifically for bringing Freya's story into the classrooms.

Huge thanks to the inimitable Ashton Myers, Jessie Marie Villa, and Stephen Keech for crafting a breathtaking song (if you haven't already, you *need* to stream "Remember Me"); to my inspiring *Pencil Test* family of Phil Earnest, Chris Haggerty, Tom Bancroft, and J.D. Spears . . . quit being so dang cool; to Samantha Olson, for sharing her boarding school perspective and experiences; to my Watkins College family (the campus may be flattened, but our bond isn't); and I must give kudos to these incredible Nashville staples: Ben at Two Ten Jack, Kyle at Fenwick's, and Kayla at Scout's Germantown.

To the writers of books, musicals, films, television, and songs—endless inspiration: John Green, Brandon Sanderson, N.K. Jemisin; Lin Manuel Miranda; Christopher Nolan, Guillermo del Toro, Paul Thomas Anderson; Josh Schwartz and Stephanie Savage; Phoebe Bridgers, Shallou, Roland Orzabal, and Curt Smith.

To my eternally encouraging parents, siblings, nieces and nephews. A true tribe of a family if there ever was one. You all teach me many things and are my biggest cheerleaders. To the Izquierdo family . . . for emigrating from Mexico and making both mi mamá's—and my—dreams come true in America.

To my beautiful bride, my muse, Katie. I don't deserve you. And to each one of my bright kiddos, Lane, Luna, Lennox, Lyvia, and Lincoln. Thank you so much for your sacrifice and unconditional love.

Finally, I am forever grateful to God—my Father in Heaven—for opening this door and giving me the words.

DISCUSSION QUESTIONS

1. In *The Memory Index*, the author has created a parallel world where forgetting your memories isn't just an inevitability, it's an ever-present threat. Are there any memories that you actively, intentionally recall so that you can preserve them over time?

2. Dean Mendelsohn talks about "memory anchoring"—hand drawing certain memories to help him recall them. Do you do a form of this? Journaling?

3. Dr. Sanders poses the question, "Are we more than the sum of our memories?" Have you ever pondered this before, and do you agree with Freya's eventual response to the essay question?

4. Freya's father says that misremembering is a greater danger than forgetting. Do you agree with this? Why or why not?

5. Once Freya arrives at Foxtail Academy, she befriends Hoa Trang (Ollie), Chase, and Fletcher. Of the four, who do you like/connect with the most? Why? How about the least, and why?

DISCUSSION QUESTIONS

6. What role does grief play in the novel? How do the four seem to navigate grief in their own ways?

7. Fletcher says, "We're so fixed on reclaiming our memories, it's like we're living for the past, not for today. It's like we've forgotten how to be in the moment." Do you ever fixate too much on the past (or future) and forget how to be present? If yes, why do you think that is?

8. Near the end of the book, Ollie shares a traumatic story from her childhood. Do you agree with her thoughts on forgiveness? Why or why not?

From the Publisher

GREAT BOOKS

ARE EVEN BETTER WHEN THEY'RE SHARED!

Help other readers find this one:

- Post a review at your favorite online bookseller

- Post a picture on a social media account and share why you enjoyed it

- Send a note to a friend who would also love it—or better yet, give them a copy

Thanks for reading!

ABOUT THE AUTHOR

Photo by Chris J. Haggerty
Instagram: @ChrisHaggertyDP

Julian Vaca has been a creative writer for over a decade. He's a staff writer on PBS's "Reconnecting Roots," a nationally-broadcast show that drew in millions of viewers over its first two seasons. He's also the co-writer of *Pencil Test*, a feature-length documentary that's being executive produced by Disney animation legend Tom Bancroft (Earnest Films, 2023). Julian lives in Nashville with his family.

Connect with him at JulianRayVaca.com
Instagram: @JulianRayVaca
Twitter @JulianRVaca
Facebook: @JulianRVaca